On Falcon Wings

An intimate memoir

crafted from journals, essays, poems and stories,

scripted over a lifetime and

compiled for posterity

Susan Morrell

Author of *The Pleasure of My Company:*
Finding the Motivation and Courage to Spend Time Alone

<u>DEDICATION</u>

This book is my legacy for future generations, so it is fittingly dedicated to my grandnephews, James Everett Adams (born January 23, 2016) and Luke Henry Adams (born August 31, 2018), the youngest members (to date) in my immediate family. You—and any children born to this family beyond this printing—*are* the future and the Future is truly in good hands if It is infused with your enthusiasm, curiosity, disposition, tenacity, intelligence, innocence and pure unadulterated joy. I entrust my words to you as sparks of wisdom from a woman who loves you beyond measure and will be with you beyond Time.

Table of Contents

PROLOGUE

Why This Book and Why Now?

Hello, Readers. Thank you for selecting my book and participating in this ambitious episode of my life. Ambitious because, as the book's title implies, I am releasing my literary works out to the world "on falcon wings" and exposing my heart and soul for all to see. The thought of doing so is liberating—and scary. I've been writing and collecting the material in this book for most of my adult life. They've been stuffed into files, stored on computers, transported from state to state, printed and reprinted, read and re-read. For the most part, though, they've never been shared.

I was fortunate to have published a book in 2012—*The Pleasure of My Company: Finding the Motivation and Courage to Spend Time Alone.* Since then, friends and readers have been asking me when my next book was coming out. *Did I have something more to say?* I wondered. *Was a second book lurking in the nooks and crannies of my mind, waiting to be put to print?* As it was, *The Pleasure of My Company* took over ten years to get published until finally, in 2012, I discovered the online independent publishing world. I chose CreateSpace (now a part of Amazon publishing) as my collaborator on this venture. When I held my first printed copy on December 3, 2012, I felt like I'd given birth after a 143-month pregnancy! Now, I ask you, who would want to go through *that* again?!

Fast forward to the 2020 Covid-19 pandemic. Ironically, the lockdown created the opportune time for me to retrieve the many individual pieces from their prisons in order to ascertain if there was, in fact, something worth developing into a new book. I had plenty of material, but what kind of book could I create and would it appeal to the masses?

I played with over 100 pieces in many formats—books, stories, journal entries, essays, poems, compositions and queries—and wondered how to organize them. Do I put them in chronological order? Do I sort them in sections by type of material? How about alphabetizing them? Maybe I arrange them randomly, in no particular order at all! During all of this, my Muses prodded me into writing new material. I kept a pad and pen by my bedside because ideas would flood my brain the minute I lay my head on my pillow. I had to do a "brain dump" before I could fall asleep—*so* I'd fall asleep—or I'd forget everything when I woke up the next day.

Before I could determine the *What* and *How*, however, it was important for me to clarify my intention for writing this book— the *Why* behind it. Was it pretentious of me to pursue this or was I being directed by my spiritual guides? I knew I wanted to enrich minds and inspire readers to give voice to their own stories and insights. I know I have a talent for writing and I felt obliged to use that talent in a way that would entertain, teach, provoke and motivate you, my readers.

Then one day, while I was typing yet another new essay, it hit me. These weren't just individual anecdotes and narratives—my whole life story is captured in these works! They were puzzle pieces that fit together to reveal my personality, my likes and dislikes, my beliefs, my relationships and my successes and failures. They explained my thought processes, exposed my emotional methodology and validated my spiritual progression. Then it *really* hit me—this book would be my legacy, what I left behind for my nieces and nephew, for their children and grandchildren. I was moved to tears. I now had my intention! I was aligned with my purpose for creating this book and I composed the brief subtitle so I'd stay focused on this purpose: *An intimate memoir crafted from journals, essays, poems and stories, scripted over a lifetime and compiled for posterity.*

This is not an autobiography. It doesn't begin at my birth and tell you in detail how my life played out in events and by dates. That would not only be boring for you to read but boring for me to write! I have arranged the essays and poems in chronological order so that as you read them—as you read *between* the lines— you'll become acquainted with me and how my life evolved. You'll learn I like to go against the grain and shake things up. That's why this book isn't a narrative with a beginning, middle and ending. It doesn't have to be read from front to back—feel free to start on the last page and move forward or open it randomly to something that may strike a chord with you at that moment. My hope is that as you learn about *me,* you'll discover facets of *you* that are yearning to be exposed.

One of the most significant things you'll come to know is that I'm a firm believer in the spiritual concept of *surrender* and the importance of *releasing* to clear out the clutter and make room for the next good thing to enter my life. So, the idea of releasing my written words as a memoir—a self-portrait of sorts—made perfect sense to me. How you, my readers, are affected by my words is between you and them—I'm just the vehicle to get them out there to you. The words were never really mine anyway— I'm just returning them to the Universe that inspired them.

Which leads to the book's title—*On Falcon Wings.* I wanted to include the word *falcon* in the title because the peregrine falcon holds a special place in my heart and soul. (The story, *The Woman and the Falcon,* clarifies this bond.) How better to untether my words to the heavens than on the wings of my beloved feathered friend, the Falcon?

I offer you, Readers, this final compilation of my works to tender whatever comfort, joy, knowledge, provocation, entertainment or other reward it can give you. All I ask is that you let go of preconceived ideas of how a book *should* be structured and appreciate my writings for what they are—the treasured musings of an untethered woman. Thank you for reading!

TIMELINE

Map of My Spiritual Peregrination

After attending a weekend workshop at the Unity of Mesa Church in the fall of 2019, the minister who was conducting it gave me an exercise that she thought I might like. She called it a "map of your spiritual journey." I've changed the name of my map, however, from *journey* to *peregrination* because of my affinity for the peregrine falcon. (I didn't even know the word *peregrination* existed until I looked up *journey* on Thesasurus.com!)

The instructions were to plot out the events that had a significant influence on my spiritual development. It was to include external circumstances that caused me to learn and grow, internal insights about how Life operates or both. It should also include the people, books, travels or other stimuli that most inspired me to look inward and follow my spiritual nature.

That minister knew me well—I love doing this kind of introspective activity! I worked meticulously on my timeline and the pages that follow are the result. I include the map in this book because it really offers a good "big picture" view of who I am as a spirited soul having a human experience. My knack for detaching myself from contiguous situations so I can analyze them from afar came in handy doing this project.

As always happens when I delve deep into my psyche, I was able to learn something new about myself, even at this seasoned stage of my life. So, I highly recommend that you try this for yourself so you, too, can put your life in perspective and discover just how incredible you are!

Significant Spiritual Experiences in My Adult Life

OH	1949	Born October 28 in Warren, Ohio; first-born child of Frank & Gloria Nyitrai and first-born grandchild in both families; liked my place in birth order until my last adult relative died in 2021—I'm now the matriarch; no one older than me
	1968	
	1969	
	1970	Sexually assaulted by co-worker [years later called 'date rape' by media]; felt confused, guilty, shamed, powerless, vulnerable; didn't acknowledge or discuss with anyone for years
	1971	
NY	1972	Moved to White Plains, NY; worked at Xerox Corporation; formed lifelong friendships; based on a friend's comment, started seeing myself as *aloof* instead of *shy*, creating a major shift in my self-confidence and identity
	1973	
	1974	Experienced my first broken heart when my relationship with Thomas McGuire, "love of my life," ended. Read "How To Be Your Own Best Friend" by Mildred Newman and Bernard Berkowitz; introspective and life-altering
AZ	1975	Experienced metamorphosis in Phoenix: learned Transcendental Meditation; embraced hiking and spirituality in Nature; learned to swim. Read "The Assertive Woman" by Stanlee Phelps & Nancy Austin
	1976	
OH	1977	Read "Illusions: Adventures of a Reluctant Messiah" by Richard Bach. Moved by the humanistic portrayal of Jesus in the T.V. movie "Jesus of Nazareth." Experienced past life regressions. Attended weekend workshop at spiritualist church
NY	1978	
	1979	Dad died from a heart attack in sleep on June 16, the day after Mom given healthy results from a lung biopsy; I wondered, *Did he pray for God to take him instead of her?*
	1980	Read "Gift from the Sea" by Anne Morrow Lindbergh; deeper appreciation for my womanhood
	1981	
	1982	
	1983	Intuitively guided to Blithe Spirit bar in Edinburgh, Scotland, where I met my future husband, Stuart Pawluk
	1984	Inner Voice said, "This is what being married to him will be like," as drunken Stuart slept in car going to Ohio for our wedding; chose to marry him anyway, believing love would prevail
	1985	Integrity shift in me as I lied to cover for Stuart's drinking; didn't share it with anyone; had unconscious effect on me emotionally and psychologically
NY & OH	1986	Fire in N.Y. apartment. Friend helped me acknowledge Stuart's drinking problem. Read my first Unity Church "Daily Word Magazine." Moved back to Ohio
	1987	Birth of niece/goddaughter Christina; spiritual awakening watching two-month-old Christina sleeping: *She's come directly from God; her soul remembers God, but she can't tell me about it; our reason to be is to remember*
	1988	Divorced Stuart; began repairing my dismantled integrity and shattered self-esteem

IL	1989	Birth of nephew Michael. Moved to Chicago suburb of Naperville
	1990	Falcon/Falconer metaphor for Mom and me. First Unity Church involvement. Read "Happiness is a Choice" by Barry Neil Kaufman; attended his Inward Bound workshop in Massachusetts
	1991	Mom diagnosed w/cancer in June and died December 9; questioned if it's better to know you're dying, like Mom or in your sleep, like Dad. Moved back to Ohio in October to be near Mom
OH	1992	Wrote "The Woman and the Falcon" story after dream about Mom; a cathartic experience
	1993	Birth of niece Rachel
	1994	
	1995	
	1996	
	1997	Compassionate Listening training at Unity Church. Read "Conversation with God" by Neale Donald Walsch
	1998	Responded positively to an internal spiritual Voice telling me to, "Sell the house and things, quit job and go west!" Synchronous events reinforced making a journey
	1999	Being fired from Liberty Industries allowed for my spiritual release from a malignant employer. Read Dr. Wayne Dyer's "Wisdom of the Ages"
	2000	Journey west in August/September; drawn to Park City, UT; winter job at Deer Valley Resort led to a full-time job that lasted 18 years; took two years to leave Ohio so the Universe could align people/events I was meant to experience in Utah
UT	2001	
	2002	Performed in an improvisational comedy troupe for six years; enriched my creative side; challenged public performance skills and comfort level
	2003	
	2004	Board member and ordained lay minister at Unity Chapel of Light (through 2010); created and led guided meditations
	2005	Produced CD of my guided meditations for Unity Chapel of Light w/musical director
	2006	
	2007	Read "Peak" by Chip Conley, leading me to his Modern Elder Academy in 2018
	2008	
	2009	Hosted 60th birthday weekend for girlfriends, both local and nationwide; felt my kinship with each separately as well as watching them bond because of me
	2010	
	2011	First trip to Hawaii; drawn to the ocean, culture and sanctity of the islands
	2012	*Life Coach:* "Why do you want to publish a book?" *Me:* "To change one woman's life the way 'How to Be Your Own Best Friend' changed mine." Defining intention led to my book, "The Pleasure of My Company," getting published in December. Second trip to Hawaii
	2013	Met a widow at a book signing who said her life was changed by my book; she was "the one;" humbling experience
	2014	Third trip to Hawaii; "Let go, let God," lead to meeting *Hawaii Five-0*'s Alex O'Loughlin and two other H50 experiences
	2015	
IL	2016	Fourth trip to Hawaii; explored the possibility of moving there for a year after retirement

	2017	One week in Hawaii for life coaching training conducted by author/life coach Alan Cohen; the ideal way to apply compassionate listening and other spiritual skills
AZ & UT	2018	Received Life Coach certification in March. Retired and moved to Mesa, Arizona, in September. Attended Chip Conley's Modern Elder Academy workshop in Baja, Mexico, in December
AZ	2019	Period of adjustment, externally and introspectively, to retirement and to living in Arizona
	2020	Sister Sandy died on March 14 after a prolonged illness. Experienced atypical anxiety from the Covid-19 pandemic lockdown, but it was a creative, introspective period; felt isolated from the family in Ohio; decided to move back
	2021	Aunt Toni died April 6—I'm matriarch now?! Released Ohio move to the Universe for guidance. Identity theft in August; felt extremely vulnerable
AZ & OH	2022	House sold in one day on January 19 for cash for the asking price and closing date--Universe at work. Realized could bequeath my legacy through my spiritually-inspired words; compiled a lifetime of my writings as a scripted memoir, hopefully for publication

Stories

This is a collection of unpublished pieces, including short stories, my earliest attempt at writing as a teen and several longer pieces that have special significance to me.

The Woman and the Falcon

(1992)

Foreword

In the early 70s, I read a romantic suspense novel called "A Falcon for a Queen" by Catherine Gaskin that takes place in Scotland in 1898. The main character befriends a local man who hunts with a peregrine falcon. Ever since, I've been intrigued by the falcon.

My encounters with falcons have been special. While vacationing on Mount Desert Island in Maine in 1995, I watched a male and female falcon nesting on a high precipice through a park ranger's telescope. She told me the birds mated for life and returned each spring to the rocky ledges. She also said that the parent falcons shared in the incubation period and the powerful lens let me see the male nesting on the eggs while the female hunted. In 2001, I took a river rafting trip down the Colorado River and one afternoon two falcons flew back and forth over the river, following my raft for a short time. The raft pilot pointed them out and commented that maybe one of them was my mom's spirit watching over me. I even held a falcon on my outstretched arm one summer during a "Birds of Prey" nature show at the resort where I worked. I feel a kinship on a spiritual level with the bird; it has become my Spirit Animal.

In January of 1991, I created a metaphor to describe my relationship with my Mom—I am the falcon and she is my falconer. Like a falconer who sets his falcon off into the skies to fly and hunt, then waits for the bird to return to his outstretched arm, my Mom sent me off on countless journeys in my life—yet was always there when I felt the need to go home. She taught me, supported me, encouraged me, but most of all, she loved me. She would often say that she was living vicariously through me.

In June of '91, Mom was diagnosed with liver cancer and died in December of that year. The following summer, I awoke around one o'clock one morning from a dream about her, crying and missing her so much. While dealing with my emotions, Universal Mind planted a seed in my mind. I immediately found a pad and pen, wrote down the majority of the story, then fell peacefully back to sleep. The experience was cathartic for me, helping me move beyond the worst of my grief. The Woman and the Falcon is that story.

I have shared this folk tale with family and friends over the years. In the spring of 1998, I showed it to Rev. Guy Lynch, the pastor of my Unity Church in Tallmadge, Ohio. I asked him if I could print booklets to give to the church's congregation as a gift. He liked the idea and took it a step further—he read it for his sermon at his two services on Mother's Day that year! I invited my brother and his family to attend one of the services to surprise them with the reading. The pastor also had me greet the members as they left the services to sign their copies and talk to them. Two members, in particular, moved me—they were both psychologists who specialized in grief therapy and asked if they could share the story with their clients. I was overwhelmed by the attention and the praise I was shown!

I hope you enjoy this story and, perhaps, understand why I've chosen the title that I have for this book. By setting my writings free, I am untethering my Spirit Animal—my falcon—and myself.

ଛ ଛ ଛ ଛ ଛ ଛ ଛ

This story is lovingly dedicated to…

Gloria Morrell
My mother, my falconer, my friend.
April 25, 1928 – December 9, 1991

"You are the wind beneath my wings."

Once upon a time, there was a Woman who lived in a small cottage deep in a forest. The forest stood between a village and the rocky hills that loomed above it. One day, while returning from the village, the Woman came upon a bird egg lying in a bed of leaves along the path.

"It must have fallen from a nest in a tree or a crevice in the rocks above," she thought. But, miraculously, the egg had not been damaged when it landed in the leaves. So, the Woman gently picked up the egg and took it home with her.

In a large basket, she made her own nest of twigs and leaves. She wrapped the egg in a small blanket and laid it in the nest. Then, she put the basket on the hearth, near the fire, to keep the egg warm.

Days and weeks went by. The Woman worried that the egg would not hatch because of the fall it took. But, one morning, she was awakened by the sound of chirping coming from the basket.

There, amidst the leaves and twigs and broken shell, was a scrawny, baby peregrine falcon! Its bulging brown eyes looked up at her as it opened and closed its beak as if begging for food. She smiled as she began to take care of her new guest.

In the weeks that followed, the Falcon grew from a bony fledgling to a strong bird. The Woman saw that it was a girl falcon and she grew to love her very much. But the Woman knew she could not keep the Falcon in her small cottage forever. As sad as she was at the thought of the Falcon leaving, she knew the time had come for the bird to learn to fly.

On a sunny spring day, the Woman walked to the top of a knoll in a meadow near her home. The Falcon was perched on her arm. She stroked the bird gently as she said in a loving voice, "Don't worry, my little friend. You are a magnificent falcon and it is your nature to soar through the skies."

The Falcon looked at the Woman, tilting her head to one side as if to say, "But I want to stay with you, Woman. You have treated me so kindly and I don't know what is up there in that great, big sky. I am afraid!"

Sensing the Falcon's fear, the Woman hugged her close for a moment. Then, holding the bird in both hands, in one quick movement, she lifted it high above her head and released it to the skies.

For a second or two, the Falcon seemed to stop in midair. Then, as she began to tumble to the earth, she spread her wings out as far as she could and moved them up and down feverishly. At first, her clumsy efforts seemed to be in vain.

But she kept on flapping until—wonder of wonders!—she actually began to go up! Her wings slowed to a smooth rhythm as she felt the wind lifting her upwards. Higher and higher. Oh, what a glorious feeling!

In the meadow, the Woman watched anxiously as the Falcon faltered, then caught the wind and was flying. She felt a tug at her heart and her eyes filled with tears. She was so proud of the Falcon, yet part of her wished it was still a baby, nestled in the basket by her fireplace.

After a short time, the Falcon grew tired. Looking down, she saw the small figure of the Woman, still standing on the knoll. Something deep inside the Falcon stirred. A feeling of homesickness swept over her.

She swooped downward. The smile on the Woman's face as she flew to the outstretched arm filled the Falcon with joy. Landing lightly, the Falcon sighed contentedly as they headed back to the cottage.

The years passed by and the Falcon ventured further and further from the meadow and woods. She would be gone for days, even months, at a time as she discovered the wonderful world around her.

Yet, whenever she felt the urge, she could find her way back to that meadow. And waiting there for the Falcon, with arms reaching out and a smile that brightened her face, was the Woman.

She was there when the Falcon returned one autumn day with the male falcon she had come to love. She was there the following spring when the Falcon and her mate returned with their four young children close behind. And she was there when the Falcon returned alone and grieving, after her mate had been brought down by a hunter's arrow. No matter when the Falcon came back to the meadow, the Woman was there, waiting, ready to share in her adventures and simply to love her.

"How does she know when I am coming home?" thought the bird in amazement each time she saw her there on the knoll.

Little did she know that the Woman visited the meadow every day in hopes of the Falcon's return. Sometimes she would go at the crack of dawn, sometimes at midday and sometimes at dusk.

She had come to love and admire the Falcon. She took pride in the fact that, because of her care and perseverance, this beautiful bird was alive. So, she waited patiently, knowing that eventually her little friend would visit her again.

Then, one spring morning, the Falcon met with a surprise as she flew back over the meadow—the Woman was not there! The Falcon looked around in confusion.

"Am I in the wrong meadow?" she thought. "No, this is the place. Then where is the Woman?"

The Falcon flew to a branch high up in a nearby tree and decided to wait for the Woman, who must have been delayed in the village. All day, the Falcon waited, but the Woman never appeared.

By nightfall, the Falcon was feeling empty inside. "Perhaps if I get something to eat, I will feel better," she thought. So, she dived down, caught a mouse in her talons and carried it back to her limb. But even after eating, the empty feeling remained.

Just then, an owl flew up and landed next to the Falcon. "Hello-o-o, Falcon. What brings you out so late at night?" asked the owl.

"I am waiting for my friend, the Woman who lives in the cottage in the woods. She is always in that meadow to greet me when I come home, but today she was not there. I have been here in this tree all day, but she did not come. Perhaps she has forgotten about me," the Falcon answered sadly.

"Oh-o-o, I know the Woman you mean. She did not forget you, my friend. You see, she died last winter."

The Falcon stared at the owl in disbelief. "Died? But that cannot be! How could she die? Perhaps you are mistaken."

"No-o-o, it was her. I remember being awakened early one morning by people in the village who had come to this meadow. Someone had found the Woman lying dead at the top of the knoll. They carried her away."

On hearing that, the emptiness inside the Falcon grew to such proportions that she couldn't stand it. She plunged down toward the meadow and into the woods. She couldn't believe it—the Woman was dead?

She flapped her wings furiously as she found her way through the trees to the little cottage. She flew in through a broken window and landed in the middle of the room.

"Woman!" she cried. "Woman, I am back! Where are you, Woman?" Her screeches echoed through the cottage. But the Woman did not answer.

The Falcon glanced around the room. The dust on the furniture and the cobwebs hanging from the rafters were evidence that no one had lived here for months.

Then, her eyes caught sight of something—there, by the hearth. She flitted closer and felt a lump in her throat at what she saw there—the basket with the leaves and twigs and blanket. Even the broken eggshell. Her nest. Her home.

"Oh, Woman, are you really gone? What will I do without you, Woman? Who will I share my life with now? You were always there for me to come home to—you *are* my home! How could you leave without saying goodbye? Woman! Woman! Mother, don't leave me!"

The Falcon's screeches filled the cottage again. Suddenly, she felt suffocated by the walls and the quiet. She flew frantically out the window and back into the night.

The creatures of the forest froze at the sound of the tormented bird. Long into the night, the Falcon flew in circles over the meadow, around and around, her mind and heart in turmoil and despair.

As the morning light slowly pushed away the evening shadows, the Falcon ended her vigil over the meadow. She flew to a tree, let the fatigue sweep over her and fell into a deep sleep.

For days afterward, the Falcon stayed close to the meadow by the woods. She couldn't bring herself to leave. Where would she go? What would she do? So much of what she did was because of the Woman.

The Woman was encouraging and playful, comforting and caring. But, most of all, she was loving. The Falcon missed her terribly and couldn't imagine life without her.

But a few days later, a restlessness began to stir in the Falcon. She found herself longing for the open skies—for the feeling of freedom she got while soaring high above the earth for miles and miles, her feathers kissed by the wind that held her aloft.

So it was that the Falcon circled the meadow one last time that spring morning. She remembered another spring day—how long ago was it now? —when the Woman had carried her to the knoll for the first time. She remembered how frightened she had been at the thought of flying—then how exhilarated.

"Thank you, Woman, for giving me my life. Thank you for setting me free to experience it fully. And thank you for always being here to share it with me."

And with that, she spread her wings and headed up, up, up. Closing her eyes, the Falcon let her instincts guide her high into the clouds, oblivious to the world around her.

"Oh, little friend, isn't it magnificent up here?"

The Falcon reeled at the sound of the voice and looked around her. "Who—what was that?"

"It is I, my friend," said the voice again.

But there was no other bird in sight! Only—no! It could not be! The Falcon stared incredulously at the apparition floating just ahead of her. It was the Woman!

"How—how did—I must be dreaming!"

"No, you are not dreaming. It is I, little friend, but not as you knew me before."

The Falcon was very confused. "Are you a bird now?"

"No, not a bird," laughed the Woman. "I am spirit now, the part of all living things that never dies. I cannot stay with you for long, though, for I must join the other spirits. But I wanted to thank you, too, for being a part of my life and giving it meaning."

"But I did nothing," said the Falcon, "except leave you all the time. I was selfish to expect you to always be waiting for me while I was off enjoying myself and seeing the world."

"Ah, but that is your nature, my friend, your purpose as a falcon. And mine was to take care of you and encourage you. It was my choice and it gave me immense pleasure."

"Then stay with me now, Woman. Fly with me and we will see the wonders of the universe side by side."

"I cannot stay," replied the Woman, "but I will always be with you. There is a bond between us that will never die, that never leaves us. That bond is our love for one another. And, like the wind that lifts you high and carries you far, this love will lift your spirits and carry me in your heart and mind forever."

"Oh, Woman, I *do* love you so and I miss you terribly. But I'm afraid to be without you. If love is like the wind, can't it hurt me like the wind can destroy the trees?"

"Only trees that resist the wind are broken by its force. Those that trust in the wind will bend with it and survive," the Woman explained. "It is the same with Love, little friend. When you do not trust in Love, you become afraid. Then, anger or self-pity, envy or hate take control of you and you *do* get hurt. But Love and Fear cannot be inside you at the same time. When fears begin to rise, just turn to the Love that is deep in your heart, believe in its power and it will keep you safe."

The Falcon thought and thought about this. Then, a strange thing happened. Suddenly, the Falcon *knew* what the Woman meant.

"It's like when I am flying," she exclaimed. "If I fly when I'm feeling depressed or angry or unsure of myself, I seem to be struggling against something and it's hard. But when I'm happy and joyful, flying is effortless and smooth!" With this insight, the Falcon felt the love between her and the Woman as if it had a life of its own and a smile radiated across her face.

When the Woman saw that the Falcon understood, she smiled too and said, "Now I must go, my friend. Think of me often and know that I am with you always. I love you, Falcon." And with that, the apparition began to fade.

"And I love you, Woman," the Falcon whispered. Surprisingly, she did not feel sad at seeing the Woman go.

Instead, she went on to live and love, ***happily ever after.***

Dear Christina

(1990)

Dear Christina,

How do I capture in words the essence of your being? What phrase will best convey the myriad of feelings you conjure up in me? You are but three years old! You've cast a spell that draws me ever to you, yet you have no idea of the power you have over me.

That's why I'm writing this letter to you now, Christina. I want to capture my feelings while I am in the midst of them, while I am experiencing your innocence and purity and love. For all too soon, Time will weave its magic on you and you will grow up. You will be introduced to logic and common sense. Curiosity and spontaneity will take a backseat to maturity and responsibility.

So, before you-the-child gets lost in you-the-adult, let me tell you about the influence that child has had on my life—and maybe we can "save" her from the trappings of growing up.

May 8, 1987

The spirit of God breathes life into the body of a baby girl in a U.S. Army hospital in Wurzburg, Germany, on March 7, 1987—and you, my niece, Christina Lynn, are born. But it would be two months before I see you when you make your stateside appearance amidst the tears and laughter and *oohs* and *aahs* of your welcoming party at the Pittsburgh airport. It's amazing how a baby can transform six mature adults into goo-gooing, babbling idiots! I want so to grab you up and whisk you away just for myself, but it was not the time or place. I would have to wait.

At home in Ohio, more relatives are ready to hail your arrival. You are so good and tolerant of all the attention and noise. But soon, your mother decides you've had enough and puts you to bed away from the hustle and bustle that is so much a part of our family gatherings.

A short while later, I see my chance. I slip quietly into the bedroom. In the dim shadows of the nightlight, I gaze down upon your sleeping form—and it is then I feel my heart and soul fill beyond proportions with a love I had never imagined possible! Tears flow down my cheeks, relieving some of the emotions that are welling up inside of me. Nothing in the world has prepared me for the rush of feelings that sweep over me! My problems dissolve, my worries and fears fade into oblivion. I feel so small and insignificant next to you, yet at the same time, at one with the universe. This is what it's all about, I thought! This child that's entered our lives is Love in its purest sense!

I know in that moment that a bond exists between us that has transcended Time. That you and I have lived and loved each other before. That we have things to teach each other, to give each other and to share with each other—this time as aunt and niece, godmother and goddaughter. Oh, what a ride lay ahead for me, with you at my helm and I can't wait to begin!

May 10, 1987

A whimper escapes your lips as the priest anoints you with holy water during your christening. Baptism is an old rite, supposedly a cleansing of original sin from the newborn's soul. How could anyone look at this precious life before me and believe in sin?

I rather think that you are without sin and we are here to acknowledge those values that we all were born with but which somehow got lost or put in the recesses of our minds as being too ethereal for the "real" world. The "sin" is in not allowing these values—love, honesty, faith, trust—to be more predominant in our daily lives.

So, I am now your godmother, officially. Our spiritual relationship began eons ago, however, and this ceremony merely celebrates our reunion. I take the role of godmother very seriously and I will be here for you, Christina, throughout your life. I will listen without judgment when you want someone to talk to. I will give you guidance when you ask for it. I will share my dreams with you and hope you'll do the same with me.

As the weeks go by, you keep us entertained with each new look or sound. You're such a happy, energetic baby! I fear I monopolize your time and try not to do so. But I know each passing day brings us closer to your leaving and I don't look forward to that at all.

But go, you must. I make a promise to you before you leave—I will be in Germany for your first birthday. Never mind that money is tight and I have no full-time job. Somehow I will be there.

Then, before we know it, your Mom and Dad are carrying you onto the plane. Whoever coined the phrase "broken heart" knew of what she spoke, for when the heart experiences overwhelming sadness, it actually feels like it's tearing apart inside your chest.

My heart breaks that day in June when your smiling face is lost in the crowd of people boarding that plan! But it mends as the days go by in thoughts of seeing you in nine months, eight months, seven…

March 4, 1988

The door of the third-floor apartment—just across from the U.S. Army base in Wertheim, Germany—opens. The fatigue of an eight-hour transatlantic flight and a six-hour time zone change fades away. For there you are, in your mother's arms, wearing the rose-print dress and pinafore that I made you for Christmas! Oh, how you've grown and is it possible you're even more beautiful than I remember?

I don't take you right away—though God knows I want to! —because I don't want to frighten you. I want to give you time to get used to me, to remember me first. But a smile lights up your face and I feel your eyes following me as I walk around the apartment, talking to your Mom and Dad.

Finally, I can't wait any longer. I hold out my arms to you—and you come right to me and we hug and kiss—and I cry. The joy of that moment lives with me to this day.

During the months of planning and scrimping and saving for the trip, someone would comment about my not having to go in March, that I could go later and that you wouldn't know the difference.

They just didn't understand—I'd made a promise to you, my first promise to you and I wasn't about to go back on my word. Besides, I'd also made that promise to myself and it was very important to me, especially at that time in my life, to fulfill this commitment for my own personal well-being.

What a great time we have that month! We spend most of our days playing and laughing and getting to know each other. Some afternoons you, your Mom and I walk to the Army post for groceries or to meet your Dad for lunch. Other days we go into the village of Wertheim or drive to neighboring cities to shop. On the weekends, we all go touring around the country.

Your first birthday party is *the* social event of the preteen set—your guests range in age from eighteen months to twelve years! From entertaining your guests to opening presents to eating your birthday cake, you have a captive audience and enjoy being the center of attention.

My favorite times are in the mornings. I share your bedroom and when you wake up, you stand in your crib looking over at me in my bed. I pretend to be asleep and watch you through squinted eyes. You amuse yourself, talking to Mr. Bunny or playing with the mobile that hangs above the crib.

Soon I bring you into my bed. We play, talk, sing, laugh and maybe even go back to sleep in each other's arms. I can still smell your hair and remember the smallness and softness of you cuddling next to me. How will I ever love a child of my own now? How could there be more than this? I honestly don't believe there is—different, yes, but not more.

The day I leave Germany, it rains and flooded roads cause us to retrace our tracks a few times so that by the time we reach the Frankfurt airport, we don't have much time to visit or say goodbye. It's probably just as well. You don't make it any easier as you cling to me.

Do you sense the sadness I am feeling, the impending separation? You have no sense of time or distance, so how can you know that I am going far away or that it will be months before we see each other again? Will you wonder what's happened to me? Will you be sad? Will you forget me? Do you cry on the way home the way I do?

Christmas 1988

Once again, there's a group anxiously awaiting your arrival in Ohio as you and your parents return to the States, this time, for good. Underlying our thoughts, though, is a nagging fear—just the day before, a Pan Am airliner, bound for the U.S. from Frankfurt, Germany, exploded over Scotland, killing all on board. Loved ones heading home to be with their families for the holidays—children, parents and friends. An act of terrorism so inhumane, so violent, that it puts us all in a state of anxiety—each minute seems like ten, each hour drags on forever, until—we see you walk off that plane and back into our lives!

They say that Christmas is a holiday for children and that no matter how hard we try, we cannot "go back" again to those years of wonder and magic. But I believe we can go back by "seeing" Christmas again through the eyes of a child.

Watching your face beam as you see our Christmas tree for the first time, seeing your eyes fill with delight at the sight of presents and candy and Santa Claus, hearing the lilt of your laughter as you play in the snow—how can I not remember and how can I not get caught up in the spirit of the season with you!

In many ways, Christmas that year is a sort of déjà vu. Because your father is fourteen years younger than I am, I have clear recollections of his childhood. And a picture comes to mind of him when he was five years old, lying on the floor, chin in his hands, staring at the manger under the tree. The lights, reflecting off the icicles, throw dancing shadows across his face. And he and I talk about the baby Jesus and that first Christmas so many, many years before. I wished then that I could freeze Time and I guess I did because that moment is so deeply etched in my memory that I can almost smell the pine when I recall it.

Now it's you I see on your stomach, chin in hands, staring at the splendor of the tree—and I thank God for being able to experience the serenity of this moment twice in my lifetime.

We really develop a bond between us that Christmas. Grandma Gloria calls us "bosom buddies," and the nickname sticks.

Once again, we share a bedroom, but this time, it's mine. And once again, your wake up and look down at me from your crib, only now you call out to me— "Susie! Susie!"— and I still pretend to be asleep. But you are relentless and I am a pushover, so soon you are in bed with me, laughing and tickling and talking. What a special Christmas that was for us all!

February 1989

"The itsy, bitsy spider goes up the waterspout. Down comes the rain and…"

Do you remember this song? We play Carly Simon's version on the car stereo all the way from Ohio to Alabama that winter when I drive you, your mom and your soon-to-be brother to your new home in Weaver, Alabama. Your father has gone on ahead to his new assignment at Fort McClellan and has found a house. You are so good on the two-day trip. You play with your Mickey Mouse characters, sing songs, read books, sleep—and make friends with all the waitresses and shop clerks along the way!

You've missed your Daddy and keep asking where he is and when you will see him—it's only been a few weeks, but to a child of almost two years, the word "soon" is unfathomable. We arrive at the house early and have to wait for your Dad to get home. When he finally drives in, you are so excited and run straight into his arms.

You have no idea what it means to me to see my "baby" brother with his own child. I felt like a sister-mother to him when he was growing up. Now we are good friends and I know that you're part of the reason for our relationship being as special as it is today.

April and August 1989

I manage to get down to Alabama two more times that year. The first time is in April with Grandma Gloria and Aunt Sandy. As usual, I go crazy with the camera, making vain attempts to record on film your magic and spirit. While an impossible task at best, I enjoy the creative channel that photography offers me and I couldn't have asked for a better subject.

The second visit, I'm by myself, "on the way" home from Chicago in August. That's when I see your brother, Michael, for the first time. He is less than three months old, but what a bruiser!

When I come in the house, you are "hiding" in your bedroom, but I see you peeking your head around the door and finally, you come running down the hall and into my arms.

Nothing of any consequence happens on these trips, but it's the ordinary times that seem to create extraordinary memories. Like the night before I leave in August.

You cuddle up to me on the sofa in your nightshirt, smelling of baby powder from your bath, your hair hanging loose and silky. It's a quiet time. The lights are dim, your Mom is nursing Michael to sleep and your Dad is watching a baseball game on the television.

Then, for no apparent reason, you turn your head and look up at me and say, "I love you, Susie." Four words send my head reeling, my heart pounding! If I had died then and there, I would have been the happiest person that had ever lived! I hug you tightly and say, 'I love you, too, Christina,' and look up to see your Mom smiling at us. She's heard the exchange and nods in understanding.

Treasured moments like this cannot be diminished by the passing of time.

October 1989

You and your family drive up to Ohio for Michael's christening. It brings back memories of your baptism. Have two and a half years really gone by since I first met you?

You stand close beside me in the front row of the church as I videotape the service, holding onto my dress or my hand, a little timid in these solemn surroundings. My little "shadow," they call you.

One Saturday, you and I go on a "buddy adventure" to the Cleveland Zoo, just the two of us. It's hard to believe that I can have such a good time with a two-year-old—that I can actually carry on a conversation with you—you ask me so many questions and answer mine with a wisdom that only children seem to possess.

I love the looks and the "what-a-cute-little-girl" comments we get as we walk around. I'm sure they think you are my daughter—and I'm not about to tell them otherwise. I'm always telling your Mom and Dad that you really are mine and that they're just taking care of you until I can take you home with me. (They don't want to hear it!) But being your aunt has special privileges—we can have fun and I can buy you things and take you places and "spoil" you to my heart's content!

April 13, 1990

Good Friday and good riddance—to the Army, that is, because today your Dad is a civilian again and you are back in Ohio! I drive home from Chicago (a new place, a new job, a new chapter in my life) and spend a long weekend. My, how you've grown up! You're becoming such an independent little woman and losing some of your baby-ness.

I begin to understand how accurate Kahil Gibran's poem about children is—you are the arrow that your parents, as the living bow, send out into the world to live your own life. I wonder what your life will be like, what dreams you will nurture, what pains you will suffer, what your purpose is for being here this time.

May 1990

I travel to Ohio for Memorial Day weekend and Michael's first birthday party. Wasn't it just yesterday I was in Germany celebrating your first birthday? Time is such a paradox! There are moments when it seems to be passing in slow motion, not at all fast enough for us. Yet, when we stop and look back over the months and years that have gone by, we ask, "Where did the time go?"

You are my travel companion on my return trip to Chicago. Your Mom, Dad and Michael follow us and you are all my first out-of-town guests in my new apartment.

In my extra bedroom, "Christina's room," is my toy chest. It's almost forty years old and Aunt Sandy, your Dad and I have all used it over the years. Now it holds toys for you and Michael to play with when you come to visit me. And in the corner is an old school desk from my grade school, with storybooks, paper, coloring books and crayons under the seat.

It doesn't take you long to make yourself right at home. I love seeing your fingerprints on my glass coffee table and your milk cup in my refrigerator and Mr. Bunny on the floor! You christen my apartment with your laughter and love—and make of it a home.

… Throughout these past three years, you *have* taken me on a ride, Christina, on a journey that has brought me full circle. For, while discovering the beauty and wonder of you, the child, I rediscovered Me, the Child. And of all the many lessons I've learned on this journey, the most valuable has been to allow that child to be free.

As we grow up, we are taught to be mature, to be responsible, to be adults—and that's as it should be. But for some unknown reason, we think that means ridding ourselves of the child inherent in us all as if one cannot exist with the other. But being an adult does not have to mean giving up the qualities of our childhood.

Think of how free a child is, how expressive, how curious, how uninhibited by what others may think of her! Don't we wish at times that we could run and jump and laugh and sing just for the sake of doing it, regardless of who's watching? Don't we feel exhilarated when we *do* let down our guard, even for a moment and let that child that's been suppressed for so long cry forth in glee?

The timing of this journey in my life was uncanny. I was in a marriage to an alcoholic that was causing me mental and emotional turmoil, as my feelings ran the gamut from anger to guilt, fear to indifference, love to hate. I felt myself becoming someone else, someone unknown to me while wondering what had happened to love; why wasn't it enough to sustain us, to make things right?

In my search for answers, I found myself focusing on you and I was reminded what the world, what this life, is *really* all about. My healing process began. Balance eventually returned to my life and I was able to put all things in perspective. And by the time I made the decision to end the marriage, I was ready to joyously celebrate life again.

Finally, this journey has brought me in closer touch with my spirituality and the realization that the child within me is the essence of this spirituality. A soul evolves from the Mother/Father God and is made incarnate in the body of a baby, bringing with it the truths and lessons that God wants us to live and share. What happens to these truths along the way? Why do we lose ourselves in the external world, making our lives more complicated than they need be?

From you I learn that it's the simple things that matter, the simple things that teach the most important lessons. You get excited about the illusiveness of a bubble and I learn to enjoy what I have, even if I only have it for a short time. You fall down crying one minute, then are running around playing again the next and I learn that I can keep moving forward in my life regardless of the 'falls' I make. You jump into a swimming pool believing that I will catch you and I learn about trusting those who love me. You ask nothing of me yet accept my offerings naturally and I learn the joy of giving for the sake of giving and the art of receiving graciously. And it seems the more I give to you, the more I receive from you.

As a child, you have no concept of Time. You carry no grudges for past indiscretions, nor do you think ahead to a time when you can exact justice for those indiscretions. Rather, you live in the 'now.' What a simple yet dynamic lesson that is—to appreciate and live each moment to the fullest! What's done is done and cannot be changed. We must forgive others—and ourselves—for failings and shortcomings because to harbor regrets or hurt or angry feelings is to be trapped in the Past. And to worry about the Future is just as futile for the future is not reality yet, therefore there's nothing to change. We must let go of regrets and worry, turn our hearts to the divine child, the God-life, within us and celebrate life *now!* Otherwise, at some point in our lives, we'll find ourselves wishing— I wish I'd told so-and-so how much he meant to me; I wish I'd spent more time with my children or with my aging parents; I wish I'd gone here or done this or said that and on and on and on. What a sad commentary of our lives if we end up with a basketful of wishes instead of memories!

In the years ahead, Christina, as you face the events that show up in your life, you have the choice as to how those events will affect you. You can let them control you and let others make decisions for you, maintaining an "It's-not-my-fault-or-my-responsibility" attitude.

The problem with that choice is that it's also not your success. You can resist each event in the fear of things being out of your control or hurting you. But then you risk becoming inflexible and stagnant. Or you can recognize the possibility that each event presents to you, the opportunity for growth, for being true to yourself, for taking full responsibility for your life and experiencing it to the utmost. Those are the kind of choices I hope you make, Christina, ones of possibility and hope.

As I look back over my life, I realize that, without consciously being aware of doing so, I have lived most of it in "possibility." Through you, I have learned to be more aware of each day, each event and to expand my horizons even further. I encourage you to do the same, Christina. Challenge yourself, grow and be open to the wonders that Life has to offer you! Challenge others. Ask questions that stimulate their minds to fresh, new thoughts and ideas. Look beyond the obvious, beyond established boundaries, to new dimensions and be creative and innovative.

Search for and acknowledge similarities in yourself and others instead of for differences. Recognize the divine child within them and realize that you share something special with every single person on this earth. And most of all, let the child within you soar and take you to heights beyond your imaginings!

If I could teach you one lesson in your life, Christina, it would be to take time for silence, for getting in touch with the God-life within you. It's there you'll find inner peace and strength, where all your questions are answered if you but listen and believe.

Take moments to stop, to relax and go to a silent, private place inside your mind and heart. Slow down your conscious thoughts and leave them 'outside' to be dealt with when you return. Instead, listen to the stillness. Let the wisdom of God flow through you and see things in a new light. Let your Inner Voice speak to you and hear its divine ideas and thoughts. Realize that there is a power within you, a power to do great and wonderful things—to love, to inspire, to teach, to learn, to heal, to create.

When I finally separated from your uncle, I got back to meditating on a daily basis, sometimes twice a day. It has great healing effects on the body as well as the mind and helped me relieve the stresses I was going through.

During one meditation, my mind wandered as it will and eventually I found myself in an attic, surrounded by dusty castaways and stifling air. I came upon a large trunk. Inside the trunk were photographs of people from my life. As I took them out, one by one, I reflected on my relationship with each person and began to sort them. Some I decided to keep for they were of family and friends currently in my life. Some were of friends I hadn't seen in a while and I decided to get in touch with them again. Some were people I said "good-bye" to as I realized that our time had passed.

Then I came upon a photograph of my father, your Grandpa Frank. Nine years had passed since his sudden death. As is so often the case, unexpressed feelings remained—feelings of bitterness, love, disappointment, joy, regret—for he and my mother had been separated for two years before he died.

As I looked at his photograph, all these emotions rushed forth and I held the picture to my heart and I cried, "Daddy, I forgive you. I'm sorry. I miss you and I love you!" Suddenly, the air cleared, the attic filled with light and a calmness settled over me. And when I looked at the photograph again, *I* was in it with him. And I knew that we had both resolved our unfinished business with each other and we could now move forward with love in our hearts.

So you see, Christina, why it is so important to be in touch with your Inner Self and listen to the silence of your heart and soul. Your conscious mind cannot hold all the memories of your life and is even less equipped to handle all the emotions related to those memories, good or bad. Instead, those memories and feelings disappear into the recesses of your higher consciousness, where they lay in dormant repose or emerge as attitudes and actions in your daily life.

You must go to the child within you, the keeper of your higher consciousness and draw upon this 'well of truths' about yourself. By facing these truths in a peaceful, quiet place, you will recognize their value and you can choose to either weave them into your conscious being or rid yourself of them. You are free to forgive, then release forever the negative feelings and bask in the light of the loving, positive ones.

I believe, Christina, that you and I have years ahead of us to enjoy each other's company and spirits. And I look forward to those years with childlike anticipation and delight!

In 1990, I wrote this letter in the form of a book for my niece and goddaughter, Christina, to celebrate her third birthday on March 7 and I gave the hardcover book to her and her parents that Christmas. Even though she couldn't read it at the time (but she enjoyed looking at the photographs of her and the family that I'd included), I wanted to share the lessons about life that I'd learned from her as well as my philosophies "just in case" the opportunity didn't present itself as she got older. I hope that what I've shared here resonates with you on some level and I hope that there are individuals in your life that impassion you in the way my niece—and her brother and sister—impassion me. If so, be sure to let them know "just in case."

Secret of the Cave

(1962)

"I hope it stops snowing by the time we reach the resort. I don't think it's stopped since we began this miserable vacation," grumbled Kathy Turner, a cantankerous, blonde girl.

"Oh, don't be so ungrateful. We were lucky we could get reservations here to have one," replied Susan Benson, her tall, beautiful companion. "Anyway, it's supposed to snow in the mountains. That's what gives them their beauty."

"Beauty, shmeautey! I still wish we were at the resort," said Kathy.

At that moment, the rooftop of their destination loomed into view. The Mountain Top Resort was a popular vacation spot for many. The bus stopped near the front entrance of the building. They registered at the desk and went to their room, where they each took a hot bath.

"You know, I feel better already," implied Kathy.

"I do, too," Susan said, who was standing by the window. "Isn't the view beautiful?" Then, "Especially what I see now!"

"What do you see?" asked Kathy, as she walked to the window.

"Take a look over by that clump of trees," said Susan.

"Wow!" exclaimed Kathy.

Standing by the trees were two handsome boys, apparently guides.

"I've got a wonderful idea, Sue. Let's take a walk through the mountains. Of course, we'll need a couple of guides since we've never been here before," said Kathy.

"That's the same thing I was thinking of doing. Let's go!" shouted Susan.

They went to the lobby and asked the clerk if the guides were available. He led the girls outside to meet them. Jim Hawks, the handsomer of the two, at once took a liking to Susan, the feeling being mutual. Ronnie Kanton became well acquainted with Kathy. The boys said they would be happy to accompany them.

A little while later they started off. The cook had packed a picnic lunch for them to eat. Ronnie and Kathy walked behind while Susan and Jim took the lead.

A couple of hours later Jim suggested that they start back for the cabin. The sky was becoming dark with snow clouds.

"I agree," said Susan. "We've never been in the mountains before, and frankly I'm frightened."

"So am I," said Kathy.

"It's nothing to really worry about," said Jim. "But we still should be getting back."

"That's right," answered Ron. "This doesn't look like a bad storm, but no storm is safe in these mountains."

They had gone a little way when snow began to fall.

"Oh, dear!" cried the girls.

"We'll have to get under cover. We can never make it back until it stops," Ronnie implied.

"There's a cave down the trail a little way," informed Jim. "We can hold out there."

Once in the cave the group settled down to eat what was left of their lunch. When they were finished, Jim took Sue aside.

"There's a dance at the lodge Friday night. Will you go with me?" asked Jim.

Sue thought a while then answered, "I'll be glad to."

Meanwhile the same conversation was being carried on between Kathy and Ronnie.

"I'd be delighted to go," Kathy was answering.

At that moment there were voices heard from somewhere else in the cave. The foursome gathered up their belongings and hid in a niche in the rock. Their movements were timed perfectly for at that moment three husky men came into view.

"Put the loot in its regular spot till we can come pick it up," ordered the man who must have been the ringleader. "Mugsy, start a fire. We can't leave till this storm lets up."

The man known as Mugsy did as he was ordered. To the group's dismay he found a soda bottle which they had thoughtlessly left behind.

"Hey, boss. Look what I found. Someone's been here recently."

"It was probably left here days ago. We haven't been here in a week. Give it to Joe. Tell him to get rid of it. He—What was that?" he asked in surprise.

Kathy, unable to hold back a sneeze, looked at her companions. Should they be caught, their captors wouldn't listen to their pleas. They huddled closer together hoping they would be overlooked. But it was too late for they had been seen. They were dragged out of their hiding place and tied up.

"Forget about the gags. No one can hear them from up here," the leader said. "We'll have to take care of them when we get back. We've got to pick up the next load of money in an hour and Tucson is 100 miles away. Let's get going."

At that moment there was a great rumble in the earth. Joe went to the entrance of the cave and came back to report what had happened.

"An avalanche blocked the entrance. It's sealed tight. No one can get out that way."

Susan and Kathy looked at each other and then at the boys. Although they, too, were trapped in the cave the thought of the counterfeiters being trapped also pleased them. But their joy was changed to grief when Mugsy said,

"Now, for sure they won't get away. But we'd better go."

The three men gathered their belongings and started off in the opposite direction of the entrance. The voices soon were lost in the silence of the cave.

The foursome sat quietly. Not until that moment had the thought of another entrance entered their minds.

"Ronnie, rub the rope against the rock," instructed Jim.

For what seemed like hours to the girls, but was only a few minutes, the boys worked at their jobs with determination. Finally Ronnie's rope gave way and then Jim's. They untied Kathy and Susan and then picked up their knapsacks.

"We've got to find that other entrance and inform the police about the crooks' plans before they're carried through," said Ron, as they headed in the direction the men had taken.

"I've been through this cave on other occasions, and as far as I know there's no other exit here," Jim said.

"What if we never get out? It'll be all my fault," cried Kathy.

"Don't worry, kid. You couldn't help it. We would still be in this jam with the avalanche anyway," comforted Ronnie.

"Yeh, it wasn't your fault," said Susan.

"Heh, we found something!" shouted the boys a little while later.

"What is it?" asked Kathy.

"It looks like a trap door. Don't you think so, Jim?" asked Ron.

"Yes, I do," answered Jim, as they opened the door.

Jimmy went down first, then Sue, Kathy and Ron. A dark tunnel led them to a flight of stairs at the top of which was another door. They opened it and found themselves in a house.

"Why, it's the old Miller cabin! It was buried in an avalanche last year!" said Jim.

"There must be a way out if the crooks used this as a hideout," Susan said. "Let's see if we can find it."

Sue and Jim looked on one side of the house while Kathy and Ronnie looked on the other side. A little while later a shout came from the side on which Jim and Susan were working. "We've found it!" they said.

Ingeniously worked into the woodwork in the corner of the house was a panel about 3 feet by 3 feet. They gave it a push and after a little effort it swung outward.

"We're free!" they yelled in unison.

"We'll have to hurry if we expect to round up the gang. How 'bout if Kathy and I stay here should the men return, while you and Sue go to the resort and call the police?" suggested Ronnie to Jim.

"That's fine with me," answered Jim. "How about you girls? Is it okay?"

"Well—" they said, looking at each other. Then with a nod of their heads they answered, "It's fine with us."

Sue and Jim started down the mountain. It was a slow, tedious job for the storm had made it slipperier and wetter. Besides that the sun had set hours before.

About an hour or so later they saw the resort. They ran toward the front door and were surprised to see a police car in front of the building.

"What do you suppose they're doing here?" Susan asked Jim.

"I don't know but we'll soon find out," he answered, as he opened the door.

In the lobby were three policemen talking to Mr. and Mrs. Raleigh, the owners.

"We captured two of them," said the sheriff. "We figure there are about five or six of this counterfeit gang left. If you should see any suspicious characters, please let us know as soon as possible."

"Excuse me, sir, but we know where their hideout is and where they've hidden some of the loot," interrupted Jimmy.

"Why, Jim! Where have you been? And how did you know about the counterfeiters?" asked Mr. Raleigh.

"It's a long story and---," He was cut short by Mrs. Raleigh, who said, "And you're hungry. Why it looks as if you haven't eaten in days! So before you tell your story, come and have a bowl of hot soup, both of you."

During the meal, the couple related what had happened.

"Our friends are up there now in case they return," said Susan.

"I'll radio headquarters and have them send a squad car up there. We'll go up now and meet them," the sheriff said.

"I'm going with you," replied Jim. "I wouldn't want to miss this for the world."

"Either would I" cut in Sue.

"Well—all right, you can come. Let's go!" said the sheriff as he went out the door. The sun was just rising as they left.

* * * * * * *

Meanwhile, Kathy and Ronnie were working out a scheme in the cabin. Ronnie, who knew a little about wiring, rigged up a loudspeaker with a telephone and radio. He connected the wires of each and put the radio near the door. Then he and Kathy took the telephone and went down the trap door, waiting tensely for their prey. The idea was when the crooks entered the house, Ronnie would talk into the telephone. His voice would be heard from the radio, which, being near the door, would make it sound as if someone were outside.

About an hour later, they heard voices above them.

"Here goes!" said Ronnie.

"All right, come out with your hands up!" Ron spoke into the loudspeaker. "This is the sheriff!"

"What's going on?" Sheriff Newton asked. "Where're those friends of yours, Hawks?"

"I don't know. They were here when we left," replied Jim.

Ronnie and Kathy looked at each other. They had mistaken their friends for enemies!

"Here we are!" they called as they got out of their hiding place.

Then Ron explained what they had done.

"Good work," complimented the sheriff.

"Someone's coming!" cried one of the policemen, who was looking out the panel.

"Quick! Everyone down into the hole. When the gang hears you talking," he said to Ron when they were hidden, "they'll think they can make a getaway by coming down here, but we'll be waiting for them. Reinforcements will be outside in case they should go out, so they're—Sh-h-h!"

A few minutes later, five men entered the house through the secret panel. Among them were the three men who had captured the foursome.

"What about those kids in the cave? Should we go get them?" asked Mugsy.

"Not yet," said the boss.

Unnoticed by the gang, a police car arrived with reinforcements. They surrounded the house.

Then a voice was heard.

"Come out with your hands up! This is the police!"

Within a matter of minutes they were handcuffed and being put in the squad car.

The next couple days went fast. Jim, Sue, Ronnie and Kathy were congratulated on their work. The reward money was split among them.

The last night the two couples went to the dance. When it was over, they all went to the girls' room.

"When will you be leaving?" asked Jim.

"Tomorrow, sorry to say," answered Susan. "We've really had a wonderful time and thank you gratefully."

"It's us who should be giving the thanks," said Ron. "Will you come back soon?"

"Not with school and all, we won't. But when we are free, you'll be sure to see us," Kathy replied.

The next day, Sue and Kathy hopped on the bus. As Mountain Top Resort was lost in the distance, they waved to their new-found friends. Their next visit wouldn't come soon enough.

ও ও ও ও ও ও ও

When we were thirteen years old, my best friend, Kathy, and I were fans of Nancy Drew, Girl Detective, books, so we decided to write our own detective stories. We had crushes on two boys in our eighth-

grade class—Jimmy H. and Ronnie K.—who naturally made it into the stories with us, just as naturally as we each wrote ourselves as the main character—the cuter, smarter and braver girl. Kathy's story was called, "The Clue in the Hollow Tree," and took place on a dude ranch.

I debated whether or not to include my story in this book, then said, "Why not?" It's my first attempt at writing and, though it was fun at the time, writing fiction never really caught on with me. My original copy of the story was typed on a Smith-Corona manual typewriter and has hand-corrected typos and crossed out words. I was so tempted while retyping the story to proofread and edit all the typos as well as improve on the plot—it was driving me crazy typing mistakes! —but I decided if I was going to include it in this book, it had to be in its original format—as written by a thirteen-year-old Susan, not the present-day version.

I hope you enjoy this little jaunt down memory lane and get a good laugh out of it—I did!

The Visitors

(1999)

Once upon a time, there lived a Man whose home was his castle. Living with him in this castle were his Wife, his Son and his Daughter. The Man would leave his castle every morning to tend to his fields and earn his living. Sometimes he would venture off for several days at a time to sell his wares or defend his lands. But whenever he returned, he would sit in his favorite chair, surrounded by his loving family, and they would entertain themselves with tales of their days or play games or read to each other.

One day, there came a knock at the castle door. When the Man opened it, he found standing there a most unusual large wooden box.

"Pardon me, sir," said the box, "but I have been traveling far and would appreciate a place to rest. In exchange, I will delight you and your family with stories and magic."

Being kindhearted and curious, the Man agreed. The wooden box was given a place in the corner of the Main Room where it rested all day long.

That evening, the family gathered around their strange visitor, who said its name was Radio. To the family's fascination, Radio entertained them with music and mysteries and games. It even told them of events happening in other parts of the country and let them hear people speaking to them from miles away. It was truly magical! So the Man invited Radio to live with them.

Every day, Radio rested quietly in its corner. The Woman kept its wood polished and its dials dusted. And every evening for a few hours, Radio was surrounded by the family who was entranced by its magical performances.

Several years passed by. Then, one day, the Man again answered a knock at the castle door, and there stood another large wooden box.

"Please, sir, I have been traveling far and would appreciate a place to rest," said the box. "In exchange, I will tell you wonderful stories."

"I'm sorry," said the Man, "but Radio already lives with us and amuses us every evening with its magical powers."

"Ah, but I have even greater magical powers than Radio," said the box. "If you'll take me in, I will gladly share them with you."

This piqued the Man's interest, so the box was invited in. It said its name was Television. And, sure enough, that evening, when the family assembled around their new guest, Television not only told them stories, but showed them pictures to accompany these stories! It truly had more powerful magical powers than Radio, and the family invited it to live with them.

Radio was moved to a room in another part of the castle, and Television was given its place in the corner of the Main Room. And the family gathered around it every evening to enjoy its wondrous magic shows.

But Television was not as patient as Radio and got bored just sitting there during the long days while the Man and Woman worked and the Children went to school or played. It didn't like watching—it thrived on being watched. And it didn't like being stuck in the corner of the room. So, it began performing its magic during the day as well, a little at a time, attracting to it one or the other family member. Eventually, the Man moved Television to a more central position in the Main Room and rearranged the furniture to face it. This pleased Television, who offered even more shows in return.

As time went by, Television demanded more and more of the family's attention. It coaxed the Children away from their homework. It captured the Woman's attention with shows that never ended but had to be watched day after day after day. It enticed the Man with colorful competitive events during his leisure time at home.

No longer did the family gather to tell each other tales of their days. No longer did they play games or read books together. These old rituals were long forgotten when Television walked in their front door. Television ingrained itself so firmly in the castle that the Man even had a room added on especially for it and they called it the "TV Room."

Television loved all this attention. It soon spawned others of its kind. Smaller versions of the magical box could be found in the bedrooms, kitchen and basement, and at least one of them was on throughout the better part of each day.

Meanwhile, Radio had been moved to the basement and, over time, was buried beneath sports paraphernalia and boxes of Christmas decorations, as tiny critters built nests and webs in its guts.

❧ ❧ ❧ ❧ ❧ ❧ ❧

I found this unfinished and forgotten story buried in my files, and I knew it had to be included in the book. Fiction isn't my forte, but I do like whimsy. I remember that I was going to add other visitors, like video games (Atari's Pong, Nintendo's Super Mario Bros. or Sony's PlayStation), computers (Mac vs. PC creates disharmony within the family) and mobile phones. I didn't have an exact ending, but I remember toying with the Visitors slaying the Man, Woman and Children—the moral being: Technology Kills the Family Unit.

Instead, I'll leave it up to you, Readers, to exercise your own writing skills and complete this story yourself. Have fun with it!

Compositions

These are compositions from class assignments when I was attending Youngstown State University in my early Forties or from non-credit classes that I've taken over the years. There may be some repetition of topics or viewpoints with other pieces throughout the book because they weren't written at the same time. The book covers over fifty years of reasoning and contemplating. Some of my philosophies took root as ideas early on, then slowly developed into the belief system that I advocate today. I've outgrown some viewpoints and adopted new ones along the way. I think that's called being human!

Death Inspires Me

(1977)

I know that I am Susan for only a short time. I know that my real life is as a soul; and my habitation in the body of Susan is temporary. But I am also aware that this existence is essential for my eternal peace and happiness. I am here to learn. I am here to experience new sensations and degrees of emotions. I must feel pain as well as laughter, hate as well as love, and sorrow with the joy. What I have done and who I have been in previous lifetimes will affect my duration here and now. There are debts to be paid from those times and rewards to collect.

I believe my soul and conscious mind are very attuned to each other. They are making me more and more aware of how I must live out this lifetime. I have learned to like myself as my "own best friend;" to be less afraid of making changes and moves; to meet people and enjoy the experience of knowing them, whether good or bad. I do not know how much longer I am to remain here as Susan. Therefore, I do not have time to waste on regrets and self-pity. I intend to live each day as Susan to the fullest as if it were my last. I am not ready to die yet. But neither am I afraid of Death. It inspires me to take advantage of the time I have left.

The following two quotes sum up my thoughts:

> *"[People] think they have eternity before them...We don't have eternity; we only have time. It is what we have to work with. There are no limits to how much we can grow and develop, but time limits us...People are often obsessed with aging, with what time does to them. Instead, they should be concerned about what they do with time."*

> *How to Be Your Own Best Friend*
> by Mildred Newman & Bernard Berkowitz

"I will greet this day with love in my heart. And how will I do this? Henceforth, will I look on all things with love in my heart and I will be born again. I will love the sun for it warms my bones; yet I will love the rain for it cleanses my spirit. I will love the light for it shows me the way; yet I will love the darkness for it shows me the stars. I will welcome happiness for it enlarges my heart; yet I will endure sadness for it opens my soul. I will acknowledge rewards for they are my due; yet I will welcome obstacles for they are my challenge."

The Greatest Salesman In the World
by Og Mandino

૪ ૪ ૪ ૪ ૪ ૪ ૪

I wrote this for an assignment in a Metaphysics class. It was the Seventies and I wasn't alone in my interest in all things metaphysical, occult and mystical. I dabbled in psychic readings, past life regressions, astrology, numerology, tarot cards and other "Age of Aquarius" practices. I gravitated toward these types of philosophies because I already possessed the deeply-rooted beliefs expressed in this essay—I was not influenced by them as much as my beliefs drew me to similar-thinking teachings. Eventually, my interests evolved to deeper, more spiritual teachings and I left the metaphysical tools behind—they'd served their purpose for me and I was ready to move on, grateful for the part they played in my spiritual development.

Tending Your Garden

(1992)

Chance pushed his way...toward the exit...Chance was bewildered. He reflected and saw the withered image of Chauncey Gardiner: it was cut by the stroke of a stick through a stagnant pool of rainwater. His own image was gone as well...

Chance pushed the heavy glass door open and stepped out into the garden...The garden lay calm, still sunk in repose...Not a thought lifted itself from Chance's brain. Peace filled his chest.

Being There
by Jerzy Kosinski

Even though I saw the movie version years ago starring Peter Sellers, I only recently read Kosinski's book, "Being There." I was moved by the way Kosinski dealt with the complexity of the human psyche in such a simple story and was even more amazed at how well the story has withstood the passage of time. When published in 1971, we were in the midst of a controversial war and social "revolution"—the ramifications of which have infiltrated the very fiber of our existence ever since. Yet, Kosinski's message is timeless, having as much value and significance today as it did then, maybe even more so. I feel compelled to express my thoughts on this tale and share them with whoever feels compelled to pay them heed.

Kosinski's Chance, the main character in his novel, is a man who has spent his entire life in seclusion. For forty years, Chance's life centers around two things—watching television and tending his garden—and he successfully manages to maintain a balance between these two aspects of his life. He is content. When circumstances force him to leave his home and he is faced with new experiences or relationships, he draws upon the knowledge he has gleaned over the years watching television, transfers it to the immediate situation and acts accordingly. It doesn't occur to him to do otherwise. It doesn't occur to him that he is, as the reader sees him, a "fish out of water."

On the surface, his encounters are comical and whimsical, bringing a chuckle to the readers' lips at the incredulity of the situations. But in the five short days that transpire, there is a change going on deep inside of Chance. The passage quoted above, which is the last in the book, suggests the first signs of his confusion and frustration. What he doesn't realize is that his life is out of balance. For the last five days, he's only been living one aspect of the life he had known for the past forty years—watching television. What's been missing is his gardening.

The book, and subsequently the film version, satirically plays up the humor of Chance's obsession with television. When Chance does talk about gardening, the metaphors are looked upon by the reader as amusing evidence that he lacks a grasp of reality. I believe, however, that the message Kosinski is conveying goes even deeper than the interactions and reactions of Chance's experiences. It's about balance in our lives—what it is, what happens when we shift off it and how we can get it back.

It is my premise that in "Being There," watching television symbolizes the external elements of life and the garden, the internal. When Chance goes for days without tending his garden, he is denied the peace and tranquility that balance the activity of his life. He's off kilter. While he may not be aware of why he's feeling the way he is, as the book comes to an end he is drawn to the garden as a place of security and peace. Even in the final scene of the film, while attending Rand's funeral, Chance is attracted to the nearby woods. He wanders off alone, reveling in nature's splendor, obviously happy in the world he has missed.

The film also offers a scene not in the book, a scene that first opened my eyes to the depths of Chance's soul and the possible intent of

Kosinski's story. It is when the doctor confronts Chance at Rand's deathbed, telling him he realizes that he really is just Chance and he really is just a gardener after all. For the first time, Chance expresses emotion and gets tears in his eyes as he affirms what he has known all along, but for which he had never been acknowledged—the simple truth of who he is. Isn't that what we all want, to be acknowledged for who we are?

Yet, all too often, we look outside ourselves for that acknowledgment. We search for external goals and stimulations, external relationships and feedback, to direct our attention. We are so engrossed in this search that when external elements are lacking, our thoughts and actions become chaotic and we experience inner disorder. When left alone, we begin to wonder about things. And unless we have control over our consciousness, our wondering turns to worrying--about health, jobs, relationships, finances and whatever potential problems we can imagine. So we search for diversions.

Television plays an important part in diverting our attention. Although the experience of watching television may generally leave people feeling passive, weak and even irritable, the predictability and redundancy of the shows and commercials keep unpleasant concerns or personal worries out of our minds. TV is turned on for companionship, as soon as we awake or return home. The same is true of the stereo or the car radio. How many people could drive for seven hours without turning on the radio or popping in a cassette? It's as if we need constant distractions from—what? Ourselves? Being alone? Just what is it we fear about being alone? About talking to ourselves? Or, more importantly, about listening to ourselves? How can we sustain balance in our lives unless we allow ourselves time to be alone, time to tend our 'gardens?'

Actually, there are times when we tend our 'gardens' without being aware of doing so. If you've ever been so immersed in a project or book or craft that you've completely lost track of time and your surroundings, you've been in your 'garden.' If you've ever participated in a sport, like running or swimming or skiing, and felt everything "come together"—mind and body working in perfect harmony—you've been in your 'garden.' In his book, "Flow: The Psychology of Optimal Experience," Mihaly Csikszentmihalyi calls these experiences 'flow,' and goes on to explain how we must develop the ability to find enjoyment and purpose regardless of external circumstances. For me, driving alone for miles and hours can be a 'flow' experience. Some may argue that we can achieve 'flow' by being engrossed for hours in a television show. But Csikszentmihalyi disagrees, contending, "…one expends a great deal of attention [watching television] without having much to show for it afterward," unlike the experiences described above.

Another way to tend our 'gardens' is to daydream. Remember when we were children and we were encouraged to use our imaginations? Remember daydreaming about being a prima ballerina or a famous ball player or an Olympic gold medal winner? The joy of daydreaming need not be confined to childhood. Take the time to sit in your easy chair, with no television or music playing in the background, and let your mind wander where it will. For some, this is actually a scary thought, which is all the more reason to try it. Just relax. The birds chirping outside the window or the drone of the neighbor's lawnmower or the ticking of your clock are not distractions, but act as lullabies to help your mind drift off…let it create something wonderful for you. Don't be limited by can'ts or shouldn'ts. If you're a writer, see yourself autographing copies of your latest novel at a bookstore. An engineer? See that magnificent building you designed reaching to the heavens. Whatever you aspire to, feel the moment—the pride, the excitement, the glee—as your mind takes you on this incredible journey. And know that these thoughts are flowers you are gathering from your garden, the beauty and scent of which will motivate and comfort you when you revert back to the external world.

Similar to daydreaming is a third method of visiting our 'gardens'— meditation. Ever since the Maharishi Mahesh Yogi introduced Transcendental Meditation to the United States in the mid-70s, more and more people are turning to some form of meditation to create the balance so necessary in their lives. There are no mystical, magical secrets or rituals to meditating. The mantras of TM and the positions of yoga are only techniques for personal preference and variation. All that's required to meditate is to sit in a quiet environment with eyes closed and body relaxed, breathing deeply and evenly and letting go of all conscious thoughts by gently focusing on one word, sound or thought.

The experience is not unlike immersing in an ocean. Imagine your external, physical, conscious self as the surface of the ocean, sometimes calm and sometimes turbulent but always moving. As you meditate, you travel down through the depths of the ocean to where the waters are calmer and the atmosphere tranquil. Eventually, you reach the ocean bed—your subconscious mind, your inner 'garden'—and the activities of the surface are far away and forgotten.

It is from here that balance is attained between our external and internal natures. It is from this perspective in our psyche that our more complex 'self' grows, a self that is able to blend its distinction and its uniqueness with ideas and beings beyond it. It is in the solitude of the 'garden' that we recognize the beauty of the Universe. For it is at this level in the ocean where the surface activity begins—first as a ripple, then a current, until as a wave, it crests and crashes on a distant shore. So, too, do our thoughts and ideas begin, at some distant place in our subconscious. And once we have achieved balance and growth, we resurface to integrate the subtle yet powerful experience into our daily lives.

This internal 'garden' I have been referring to is known by many different names—subconscious, soul, inner child, creative mind, divine life, higher self—whatever we chose to call it, it's the center of our being, the place from which come all our ideas and feelings. Now, I'm not talking about a religious belief here. Religion is an external faction, created and controlled by people for the purpose of sharing common beliefs. What I'm referring to is our metaphysical essence, that central part of us that is connected to the Force that governs the Universe. It is Yin to the Yang, passive to the active, spiritual to the corporeal.

We have an abundance of external stimulation and activities available to us. Our society emphasizes and thrives on them, and that's not necessarily bad. What is detrimental to our well-being as a people is when we shun the complementary activities that would allow us to maintain the balance we so desperately need. Chance recognized this. While we can't help but be amused by his antics as the mysterious, comical hero of "Being There," we have a hard time relating to him or feeling comfortable with the idea of someone like him. Yet Chance, in his own naïve way, has the secret to leading a happy, balanced life. He knows himself better than most people could admit to and he can teach us a lot. Perhaps a visit with him to our inner 'garden' would be just the remedy we need to relieve ourselves of the fear we have of being alone.

∾ ∾ ∾ ∾ ∾ ∾ ∾

This was written for an English Literature class at Youngstown State University. We were reading books that had been made into movies, like Ragtime. We discussed whether the author's story had been lost in translation when taken to the big screen; how using our imaginations while reading differed from seeing someone else's vision of the story play out; and whether the changes made to the storyline to make it "better" for the film version worked or not. I preferred Being There, the book, over the movie. While the movie was enjoyable on its own if you hadn't read the book to compare it to, there was an expectation of comedy because Peter Sellers was playing the lead character. The book provides so much more insight into what the characters were thinking and saying, and the humorous moments don't overshadow the serious ones. Of course, that happens a lot with book-to-movie adaptations.

What I realized while re-reading this essay is how attuned I was in 1992 to the value of spending time alone. This theme has manifested itself into a lot of my work, especially the book I published twenty years after I wrote this essay. It's entitled, "The Pleasure of My Company: Finding the Motivation and Courage to Spend Time Alone."

The American Dream

(1992)

The widow asked my father if it would be all right if she read aloud some poetry. Naturally, he agreed. She went into another room, came back with a bound book and, for many minutes, read selected pieces of beautiful poetry. When she finished, my father commented on how beautiful the poetry was and asked who wrote it. She replied that her husband, the millwright, was the poet.

It is now nearly sixty years since the millwright died, and my father and many of us at Herman Miller continue to wonder: Was he a poet who did millwright work or was he a millwright who wrote poetry?

Leadership is an Art
by Max DePree

Did it ever occur to them that he was both a millwright and a poet?

The American Dream. There are as many as there are American dreamers. For me, it's the freedom to become any and all things that I choose to be. We are not one-dimensional beings. So why are we so inclined to put labels on people? To put them in tidy little boxes?

There's a puzzle that instructs you to connect nine dots in a square formation with four straight lines without lifting the pencil, going through each dot only once. Most people struggle with it, trying unsuccessfully to stay within the implied borders of the square. But the imaginative person, the visionary, sees beyond the obvious and moves outside the box to solve the puzzle.

I live outside the box. I sit at my life's loom, weaving the yarns that are my experiences into a tapestry, selecting colors and creating patterns as I go. I can even pull out the yarns and change my past by changing my attitude toward it, by not giving it the power over me now. The tapestry is continuously developing. I follow no pattern except the immediate desires of my heart and mind.

I enjoy living outside the box. So far in this lifetime, I've been a teller, office manager, computer programmer, corporate trainer, production manager, consultant, traffic manager and entrepreneur. I've worked in advertising, banking, pallet brokering, large corporations, small companies and my own businesses. Since I was twenty-five, I've learned how to swim, fence, ice skate, ballet dance, meditate, read tarot cards, sign language, act, Tai Chi--the list goes on. And I am a consummate traveler, a gypsy by blood and inclination.

Through all these professions and ventures, one love has remained constant--writing. Whether writing training manuals for Xerox, a supplier newsletter for a General Motors division, correspondence, reports, poetry, essays or memoirs, expressing thoughts, images and emotions through the written word always delights me. Someday, like many an amateur writer, I'd like to be published and see my work in print on a shelf in Borders, gracing someone's coffee table or peeking out of someone's briefcase. But regardless, I'll continue to put pen to paper even if I'm the only audience.

I tell you all this not to boast, but to offer encouragement and motivation. Our lives need not be limited to one career, one track, one box. And even if the life's work that we choose requires a commitment to one field, that does not limit our ability to interweave other 'lives' within that choice. Neither time nor age decrees when we can, or cannot, do something—we are in control. Nowhere is it written that we cannot change our minds and move on to something different and new.

The American Dream? It has taken on many faces over the years. No longer can we expect to work at the same company for thirty years—the era of the gold watch at retirement may be lost forever. No longer do children follow in their parents' footsteps or take over the family business—they're hearing the beat of different drums. But regardless of the form the American dream takes, the basic content is the same—freedom, our fundamental right. It is embodied in all of us from our first cry to our last breath.

We are as diamonds in the rough. We must remove the outer layers, the mental boundaries, and expose the multifaceted, brilliant gems that lie within. And we must remember to behold others as gems also. We mustn't assume that we know a person simply because we've seen one aspect of his or her life. If we see only the millwright, we risk missing out on the poet.

❧ ❧ ❧ ❧ ❧ ❧ ❧

This assignment for an English Composition class at Youngstown State University instructed us to write our take on the American dream. The opening passage is from a popular book on leadership, published in 1987. Max DePree was an American businessman and writer. His father, D.J. DePree, founded the Herman Miller office furniture company in Michigan. When a millwright died on the job in 1927, D.J. DePree visited the family and was moved by the widow's reading of her husband's poetry. He makes a commitment to treat all workers as individuals with special talents and potential, and the story of the millwright became part of Herman Miller lore. I thought this company's progressive philosophy to acknowledge the value of its employees created a working environment where workers could fulfill their American dreams.

The Last Temptation of Christ

(1992)

This book was written because I wanted to offer a supreme model to the man who struggles; I wanted to show that he must not fear pain, temptation or death—because all three can be conquered, all three have already been conquered. This book is not a biography; it is the confession of every man who struggles. In publishing it, I have fulfilled my duty, the duty of a person who struggled much, was much embittered in his life and had many hopes. I am certain that every free man who reads this book so filled as it is with love, will more than ever before, better than ever before, love Christ.

Nikos Kazantzakis, from his prologue
to the novel, *The Last Temptation of Christ*

It was never my intention to set out and shake anyone's faith, but rather to ignite faith. The side issue in my mind was for me, as a filmmaker, to get to know God and in making Jesus more accessible to myself and people like me. If you already have faith you are fine, but we're the ones who need it, and maybe this film will be some consolation.

Martin Scorsese, Director of the film,
The Last Temptation of Christ

The Ayatollah Khomeini, in early 1989, pronounced a death threat against the author, Salman Rushdie, for his portrayal of Mohammed and Islamic tradition in his book, The Satanic Verses—and an uproar of dissent was heard the world over and no less so here in America. Thousands of Americans protested this despicable attack, this extreme censure that violated the fundamental right of freedom of speech.

Yet, ironically, many of these same American protestors, just eight months earlier, had unleashed a censorship campaign of their own against Martin Scorsese's film of Nikos Kazantzakis' book, The Last Temptation of Christ. In one case they drew a line in defense of freedom of speech; while, in the other, they crossed over it. Why was such a furor raised about this particular movie? In order to answer that, one needs to know some of the circumstances leading up to its production.

Nikos Kazantzakis was born in Crete in 1883, and raised in the Greek Orthodox Church. An intellectual who knew and loved ordinary, uneducated people, his entire life was spent in the battle between spirit and flesh. Traveling the world over, he studied the philosophies and religions of the many cultures he visited, searching untiringly for his true savior and the meaning of his, and our, existence. One after the other, he would adopt, then renounce, allegiance to their ideologies—Catholicism, Darwin, Plato, Nietzshe, Bergson, Buddha, Lenin, Odysseus. When he finally returned to Christ, it was to a Christ that was enriched by everything he had experienced during his life. The quote cited above explains in Kazantzakis' own words how the culmination of his internal search evolved into the writing of his book in 1955.

The book is a novel based upon the adult life of Jesus of Nazareth. It deals in depth with Jesus' human nature and its conflict with his divine nature, which he finally comes to accept after years of temptations and struggling between the two. Kazantzakis tried to portray Christ in terms "…meaningful to himself and thus…make Jesus a figure for a new age, while still retaining everything in the Christ-legend which speaks to the conditions of all men of all ages."[1]

It was this struggle of the human side of Jesus accepting his divine nature that interested the renowned filmmaker, Martin Scorsese, when presented with a translated copy of the book in 1972. Scorsese was raised a Roman Catholic and even spent part of his teenage

---

[1] A Note on the Author and His Use of Language, P.A. Bien's commentary at the end of his translation of the book.

years in a seminary studying for the priesthood. Like Kazantzakis, he examined the inner turmoil of man and portrayed it through the vibrant characters and melodrama of his films, including Raging Bull, Taxi Driver and Mean Streets.

Bringing Temptation to the screen was a pet project of Scorsese's for years. Paramount originally was to produce it in 1983, but backed out just weeks before the filming began. Universal Pictures agreed to produce it as part of a three-film deal with Scorsese, which allowed him to make one film of his choice for two major productions of their choosing. Intended as a fairly low-budget art film, not a big commercial moneymaker, the movie was, according to Scorsese, his "...way of trying to get closer to God."

But while the film was still in production, the protests began to pour in. Many complainers were responding to a bootleg copy of an outdated script, containing several distasteful lines not used in the movie, being circulated by a group of ultraconservative Protestant women called the Sisterhood of Mary. In an effort to alleviate these anticipated objections, Universal Pictures invited a group of forty church leaders to a screening of a rough cut of the film prior to its release, a group representing a cross-section of Protestants, Catholics, Jews, Fundamentalists and a constituency ranging from Morality in the Media on the right to People for the American Way on the left. The Fundamentalist faction refused to attend, however, and ninety-nine percent of the people raising complaints about the movie didn't even see it.

The responses to the viewing were mixed. Conservative Christians proclaimed it blasphemous, staged demonstrations and organized a national campaign to have the picture destroyed. Fundamentalist leader Jerry Falwell called for boycotts against Universal's parent company, MCA, as well as their products and subsidiaries, such as Grosset and Dunlap publishers and the video release of E.T. The most organized campaign, headed by Methodist minister Donald Wildman, head of American Family Association, sent out 2.5 million mailings protesting the film and did anti-Temptation advertisements on 700 Christian radio stations and 50 to 75 television stations.[2]

The resistance took an ugly turn when anti-Semitic incidents and threats were issued against "non-Christians" at Universal Pictures. Reverend R.I. Hymers, Jr., a Christian extremist in the Los Angeles area, staged a demonstration near the Beverly Hills home of Lew Wasserman, the chairman of MCA. An actor portraying Wasserman stepped on the bloody back of another actor playing Jesus carrying the cross, while an airplane flew overhead with a banner reading, "Wasserman fans Jew-hatred with Temptation" and the crowds chanted, "bankrolled by Jewish money."[3]

Those who did not find the movie irreverent rated it anywhere from "a work of art which emphasizes certain aspects of Jesus" to "people who go to the movie are going to come out bored and leave before it is over." Bishop Anthony Bosco, of the National Council of Catholic Bishops, felt the movie should be allowed to just expire quietly, stating, "This too shall pass." Reverend Paul Moore, Jr., an Episcopal bishop, offered some of the strongest defenses of the film, calling it "theologically sound." Michael Morris, a Dominican priest who holds a doctorate in the history of art, concluded his extensive theological and artistic analysis of the film with the statement, "More than any other film of its type, Scorsese's Last Temptation measures the magnanimity of Christ's sacrifice in terms of moral choices. This, above all, is the value of the film, and for that, one can tolerate its theological deficiencies."[4]

Interestingly, what incensed so many about this movie is what appealed to so many others. The artistic merits of the film would

---

[2] The movement continues long after the film appeared in movie theaters. Nine months after the film's release in August 1988, it was released on video; and Blockbuster Video, the largest retail chain in the country, refused to stock it. In October 1990, Cinemax aired the movie as part of its "New Wave Film" series. Some local cable companies across the country provided an "extra service" to their subscribers: They "blacked out" the film during its slotted air times.

[3] John Lea, "A Holy Furor," Time, August 15, 1988

[4] Michael Morris, O.P., "Of God and Man," American Film, July/August 1989

warrant a separate essay, but the context—seeing Jesus portrayed as a virile, energetic human, who laughs and cries, sings and dances—was a refreshing change from the starchy, overly-reverential characterizations of the past. He was a character to whom people could relate. Randy Pitman, writing for the Wilson Library Bulletin, explains, "The major points of controversy that surround the film don't crop up until the final third, when, in a fantasy sequence, Christ is allowed to step down from the cross and live out the remainder of his days as an ordinary man. He weds, and makes love to, Mary Magdalen. When she dies, he moves in with Martha and Mary [whom he marries] and continues to ply his former trade as a carpenter. Only on his deathbed, when confronted by Judas…does Christ realize that he had been tricked by Satan. Understanding this, he crawls back to the cross so that he can complete God's plan for man's salvation."[5]

The outrage was based upon its being an 'interpretation' of Christ's life instead of the 'facts' presented in the Bible. Then why were no such assaults made against other theatrical portrayals? According to Michael Morris, the 1961 MGM production, King of Kings, omitted all the major miracles of Christ's ministry and his character was watered down "in an effort to make him digestible to an intended large and diverse audience. No mention of Christ's divinity was made in the film and the resurrection was only hinted at…" Then there are the other movies, based on the Broadway plays, Jesus Christ Superstar and Godspell, where Jesus is portrayed as a rock star and a clown, respectively. It seems as long as Christ is portrayed as a 'good,' one-dimensional man, then cinematic omissions and broad interpretations will not offend Christian sensitivities, but it is considered taboo to create a deeper, more complex personification of the man. Such was Martin Scorsese's intent when he said, "I wanted to show a Christ you could argue with, one who eats and drinks with prostitutes and sinners, a real earthy Jesus."

---

[5] Michael Morris, O.P., "Of God and Man," American Film, July/August 1989

I believe what happened here was a sad commentary on how self-righteous, narrow-minded prejudices have become entirely too prevalent in our society. People were so afraid of their religious beliefs being blasphemed they failed to realize that their own actions were blasphemous to the ultimate meaning of Jesus' life and death—love. Personally, same as for Scorsese, I feel closer to my own divinity when I am allowed to relate to Jesus as my example and way-shower, my brother and teacher. Newsweek tells us of a statement made by the Reverend Charles Bergstrom, a Lutheran minister, who said, "There's no way this film can be considered blasphemous or an attack on the Holy Scripture. I think for people who really believe there is a God, this could in fact, help in their faith."

Censorship, when taken literally, has value in that it allows for the examination of documents or other materials in order to determine their content and worth. This is done with the movie rating system, for instance, which gives an indication of the nature of a film for discretionary viewing audiences. To be sure, the First Amendment affords the objectors the same right to express their views as it does to the author and filmmaker. But to blatantly use censorship as a way to control what is produced based on personal beliefs is a violation of that basic freedom.

In my opinion, the people who protested so vehemently against the film missed an opportunity to discover for themselves a multidimensional savior who is within reach, instead of revered and held at arm's length. In his day, Jesus was considered by some to be a rebel, a revolutionary. I wonder what he would have thought of all those intolerant protestors crying out for censorship in his name. I like to think that he would have reiterated the petition that he made to his Father while dying on the cross— "Father, forgive them, for they know not what they do."

∾ ∾ ∾ ∾ ∾ ∾ ∾

This composition was assigned in an English Honors class. The professor gave us a list of topics from which to choose, and I selected Censorship. Anyone who knew me, knew how incensed I could get when someone had the audacity to tell me I had to think this or I couldn't read that. Seriously? So when deciding what angle to take on this subject, the semi-successful censorship of the movie, The Last Temptation of Christ, *was perfect fodder for my confrontational appetite.*

Rose: A Biographical Sketch of My Grandmother

(1993)

"...and then there was the time I talked George [Washington] into cutting down that cherry tree—boy, did he get into trouble for that!" Fact? Hardly. Senility? Not a chance. This typifies the humor one can expect from the eighty-seven year "young" woman known as Rose Nerad Morrell.

Rosella Frances Nerad's life began on October 9, 1906, in a second-story bedroom in a section of Cleveland, Ohio, known as Shantytown. But, due to the circumstances of her birth, it was not recorded until December of that year. "Is she dead yet?" the midwife would ask each day when she checked in on mother and infant. Rose was premature, you see. Her mother, Mary Kadlececk Nerad, went into shock-induced labor after having a finger on her left hand amputated—over the kitchen sink without anesthetics! She had slammed a window down on the middle finger a few weeks earlier, and chips of glass and bone had embedded in the digit to the point of becoming gangrenous. Hospitals and anesthetics were the exceptions in Shantytown in 1906, hence the crude operating conditions.

Rose was born the next day, but she was a feisty baby and survived, much to their surprise—and, despite her diminutive five feet, one-inch frame (or maybe because of it), she's been feisty ever since. *"I come from sturdy, stubborn Bohemian stock,"* she'll tell you proudly.

Rose's father, Frank Joseph Nerad, was born in 1867 in Prague, Bohemia—before it became Czechoslovakia. He was a tall, thin man with wavy black hair and mustache, blue eyes and a straight patrician nose. He loved music and could play the piano and the accordion. What he didn't like was work, and managed to avoid it more times than not. On those rare occasions when he did work, he was an iron molder. He also picked mushrooms and sold them to the neighbors. *"Everyone wanted my Dad's mushrooms. He really knew how to pick the best ones."*

Mary Kadlececk married Frank Nerad at the age of sixteen. She, too, was Bohemian, but was born in Detroit, Michigan, in 1874. She was of average height and had blue eyes. Her crowning glory was her long, lustrous, chestnut hair. Rose remembers being mesmerized as she watched her mother brush it every night. She even has a braid of it that had to be cut off when Mary died so the body could fit in the coffin. Mary was a gentle, hard-working housewife and mother who took in ironing to support the family during those long periods of her husband's unemployment.

Frank and Mary had thirteen children, but only eight survived past infancy. Rose, the ninth baby and fifth of the survivors, was born when Mary was 32 years old. She had four sisters—Molly (1), Maude (3), Julia (4) and Anna (6)—and three brothers—Joseph (2), Edward (7) and Hank (8). Today, only she and Anna are living.

Shantytown mirrored so many cities across America in the early twentieth century, a blend of European immigrants sequestered away from the Anglo-Saxon middle-class and upper echelon. There was Mrs. Black, the Scots woman; Mr. Kisch, the Hungarian shoemaker; Frank Turner, the Englishman who married Rose's Aunt Anna; the Rothenbergs, the Kesslers, the Vainers. There was even a divorced woman— *"Scandalous!"*—who lived down the block and *"...none of us kids were allowed to speak to her."*

Rose attended Quincy Elementary School, where her best friends were Margaret Kessler, a Hungarian who took her to a Catholic church for the first time, and Marie Vainer, whose father came over on the same boat from Bohemia with Rose's. When it came to playing, Rose never cared much for dolls. One Christmas, when her sister, Maude, gave her and Anna a doll to share, Rose let Anna keep it. She preferred to shoot marbles, play baseball, hit a tennis ball on the sidewalk or play tag with the boys. Once, while playing hide-and-seek, she ran between two houses in the neighborhood, passed a doghouse. She didn't know there was an old bulldog inside, but she found out soon enough when it bit her left leg. She hobbled home, where her mother treated the bite with peroxide, which made it foam and *"...hurt like the dickens!"* Rose did learn to embroider and crochet. She will gladly crochet you a lap throw or hammock cover today, although it may take a little longer because of her arthritic fingers.

In 1920, during Rose's second year at Central Junior High School, Mary Kadlececk Nerad died of lumbar pneumonia, at the age of forty-six, in her daughter's arms in their home. There were no funeral homes in those days. The undertaker came to the house and embalmed the body in the basement. Rose remembers sitting on the back porch when he walked out with a pail of blood to throw in the ditch! *"To this very day, I'm squeamish at the sight of blood."*

After Mrs. Nerad's death, the younger children were separated and sent to live with relatives. Anna and Hank were sent to St. Paul, Minnesota—she to live with their maternal grandmother and he to live with their Uncle Charlie. Ed moved in with their brother, Joe, and his wife, Dolly. Julia got an apartment with a girlfriend, and Molly and Maude were already married.

Rose, on the other hand, had to drop out of school at the age of fourteen and move in with a Jewish family, the Rothenbergs. She did housework and babysat their two sons for room and board and two dollars a week in wages. She recalls the time when she was dressing the younger boy near the fireplace in the living room, and the hem of her long house dress caught on fire. She ran to the kitchen and tried to douse the flames with glasses of water. She could see her reflection in the glass cupboard doors, flames shooting up behind her. Her screams brought Mr. Rosenberg downstairs, and he rolled her in a blanket on the floor. A doctor was called, and he had Rose sit in a hot(!) bath. Blackened skin floated in the water, and she almost passed out from the pain. When she stepped out of the water, her left hip and thigh were raw, bloodied flesh. The doctor put ointment on the burn and wrapped it in cheesecloth. The house visit cost two dollars, which Rose paid off herself in two installments of a dollar each.

Rose stayed with the Rothenbergs for just over a year. Then she moved in with Joe and Dolly to help take care of their newborn first child, Joe, Jr. She only had Thursdays off, and she and Dolly didn't get along. When, after living there about a year, Dolly called her and her mother *whores*, she moved out and went to live with her Aunt Rose and Uncle Gus, *"...a big, burly German who looked like the actor Edward Arnold."*

At this time, Rose got a job at Thompson Products as a tip grinder. Thompson manufactured valves for locomotives, automobiles and airplanes, and she and Louise— *"I can't for the life of me remember her last name!"*—were the only two women working in the entire plant. Surprisingly, there was not a problem of unequal pay based on sex—all the employees were paid the same low, piecework wages. She recalls one of her "big" pays of seventy-two dollars!

About ten feet away from her machine worked the "new guy." Louise checked out his timecard and learned he was an Italian named Anthony Todd Morrell. She declared, "I'm going to marry that man," but Rose could care less. In fact, she was a little afraid of him because she often caught him staring at her while they were working or in the lunchroom. He did neck grinding on the valves, and when he finished a pan, he had to take it to her station for the tips to be ground. One day he offered to lift her pan of completed valves and said, "I don't like blondes. My real estate partner ran off with a blonde and left me high and dry. That's why I had to take a job at this place." Rose was not concerned or impressed. [She later learned that the *real* reason he had a job there was because the owner saw him bowl and wanted him on the company team—so he hired him! Todd had moved to Cleveland from Ashtabula and was living with his cousin.]

Rose had to take two streetcars to get to work, leaving her house at 6:30 in the morning. One morning, Todd "happened" to be driving by when she was walking to the streetcar stop and offered to take her to work. Of course, he brought her home, too; and, despite Rose's initial apprehensions, their relationship began to grow over the weeks that followed. *"He wasn't so bad after all. In fact…"*— and here her eyes roll heavenward and a youthful blush radiates her cheeks— *"many mornings we would take a 'short cut' down a dead-end street that we nicknamed 'Kiss Me Street' so we could…well, you know."*

About a year after they had been dating, Julia invited Rose to return with her for a visit to Detroit, where she now lived. Todd said she couldn't go, to which Rose replied, "That's what you think! She's my sister, and I can visit her any time I want." They sat on the front porch swing for hours arguing, but she won out in the end. He took her to the boat docks the day of her departure, giving her a small box of candy to open on the boat, with a note that said to expect a surprise when she returned.

She swears he jinxed that boat because the trip across Lake Erie to Detroit was rough. High winds caused the Cleveland skyline to disappear, then reappear, as high waves tossed the vessel to and fro. Feeling a bit seasick, Rose left the dry, warm cabin and huddled in a deck chair on the top deck and dosed off. Unbeknownst to her, the chair slid precariously close to the edge of the boat with every other wave, then back toward the cabin. Julia became worried at her absence and sent a purser to look for her. He found Rose and took her inside, amazed that she hadn't been swept overboard!

Upon her return to Cleveland a week later, Rose purposely sat inside the cabin and waited until everyone else had disembarked. She could see Todd standing on the dock, nervously wiping his face and arranging his homburg as he checked each passenger that stepped off the boat. Finally, she decided she'd kept him waiting long enough and got off, pleased at the relief and love she saw on his face. As soon as they got in the car, he put a diamond ring on her finger and said, "Now you can't go to Detroit anymore!" She didn't object.

Todd's mother, Josephine, didn't approve of Rose. She was an American girl, you see, not the nice Italian girl his family had arranged for him to marry. But Todd had been forced into a 'shotgun' marriage two years earlier, only to have his wife leave him for another man after his daughter, Marian, was born. He was separated when he met Rose, and the divorce was finalized one month before their wedding. This time he was marrying for love.

Rosella Frances Nerad married Anthony Todd Morrell, twelve years her senior, on April 8, 1926, in Mount Carmel Church in Ashtabula, Ohio. The bride was dressed in her favorite colors of pastel purple and green. The reception was held at the groom's family's house, and as was the custom, handfuls of candy-covered almonds were thrown at the couple when they entered the house to signify a fertile new beginning. A friend of the family, Tony Rose, played the accordion, and there were lots of relatives, friends and neighbors in attendance to wish them well. The only member of Rose's family who could attend, however, was Julia.

The honeymoon was spent in their new, second-story apartment in Cleveland, which they had fully furnished, including appliances, for two hundred dollars! That first night, a nervous Rose changed into a self-embroidered orchid nightgown in the bathroom, waiting for Todd to fall asleep before coming out. But he never did! However, they had to contend with tin cans under the mattress—courtesy of Julia and Aunt Rose—before *"...getting down to the 'serious business' of the wedding night."*

Eventually, Rose and Todd settled in Ashtabula, where Todd got into the insurance business. Rose had difficulty getting pregnant at first. Dr. Collander stretched her— *"So much pain!"*—and gave her pills. Yet, when she finally did get pregnant, he saw her once and then instructed her, "I'll see you in nine months." She gave birth at home, with no anesthetics, on Wednesday, April 25, 1928, to a black-haired, brown-eyed baby girl whom they named Gloria Marie. Todd was a little disappointed when he heard—like most men of that generation and nationality, he wanted a son first—but it didn't take him long to get over it once he saw his beautiful daughter.

Two years later, on Wednesday, July 23, 1930, they had their second and only other child, another daughter whom they named Antoinette Josephine. The two girls were as different as night and day in looks and personality. Gloria had Todd's dark, sultry Italian looks, while Toni's fair hair and complexion resembled the Nerad's. Gloria had colic for eight months as a baby, and cried and cried and had to be held all day, taking short naps. Toni, on the other hand, slept most of the day. But the girls got along well together, except for the usual sibling confrontations, like when Gloria pulled the knob off the radio and quickly put it in Toni's hand when she heard Rose coming down the hall. Toni cried and denied having done the dastardly deed, while Gloria looked innocently at her mother. Rose admits having been a pushover when it came to disciplining her daughters— although to hear them talk, she was a formidable woman to face when caught in some indiscretion.

Rose and her family were lucky during the Depression because Todd was able to keep his job selling insurance, although it was difficult collecting premiums. Their friends and neighbors thought they were rich since he was working. *"Imagine, they thought we were rich because we were able to save five dollars a week!"* They were a tight-knit family, doing lots of things together, like going to movies and carnivals, bowling [Todd was the first bowler inducted into Ohio's new Bowlers Hall of Fame, posthumously, in the late 70's.] and taking vacations for a week every August to such places as Hershey's chocolate factory in Pennsylvania or Lake Riley.

In 1932, a national tragedy precipitated a paralleling family tragedy. Charles and Anne Lindbergh's two-year-old son was kidnapped from his second-story bedroom, later to be found brutally murdered. The country was in shock, moved by the Lindbergh's grief. At the same time that the headlines told of the missing baby, Todd's six-year-old nephew, Jimmy, was kidnapped on his way to school with his older sister. The DeJute family lived in Niles, Ohio, where Jim

DeJute had a successful contracting business. The kidnappers demanded a $25,000 ransom. In the meantime, a woman called the police and told them where two men were hiding little Jimmy. When the police checked out the deserted house, they didn't find anyone at first. Then, one of the officers spotted a schoolbook on the floor and called out. Young Jimmy responded, and they found him in a secret panel in the wall. The two men were apprehended, as was the ex-housekeeper who had tipped them off when she realized what her friends had done. Fortunately, the incident had a happier ending than the Lindbergh case. Years later, while touring the Ohio State Penitentiary, Rose and Todd had the two kidnappers pointed out to them by the guard.

Nineteen thirty-two was also the year Frank Nerad passed away. He was sixty-five years old, and he died of a stroke after a fall down a flight of stairs in his son, Joe's, home. He had been living there for seven or eight years when it became apparent that he couldn't live by himself without Mary to care for him.

From the year Rose's mother died, through her courtship and marriage to Todd, through the birth of her two daughters, to the death of her father, the country had been living under Prohibition. Rose remembers being nervous about going to her friend Louise's house because Louise's mom ran a speakeasy, and Rose didn't want to get picked up in a raid while visiting her. But she wasn't able to avoid the "long arm of the law" entirely. In 1933, Todd was arrested for having a still in his upstairs bathroom! Actually, the contraption belonged to Todd's cousin, Albert, who was living with them temporarily. The police tracked it down from the fumes that traveled down the plumbing and seeped out into the sewers. Todd wasn't home when the police arrived and confiscated the still, but he drove up as they were leaving. Rose tried to signal him from the front window, but to no avail. That evening, Todd's father bailed him out of jail for $700. He had borrowed the money from the local Mafia boss in Ashtabula, Nick C. Nick told Todd to take his family out of town for a night, and he would handle everything. Todd obeyed, and, sure enough, when they returned the next day, the file had "disappeared"—no arrest, no police record and no more bootlegging for Todd! As it turned out, prohibition was repealed later that year.

The Forties and World War II. Men were off to war, and women replaced them in the workplace—and Rose was amongst them. She got a job in 1944 at the ordnance plant working the 4 p.m. to midnight shift. She got a few hours sleep each night, then woke up early to get the girls ready for school. (Todd had moved to Warren, Ohio, to manage the Club Center Bowling Alley, but more of that later.) Rose would leave a dinner started on the stove for them to finish cooking and eat when they got home from school—latchkey kids were prevalent before modern day! *But do you think they would bother to wash the cruddy pots and pans? No, sir. Dishes, yes, but I'd come home to cold water sitting in greasy pans!"*

Rose's brother, Hank, was an M.P. in the army and got a purple heart when he was wounded serving in Germany. Gasoline, sugar and coffee were some of the staples being rationed. But, all things considered, the Morrell family got through the war unscathed. As stated earlier, Todd moved to Warren in 1944 after his insurance job was eliminated. Rose would take the bus down on weekends, sometimes alone and sometimes with the girls. Todd earned twenty-five dollars a week at the Center, and sent $15 home to Rose. One week, Rose met his boss, Sam C., and told him they couldn't afford to live on just $25 a week, especially since they were paying for two households. Sam agreed, and gave Todd a five-dollar-a-week raise. Every time after that, Rose managed to finagle more out of Sam until, having reached the incredible sum of fifty dollars, Sam told Todd, "Let me know when she's coming again so I can be sure not to be here!"

Finally, Todd got a job at another insurance company in Warren and made arrangements for his family to join him there. Since Gloria was in her senior year of high school, she stayed with relatives in Ashtabula so she could graduate with her class. But Toni and Rose joined Todd, and Gloria would take the bus to visit them on weekends. They moved into a rented house on East Market Street.

It was a big, rambling structure with a garage as large as the house and large crates in the lofts. Rose wondered about the oversized basins and tables in the basement and the many painted-over nails and hooks in unusual places on the walls in the living and dining rooms. Her curiosity was satisfied when she came upon an old calendar one day. There on the cover was an artist's rendering of her house—advertised as a funeral home! She quickly put two and two together—the deep sinks and long tables in the basement… *"where they embalmed the bodies!"*; the high, double garage doors… *"for the horse-drawn hearses!";* the large crates… *"coffins!"*; and, the nails and hooks…*" for hanging flower arrangements!"*—and within a month they moved out.

On January 24, 1948, Gloria married Frank Nyitrai, a catcher in semi-pro baseball and an electrician at Ohio Edison; and, on July 5, 1952, Toni married Remi Rechedy, a trumpeter and truck driver. The national events of this time period—the Korean War, the Communist threat, McCarthyism—didn't impact Rose's life in any significant way that she could recall or cared to comment on. She did, however, experience her first hospital stay and surgery in 1953.

She and Todd were celebrating their twenty-seventh wedding anniversary when she developed sharp pains in her stomach. Thinking it was something she ate, she went home and put a heating pad on her abdomen. A day or two later, her pain having become excruciating, they called their family doctor, but he was out of town. Todd got in touch with a doctor he knew from the Elks club, who gave Rose a *"…shot that would knock out a horse."* But it didn't affect Rose. They were finally referred to a Doctor Trimbur who, upon examining her at their home, ordered her to the hospital immediately. She had a ruptured appendix! He performed surgery and discovered it was beginning to turn gangrenous and peritonitis had set in. She was close to death for a few days, but her Bohemian robustness and tenacity pulled her through—only to find out later that, coincidentally, the physician who had administered the shot was the county coroner!

Rose and Todd became grandparents for the first time on Friday, October 28, 1949, when Gloria and Frank gave birth to a daughter, Gloria Susan. They were living with Rose at the time; and Gloria, never having had *any* experience with babies, gladly accepted her mother's assistance with, and assumption of, the duties of raising her daughter. Susan grew to be a constant companion of Rose and Todd's during her youth, joining them on summer vacations and weekend excursions for Todd's bowling tournaments, showing up for dinner a few nights a week—the two family's now lived in two houses next door to each other—and sleeping at their house every Monday and Saturday evenings, when they would play Scrabble or cards.

Over the fourteen years following Susan's birth, four other grandchildren were born: Susan's sister, Sandra Rose, in 1952; their cousins, Lorraine (Chickie) and Lynette (Tina) in 1953 and 1955, respectively; and, finally in March 1963 (to Todd's delight), the first boy child, Gloria's son, Anthony Michael. The five cousins were as close as siblings and remain so to this day, a tribute to the strong family values passed down from Rose and Todd.

Those values are now being taught to a third generation of Morrell offspring, their five great-granddaughters and three great-grandsons. Unfortunately, Todd did not live to know any of these children. On July 3, 1973, he died of an embolism at the age of seventy-nine. Rose's grief seemed insurmountable, yet her fortitude got her through the worst of it, even though a part of her seemed to die with Todd. But she was to experience an even greater loss eighteen years later when liver cancer claimed her first-born child, Gloria, on December 9, 1991. *"No child should die before the parents. I'll never get over it, but I have to live with it. No minute of the day goes by that I don't think of her. Why her, why not me?"*

Yet, despite these tragedies, Rose hasn't succumbed to her grief or depression. To this very day, she remains a model of survival and perseverance. She lives alone in her two-bedroom Cape Cod house that she and Todd moved into forty years ago. Her daily routine may include any of the following: reading the Ashtabula paper with her breakfast (She's had the *Star Beacon* mailed to her for as long as she's lived in Warren); performing a household task or two ("Friggin' Friday" is reserved for major cleaning and ironing.); getting picked up by her hairdresser to have her hair done; reading whatever novel she's engrossed in over a cup of tea (She's an avid reader, going through books at a rate that would put the average college student to shame. She especially enjoys thrillers and murder mysteries.); watching her favorite soap opera, *Guiding Light* (which she first listened to as a fifteen-minute radio show over fifty-five years ago); writing letters to her sister, Anna; or, finally settling down in her nightgown and robe around six o'clock to watch the evening news and television shows. On the table next to her rocking chair you'll find her nocturnal glass of white wine, a long-standing tradition. Saturday mornings, Toni and one or more of the grandchildren usually stop by for coffee and donuts. Sunday dinners are often spent at Susan and Sandy's house, where a few games of cards may follow their repast.

Her movements are slower, she needs help climbing stairs and getting in and out of cars and she has slight difficulty hearing, but none of these impediments have impaired the spirit of Rose Nerad Morrell. She's still the feisty, little Bohemian that first graced this world on October 9, 1906, in that second-story bedroom in Shantytown.

* * * * * * * * *

As the reigning matriarch of my family, Rosella Frances Nerad Morrell asserts an inner strength that is unparalleled in any other woman I know. Her devotion to her family is incomparable, and she is a constant source of encouragement and love for us all. She isn't profusely vocal about her view on national or international events. When you ask her about specific incidents of historical significance, her responses are succinct. This is not to imply indifference on her part; but, rather, it exemplifies the fact that her family is the center of her universe and whatever happens outside of it is of lesser consequence. However, I was able to secure some comments about events and issues that occurred during her lifetime.

World War I: "There was bedlam downtown… crowds… ticker tape parades… celebrations… when armistice was declared.

Vietnam War: "Shouldn't have been there…too many good guys got killed for nothing at all…waste of good men."

Abortion Rights: "It's their bodies…they should be able to do what they want. People shouldn't meddle in other people's business or bodies."

Civil Rights Movement: "He [Martin Luther King, Jr.] had good ideas…for unity and non-violence…a good heart. Integration is necessary…segregation isn't right."

Airplanes: Her first plane ride was in October 1973, three months after Todd died. She went to Las Vegas with Sandy and was *"…scared at the thought of flying…when the plane taxied, it was great. Then we took off—I thought I would die!"*

Politics: "Never argue or talk about politics or religion…Full of unfulfilled promises."

Women's Movement: "Pay for talent regardless of sex."

First Man on the Moon: "They looked cute walking on the moon! Made me tired to watch them."

Assassination of JFK: "So sad…such a waste…Gloria called me to turn on the TV… 'They just shot Kennedy!' she screamed into the phone."

The living legacy that Rose Morrell leaves her family is her youthful outlook on life. To her, age is a state of mind, *"…just another number. You can be old at 21 if you think so."* She attributes her young-at-heart attitude to having been around young people all her life because she *"...always had kids at the house visiting my daughters."* There is nothing about her life that she would change or do differently—she describes it as satisfying, enjoyable and happy. Even when asked how she would like to be remembered, she first offers a quip— *"The wicked witch is dead!"*—then adds seriously that she wants to be remembered for *"...helping people."*

On October 22, 1993, the newest member of Rose's family, Rachel Marie Morrell, was born. When asked what advice she would give to Rachel as she embarks on her life, Rose's response epitomizes her own existence and the heritage she gives her entire family: *"Be good, respectful, a good listener, keep some of that sweet innocence—and just be happy."*

↝ ↝ ↝ ↝ ↝ ↝ ↝

I wrote this for a long-term assignment for a Family Development class at Youngstown State University. We were instructed to interview a person over the age of sixty-five, so I chose my maternal grandmother. I had to include a list of questions assigned by the instructor related to historical events that would have taken place during her lifetime while also getting her personal story. We sat at her kitchen table for over three hours, two of which I videotaped, and she was in her element. Some of the stories I'd heard while growing up, but others were new to me. This assignment turned into a labor of love, and I'm proud to say I aced it and got the full 100 points grade for it—but that's insignificant compared to the memory of that afternoon in her kitchen when I fell in love all over again with my Grandma Rose.

Growing Old

(1993)

[People] think they have eternity before them…We don't have eternity; we only have time. It is what we have to work with. There are no limits to how much we can grow and develop, but time limits us…People are often obsessed with aging, with what time does to them. Instead, they should be concerned about what they do with time.

This excerpt from the best-selling book of the Seventies, How to Be Your Own Best Friend by Mildred Newman and Bernard Berkowitz (61), has been an inspiration to me since I received the book in October of '74 for my twenty-fifth birthday. In retrospect, I realize I was on the threshold of an introspectively metamorphic period in my life, and this passage was only part of the compelling force that propelled me forward on my journey. As I got in touch with my spirituality over the ensuing years, I've come to believe that my possibilities are endless. I feel unfettered by conventional or traditional paradigms. Instead, I am free to discover new and diverse models and to create a life that satisfies all my heartfelt and soul-felt desires. I have the freedom of choices, and one of the most important choices of my life has been to use my time here to its fullest, wanting never to look back one day and say, "I wish I had done this" or "If only I had done that."

Growing old is a natural, inevitable phenomenon. There's nothing disastrous about it, nothing conspiratorial or limiting or judgmental—it is a fact of life, pure and simple. Yet, for some reason, our culture views "growing old" as some form of affliction in and of itself, something to avoid or fear or delay as long as possible and at any cost. We pursue the "fountain of youth," purchasing remedies, treatments and other miracle paraphernalia in an attempt to force our bodies and minds into perpetual youthfulness. We deny our actual age, considering our lives some tortuous, uphill climb that peaks at 30, 40 or 50, depending on one's proximity to each decade. Then, we're "over the hill" and, God forbid, o-l-d.

Am I missing something here? It seems to me going downhill would be a lot easier and more fun than going up! Better yet, why even consider life a hill at all? Why not see it as a plain, made up of many pathways, bridges and terrains on which we can journey? We need not travel in a straight, vertical direction either, but can venture off a "beaten path," forge new roads through virgin territory and discover new dimensions. We can even revisit our past, changing it if we chose to by seeing it through older and wiser eyes. We are the pathfinders of our destiny. We should have more respect for ourselves, for the years we cultivate so resolutely and the wisdom we reap from our experiences.

I attribute much of my outlook on aging to my maternal heritage. My Grandma Rose is a perfect example of someone whose heart is forever young, even in her advanced years. My mother was the same way. She encouraged me throughout my life, never pressuring me to "act my age" or conform to the conventional expectations of marriage, settling down and having children. She was my falconer, living vicariously through me; and I was her falcon, going forth to savor life—to learn, to grow, to teach, to give—and yet always able to return to my home and be sure of her love and support.

I have no qualms about growing old. I can't be bothered worrying about something over which I have absolutely no control. I can, however, control the quality of my existence. I prefer to enrich my life with the wonders that each new year brings. I look forward to completing my degree and opening or directing a preschool, preferably in some metropolitan area like Chicago, Denver or New York. I intend to tour the Orient one day and to return to Britain so I can go horseback riding across the Devon moors once again. I'm excited about the books I'll publish someday. And the pièce de résistance? Why, seeing my photograph flashed across the television screen for all the nation to see when Willard Scott wishes me a happy 100th birthday!

❧ ❧ ❧ ❧ ❧ ❧ ❧

This composition was part of a Life Span project assigned in my Family Development class at Youngstown State University. The primary part of the project was interviewing a person over 65 years of age, asking them their views on historical events that happened during the span of their lives while garnering personal information about their life as well; then writing a paper on the results of that interview. I chose my maternal grandmother, Rose Morrell, and you can read that paper in this book—it's entitled Rose: A Biographical Sketch of My Grandmother. This composition was the final part of that project, writing about my feelings on growing old.

Almost thirty years have gone by since I wrote this and, while my perspective on growing old is the same, my experience of actually getting older has sometimes been a rude awakening. I often have to remind myself of my current age (73 years 'young') when I see or hear people's reactions to things I say or do; or when I'm reminded of my advanced age every time I look in the mirror—my hair is now all gray and white, which still shocks me! So, while the concept of being ageless still applies, the reality is I have to remind others and myself of that concept because I'm being judged on outward appearances. Does this confusion on my part make sense or am I overreacting? Regardless, I'm (thankfully!) still sound of body and mind, so I say 'thanks' to Mom and Grandma Rose for the female genes I inherited that keep me feeling great!

Riding the Wooden Waves

(1996)

Graduating from kiddie rides to the Wild Cat at the sophisticated age of seven years marked a milestone in my life, and the beginning of a lifelong love affair with the roller coaster. Standing in line on that June day in '57, I clung to my Dad's hand as if he were my anchor in the sea of bodies that crammed around me. Behind us were my Mom and Aunt Toni, seasoned veterans of this monstrous latticework of wood. A train, returning from its harrowing journey, emptied its joggled cargo to make room for the next band of eager passengers. Wide-eyed, toothy expressions were frozen on the faces of those disembarking, as they scurried down the exit ramp to solid ground again. As we inched closer to the front of the line, I came to the sudden realization--soon it would be my turn.

Nestled in a residential neighborhood of Youngstown abutting Mill Creek Park, Idora Park opened its gates in 1899. Originally known as Terminal Park, it featured a merry-go-round, a dance hall, trolleys and a variety of outdoor entertainments. When the Wild Cat roller coaster was added later that same year, the park took on its new name and, over the years, grew to a full-fledged amusement park. Eighty-five years later, the park closed down when a fire destroyed a section of the midway, including half of the Wild Cat. The merry-go-round was sold intact and resides now in a waterfront park in Brooklyn, New York. The ballroom is used now and then for special fundraising events. But, for the most part, the park lies dormant like an old western ghost town. The wind floating through the charred remnants echoes the laughter and screams of bygone visitors.

Unlike the computerized, steel structures in amusement parks today, the rides in Idora Park in 1957 were constructed of wood and manually operated by grungy carnie-type men with Brylcreamed hair and tobacco-stained smiles. Though tame by present standards, these rides still packed a wallop for thrill seekers of every age. Lost

River Ride, with its log cars lurching through a water-filled chute toward a climactic plunge down a steep incline. The Caterpillar, its rapidly-increasing momentum crushing riders against the outer side of the cars before enveloping them in a tarpaulin cocoon. Bonnet-shaped Tilt-A-Whirls jerked bodies back and forth as the cages spun on their tracks around the slanted, wooden floor.

But rides weren't the only entertainment that the park offered. On the midway, barkers enticed passers-by with promises of stuffed animals in all sizes and colors for "simply" knocking down the weighted wooden bottles. They lured curious onlookers into darkened tents to observe nature's aberrations: the Bearded Lady, the Reptile Man, the two-headed calf. The Penny Arcade held guests captive for hours as they deposited token after token into the skeeball, foosball and pinball machines. Others tried desperately to grab a silver-plated lighter by manipulating an unwieldy steel claw or to collect a treasure in coins that hung precariously suspended over the edge of a slowly shifting tray.

Vendors sold sweet-smelling, gossamer-light cotton candy at every twist and turn along the park's pathways. A shiny red apple, dipped in a warm, sticky glaze and balanced on a pencil-thin stick, satisfied many a "sweet tooth," as did a cup of crushed ice soaked with blue and red syrup. My favorite was the French fries, fried in their skins and served in thin paper cones. I'd add a touch of salt and a squirt of ketchup before devouring the hot, greasy strips.

Sometime during the subtle change in the shift between the sun and the moon, the park transformed into another world. Buildings and rides were decorated in multi-colored bulbs that shone as brilliantly as gems. Their imperfections and inner workings were disguised in the shadows, like wrinkles and blemishes masked by dim lighting. The trains on the Wild Cat resembled glowworms crawling hurriedly along the coiled body of a fluorescent serpent. These and other threads of childhood memories at Idora Park are deeply woven into the fabric of my being.

Daddy nudged me forward into the yellow third car of the Wild Cat's train. I was too young to wonder at the fascination Americans have for the roller coaster. Too young to question what compels us to wait in long lines, board an open train with only a metal bar to restrain us and climb up a steep hill with the deepening sensation that something awful is about to happen. All this only to be hurtled down that steep hill and whipped around sharp turns at breakneck speeds. Knuckles turning bone-white as they lock around the lap bar. Hair flying every which-way in wild abandon. Faces going taut from G-forces that approach aeronautical proportions. And anything that isn't strapped on or tied down being propelled to the outer regions of the park, never to be seen again.

The jerking cars. The clanking chains. "I think I can! I think I can!" I prayed we could, as the train sluggishly ascended the first hill. Approaching the top, I wondered if this was such a good idea after all! We paused in midair--for a split second that seemed like eternity--before plunging forward like a car speeding off a cliff. Without giving it a second thought, my hands shot straight up above my head, my mouth opened as wide as it could, and my voice pierced the air with the ancient cry of roller coaster enthusiasts the world over—A-A-A-A-A-H-H-H-H-H!!!!!!

☙ ☙ ☙ ☙ ☙ ☙ ☙

This essay was written for an English Composition class at Youngstown State University. The assignment was to take a vivid memory of our childhood and embellish on the sights, sounds, smells and feelings of the memory. My father worked for Ohio Edison, the state's public electric company, and every summer they held a family day at Idora Park. Dad worked in the morning until eleven o'clock while Mom fried her breaded chicken and packed her wicker picnic basket with potato salad, baked beans and other delicious foods to be shared with other families we'd meet in the Park's pavilion. My sister, Sandy, and I waited frantically for Dad to get home so we could leave. Many of my fondest childhood memories took place at those Ohio Edison Family Days at Idora Park.

One Minute in Time

(2001)

The nurse beckoned us from our vigil in the hospital waiting room. We'd been sitting there in virtual silence—my brother, Tony; his wife, Patty; and I—each lost in thoughts both deep and fleeting. I remember thinking that the color scheme of the small sitting area was blasé in its shades of gray and mauve. It did, however, mirror the view outside the ceiling-high windows. The gray sky was typical for Ohio in December. Hell, it was typical for Ohio most days of the year. I guess the colors and the December sky mirrored my mood as well. Knowing your mother is dying of cancer can make even the bluest sky seem gray.

Tony, Patty and I stood and paused, none of us wanting to go first. None of us ready to take that short walk down the hall to her room to view Destiny's handiwork. Dead man walking. God, why did I think of that phrase at a time like this? Why, indeed!

"*Iron* is a four-letter word!" my mother would say, as she admonished my sister or me for admitting we were ironing something. To her, permanent press was the greatest creation of the modern world. She had long ago relegated her ironing board and iron to a corner of the basement, where they became an intricate part of some spider's elaborate web.

There were other four-letter words that she hated--well, perhaps hated is too strong a word, but she certainly had a strong aversion to them. Words like *cook, wash* and *bake*. And she claimed that *clean* was really a four-letter word, but they'd put the silent 'a' in it to fool her. But you couldn't fool her very easily. Lord knows, I tried!

I don't want to give the wrong impression of my mom, though. She did her share of all those chores, and she did them quite well in my estimation. But, unlike some mothers who actually seem to flourish in the Zen of housework, my mom performed those tasks out of duty. She genuflected to a different idol--Life. It seemed that her idol was turning on her now though.

The nurse walked ahead of us, her rubber-soled shoes squeaking as they moved across the linoleum floor. More shades of gray surrounded us in the sterile hallway. It's amazing how clear my memories are of that hallway, as if my mind was taking inventory as a way to keep it from thinking of where we were headed. Someone had a television on in the room on the right--I could hear a commercial for a local car dealer playing. On the left was a cart with little plastic cups of medications all lined up and ready to be administered to the appropriate patients. A candy-stripe volunteer passed us, her bouncing gait, perky face and cheery smile in shocking contrast to the steel and white and gray surroundings.

As a child, my mother used to sit with her finger pressing on the tip of her nose. When asked why she did that, she said because she wanted to have a perky nose like some of the other girls in her class. She found her Italian proboscis unattractive, just like most children find something about their physical features 'wrong' and in need of dire change. But, looking at photographs of her as a teenager and at her wedding picture at the age of twenty, I am reminded of Elizabeth Taylor's dark, striking looks. As a child, I thought my mother was beautiful on the outside. As an adult, I knew my mother was beautiful on the inside.

I'd be hard-pressed to tell you what one thing I admired most about my mom. Certainly, her sense of humor. She knew how to see the humor in the most aggravating situations, how to enjoy the moments, how to laugh. She left my friends in stitches with her antics, and I've heard them recant tales of their encounters with her to others on numerous occasions. She wasn't afraid to laugh at herself either, never taking things too seriously. I think that's what was so special about her. She taught us how to be young at heart and light-hearted as well. She taught us how to laugh.

I wasn't laughing as we approached her hospital room. My heart was heavy with the impending scene that awaited us in that room. I had left the hospital about an hour earlier. In need of some fresh air, I'd gone for a walk around the block. The parking lot and sidewalks had tell-tale patches of snow and ice, but for the most part, the pathways were clear and I was able to walk at a brisk pace, paying little attention to where I stepped. I remember distinctly how, when I turned onto Meadowbrook Avenue, the tears that I had been fighting off since yesterday morning began to cloud my vision.

Mom was diagnosed with cancer on June 26 of that year, 1991. The prognosis from her simple operation to remove some growth from her colon had turned into her death sentence. The malignancy had eaten at a good portion of her colon, enough so that they had to remove nine inches and install one of those hideous, undignified pouches. But the disease had not stopped there. If it had, we would not have been making that one-minute walk down the hospital corridor. No, it had invaded her liver as well. Invaded it in such an insidious way that no surgeon's knife could repair it. It was impossible. Incurable. Inevitable.

As much as I admired my mother's sense of humor, it was her tenacity that stands out to me as her best trait. Oh, there were times this trait could drive me crazy! She was, after all, a Taurus. Bull-headed. Stubborn. Inflexible. But this characteristic proved beneficial when she needed a strong resolve to get through the bad times. Like her father's sudden death from an aneurysm and her mother's grief and dependency. Like my father's gambling and their eventual separation. Like my sister's suicide attempt, then her emotional and financial dependency on Mom. Like the never-ending struggle to make ends meet, balancing her small income with the day-to-day and unexpected expenses that eat away at the funds put aside for special occasions. She had a lot of "rainy days" in that regard. Yet, the combination of her inner strength and her way of looking for the humor in Life served her well. And taught me well. I'm proud to have inherited some of that strength and humor, though I could never hope to master it as well as she had.

As I continued my outdoor walk, I talked to Mom. Earlier that year--before the operation, before the cancer, before our lives were turned upside down--I had come up with a metaphor during a week-long seminar that described my relationship with my Mom. She was the falconer and I was the falcon. The peregrine falcon is my favorite bird, and I saw myself as a falcon who ventures out into the world, flying free and far. Yet, whenever the spirit moved me, I could return to my home base, to my falconer, to Mom. She liked the metaphor for she'd often said that she was living vicariously through me. Her support and love over the years were truly "the wind beneath my wings," my falcon wings.

So, as I walked around the block that Monday afternoon in December, I talked to Mom. As the unrestrained tears flowed down my cheeks, I told her how much I loved her and how much I appreciated her support. As the tears seeped into the recesses of my breaking heart, I told her it was now time for her to fly, time for her to free her spirit and soar. I would be okay. I had, after all, been taught by the best of them. She need not worry about me. "Let go, Mom, and fly," I cried.

We'd brought Mom to the hospital the morning before. She'd had two restless nights. I'd been up with her almost all of Saturday night, trying to get her comfortable on the sofa where she'd been sleeping for weeks because it was easier to get up and down from there than from her bed. I'd given her ice cubes to suck on and held her close to me when she cried out in pain. I did all this as if I were another person, not wanting to believe that this was my mother who was fading away, whose body was black and blue from lying down so long, whose eyes seemed to look through me to some distant place only she could see.

I finally called her doctor at dawn, and he said to get her to the hospital. I called my brother, who lived two houses away, and I rode over in the ambulance with her while he notified the other family members. After getting her through Emergency and getting her admitted, we gathered around her bedside, acting as if this was just a temporary setback, as if she'd be home with us soon. Her sister, my aunt Toni, was almost adamant about keeping up these appearances. Her mother, my Grandma Rose, didn't realize how close she was to losing her first-born child, didn't understand the severity of what was happening. How could she be expected to understand? She was 85 years old. She was supposed to die first, not her 63-year-old daughter. She still doesn't understand to this day.

At dawn on Monday, my mom went into a coma. When we arrived at the hospital, the person we saw lying in that bed was not my mom. That shriveled-up body belied the energetic, boisterous woman we knew. Those dead-pool eyes concealed the light and laughter of the woman we loved. For all intents and purposes, she was gone. Yet, my grandmother sat there all day long. Holding her hand. Brushing back her hair. Talking about nonsensical things. Not letting go.

The nurse pushed open the door and stepped aside so we could enter the room. I went first. My grandmother looked up at me, her eyes wet, questioning. "Susan, I've lost her. I've lost my little Gloria." And she bowed her head and cried. But I barely heard her. I was looking at the form in the bed and wondering why I didn't feel anything. Why I wasn't overwhelmed by what had happened here a minute ago. My mother had died. She was gone. Yet, it was anti-climactic to me. We'd had our goodbyes a short time before. We'd walked together on that December afternoon, and she'd taken off to fly beyond the gray winter clouds. The tears and grief would come in time, but in that instant, I knew she was free and I was so happy for her. And, for a brief moment, I lived vicariously through her.

ৡ ৡ ৡ ৡ ৡ ৡ ৡ

This essay was written for an assignment in a Writing Memoirs class offered by the University of Utah's Lifelong Learning program. We were instructed to write about something we experienced for just one minute in time, but expand it into a full essay. It tells about the minute it took to follow the nurse down the hall to my mom's hospital room on December 9, 1991.

Essays

These essays are reflective pieces I wrote for many and varied reasons over the years, covering many and varied topics. Some are informative, some are whimsical, some are sentimental and some address serious subject matters. As with the Compositions, there is some repetition, which contributes to the fabric of my life's story.

The Art of Moseying

(1971)

Life in our culture is often one big blur: the streaked image of a photograph taken through the window of a speeding car, lines smudged and colors smeared. We move in high gear, hurry from one place to the next, and cram as much into an hour as is humanly possible--then lament the lack of enough hours in a day. We're a fast-moving, constantly active society. We don't take the time to mosey anymore.

"To move along slowly; to amble" only defines the *act* of moseying. If performed properly, moseying is a true *art* that leaves you feeling relaxed physically and exhilarated spiritually. Take an imaginary mosey with me, and you'll see what I mean.

We're standing on a sidewalk in the downtown district of a large city. It's mid-week, and it's high noon. People pour out of office buildings like cereal out of boxes. They dash off in every direction--to the post office, the dry cleaners, the card shop, the dentist, the department store, the travel agent. If they have time, they grab a quick sandwich at the closest deli before returning to their offices for a few more busy hours of work before the evening rush hour. It would be easy to get caught up in their frenzy, easy to be jostled and swept away from our intended course of action, so stay focused.

Before taking your first step, inhale deeply through your nostrils; imagine your body is a balloon filling up with air. Hold it for a moment, then slowly let the air escape through your pursed lips. Try it again and notice how light you feel. Continue breathing in this relaxed manner as your feet tread lightly and you find your natural gait. Resist the urge to fall into step with the madding crowd, moving instead at a leisurely pace.

Let your hands do what feels most comfortable. Slide them into your coat or pants pockets. Clasp them behind your back. Let them just swing at your sides, conforming to the natural rhythm of your stride.

With your head held high, look ahead of you, not down at your shoes. Observe the faces rushing past. Catch someone's eye, then-- don't look away. Hold the other person's glance for one second. Two seconds. A curious thing happens. The muscles in your face shift. The ends of your mouth curl up into a grin. Done often enough, the smiles will infuse you with a wondrous aura of well-being.

Once you've mastered the *act* of moseying, you're ready to refine it to an *art*. This involves heightening your senses, noticing things you disregard in your normal haste. See beyond the obvious. A half-dressed mannequin, frozen in an unnatural pose. Faded travel posters and cardboard ocean liners. Graffiti art on a bus-stop bench. A bird's nest in the recesses of an awning. An outdated calendar on a barbershop wall.

Breathe in the street smells. The earthy scent of leather and shoe polish; the stinging odor of hair dyes and permanent solution; the stench of diesel fumes; the fragrances of floral bouquets--all blending with a smorgasbord of aromas flowing from restaurants, taverns and sidewalk pushcarts.

Tune into the sounds. A street musician plays jazzy notes on his saxophone. Passers-by toss clinking coins into his velvet-lined horn case. Bells toll from high steeples. Engines rev. Horns honk. Drivers curse. Tires screech.

At first, your senses may reel from the barrage of stimulation. This is where the art of moseying comes into play. What distinguishes the *art* from the *act* is an attitude of detached awareness. Take a moment to become aware of a specific scene or sound, to appreciate it and to experience it. Then, release it and proceed to the next one. It's like looking at your surroundings through the lens of a camera. You select a subject, bring it into focus, determine the best composition and snap the picture. When complete, you advance the film and proceed to the next photo opportunity.

So, the next time you go out for lunch in a large city--or to a shopping mall, your own neighborhood or your town's Main Street--treat yourself to a mosey. Shift your mind from "going somewhere, doing something" to "just being here and now." The effects are astounding, and your life will be enhanced in subtle, yet powerful, ways.

∾ ∾ ∾ ∾ ∾ ∾ ∾

This essay received a second-place award at the Midwest Writer's Conference in Canton, Ohio, in 1998. I was inspired to write it many years ago when a co-worker, Sam Bixler, would chide me on how fast I walked when we'd go out to lunch around town. He'd grab my arm and say, "Slow down, Susan. Let's just mosey a while before we hurry back to work." I find myself telling people to mosey now when walking around. I think of moseying as a walking meditation!

April Fools!

(1986)

Tuesday, April 1, 1986. April Fools' Day. Only the joke isn't very funny. Waking up to a sharp pain in my lower abdomen makes me moan, not laugh. Being prodded repeatedly in that area by nurses, physician's assistants, doctors and the surgeon to see "Does that hurt?" is definitely not my kind of humor. As they wheel me down the hospital hallway on a gurney and I slowly succumb to the drugs they've given me, I keep waiting for someone to say, "April Fools!" But that never happens.

Monday, April 14, 1986. Thirteen days after my appendix has been removed, I am finally allowed to leave the convalescent confinement of my home and go for a car ride, although I can't drive myself. My husband, Stuart, takes me with him in his pickup truck to visit a couple remodeling projects his crew is working on. It is a sunny spring morning, perfect for escaping our little one-bedroom apartment on the first floor of a duplex at 5 Milan Avenue in Bedford Hills, New York. I love feeling the fresh air blowing in my hair through the opened windows and feeling the sun on my face as I lean against the truck while Stuart checks his projects. That done, we go grocery shopping, then head home.

As we're driving down Babbitt Road, we can see cars stopped up ahead, then a police car and finally some firetrucks. As we crawl forward, we exclaim together, "Oh, my God! Are they at *our* apartment?" Sure enough, a fire had started in the kitchen during our absence! By the time we park and exit the truck to tell the firemen it's *our* home, the fire has been extinguished. Only some smoke hangs in the air above the building, and the smell is atrocious.

Stuart and I watch in shock as we look in the kitchen windows at the fire marshal holding up gobs of melted plastic to identify items in the kitchen. The green blob? Our blender. The yellow one? A breadbox. Yes, all that broken crystal was the glassware we'd received as wedding gifts. Almost nothing in the kitchen is salvageable, and a few things in the living room are damaged by the water that surged through the apartment from the firehoses. On a detached, subliminal level, I am fascinated by the power of the fire and the aftereffects of the smoke and water.

In the weeks that follow, Stuart and I pack up our belongings, live with some friends for a few weeks while we search for a new apartment, then eventually move to Ohio in October to be near my family. That appendix attack on April Fools' Day starts a series of events that has Stuart and I in the best possible places to avoid the worst possible scenarios from a fire happening in our home. So, though not funny, we survived and we had the last laugh.

I wrote this in my journal in November 1986. Stuart and I had been living with my mom and sister in Ohio for six weeks. We ended up remodeling half of the basement into a small apartment—bedroom and living room—while we shared the bathroom and kitchen with them. Stuart started his own remodeling business and I got a job with a temp agency.

As it turns out, that fire was a catalyst that the Universe created for me. I'd been procrastinating and vacillating about what to do about Stuart's increased drinking. While staying at my friend Dorothy's house after the fire, two pivotal incidents occurred that would help me deal with the problem. The first was a conversation I had with Dorothy the second morning of our stay, when Stuart hadn't returned home from going out with his friends the night before. She shared that her father was an alcoholic when she was a child. As she described his actions and the family's reactions, I realized that she was also describing Stuart's behaviors. I loved that she didn't just come out and tell me, "Stuart's an alcoholic." Instead, by sharing her story, she allowed me to come to the realization myself. The second incident was finding a basket in my guest room with little books called, "Daily Word." They had daily inspirational messages based on a word for that day, and reading them during this traumatic time in my life was very comforting. I ended up subscribing to them myself and to this day I read it every morning before I do my daily meditation. I've also occasionally been involved with the spiritual community, Unity, that publishes the magazine.

The point is, I wouldn't have received those two "gifts" had we not had the fire. I needed a push in the right direction and the guidance to move forward, so God literally and figuratively "lit a fire under my feet." Extreme? Perhaps, yet we were lucky. The fire happened during the day, not at night while we were sleeping. It was contained to the kitchen with only water and smoke damage to the living room, bedroom and bathroom. The upstairs apartment wasn't damaged, although the neighbors' cat was freaked out. In fact, the cat going crazy is what tipped them off that something was wrong. When they saw smoke coming out of our kitchen windows, they immediately called the fire department.

To this day, I have "souvenirs" from that fire—photographs that were partially ruined by water that blurred their colored inks; and smoke-damaged Monopoly and Clue game boxes that were stacked on top of one another in the bathroom closet and furthest from the fire itself. Five years after the fire, when I opened boxes of items that I'd had in storage the whole time, I detected whiffs of smoke—or were those just residual memories conjuring up illusory smells?

Solitary Refinement

(1988)

Today is the first time I've woken up a single woman in three years and ten months. A divorced single woman. And it feels—what? What am I truly feeling?

Relieved. Happy. A little sad for what should have been. A lot glad for what will be. Mostly relieved that I no longer have to worry about what Stuart is doing. Is he drinking? I don't care. Is he coming home tonight? I don't care.

Now I'm alone again. I've been on my own a lot in my adult life so it's something I value. Being by myself. Better to be by myself than in a marriage with a man who drinks too often and too much and causes me anxiety. With a man who tells me I'm getting fat when he can't make love to me because his drinking has left him impotent. A man who had me lying for him to cover up for his binges.

God, how did I let that happen? I've always been an honest person, intolerant of liars, yet I had become what I least admired. How? The simple answer—I loved him. The more complex answer as I look back on those three plus years—well, when you're in the midst of changing you're too close to see what the change really looks like. What's that saying—you can't see the forest from the trees? Stuart's drinking and my lying for him were giant sequoia trees blocking my view of the forest that was my marriage and my integrity.

Was it always like that? Did I enter that forest when I first met Stuart at that pub in Edinburgh five years ago? Did I venture further when I ignored my Inner Voice telling me "This is how it will be with him. You don't have to go through with it" on that drive to Ohio for our wedding with him sleeping off a drunken stupor in the passenger seat? The deeper I went—the more in love I was—the blinder I became to what was happening to us, to him and to me.

Stuart's drinking reared it's ugly head for the first time the weekend we made that drive from New York to Ohio for our wedding in November of 1984. We'd met while I was vacationing in Great Britain in 1983, and he courted me for ten months via transatlantic calls and snail mail. During a month-long visit in July, he met my friends in New York and my family in Ohio. He proposed to me at the Newark Airport before he returned home, then returned in November to go through the immigration process before the wedding.

Our plan was to leave at 4:30 on Thanksgiving morning so we'd arrive in time for the holiday dinner. That's when things got messy. Stuart's boss and a couple co-workers took him out for drinks after work as a sort-of bachelor party that Wednesday evening. He promised he'd be home at a decent hour since we had to get up so early the next day. That was the first promise he broke.

As the hours passed and no Stuart, I called the boss's wife but she hadn't seen her husband either. I went from mild concern to he's-having-fun-with-his-new-friends acceptance to worry to major concern to fear until, at four o'clock a.m. he was dropped off at the apartment so drunk he could hardly walk. Now I was angry! I told him not to go to bed because we were heading out as planned at 4:30—and we did. It was while entering Pennsylvania on Interstate 80 near Stroudsburg that a sleeping Stuart yawned and the stench of alcohol reeked throughout the car—and that's when I heard that Inner Voice warning me of what was to come.

That's when I stepped deeper into that forest because, after mentally deliberating, calculating, rationalizing with myself, it was my heart's pleading—"But I love him!"—that won the argument. So the wedding took place as planned and over the next three years, Stuart's drinking was contained for the most part, at least that's what I told myself. Eventually and in hindsight, I saw the patterns— Stuart was a binge drinker. He could drink normally when we socialized, but I came to know the signs when a two- or three-day binge was coming. He'd play harder rock music and wear one of two shirts—a white tank top or a black T-shirt.

I hadn't known the extent of Stuart's drinking problem when I married him, but during one of his binges his Mum called from Scotland. I tried to cover up for him, but when she asked me, "Is he out drinking, dear?" I broke down and cried. "I'd hoped that the move to America and being married to you would be good for him. I'm so sorry!" she sobbed.

The worst thing about Stuart's drinking wasn't what it was doing to him or his business relations—it was the change that I was going through at a slow, subtle pace. I started lying for him to clients and friends when his drinking caused him to miss appointments or social events. That so went against who I was and warped my integrity! Our sexual relationship suffered because drinking made him impotent, but he blamed his inability to perform on me because I was gaining weight as a result of stress eating. My self-esteem was shattering but I was too close to see it.

In the fall of 1986, we moved to Ohio after experiencing a fire in our home in April. Stuart joined a group similar to Alcoholics Anonymous and I found a support group for significant others of alcoholics. We tried our best to create a new life near my family, although we didn't tell them about the problems we'd had in New York because of his drinking. However, it wasn't long before he slipped into old habits and it became apparent to my family what was happening.

I left that forest for good when I signed those divorce papers yesterday, but I've been standing at the edge of the forest looking out for the past year. Ever since Stuart went to Scotland to visit his family and I told him to give serious thought to his drinking problem and our marriage. Ever since I heard the new woman in my Significant Others support group say she'd been married for twenty-two years to an alcoholic.

Twenty-two years? That's when the light bulb went on in my mind and I realized I didn't want to be with Stuart another twenty-two *days,* let alone years. But he came back ready to commit to a treatment program and make this work, so I felt obliged to give him a chance. And, since I took my marriage vows seriously, I felt I owed it to myself to see if anything was salvageable even though something told me I was postponing the inevitable.

I lived the next nine months waiting for the other shoe to drop. I slowly detached myself from the relationship, going through the motions, watching for the signs that another binge was about to happen. The shoe dropped in June and I felt a load lifted from my heart and mind—my obligation was over. I'd allowed myself time to prepare mentally and spiritually for the solitary refinement that was long overdue.

The smile on my face this morning feels so genuine, so authentically me again! Oh, Stuart, I really wish you the best of luck. We did love each other—we just couldn't be together. One thing I've learned from this is that it's not about love. Love is an abused, overused word. We expect it to be the end-all solution when it's not. It permeates everything and never dies but it shouldn't be used as an excuse to stay married when you no longer *like* the person to whom you're married. When you no longer *trust* the person to keep his promises of sobriety. When you're being mistreated and abused, either emotionally, psychologically or physically. No one deserves that. So I wish you well, Stuart, because you're not a bad man. We've had our time together and will be better individuals apart, at least I know I will.

Wow, that felt good writing all this down! I feel as if I've swept away the last particles of dust from my tarnished heart. I needed to purge all this from my mind and soul once and for all so I don't second-guess myself or wallow in self-pity because the marriage to my romantic Scotsman had perished at the bottom of a shot glass. It's now time for the old Susan to be resurrected with her self-esteem, sexuality and integrity intact. Thanks to the Powers That Be for guiding me through this relationship, this marriage, this divorce and now this next phase of my life.

I wrote this in my journal on Tuesday, September 20, 1988, the day after Stuart and I signed our divorce papers. It was an amicable divorce—no bitter words, no fighting over money or property. I even teased when the lawyer asked if there was anything I wanted and my reply was, "Is there any way I can get custody of his Scottish accent because that's what I really fell in love with!" Stuart laughed because it was an inside joke between us. It was good to leave that office laughing.

We went our separate ways. He stayed in Ohio for a few years while the following year I moved to the Chicago area. Then sometime in the mid-nineties, I got a phone call from him. He was back in Britain, living in Liverpool, England. We got past the initial awkwardness and brought each other up to date on our lives—my mom had died, one of his brothers had died, we'd each had some health issues we'd overcome. I didn't ask if he was sober or drinking—I figured I'd lost the right to ask. We laughed as we reminisced about some things and, for a short period of time, it felt comfortable and reminded me of those courting calls he made to me from Scotland after we'd met and before he'd moved to New York to marry me. But eventually, it became awkward again as we ran out of things to share. When he asked if he could call again, I almost said, "Sure," from habit. But I caught myself and knew I had to be honest with him. "No, Stuart, I don't think so. It's been nice talking to you and I'm glad you're doing well. But it's time we both move on." I haven't heard from or about him since. Am I curious? Sure, but not enough to track him down. That wouldn't be fair because I chose to cut those ties and I really don't want to see him again.

Carpe Diem

(1989)

As I lay here in my bed, the sounds of a babbling brook echoing from my tape player, it suddenly occurs to me that what I want to do most right now with my life is create. I want to make something. I think about Chicago and what path I want my career to take. I wonder if I should put together a portfolio of my photographs on the chance that some prospective employer might be interested in my work. "This is my brother with his daughter, Christina, at two months. She's my goddaughter and my favorite subject." As I imagine showing these pictures, my mind goes to the movie I saw this evening, "Dead Poets Society." The cinematography was breathtaking. I remember thinking as I watched it that I would like to learn filming, to go beyond still photography.

As the refrains of the music and brook fill the background, my mind imagines working in such an environment. To work with filmmakers, with photographers, in a media that promotes and encourages creativity on a daily, regular basis. To do something that my heart and soul could share in the experience. To create.

Where does this sudden urge, this desire, come from? It feels deeply rooted, yet so obvious, as if I knew it all along but hadn't recognized it. At this point in my life I want to embark on a career that's really "me," that uses my fullest abilities and allows me to feel and experience my talents, those I've learned in this lifetime as well as those I've brought with me from past ones.

I wonder, too, if the physiological makeup of a woman close to forty years old who has never born a child causes her to feel this need to create. Is it Life I want to create? Will I ever have a child of my own? Am I trying to find another channel for this life since it cannot take the form of a baby? And if I do, will it satisfy this need to create? Or is it a need of my soul, a need to give back some of that which has been given to me over my lifetime?

I believe that the movie I saw this evening influenced my thoughts more than I'd realized. The students were told to "seize the day," that we must pursue our dreams and make something of our lives, if only to please ourselves.

Have I pleased myself with my life? In most ways, I think I have. Although I think I began at a late age, consciously that is. For subconsciously, deep within my being, I was who I am now. My life does not have a lot of the outer elements that so often are used to measure a person's successes at certain given times in one's life. No house, no furniture to speak of, no children, no financial securities. I haven't moved steadily "upward" in a career or in a social standing. Rather, I've moved around--sometimes up, sometimes down by outward appearances. Oh, there have been the occasional pauses, the times when things seemed to stand still, become stagnant even. But in retrospect, even those times were needed in order to gain stronger momentum to move ahead again.

What's driven me, what's kept me on this journey for thirty-nine years, has been my own self-love—the inner strength that somehow gets me through all situations, good or bad, stressful or languid. And this strength and love come from my soul and its affinity to God. My spirituality has manifested itself in many ways. It's been my comfort and my friend. Perhaps that's why I like being alone, in a quiet place or on a long drive. I'm not afraid of myself, of my thoughts or fears. In any case, I know that this sudden urge to be creative, to apply myself in such a manner, comes from the center of my being.

And having faced it, written about it, thought about it, I am confident that somehow I will be able to do it. The method isn't important. It will happen. I feel relieved—and ready to sleep.

ॐ ॐ ॐ ॐ ॐ ॐ ॐ

I wrote this at 12:22 a.m. on Saturday, July 15, 1989, while lying in bed trying to fall asleep. I grabbed a pad and a pen and started writing down these flitting, capricious thoughts, just to get them out of my mind so I could go to sleep. It's how I process things sometimes. Stream-of-consciousness writing. Brain dumping. I recently found it tucked away in an old journal, and I realized that so many of my views about myself and my life remain the same today—although it turns out that I didn't really want to become a filmmaker! I did move to the Chicago area shortly after writing this, however, where I discovered some incredible outlets for my creativity and nourishments for my spirituality.

Mates

(1996)

Barb Murray Heiss and I have known each other since before we were born. What I mean is, our parents were friends, so we've been in each other's lives since we were mere "twinkles" in our fathers' eyes. She was born in Warren, Ohio, on December 25, 1948; and I came along on October 28 of the following year. Her mom, Pat, and my mom, Gloria, were constant companions; so it was only natural that when our families would get together, along with our aunts, uncles and cousins, we were *playmates*.

When I was ten, my family moved and I found myself at a new school--the same school that Barb attended. So we also became *schoolmates*. But she had her friends and I made my own. We'd hang out together, but she and I weren't particularly close. In 1967, we graduated from John F. Kennedy High School. After spending the summer with my aunt and uncle in southern California, I came back to Warren and got a job in the loan department at a local bank. One floor up, in the bookkeeping department, was Barb. We were now *workmates*. But like in school, we went our separate ways with our own circles of friends over the next few years.

Barb married Paul Heiss, a co-worker at the bank, in October of 1970. She'd chosen the path of wife and mother. I left Warren in 1972, moving to White Plains, New York, with my good friend Kathy. I chose the path of career and travel. When her first daughter, Tish, was born in 1974, I was working for Xerox Corporation and in love with a man named Tom. When her mother died in 1975, I was in Phoenix and dating a man six years my junior. In 1976, her second daughter, Katie, was born while I was spending the summer in Las Vegas before moving back to Ohio to be with my parents, who were on the verge of separating. When my dad died in 1979, she and her family were living in Sharon, Pennsylvania.

From 1978 to 1994, my life can be summarized as follows: moved to New York (1978); married (1984); moved to Ohio (1986); divorced (1988); moved to Chicago (1989); moved to Ohio when Mom died (1991); started college (1992). I spoke with Barb one time during all those years, in 1992, when I called to see if she'd be attending our 25th high school reunion. She didn't.

Then, in January of 1994, I walked into a Sociology class at Youngstown State University—and there was Barb. We exchanged pleasantries, discovering we were in the same Early Childhood Education program. *Classmates,* with similar work goals.

Over the next few weeks, our meetings were limited to two mornings a week when we'd chat before and after class and during the break. Then, on a Monday in February, she told me Paul had left her. No warning. No explanation. Just a quick "I-can't-take-any-more-of-this" and out the door. Barb had no clue what "this" was; she was in shock, then anger and guilt and the other separation stages you'd expect her to experience. We met for lunch shortly after that and discovered that, although we had taken such diverse directions with our lives, we had one thing very much in common--we had both married alcoholics. For the first time, I had someone to talk to who truly understood what I had gone through in my marriage to Stuart. As good-intentioned as my family and friends were, they couldn't grasp what I was experiencing. They just didn't get it, the heartache I went through, but Barb did. We were *heartmates.*

We started socializing more and more after that. A dinner here, a shopping trip there. One Sunday, we spent nine hours at one restaurant, sitting through the lunch and dinner hours, talking and laughing and crying and eating and drinking and talking some more. People don't believe us when we tell them about it--we even find it amazing!—but I think that was when we began our renewed relationship as *playmates.* We progressed to weekend jaunts and a ten-day vacation to Maine without an argument or stressful moment.

I love Barb. Not in the romantic or physical sense, of course, but in the deepest sense possible--spiritually. We've evolved from playmates, schoolmates, workmates, classmates and heartmates to *soulmates.* I guess we've been so all of our lives. We didn't have to spend all those years together or share the same lifestyles. Actually, it's the diversity of our past lives that enriches our newfound friendship. We've each matured in ways that are beneficial to the other at this time in our lives.

Barb is concerned that she is the only one reaping benefits from our rekindled relationship. She fears that she doesn't give *to* me as much as she gets *from* me. How can I make her see how valuable her friendship is to me? What words can I say that will express the joy she brings to my life? I've formed some very special friendships over the years. None of them are "best" because each fulfills a need within me and provides me with an outlet for giving of myself in different ways. But Barb's friendship is a rare treasure in that it comes at a time in life when most friendships have already been developed. As we embark on what author Gail Sheehy calls our "second adulthood," we've found in each other a kindred spirit. We are mature yet arouse our girlish feelings that lie just below the surface. We are confident about where we've been, yet apprehensive and excited about what lies ahead for us. We picked up where we left off over twenty years ago, yet at a level higher than either of us has ever been before.

We've often commented to each other about how we are now behaving in ways that used to embarrass us when our mothers acted the same. We've "become" our mothers! In the spirit world, Pat and Gloria are rejoicing in the bond Barb and I now share, and probably taking credit for having brought us back together. The only thing that could improve on our friendship would be to have them here to share the good times with us.

Assume...Not!

(1997)

I'm sure you're familiar with the adage, *Don't assume because it makes an* ass *out of (yo)*u *and* me*!* One of the dictionary definitions of the word *assume* is: "To think something is true or suppose that it's probably true without knowing, in fact, that it is true." Assuming creates expectations, and expectations without verification can lead to disappointment. Let me share an experience that supports that statement.

First, I'll set the stage. It's 1981 and women were being advised in magazines, movies, television, classrooms, lecture halls, etc. that we could, and should, assert ourselves. We were being encouraged to take the initiative, whether at work, school, home or in society. It was not meant as a license to be overly aggressive, but to be assertive, to stand up for oneself, voice honest opinions and act without waiting for someone's (translation: a man's) approval first.

I was working at Xerox Corporation in Greenwich, Connecticut, and my new manager invited me to the Halloween costume party that she and her husband hosted every year. At the party, I met this guy named Bill, who I was interested in seeing again. But the introvert in me, despite doing my best to be more assertive, didn't "close the deal" with Bill that night. I just hoped that I'd see him again at another social gathering.

The next week, I received an invitation from a local New York winery to a wine tasting party where I could bring nine friends with me—one of their usual marketing promotions that I'd attended before as a friend's guest. Anyway, the light bulb went off in my head—I could invite Bill to the party! All I had to do was fill in the rest of the group with some of my friends, which would take away some of the insecurity of going out alone with him.

I have to admit that I was nervous as all get out when I placed that phone call to him! First of all, I had to get his phone number from Patt, my manager, since Bill was a friend of her husband, Richie. So I invited them to the party, as well as my friends Chuck, Don and their dates. Seven down, three to go. As I was punching in Bill's phone number on my phone, I had a newfound respect for guys for having to be the "inviters" all these years—the fear of rejection can be debilitating!

Bill answered, I asked if he remembered me from the Halloween party and he said yes! So far, so good! I explained the invitation and asked if he'd like to go with me and some other friends. Then I asked if he had a friend he could bring because my friend Gail was going by herself. He said, sure, he'd get someone, which would total out the ten people I could bring. I suggested we meet at the winery since I lived in Westchester County, New York, on the east side of the Hudson River while he, Patt and Richie lived in New Jersey and the winery was about an hour north of Jersey. We made plans to meet at the front gates of the winery.

Then I called Gail to tell her it was a go and that she'd have a date, too. As we were driving over together on that Saturday in mid-November, Gail asked me what her date was like. Of course, I had no idea, but she kidded, "I hope he's not blonde. You know I prefer them tall, dark and handsome!"

We arrived, parked and stood by the front gate. Being taller than Gail by about six inches, I looked over the heads of the people walking up from the parking lot. Chuck, Don and their dates arrived first and went inside. Finally, I saw Patt's head over the crowd, then Richie, then Bill, then—*Oh, oh! Gail won't be happy,* I thought. She asked me what her date looked like, but I didn't respond. I just watched her reaction when they all approached us.

"Oh, darn, my date's a blonde!" she moaned.

Sure enough, walking next to Bill was his friend—a perky, petite blonde *woman!* My date had brought a date! Well, so much for being the modern, assertive woman inviting a guy on a date.

Gail and I never let on that Bill had blown it—we were too shocked, I think, and too embarrassed! Obviously, I hadn't been clear enough that *he* was *my* date and he was supposed to bring a *male* friend as Gail's date. Throughout the party, and dinner later, Gail and I shared the inside joke and made the most of it, including little jibes about the situation.

"Hey," she quipped. "Your date just kissed my date on the cheek!"

"Whoa, tell your date to get her hand off my date's ass!" I grumbled.

Needless to say, there was a major breakdown in communication. The problem was, I'd *assumed* Bill knew his role when I called him. What I learned from this: Be specific. Get clarification. Don't assume! That old adage, *Better to be safe than sorry,* made lots of sense.

You may be asking, what's wrong with Bill that he didn't realize I'd called him as my date. What a jerk! There's some truth in that, but it wasn't worth making a big deal about. I did tell Chuck, one of my best friends, about what happened and he couldn't stop laughing— so much for emotional support! Lesson learned.

Fast forward from the November fiasco to the Christmas tree lighting at Rockefeller Center in Manhattan in early December. A bunch of us Xerox folks would travel there annually from Connecticut to watch the lighting, then go down to Little Italy for dinner. As it turned out, Patt and Richie had invited Bill. Oh, joy! Luckily, he was alone—no perky, petite blonde on his arm. In fact, he sat next to me at dinner and we had a great time. He was clueless about what had gone wrong in November. Should I tell him? As the night wore on and the group imbibed several bottles of wine, I finally turned to him and asked:

"Bill, do you remember when I called and invited you to that winery party?"

"Sure. That was fun!" he said, with the cutest grin.

"Do you remember that I told you to bring a friend because my friend Gail was coming alone?"

"Yeah, of course—oh, no!" he said, eyes wide with the sudden realization. "You meant for me to bring a guy friend? And I brought Becky? Oh, sh#&!" he exclaimed.

"Yeah, no, sh#&!" I replied.

"I'm so sorry…and so embarrassed! I want to make it up to you. Let's go out to dinner together soon."

While tempted to say *yes,* I realized in that moment that my initial attraction to him had waned and I figured I could do better than a clueless guy, even if he was cute and nice. "Thanks, Bill, but no thanks. Our moment has passed." We ended up being friends with no hard feelings, which was good because he hung out with the Xerox group a lot that winter. He'd even tell the story himself to the others with self-deprecating laughter.

So, the moral of this story is what? Don't assume, right? Are we clear on that? Am I being specific enough for you? Do I need to explain further? The way I see it, if we can't laugh about stuff like this, we're taking life much too seriously!

Midair

(1999)

My ties with Liberty Industries are over today because I received my last paycheck for severance from them—and I am truly on my own new path financially. I am now free to receive my abundance and prosperity from new sources, sources that will enrich my life and advance me forward on my journey.

I'm sitting in my living room, reading Wayne Dyer's book, "Real Magic." I've been having thoughts about the status of my journey, the status of my job hunt and house sale, and contemplating what this present moment, this Now, is about. What meaning does it have in the bigger picture of my journey?

Unexpectedly, the image of a trapeze artist came to mind—flying through the air on one trapeze, back and forth, back and forth, feeling the air and speed of her actions. Ahead of her is the next platform she must land on. Behind her is the one she's just left. In order to reach the next level, she must grab hold of the empty trapeze that swings back and forth toward her.

But, in order to do that, she must let go of the trapeze she is on. For one quick moment—a moment that can seem like a lifetime—she must be suspended in midair, not holding on to either trapeze, trusting in the laws of the Universe that will carry her forward in time, in the motion required, to be in the right position to grab the new trapeze and move forward. If she doesn't let go, she can't transfer and can't go forward. She can swing forever on that first trapeze or go back to the first platform, never to move to the next one—and feel a sense of loss and regret and know that someday she'll have to try again.

Right now, I am in that moment of being in midair. As of today, I have let go of the first trapeze, the last finger coming uncurled from the bar as I receive my last paycheck from Liberty. I am floating. I am light-headed. I am suspended in time and space at the same time as I am propelling forward at a tremendous speed. Is there a net? Yes, God's love is my net, always there to catch me should I experience doubt or fear and miscalculate the switch from one trapeze to another.

I am flying! Unencumbered. Unfettered. Free and light and smoothly and exhilaratingly! I am the Falcon being thrown into the air by the Woman, at the point when she catches the wind and is neither flying up nor falling down. She is just "there," in midair. In God's hands as I am transferred to the next level. God is with me now, transferring *me* to the next level of my journey. The other trapeze is in my sight—the sale of my house, the new job wherever, the journey—all are there as I float toward the bar. I reach out now— thank you, God! —and go to the next trapeze. I am ready!

∾ ∾ ∾ ∾ ∾ ∾ ∾

It's April 30, 2022. As I'm reading this journal entry from 1999, I realize that I'm in midair again! I closed on the sale of my house in Mesa, Arizona, on April 15, having lived there for three and a half years after my retirement from Deer Valley Resort. Then, on Sunday, April 17, with my younger niece Rachel as my navigator and traveling companion, we made a four-day cross-country road trip to Hilliard, Ohio. I left the first platform in Arizona and headed toward the other platform—a new home and life in Ohio. But I'm temporarily staying with my brother and sister-in-law and my belongings are stored in three shipping containers at a United Van Lines facility as I search for a condominium or house to move into. As I said, I'm in midair again!

Reading this essay and knowing that my 'net' truly did support me back in 1999 gives me the confidence and patience that I'll need until I'm finally settled into my new home and starting my new life in Ohio. Near my family. In somewhat familiar territory--I grew up three hours northeast of this Columbus suburb in Warren, Ohio. It's scary. It's slow-moving. It's not in my control. And it's a perfect opportunity to 'let go and let God' deliver me to the next trapeze and the next platform of my life.

Kudos to Dickens and Puzo

(2000)

I hope that Charles Dickens and Mario Puzo didn't roll over in their graves when my family recently filmed a combination of their two masterpieces—*A Christmas Carol* and *The Godfather* trilogy. I'm sure that Francis Ford Coppola won't be threatened by my screenwriting and directing of the Morrell family classic, *The Godfather's Christmas Carol.* But I doubt that anyone involved in the film versions of their books had as much fun as we did when we created our twenty-minute film last December.

It all started around the table at Denny's on a Sunday morning in November 1999. My brother Tony, his wife Patty, their three children—twelve-year-old Christina, ten-year-old Michael and six-year-old Rachel—and I were enjoying breakfast after going to morning mass. As the conversation jumped from topic to topic, as usually happens at these kinds of gatherings, Tony and Michael entertained us with the garden scene from *The Godfather* that they'd memorized verbatim. It's the scene where Don Vito Corleone is explaining to his youngest son Michael how he never wanted him to get involved in the family business and what to expect from a family enemy.

Tony could probably recite the entire dialog of any of the movies and would agree with Tom Hank's character, Joe Fox, in the movie "You've Got Mail" when he says, *"The Godfather is the I Ching. The Godfather is the sum of all wisdom. The Godfather is the answer to any question. What should I pack for my summer vacation? 'Leave the gun, take the cannoli.' What day of the week is it? 'Monday, Tuesday, Thursday, Wednesday.'"* My nephew Michael seems to have a knack for acting because he not only remembers the lines, but he mimics Al Pacino's inflections and mannerisms to a T.

Back to the breakfast table. As I said, the conversation was jumping around and, with Christmas about a month away, somehow talk of Scrooge and Corleone crisscrossed until we were saying how funny it would be for someone to make a version of *A Christmas Carol* with Don Corleone as Scrooge. The next thing you know, we're throwing out ideas— "Tiny Tim could get killed in the crossfire of an ambush" or "The ghost of the horse, Khartoum, could be Marley's ghost" and finally, "Tony and Michael could do the garden scene as part of Scrooge's visit to his past!" That led to the name changes—Scrooge to Scroogeone, Bob Cratchit to Luca Cratchitto and the Ghost of Christmas Future to The Ghost of Christmas What We Ain't Done Yet. We were on a roll! The pens came out and we started scribbling on napkins. By the time we paid our waitress and left the restaurant, we had a fist full of napkins with a kazillion notes and the brilliant idea to actually film this ourselves!

Now, we weren't so far gone as to think this would be a real, full-length movie. We just wanted to make something to show the rest of the family at our annual Christmas Eve gathering. So, I took all the notes home with me and put together a first-draft screenplay that I presented to Tony and Patty for review. A few days and a few edits later, we had a decent script. The three of us also discussed the parts we all would play and Patty said she'd ask her younger brother, Gary and his family (Debbie, Dustin and Sarah) to be the Cratchitto family. Next, we worked out the locations in and around their house, then the costumes, props and music. I created a spreadsheet of scene numbers, time/day, setting/location in the house, action(s) and characters/actors needed per scene, as well as placards for title, credits and cast. Hey, if we're going to do this, let's do it right, right?!

Finally, the day of filming arrived—Saturday, December 11. Yes, we were going to film it all in one day, from beginning to end. Remember, we're amateurs and we don't have all that fancy filming or sound equipment. We couldn't dice and splice it, nor could we add a soundtrack after the fact. We had Tony's humongous video tape recorder and a portable CD player. I had a camera tripod for the recorder, but I ended up propping it on my right shoulder the whole time so it wouldn't be so static and the actors could move around more. It was primitive, for sure, but we made it all work. We gathered at nine o'clock that morning in their dining room where the costumes and props were set up for each scene change and did a couple of read-throughs of the entire script—I'd given everyone copies of the script the prior week so they could study and memorize their lines, etc.—then I called "Action!," and we were off and running.

What a crazy, fun-filled day! We worked hard and took that silly little project seriously, but we also managed to keep things enjoyable as we laughed between scenes. What amazed me were the kids--how dedicated they were to their roles, how well they'd remembered their lines and how animated they were with their characters. Finally, I called, "That's a wrap!" around four o'clock and we chowed down on some pizzas we'd had delivered and guzzled some nice cold beers—well, the adults did anyway!

I am so blessed to be a member of this crazy, loving, funny and creative family! Wow, what an experience this will be to talk about in the years to come! I can just imagine adding the showing of "The Godfather's Christmas Carol" to our annual Christmas Eve activities. Boy, I wish Mom, Dad and Grandpa Todd were alive— how thrilled they would have been to watch their children and grandchildren perform. As it was, the rest of the family—our sister Sandy, Grandma Rose, Aunt Toni and Uncle Remi, our cousins Chickie (Lorraine) and Tina (Lynette) and their families—were awestruck by what we'd done and thoroughly enjoyed it.

So, Charles and Mario, thanks for writing such timeless classics that lent themselves so easily to our little parody of rookie screenwriting, rudimentary filming and amateurish acting. They say impersonation is the highest form of flattery. Well, consider yourselves flattered!

❧ ❧ ❧ ❧ ❧ ❧ ❧

I'm so glad that I wrote about the making of this little flick the January after we "premiered" it for our family on Christmas Eve so I could share it in this book. I thought about including the entire script but decided that it's not interesting to read because there are too many 'AD LIB' and 'Quote Godfather movie scene' directions. In the winter of 2001, I was working at Deer Valley Resort in Utah and showed it to a ski instructor, Johnny Cocca, who was in town with two friends to premiere their first movie at the Sundance Film Festival—he cracked up and appreciated the efforts of us amateurs. I've since converted the VHS tape to a DVD disk so we can continue to enjoy it on newer technology.

Learning to Trust

(2001)

Lesson 1:

Loving someone is not enough, not when trust is gone. Caring and feeling are ethereal and illusionary for they cannot recreate trust in a person once something happens that shatters that trust. I loved him, Stuart, my husband. Yet, I couldn't trust that he wouldn't drink again. I couldn't trust that his words to me held any substance. I couldn't believe his promises when he'd broken so many promises before. His words over the few short years we were married had torn me apart, without me even knowing, cracking through my strong self-esteem and leaving me feeling less about myself than I'd ever— *never*—felt in my life. They had caused me to doubt in myself, in my attractiveness, in my womanliness, so that I looked for ways to make *me* better so as to please him. What a change from who I'd been when we'd first met!

But I was lucky. I had a breakthrough when a woman in my support group talked about recently leaving her alcoholic husband after putting up with twenty-two years of his verbal and physical abuse. Twenty-two years! My, God, I wasn't about to invest that much of my life into someone who I realized I didn't even *like* any longer! Because loving someone is not enough. You have to like him and trust him. He'd abused my trust, and now I would have to work at being able to trust again, without him.

Lesson 2:

"Sell your house and things. Quit your job and just go west!" These words were shouted at me by my Soul's voice on September 4, 1998. One year, eleven months and twenty days later—on August 24, 2000—I obeyed that voice, left Ohio and headed west with no definitive final destination in mind. After three weeks on the road— visiting friends in Chicago, Milwaukee and Minneapolis, touring

places like Sioux Falls, the Black Hills, Little Bighorn and Hole in the Wall—I stopped for a two-day stay in Park City, Utah. That was five months ago. I have landed in some kind of "twilight zone" where people come to visit and never seem to leave! But it's a good place. A healthy place. A place where I am meeting some wonderful people. A place where I am working at a ski resort that knows how to empower its employees while providing specialized care to its guests. A place where I have come alive again from the depths of my soul.

And, because of that alignment, I am healthier—having lost thirty pounds—and I am more confident and more trusting that the Powers That Be behind that voice I heard two years earlier have brought me here for a reason, one that has yet to be discovered in full. But I'm actually living my dreams, like working on a film promotion for the Sundance Film Festival in January. Like flirting with some funny, attractive and interesting instructors at the resort. Like possibly staying on here in Utah after the season ends in April. And I absolutely love the locale! The mountains and the snow are so—I find it hard to describe them adequately, the words do not come. I am still blown away by a sunrise coming over the Uinta mountain range as I drive to work. I am moved to stillness by the sight of a sky full of stars that seem within my reach. The metaphor comes unbidden, for my stars *are* within reach. I remind myself daily to just trust in the forces that brought me here and I will become aware of the path I am to take. So I do, I let go and I trust in myself and in the Spirit that is guiding me now.

Lesson 3:

It's our last run of the day. The sun is descending behind the trees atop Flagstaff Mountain, casting evergreen shadows along the snowy trail and causing the temperature to drop a few degrees. We make our way down the Ontario slope, Eric and me. I've trusted him all day—an unusual thing for me, who likes to be in control, who likes to decide for myself what, where and when I'll do something. He's taking this novice skier on her first ski excursion up into the

Deer Valley mountains. Why would I not trust him now, when he says, "Promise me you'll follow me and do exactly what I do, okay?" I nod, and we start down the Trump Trail section of Ontario, he in front and me right behind.

First, some wide turns, which I take smoothly and effortlessly. Gradually, they become tighter and swifter, yet I'm still on his tail. The snow crunches under the edges of my skis, echoing in the quiet of the late afternoon. I feel as one with the snow and the mountain and the world around me—until I see where we are headed—up a 20-foot mound to the left of the slope. Like a skateboarder whooshing up a wooden tube, Eric ascends the white mass, twists his body sharply to the right, descends and returns to the slope. For one brief millisecond, I think, "NO!" But I never hesitate in my movements as I continue in his path. I let go and trust him. I trust that he will not take me where I cannot go. I trust in myself. A thrill flows through me as I speed up the mound, make a 90-degree turn and race down again, skiing directly toward Eric, feeling oh so giddy! In mid-slope, we stop and I teasingly chide him that I can't believe he took me up there. I can't believe he did that! "Yes," he says, "and *you* did that." I did that? My God, I did!

So, trust has found its way back into my life. Trust in another person, that he will not hurt me or abuse my reliance on him to get me safely down the mountain. Trust in myself, that I can achieve whatever I set out to do. Trust in Life, that it will open up to me and provide me with all that I desire in my stay here in Utah. The giddiness I felt as I overcame that 20-foot hill stays with me for days and makes me feel invincible!

Leather and Love

(2001)

I don't pretend to follow baseball so fervently that I can rattle off statistics or distinguish between a slider and a curve ball. Nor do I keep tabs on the summer standings religiously, except to check the paper now and then to see how my New York Yankees are doing in the standings. But baseball occupies a special place in my life, forming a fiber that binds me to two men whom I value tremendously--my dad, Frank, and my brother, Tony.

If such a thing as a "baseball chromosome" exists, I have no doubt you'll find one deep within my DNA structure, somewhere between the hiking molecule and the writing gene. I don't play baseball, mind you, although over the years I've taken my turns at bat, stood on the pitcher's mound and listened to the grass grow in the lonely reaches of right field. Most of these experiences were at picnics or on the Xerox softball team in White Plains, New York. Growing up, I didn't have the opportunity to play girls' Little League simply because there *wasn't* a girls' Little League! In fact, there wasn't much of a girls' anything as far as sports were concerned. I doubt I'd have played anyway because I was shy and not very athletic.

However, I come by my interest in baseball honestly. My Dad loved the game. He loved it so much that he was a catcher for the Cleveland Indians' semi-pro team when he was just eighteen. He played with them until the responsibility of a wife and daughter-- yours truly! --found him trading in his baseball uniform and catcher's mitt for an electrician's uniform and lunch pail. But that didn't keep him off the diamond.

I remember, as a little girl going to the local ballpark, Perkins Park, in the early summer evenings to watch Daddy play ball. Actually, it's hard to say if the memories are truly memories or just mental souvenirs that I've created from stories I've heard over the years. Probably a little of both. They're like peripheral images I see out of the corner of my eye that disappear or move when I turn and try to look at them directly. I cherish them regardless of their origin.

I do remember wooden bleachers that seemed so high and open and scary to a four-year-old. I remember the Halsey-Taylor drinking fountain, made right there in Warren, Ohio--just check out the drain ring on an old fountain sometime! It stood in a puddle of muddy water created by misdirected spurts and dribbling chins.

Somewhere deep in my olfactory memory is the smell of my Dad when he'd pick me up in his arms at the end of the game--a blend of dust and sweat and leather and love. I may not have understood the game back then, but those images are carved on my heart like "Louisville Slugger" is carved on a wooden bat and woven into my soul like the stitches on a baseball's seam. I don't need to spout off RBI or ERA numbers to realize the significance of baseball in my life. I need only hear the crack of a bat whacking a ball into deep center field or the smack of a ball plunging into a well-oiled mitt to sense the ancestral passion coursing through my cells.

Despite living his entire life in Warren, Ohio, only fifty-some miles from Cleveland's stadium and deep in the heart of Indian's territory, my Dad was a die-hard, tried-and-true New York Yankees fan. Many a summer Sunday would find our family sitting in the stands in Cleveland, rooting on our boys from the Bronx.

My Dad died of a heart attack in his sleep at the young age of fifty-one. It was years later, however, that we found out from his brother, our Uncle Elmer, that Dad once caught for the Major League pitcher Satchell Paige. Paige was traveling through the area, doing exhibition games for the Negro League. He was warming up for some photographers, and Dad was called in to catch for him during the shoot. Tony, Sandy and I were flabbergasted because Dad had never told us about this! I wonder why. More than likely, he *had* told me when I was too young or too disinterested to appreciate the importance of the event and what it must have meant to him. I wish he were still around today so I could ask him about it.

I wish I could ask him about his dreams. Did he dream of being a major league player? Did he imagine wearing the Yankee pinstripes and crouching behind home plate in the "house that Ruth built?" Would he have pursued the dream had he not decided to settle down and raise a family in that little corner of Ohio where he lived his whole life?

When I lived in New York, Tony came to visit me during his summer vacations. Seeing him walk down the airplane runway, a smile lurking behind a nonchalant expression, the sibling feelings stirring deep inside of me seemed likely to implode. Yet, I wasn't so naïve as to think his joy at being in New York stemmed from his desire to see me. Oh, no! He planned his visits based on the New York Yankees' longest stretch of home games! Tony would spend afternoons watching the games on television in my apartment while I was at work. Then, we'd go to the night games, sometimes alone and sometimes with a few of my friends, and wait afterwards to get the players' autographs when they left the stadium.

Waiting for autographs with Tony is a memory that paints a smile on my heart, and it wasn't limited to those summer vacations. When I lived in Ohio before moving to New York, I'd take him to see the Yankees whenever they were in town to play the Cleveland Indians. After all the cars had pulled out of the parking lots, after all the vendors had wheeled away their carts, after all the lights had been turned off over the field, Tony and I stood waiting with a handful of other fans at the "stage door" for his stars to appear. One by one or two by two, they'd walk out, fresh from the showers, leather jackets and leather shoes replacing their jerseys and spikes. They'd graciously accept the outstretched pens and sign programs and books before boarding the bus waiting to take them to their hotel.

Tony would stand out there, patiently waiting for the right moment to extend his program, not wanting to be too pushy or disrespectful, yet not letting the celebrity of the players intimidate him. He usually managed to engage a player or two in conversation, citing some play or statistic from that night's game or from a game played a year or two earlier, amazing them with his ability for recall.

From the time he learned to count, he could read baseball statistics, reciting them like a veteran Shakespearean actor recites *Hamlet.* He still has the spiral-bound notebooks from his youth, when he'd cut and tape box scores, articles and scorecards onto the ruled pages, a book for each season. It astounds me how he can rattle off the plays, players and scores of games we attended during his New York visits as if they happened yesterday. I'm lucky if I can remember who won the World Series the previous year, although it's been easy the past few years with the Yankees winning the pennant so often!

The final scene of the movie *Field of Dreams* tapped a wellspring of tears that flowed like a stream's spring thaw running down the face of a mountain. I tried to blink them back, but to no avail. Luckily, I was watching the movie in the privacy of my Chicago home, courtesy of the local video store, so my crying didn't disturb anyone but me. In that scene, when the catcher for the mystical team, dressed in a New York Yankees uniform, slips off his mask, turns slowly to the camera, and Kevin Costner's character recognizes him as his deceased father, I sobbed, "Daddy!" For that character *was* my Dad, and Costner's character was my brother. My brother, who by then was married and had a daughter the same age as the daughter in the film. My brother, who was fourteen when our Mom and Dad separated. My brother, who was sixteen when our Dad died, before the two of them had a chance to reconcile differences that were inevitable between a father and a teenage son who felt protective of his mother after his parents' separation.

The next time I spoke with Tony, I told him he had to rent *Field of Dreams,* without telling him anything more than that it was a great family movie about baseball. A few weeks later, the phone rang one night, and it was Tony. I could hear the emotion in his voice as he told me that he and Patty, his wife, had just finished watching the movie. Awestruck by the parallel between his life and the imaginary lives on the film, he thanked me for telling him about it and said it had bumped *The Godfather* out of first place for his favorite movie--not an easy trick. Today, he owns his own copy and practically knows it by heart. He and his family have even been to the cornfield in Iowa where the movie was filmed and have photographs of them sitting on the bleachers overlooking the baseball field. Most importantly, he's since been able to reconcile posthumously with our Dad now that he, too, is a father of three children and has outgrown the immaturity and inflexibility of his teenage years.

Tony's favorite player was New York Yankee's outfielder, Roy White, number six. He would imitate White's stance in the batter's box, and he always asks for that number jersey when he plays on a local ball team. The tradition is being carried on by his daughter, Christina, who also sports the number six on her jerseys. She's been playing baseball since she was six and joined the Howland T-ball League. Now fifteen, she's played fast pitch for three years and talks about getting a baseball scholarship to Notre Dame or some other university.

I attended her games every summer when I lived in Ohio, and couldn't help but think about Dad and how much he would have enjoyed watching her play. I believe his spirit is at every game, but I would still like to watch him watching her. I want to see the gleam in his blue eyes as she fields a play at third base. I want to hear him cheer her on as she hits a line drive between the second baseman and shortstop. Now her little sister, Rachel, is following in her footsteps. At eight, she's got two years under her belt and seems to take to the game as easily as her sibling. It appears that the "baseball chromosome" lurks somewhere in their DNA ladders, too.

In October of 2000, when the Yankees played the New York Mets in the World Series, I had been living in Park City, Utah, for less than a month. I learned quickly that Utah is *not* a baseball state when I couldn't find anyone interested in going to a sports bar with me to watch the games! So, I went alone to the Broken Thumb Bar and Grill in the Park City Racquet Club down the street from where I was living. I actually had to ask the bartender to turn the channel on the TV to the game! I decided to call Tony back in Ohio--I knew *he'd* be watching the game. The last few years he had hosted World Series Opening Night parties and showed videotapes of the previous years' Yankee victories.

I love watching those with him! I love listening to the enthusiasm in his voice as he tells of the triumphs of his heroes. I love to hear his laugh as we watch baseball blunders or he recites Yogi Berra's quotes from the veteran catcher's book. I love sharing this game with him, not because I love baseball so much, but because I love *him* so much. We have our differences--he's the conservative "Alex Keaton" to my liberal "Elise Keaton" --but baseball is the great equalizer that creates a joyous environment in which he and I can talk and laugh and cry and reminisce. With my nieces now sharing in our revelry, the joy is even sweeter. I have no doubt that somewhere close by, Dad is joining in our revelry as well, asking, as the father in *Field of Dreams* asked, "Is this heaven?" Yes, Dad, it surely is!

‽ ‽ ‽ ‽ ‽ ‽ ‽

In the summer of 2019, my brother got to live that last scene from the movie by playing catch with Dwier Brown, the actor who portrayed John Kinsella, the deceased father in the New York Yankees uniform. Brown was at the Columbus (Ohio) Clippers minor league baseball game to celebrate the 30th anniversary of the movie, and Tony paid to be on the field after the game to meet him and "have a catch." He told Brown how the movie, and especially that last scene, had emulated his own relationship with his father. A television reporter heard the exchange and interviewed Tony for the evening news. Tony told him, "I felt like I was playing catch with my Dad, who's been gone a long time." I have no doubt that our Dad had come out of the cornfield and was on the field with them.

Souvenirs

(2001)

What are you taking back? Scott asks, as we sit on black-rock perches in the outdoor auditorium on this, the last morning of our river journey. What, indeed, I ponder, listening to Chris' guitar strumming as it drifts up from the beach. Ah yes, I'll take back his song, so it can echo through my soul when noises attack me from without. I'll take the *OM* of the canyon's breath that blows across my face and toes, the rattle of the cool rocks beneath my sandaled feet and the warmth of the sun's shafts as they caress my bare shoulders. I'll take the scents of Nature and Time to tantalize my olfactory factory when the stink of exhaust fumes in traffic pervade my space. I'll take sour and salty and sanguine morsels to nourish my body, mind and spirit when hunger calls. I'll take vibrant Crayola vistas to color my world when I'm having a gray day.

What are you taking back? my Body asks, mimicking Scott's original question. I'll take for you a deep appreciation for cool sheets, hot showers, clean-shaven legs, cold beers, fluffy pillows, electric toothbrushes, ice cubes, tweezed eyebrows, indoor plumbing and melt-in-your-mouth chocolates. I'll also take an abiding respect for healthy muscles, strong bones, supple joints and calm nerves.

What will you take back for me? My Mind insists on knowing. For you, I'll take back vivid memories of "whirling dervish" bats fluttering past my face; fudgy river mud oozing between my toes; baritone bullfrogs bellowing morning serenades; and carnivorous black flies gnawing at my legs. To them, I'll add feeling the planet revolve while meditating under the full moon; writing from a place inside of me that yearns to be heard; playing "Two truths and a lie" with newfound friends at the river's edge; washing dishes in the revolutionary four-stage dishwashing system; cherishing the vision of falcons soaring like circus aerialists off monolithic rocks;

washing my hair in the river's current; awakening beneath Heaven's star-studded spectacle of the evening sky; and last, and certainly least, using the shiny new, all-improved, state-of-the-art groover!

What else will you take back? my Heart quietly queries. I'll take back Scott's humble wisdom, Doug's infectious laugh, Erin's sassy smile and Jason's sardonic wit. I'll include J.P.'s cowboy twang, Kristine's graceful saunter, Mark's gentle strength and Russell's engaging smile. And I could never leave without Karla's tender tenacity, Jeff's quiet mastery, Chris' soulful eyes and Linda's sheer delight.

What are we *taking back?* My Spirit finally asks. We'll take back a requiem for the archaic shards of self that willingly went to their demise on a fiery desert pyre. We'll take back the phoenix rising from the ashes of that pyre, its wings spread wide to embrace the in and out, the hard and soft, the physical and ethereal *all* of me. We'll take back the shiny new, all-improved, state-of-the-art Me, Myself and I.

ৡ ৡ ৡ ৡ ৡ ৡ ৡ

I wrote this upon my return from a four-day, Class II river-rafting trip from Grand Junction, Colorado, to Westwater, Utah, in July 2001. The trip was a writing workshop for beginner rafters with novelist and essayist Scott Sanders. Scott instructed us during morning campfire sessions; we rafted and observed the gorgeous panoramas that surrounded us; we wrote our essays; and we shared our handiwork at the evening campfire gatherings. It was the first time I had ever river-rafted and the first time I'd gone camping—a true adventure for this gal from the suburbs of Ohio!

Waters of Timpanogos

(2001)

The stream flows from Mt. Timpanogos, meanders through Sundance Resort, drifts beside the two-mile stretch of Highway 89 to Route 189 and eventually merges with Utah's Provo River. For miles and miles, it dances down the mountain and through the valley, skipping over boulders, pirouetting around protruding tree roots and waltzing through river grass, oblivious to the human world assembled along its banks. As I sit in my collapsible chair in this secluded spot along those banks, I, too, am oblivious to the stream's prestigious origin, bountiful destination and man-made encroachments. I am suspended in time and place like a figurine in a snow globe.

I've taken a detour off the path winding its way through the resort's acreage, past cottages and meeting rooms, restaurants and gift shops. Occasionally, I'll hear the muffled drone of a car engine or the hum of visitors' voices somewhere in the distance, but mostly it's the drone of insects and the hum of the stream that fills the air.

The sun, high in the mid-afternoon sky, reaches between the needles of the tall pines shading me and touches my leg. I shift my chair to the left a bit. But the sun is in a playful mood and soon it finds me again, fondling my leg with warm fingers. I shift again; it follows me minutes later, relentless in its game of tag. Finally, I succumb to its persistence and let its warmth caress me as it seems to cry out, "You're it!"

Answering some ancient calling, the stream flows ever onward, bubbling over fallen logs and licking moss-covered rocks as it parades past this silent spectator. I watch a leaf float by and am reminded of a character in Richard Bach's book, *Illusions: The Adventures of a Reluctant Messiah.* A member of a colony of creatures that cling tenaciously to rocks and plants below the river's surface wonders what it would be like to let go and follow the river.

Other colony members ridicule this lone creature and warn against such a perilous notion. But one day, it *does* let go, and is immediately tossed against rocks and dragged through the water at a tremendous speed, causing it to wonder at the wisdom of its decision. Eventually though, it learns to relax and trust the river and experiences wonders beyond its imagination. Sometimes I feel like that creature. My life has been a series of clinging moments and letting-go adventures. I've felt tossed to and fro by the waters of Life, battered against rocks of resistance, breathless in the depths of my surroundings. Yet I, too, have experienced wonders beyond my imagination, and I couldn't conceive of trading any of them for a lifetime of tedious clinging.

My wanderlust can be attributed to two sources—my Hungarian "gypsy" blood and road trips with my grandparents in my youth. The latter spawned in me a strong desire to be behind the wheel of a car, driving for hours on end, stopping here and there to explore new places. The road is my river, and the desire is the strong current carrying me forward along highways and byways. Driving is a time of contemplation for me, a time when my mind mulls over sensical non-sensical notions, like plans for a trip to Britain, words for poems and essays, ideas for home décor and major life decisions.

Being in Utah on this summer day in 2001 stems from one of my most significant decisions, a decision born from a message I received while driving to work one September morning three years ago. As I turned onto the road where my office was located, a voice deep within me cried out, "Sell your house and things, quit your job and go west!" Having learned to trust that voice over the years, that intuitive spirit resonating from the depths of my soul, for all intents and purposes, my journey began at the moment I responded, "I will!" It took two years to work out the external logistics, but finally on a hot August day in 2000, I settled behind the wheel of my Jeep Cherokee Sport and hit the road.

I let go of the "rocks and plants" of my life—my family, friends and home—that had been comfort zones for me following my mother's death nine years earlier. I trusted in the "river of Life" to carry me forward to wherever I needed to go. For three weeks I drove on, making a two-day stop here, a four-day sojourn there. I visited friends in Chicago, Milwaukee and Minneapolis. I took in the sights, sounds and sensations of the Badlands, the Black Hills and the partially-constructed Crazy Horse monument of South Dakota; Little Big Horn in Montana; and Devil's Tower and Hole in the Wall in Wyoming. By the time I drove into Park City, Utah, in mid-September for a two-day rest stop, however, the "current" had slowed down. The river deposited me on its shores in a place where I could soothe my weary body, mind and spirit. The voice deep inside that had prompted me to make this journey was now telling me, "Stay." I felt at home immediately in these desert mountains, and continue to feel at home to this day.

The sun tags me again, and the heat of its kiss on my exposed arm contrasts sharply with the cool breeze tickling the skin of my shaded arm. Held captive in this chair by shackles of light and air, I am a willing prisoner. Closing my eyes, I let the sound of the stream keep time with the sound of my throbbing heart. Each slow, quiet breath is like a brush stroke, smoothing the sharp edges on a canvas until one image blends with another. I can no longer tell where my body ends and the chair begins. Feet and shoes and earth are one. My heart's blood flows downstream to merge with the Provo River as Mt. Timpanogos' water flows through my veins to merge with my soul.

Time takes on new meaning, for I am at once a billion years old and a newborn. I am ageless. Unlike the measurements created to confine Time to a single, linear path, I experience Time as a spiraling, three-dimensional web, moving up and down, forward and backward, over and under. The same brush that stroked my body to its blurred sense of existence paints Time with no beginning and no ending—just an infinite state of being.

Gradually, I drift out of my meditative state, aware once again of the separateness of chair and body, earth and feet, water and blood. The sun now radiates on my whole body like a spotlight on an actor at center stage. Folding my chair, I move upstream where the trees are denser and a cluster of boulders hugs the shore. I climb atop the largest boulder, stretch out my legs and, through their bareness, absorb the coolness of this perch above the stream.

The rocks in the stream entice my imagination. In the rough, dimpled rocks, I see pock-marked faces of adolescents and gangster thugs. The smooth, shiny ones are dolphins and porpoises, seals and otters, playing together in the shimmering waters. I am transfixed until something touches my shoulder and brings me out of my trance. The limb of a leafless, dead tree curls down like a withered arm, its skeletal fingers reaching for my flesh as if to take it for its own. I grasp the offered twigs gently in my hand and greet this wizened lady of the woods who welcomes me to her home. *How are you? I ask. How came you to be here along this stream in such a decaying state?*

I think of Grandma Rose, her 94-year-old bones diminished with age and her body bent from the weight of burying too many loved ones. Her arthritic hands are not unlike the knotty twigs, except their gnarled bones and purpled veins are covered with soft, loose, white flesh, reminding me of orchids in their translucency. She wonders why she's still alive, why she's had to live these twenty-eight years without the man she loved, and why she had to experience the heartache of burying her first-born child nine years ago. I have no answers for these questions, except to selfishly say that I need her here. Both my parents are dead, my mother being that child who died much too soon. I need to know sometimes, as fanciful as it may seem, that I am miles and miles from Death's door, that I am still a child who can live forever. How can I be that child when adults who I turn to for reassurance, who the child sees as indestructible, are no longer alive?

Tears blur my vision as I dwell on my own mortality and loss. I continue to clutch the dead branch, remembering my mother's cancer-ridden body in those last weeks of her life. I try to shake the sadness from me, not wanting to spoil the magical mood of the stream and the woods. A few moments later, my melancholy vanishes when I turn and see a most beautiful sight not three feet from me. Twigs of the same lifeless tree stretch out to form a three-sided frame about a foot across it's center, and strung out between the twigs is a magnificent spider web! The fibers are so fine I must shade my eyes from the sun's light and tilt my head to see the intricacies of the delicate pattern. So delicate, and yet so strong. It flutters in the gentle mountain breeze, yet can withstand the harshest of winds. Sunlight shimmers off the labyrinthine design, and I long to meet its creator.

I love spiders—I always have. I love their resilient natures and their matter-of-fact attitudes. The daddy-long-legs is my personal favorite, amusing and amazing me as it walks on spindly legs thinner than strands of hair. What I admire most is the way spiders diligently and painstakingly go about the utilitarian task of web weaving, putting such passion into their work, unaware of the masterpiece of art and engineering they are creating. How many of us can admit to such passion for the work we do, day in and day out? How many of us drudge along in mediocre jobs when our hearts yearn to be doing something else, somewhere else? And there's the other side of the query—how many of us bring no passion to our work, creating the drudgery we wallow in with our own dispassionate attitudes? It's not always easy or practical to find a means of financial support that coincides with our heartfelt passions. Yet, it can be done. We must let go of stale visions and create fresh ones that allow our passions to come alive.

As I reflect on these matters, the creator of the labyrinth makes its appearance in the upper corner of the web. I am overjoyed and humbled in its presence. Slowly, it crawls down the precarious strands of the web toward the center, no doubt hoping to find an unsuspecting insect ensnared in its sticky trap. But nothing awaits the vigilant vagabond, so it scales the silken ladder, stretches its many legs up to the wooden ledge and waddles back along the branch, perhaps to build another web somewhere nearby.

I, too, stand and stretch my legs, pack up my chair and backpack and depart my refuge of solitude and solace.

⅘ ⅘ ⅘ ⅘ ⅘ ⅘ ⅘

Whenever I read this essay, I am proud and humbled at the same time that, like the spider, I was able to weave my thoughts and feelings into the words and images here. This is one of my favorite essays and it doesn't really need any further explanation, does it?

Listen to the Music

(2004)

If a man does not keep pace with his companions, perhaps it is because he hears a different drummer. Let him step to the music which he hears, however measured and far away.

Walden
by Henry David Thoreau

Within each of us there is a voice that whispers, "Take the risks, pursue your dreams, live life to the fullest, as long as you're not hurting anyone else, why not?" Then, outside of us are voices that scream, "Don't be a fool, you're going to fail. Be like everyone else. If you do what you want, you're being selfish and hurting others." These loud incessant dictates of our companions urge us to keep up with them and threaten to ostracize us when we fail to do so.

Society in general always seems to honor its *living conformists* and its *dead non-conformists.* All those who have ever made a difference in any profession have listened to the music they hear and proceeded independent of the opinions of others. For doing so, they are labeled troublemakers, incorrigibles, even misfits. Yet they become highly respected after death.

Henry David Thoreau, who wrote the opening quote in his book *Walden*, was criticized for his position in his essay *On the Necessity of Civil Disobedience* and jailed for refusing to obey what he considered absurd rulings. Yet today, he is required reading in virtually all high schools and universities.

The beat that you hear within yourself is your connection to your soul's purpose. We all ask at some time in our lives, "Why am I here? What's my purpose in this lifetime?" We only need to listen to our inner music to identify that purpose. It will continue to plague you when you ignore it or suppress it in an attempt to conform with society.

Those who implore you to march to the beat *they* hear are often well-intentioned and coming from a position of love for you. They may even have your best interest at heart and tell you they are the voice of experience and that you'll be sorry if you don't follow their advice. You may listen and try hard to be just what everybody wants you to be. But that nagging drumbeat that no one else seems to hear faintly thumps in the farthest reaches of your awareness. Continuing to ignore it means a lifetime of frustration; you may even learn to "suffer in comfort," the best you'll achieve.

It's important that you understand that, in following your inner urges, you may look like you're conforming simply because those urges are the same as a larger group's. That's okay. As long as you're being true to yourself, there's nothing wrong with being part of the whole and expressing your beliefs with others who believe the same way. Whatever it is that you feel compelled to be or to do is the voice of your soul pleading with you to have the courage to listen and act upon the melody only you hear, as long as it doesn't interfere with anyone else's right to pursue his or her dreams.

Thoreau is speaking directly to you from the mid-19th century, speaking about *your* own self-sufficiency and happiness. Imagine what it would have been like walking through the woods with Thoreau back in the 1840s, before the Civil War. His observations were based not on some philosophy he'd read in a self-help book or heard on a television show, but on his own direct experience of feeling outrage of conformity and seeing the horrors of how native Americans were being treated by the white man and removed from their lands. He left to live in nature and experience self-sufficiency away from the pressures of the larger group. He did not keep step with his companions and at the time was criticized for it.

There are many others throughout history who we honor today for their acts of nonconformity—Buddha, Gandhi, Jesus, Mother Theresa, Martin Luther King, Jr., the Wright brothers, Nikola Tesla,

Betty Friedan, David Bowie to name but a few. Many of the religious or spiritual organizations in the world today were started by nonconformists who, having been raised in a strict, formal and structured religion, questioned the rigidity and exclusivity of these religions. They evolved beyond those restrictions to embrace a spiritual path that honors *all* paths to all Gods—or that chooses to forego a belief in a deity or Universal force.

In closing, I'll share one of my favorite passages, *On Creativity,* by Alan Ashley-Pitt—you may recognize some of the words.

> *The man who follows the crowd will usually get no further than the crowd. The man who walks alone is likely to find himself in places no one has ever been before. Creativity in living is not without its attendant difficulties, for peculiarity breeds contempt. And the unfortunate thing about being ahead of your time is that when people finally realize you were right, they'll say it was obvious all along. You have two choices in life: you can dissolve into the mainstream or you can be distinct. To be distinct, you must be different. To be different, you must strive to be what no one else but you can be.*

The Mystery in the Bedroom Closet

(2007)

My favorite room in the house we lived in at 1959 Irene Avenue was my closet. The brand new, ranch-style house was the fifth home I'd lived in during my ten long years, and it was also the largest my family had lived in, which meant I would now have my very own bedroom! No more sharing with my younger sister, Sandy. (At least until my baby brother came along four years later and forced us back into the large bedroom together, but that's another story.)

We were the first family to move into the new housing development in Warren, Ohio. Over the next year, houses on the street started popping up, one after the other. Most were ranches like ours with the occasional two-story Cape Cod thrown in here and there. Irene Avenue was what we called a "double dead end"—one end curved and stopped at a woods and the other stopped at an Ohio Edison power station. Access to the street was from two side roads that ended at our street. So, there wasn't any through traffic, which afforded us kids the benefit of the street as a playground. The manhole cover in front of our driveway was home plate in many a game of kickball. There was talk of continuing the road through the woods someday, but fortunately, that never happened.

But back to my closet. My bedroom was in the front of the house between the living room and my parents' room. While measuring only about ten feet by eleven feet, to me at the time it was as spacious as a mansion. The walls were the color blue of an early summer sky before the sun saturates it with brilliance. A white chenille bedspread with pink and yellow flowers swathed my single bed, and a dresser, a desk with a bookcase and my toy chest finished off the décor. However, as much as the room thrilled me, it was the closet—one of those long, narrow, double sliding-door styles—that soon became my refuge.

Now, I don't want to mislead you here. My parents didn't relegate me to the closet as some sort of strange punishment. Nor was I weird or anti-social. I played with my sister and my friends, doing the things that most kids liked to do who grew up in the Sixties. Monopoly on Saturday mornings with Sandy was a favorite. In fact, any board game could keep us busy for hours. Then, there was the clue game we made up. Each of us would take a room in the house and hide a small "treasure" for the other to find. We'd write clues in the form of riddles and hide them throughout the room, eventually leading to the treasure. Handing off clue number one, we'd race to see who could find the other's treasure first. This treasure could be a piece of jewelry, a small bank, a figurine--whatever we fancied. Depending on our moods and the time we had, we'd decide on a 10, 15 or 20 clue game. What fun we had!

The point I want to make is that I could just as easily entertain myself and, contrary to my second-born, socially-adept sister, often preferred to do that. For instance, sometimes I'd put on my roller skates—the metal kind that you put on over your shoes and used a key to tighten until your pinky toes were scrunched—and I'd skate around the basement floor to Grieg's "In the Hall of the Mountain King" from the Peer Gynt Suite. Arms swinging from side to side like pendulums in front of my body, I'd increase my speed as the metal wheels clacked over the cold, cement floor. Sometimes, I'd grab a gray support pole and swirl around and around it, my head tilted back, my hair flying out behind me. The gradually-increasing tempo and cymbal-crashing finale made for an exhilarating skating session. Unfortunately, this came to an end when my parents laid carpeting and furnished most of the basement for entertaining friends.

At the age of eleven, a year after we'd moved into our new home, I discovered a whole new world in my closet. It's the year I met a new 'best friend.' Her name was Nancy Drew. You see, for my birthday, my Mom gave me two of her own Nancy Drew books that she'd saved to pass on to her daughter someday. I read "The Haunted Mansion" first and was hooked! From that point on, I'd spend hours with my nose in a book trying to figure out the mystery with Nancy and her friends, Bess Marvin and George Fayne.

You'd think that my very own bedroom would be ideal for reading, wouldn't you? Yet, as private as it was, it did not afford me enough of the seclusion I wanted when getting lost in one of Nancy's mysteries. So, I set up my closet as a sort-of library. I lined my Nancy Drew books on the floor against the back wall. Then, I hung a flashlight from a belt between my clothes and put some well-placed pillows on the floor and against the wall. Sliding shut the door, I'd seclude myself for hours reading. Sometimes I'd put a glass of water and a Hershey bar outside the door (there wasn't enough room inside) and I'd open the door to get a bite or a sip. Before I knew it—and often long before I'd taken notice—my derriere would get numb and my legs would get cramped. But that didn't deter me. Nancy and I were comrades, you see. Her independent nature appealed to me, and I believe that a lot of who I am today is because of the time I spent with her in that closet, imagining myself in the role of girl detective.

Where's Grandma Rose?

(2008)

According to the passage in my journal, I awoke around 4:30 the morning of December 11, 2007, to visit the "little girls' room." In my half-asleep state, a voice in my head said, "Go write." While part of me wanted to get back into bed and snuggle under the covers for another hour and a half before the alarm went off, I listened to the voice. I grabbed my glasses, a notebook and pen and settled on the couch to do some stream-of-consciousness writing. I had no idea what to write—I just let my hand move across the page and the words flow out of the pen. Scattered thoughts. Nonsensical phrases. Incomplete sentences. Yet in the midst of all that mumbo-jumbo, some feelings were expressed and thoughts conveyed, mostly about my Grandma Rose. A few minutes later, as I snuggled in bed and was dozing off, those thoughts centered around one question that was gnawing at me for some time now—*Where's Grandma Rose?*

On October 9, 2006, my Grandma Rose celebrated her 100th birthday. Since her 99th birthday, I thought a lot about the fact that she was living her one-hundredth year on this earth. I also thought about her because her health has taken a couple downhill turns. When I get a phone call from home, I often wonder before answering if this is the one where they inform me she has died. But mostly, that same question—*Where's Grandma Rose?* —keeps running through my mind.

Now, I know where she is physically—Room 124 at the Autumn Hills Care Center in Niles, Ohio. She's been a resident there for four years now, when it became evident that she could no longer live in her little Cape Cod house all by herself. She doesn't know it, but she'll never go back to that yellow house on Bonnie Brae where she lived for over forty years. We haven't had the heart to tell her that my Aunt Toni had to sell the house to pay for her expenses at the nursing home—we can't imagine what that would do to her spirit, so we let her think that as soon as she gets a little better, she can go home. It breaks our hearts to keep this from her, but better our hearts than hers.

Anyway, as I was saying, I know where Grandma Rose is physically, but as her body and mind have succumbed to the ravages of old age, I wonder where she is mentally and spiritually. I visited her last April and she recognized me and we had some laughs. But it was evident that her body is slowly deteriorating. She can no longer walk with her walker and is confined to a wheelchair. Her hands, gnarled by arthritis for years, have become even more misshapen and unable to function, making it difficult for her to feed herself without spilling food in her lap. Her hearing and eyesight have weakened so that we have to speak louder to her and stand closer so she can see who's talking to her. There are days she doesn't recognize her own family members who come to visit her, yet she'll speak of family or friends who have died as if they were in the room with her or she'll converse as if she were in another time and place.

Last May, my aunt called to tell me about an episode Grandma had experienced that left her bedridden with a very low oxygen count. I was told to expect a call soon that she had passed on. The nursing home staff wanted to send her to the hospital, but my aunt wouldn't allow it on Grandma's wishes. "But we can do things there to figure out what's going on," they explained. "What's going on," replied my aunt, "is old age. Just let her be and go in peace. It's what she wants."

Rose Nerad was born in the family's home in Cleveland, Ohio, on October 9, 1906. She was so puny that the midwife didn't expect her to live more than a few days. Two months later, they finally filed her birth certificate when it was evident that the puny baby was, in truth, a feisty one. Her feistiness for life is what prevailed that May because she pulled through yet another medical crisis, surprising the staff but not her family.

However, this bout took its toll on her in very marked ways. When I visited her a few months later in August, she was a shell of the woman I'd seen in April--more slumped in her chair, eyes less focused, mind less alert. For the first time in all the years I've known her, her skin felt dry when it had always felt as soft as a baby's. An oxygen tank was attached to her wheelchair with the hose inserted into her nostrils like a bridle on a horse's mouth. It takes longer for her to recognize someone, if at all, and she rarely initiates a conversation. When she does, it's often to repeat a statement or question she's spoken several times already. Yet when I was there she was lucid enough to ask me the question she always asks me, "Do you think you'll ever move back to Ohio?"

There's another question she's been asking these past few years—*Why am I still here?* That's one none of us can answer for her, yet we wonder it ourselves. I was wondering it that December morning as I sat writing. *Why is she still alive? What purpose does her being alive serve on a spiritual level? What else does she have to do as Rose Morrell and how can she do it in the state she's in?* This is where my spiritual lessons and beliefs come into play.

We all know that our bodies have DNA that acts as blueprints for our existence. Yet, according to Neale Donald Walsch's book, "Home with God," our souls have DNA as well—Divine Natural Awareness. The soul has a blueprint for its existence here on earth in the embodiment it has selected for this experience.

I liked this explanation—while not a new concept to me, it made the concept easier to explain and understand. I like to think of it this way: Our soul makes an agreement with God as to when it will enter a human body, what it will do during that body's lifetime for its spiritual growth and when it will leave the body. In other words, when it will be born and when it will die--it dies when it's completed its reason for being here in the first place. Not necessarily the humanly-calculated *when* and *how* of the death, but the spiritual *why* of it.

There comes a time as adults when we look for deeper meaning to our lives. We've gone to school, learned a trade, married, had children, succeeded at our career goals, accomplished our athletic goals and whatever else we set as milestones. Now we're wondering, *What now? What else is there for me to do? What's my real purpose for being here? Who am I?*

The answers to these questions can come to us in a number of ways. A sudden-life threatening event or witnessing some incredible feat that someone else has accomplished are possibilities. But we are given clues about these queries every day that we rarely take the time to notice. The answers come from our own spirits and from Universal Spirit, yet we need to be in a still state in order to hear their quiet voices. Meditation and prayer are excellent ways to get in touch with these issues. In prayer, you ask God for guidance; and in meditation, you listen for the answers. Moments of stillness, of being in absolute silence, need not come in some secluded room with candles lit and soft music in the background. You can 'hear' God's voice while skiing down a perfectly-groomed run when everything in your movements and the moment are in sync. You can 'hear' your spirit while hiking a mountain trail or playing a musical instrument or driving down a tree-lined country road. If you allow yourself moments alone with no outside distractions, like cell phones, CDs or companions, you create an atmosphere where God's whisper can be heard.

When I think of Grandma Rose, I think about Life and Death and how the whole progression works. I know that death is a natural part of the life cycle. I don't dwell on it out of morbid curiosity, but out of intellectual inquisitiveness. We can't be afraid of Death, for to do so is to be afraid of Life. They are flip sides of the same coin, existing hand in hand. If we fear Death, that fear extends into how we live our lives and we won't live purposefully as our soul intended. We'll end up regretting what wasn't experienced.

As I think about Grandma, I reflect on my own life and mortality, which makes me think about my parents' early deaths. My dad died in his sleep of a heart attack at the age of fifty-one. My mother died 12 years later at the age of sixty-three after a seven-month bout with liver cancer. I can't help but wonder which way was better—

knowing or not knowing that Death was ready to return me to my spirit form. Perhaps somewhere in between their experiences because I want to experience it intellectually and to know so I can say goodbye to my loved ones, but without prolonging the physical or emotional agony of the experience.

So it still leaves Grandma's question unanswered—*why is she still here?* Just how conscious is she of her state? I'm told that more and more she confuses family members for someone else, often those who have died, and she talks about things she's done that have nothing to do with her current life. I can't help but wonder if the soul isn't softening the transition for her by letting her relive past moments or communicate with passed loved ones so she doesn't have to sit in the shell of her body, day in and day out, lamenting her inabilities. What a gentle way to ease out of the human life back into the spiritual realm! Although it may be hard for us to witness—we tend to project ourselves into her condition and feel uncomfortable and pained by it—hopefully, she is unaware, at least most of the time, of how much she's changed.

With that in mind, I decided that I needed to let go of my own pain about Grandma Rose and, instead, discover what lessons there are for me and how I might grow spiritually from this experience. I find myself examining my own life—*Is the quality of my life what I truly want at this stage in it?* I'm coming to terms with my dreams, beliefs and desires—deciding which ones to keep, which ones to discard, which ones need to change and which new ones to add.

I think that the younger members of our family, Grandma's great-grandchildren and great-great-grandchildren, can learn from her now as well. They can learn that old age is not to be feared or shunned out of discomfort but embraced as a natural part of life. While the adults can share memories of a Grandma Rose who was vibrant and feisty, loving and healthy, the children can also share with the adults their feelings and thoughts about the Grandma Rose they know. We can learn from each other because of her.

I don't pretend to have all the answers, but I have found the answer to that gnawing question that prompted all this. I *know* now where Grandma Rose is—I found her—she's in my heart and always will be! Even though we're separated by thousands of miles and differing states of consciousness, she'll always be with me.

It's not a time for sadness—it's a time for joy and for celebrating the sweetness of her life and the blessedness of her eventual transition. It's a time for remembering and being grateful for the grace she's brought to my life and the lives of all who know her. I close now with the words of a poem that was on a sampler in the bedroom I slept in as a child at her house. While I never consciously memorized this poem, I read it so many times during so many sleepovers that it's imprinted in my mind forever:

> All to myself I think of you.
> Think of the things we used to do.
> Think of the things we used to say.
> Think of each happy yesterday.
> Sometimes I sigh and
> Sometimes I smile,
> But I keep each olden, golden while
> All to myself.

-- Wilbur Dick Nesbitt

❧ ❧ ❧ ❧ ❧ ❧ ❧

Grandma Rose lived another three years and two months, dying peacefully in her sleep on February 17, 2010, at the age of 103. Since then, the rest of my adult family members have died, my Aunt Toni being the last on April 6, 2021. I'm now the matriarch—a very strange role, having no one to talk to about the family's history. I've been blessed with strong, loving women as role models: Lena Galambos (paternal great-grandmother); Rose Morrell (maternal grandmother); Emma Nyitrai (paternal grandmother); Gloria (Morrell) Nyitrai (mother); Toni Rechedy (maternal aunt); Eleanor Gearheart, Emma Clark and Dee Nyitrai (paternal aunts).

Sassy, Sexy, Silly Sixty

(2009)

It's Friday, October 30—two days after my sixtieth birthday. *Sixty.* *Six-Zero. 6-0.* Nope, no matter how I type it, the number sounds foreign to me. I kind of like writing it, though, the roundness of it, no sharp edges or straight lines, just fluid curvy numbers. Kind of like me—fluid and curvy! Hmm, the number's growing on me.

Last year when I turned 59 and realized that my milestone 60th birthday was just 365 days away, I started thinking about how I could celebrate the event. Then I got this crazy idea—why not celebrate with all of my girlfriends? Thus commenced my Sassy, Sexy, Silly Sixty Girlfriend Gathering!

I created a fun invitation that I mailed to my friends near and far, inviting them to plan on taking a special trip in 2009 to attend my Gathering. I researched resorts and locations around the country to see where we could meet. My friends live all over the country, from Greenwich, Connecticut, to Bremerton, Washington, and many cities in between. I've lived and worked in a lot of places as an adult—Ohio, Pasadena, NY/NJ/CT area, Chicago, Phoenix, Las Vegas and currently in Park City, Utah—and I've created some incredible, long-lasting friendships. I make a point of keeping in touch with these friends, even if it's just a birthday card every year and the occasional phone call. You can tell they're good friends because when we get together, no matter how long has elapsed since we last saw each other, we just pick up where we were left off like no time had passed at all!

Unfortunately, the plummeting economy last fall and winter prohibited going to some of the places I'd been looking into—Napa Valley, Hawaii, Santa Fe, Bar Harbor. In the spring of this year, a friend suggested that I hold it in my new home in Park City so those friends who lived outside of Utah could see the special place that had captured my spirit on my cross-country journey in 2000. Great idea—Park City, Utah, here they come! Now, to get down to the details of the Gathering.

Even though my birthday is October 28, I chose a weekend in September because it's a better time to visit Utah both for the weather and for things to do. I decided on Friday to Tuesday, September 11 to 15, and I got the word out to everyone to mark their calendars and R.S.V.P. A.S.A.P. I sent out twenty-nine invitations and was pleased to learn that sixteen gal pals were going to attend, including five of the twelve out-of-state ladies. I booked two 2-bedroom suites at the Marriott Summit Watch on lower Main Street in Park City. Mary and Edo Bernasconi, local friends, offered me their timeshare at the Marriott—I told you I've got great friends! — so we only had to pay for one and divvy it up between the six people staying there.

The year 2009 proved to be an eventful one for me. Besides organizing my special weekend, I underwent three surgeries. The first two were cataract surgeries, each eye done separately a month apart. They were the easiest, practically painless medical procedures I've ever experienced! The third surgery was to have my protruding eyelids, which were affecting my peripheral vision, cut back. A good friend, Dr. David Teasley, is a reconstructive surgeon who did the procedure for me. This operation left me with stitches for a week and black-and-blue eyes for a month, but boy was it worth it! I was ready to show off my new eyes to my friends in September.

First to arrive for the weekend was Kathy Reuschenberg (Katonah, New York), who got to town on Thursday, September 10, and spent the night at my apartment. We had a chance to catch up before connecting with everyone else. Kathy and I have been best friends since seventh grade and carry on one of those "pick up where we left off" conversations I mentioned earlier. She helped me check into the Marriott on Friday and we set up the suites. Friday night we had dinner at the Baja Cantina Mexican restaurant with Jean Miles (Stone Ridge, New York) and awaited the arrival of Virginia

McDonald (Bremerton, Washington) later that evening. Three here and two to go!

Saturday, September 12, while the four of us were having lunch at Red Rock Brewery, my local friend Kathy Stanger picked up Gail Wallace (Greenwich, Connecticut) at the airport in Salt Lake City. They called in their drink order on the way up the mountain—my kind of friends! After lunch, Kathy R, Jean and Virginia headed to the Utah Olympic Park while Kathy S took Gail and me back to the Marriott so Gail could settle into her room. Later that afternoon, Mary Holt (Lisle, Illinois) arrived and all six Marriott guests (including me) were here. That evening, we went to dinner at my favorite Italian restaurant, Cicero's, and window-shopped on Main Street.

Sunday's plans were to take the chairlifts at Deer Valley Resort (where I work) from Snow Park Lodge to mid-mountain Silver Lake Lodge, then a second lift up to the top of Bald Mountain. But it was chilly and windy on the first lift ride, so we opted to skip the other lift ride and hang out around Silver Lake Lodge a while before heading back down to have lunch at the Stew Pot. The afternoon was relaxing as I got things ready for the birthday party that evening.

And what a party it was! Seventeen of us gathered for food and drinks and talking and laughing and bonding! The party was catered by Debby Turkington, a co-worker at Deer Valley Resort, and I ordered my favorite cake from the Resort's bakery, German chocolate.

What I loved the most about the evening was watching my girlfriends get to know each other. These women are such valuable parts of my life for so many reasons, and having them all in one room gave me a feeling that can't be expressed in words. During the festivities, they had me explain how I knew each person, and I recited the "All To Myself" poem. I explained that the common denominator between all of them was the joy they each brought to my life—so I gave them each a little joy in the form of a memento stone with the word "Joy" carved on it. As they say, a good time was had by all!

Monday, we took it easy. Three of us had an in-room massage that evening. We said our goodbyes to Mary H, Kathy R and Gail that night because they had early morning flights on Tuesday and were out the door between 4:30 and 7 a.m. Virginia stayed an extra night, and Jean took her to the airport on Wednesday, then went to her condo in town for the rest of her stay. I stayed in the timeshare suite by myself for two more nights since we had it booked for the week. It gave me time to reflect on the weekend and how truly blessed I am to have these amazing women in my life, as well as those who could not make it to the Gathering but were there with me in spirit.

Even though it's been over a month since my birthday bash, I'm still feeling the love from that weekend. I made sure to have a photo taken of me with each person at the party so I could create a photo album afterwards; then I had them each sign something next to where their photo would go in the book. And, to capture the celebration for perpetuity, I created a 12" x 12" book of photos, text and captions through HeritageMakers.com. I included my invitation verbiage and some poems that I shared with everyone that express how I feel about our relationships.

So, what will I do for my 65th birthday…

Improvisational Living

(2001)

When I signed up for the improvisational comedy class in the fall of 2001, I had no idea the incredible effect it would have on my life. The four classes in four weeks expanded to weekly lessons with the instructor in our homes and finally to performing in public as a comedy troupe a year later and for the next six years. *Off the Top* was the name of the troupe and we performed games and skits off the tops of our heads without a script, without rehearsals, never the same show twice, similar to the television show *Whose Line Is It Anyway?*

A show consists of a series of games or comedy sketches. Some are guessing games, some involve audience participation, some are musical numbers, some are tag-outs and some are straight scenes. Games have names like A to Z, Emo Party, Excuse Yourself, Gibberish Expert, New Choice, One Word, Question Tag, Soap Opera, Superheroes and Day in the Life. Sometimes it requires suggestions from the audience, like *an object found in your grandmother's attic, non-geographical location, a relationship between two people or objects, film genres, emergency situations,* etc. Even though improvised, there is a structure to each show. A director decides on 14-15 games to play that mix up types—physical, guessing, musical, etc.—to fit within a two-hour timeframe.

Does any of this sound familiar? Perhaps you've tried your hand at improvisation? I'd venture to say you have for, in truth, our lives are improvisational. We're constantly making it up as we go, off the tops of our heads. We play games throughout our lives, if you allow that by games, I mean interactions that require participation, decisions, choices, giving and taking, maybe winning and losing and that have an objective. Some life games include childhood, teen years and adult stages. Love relationships, friendships, business relationships, political agendas and community involvements—our roles in these interconnect and change over the years. Some stages have beginnings and endings while others go on throughout.

There is a structure to our lives as well, a master plan established between the Universe and our spiritual selves before we took on our human life. We come to Life with a purpose or a series of purposes to fulfill. We'll be involved with certain people, experience certain events, have certain things to learn and teach in this lifetime. Free will and choices are the improvisational aspects of our lives.

One of the first things we learned on the first night of class was the Rules of Improvisation. *Rules? Isn't that contradictory?* However, it turns out that the rules are very important in order to maintain the integrity of improvisational comedy—there is a *method to the madness.* The idea is to apply the Rules of Improvisation so well that it appears as if there are none at all, that everything is completely freeform. Interestingly enough, the Rules of Improvisation can also apply to our lives…see if you don't agree with me.

Rule #1 – Listen and watch others. By listening to the other players, you're able to respond to their lines and come up with your next line, one that moves the scene forward. If you don't listen but are thinking about what you're going to say or do next, you don't honor the others and you miss opportunities to create a cohesive scene.

It's the same in life. We need to listen to the people in our lives, to honor their presence and be prepared to respond to their words and actions in order to help them or to move the relationship forward. If we're constantly thinking about ourselves, we are disconnected from the people in our lives and are living a solitary existence even though surrounded by people.

Rule #2 – Don't deny. Accept information, verbal and physical. Go with what your partner or partners are saying and doing, no matter how crazy or different from where you thought the scene would go. Don't preplan your next move, but follow the lead of the others. Allows for funnier, more spontaneous scenes. For instance, if a player says to you, "I think our new neighbor is from Mars," don't deny it; go with it. Respond with something unexpected like, "Well, that would explain those candy wrappers all over their yard!"

In life, don't be ready to disagree with others, especially if their position is different from yours. Accept that what they say or do is true for them and be open to their ideas as possible alternatives. This doesn't mean complying with everything or changing your principles. It means recognizing that there are other points of view and giving permission to others to voice theirs. Find compromises. Don't *need* to be right.

Rule #3 – Establish information early. Define who, what and where. This means not to take a lot of time and energy with extraneous discussion that leaves the audience wondering what's going on and who the players are supposed to be. It means *being* the characters, not *explaining* them.

Rule #4 – Make assumptions and avoid questions. Enter a scene as if you know what's happened before it. Enter in the middle and assume that what you're doing and saying is already known. If the scene is a series of questions between players, it won't move forward. It's boring to the audience—they want action, so just do it!

Rules three and four often go hand in hand, as they do in life. We're defining and redefining ourselves all of our lives. When we meet others, we should let our true selves be seen, not some face we hide behind. That's not to say we reveal everything at once, but we do reveal truths. We don't reveal what others expect, but who we truly are.

We've all heard that we should *not* assume things, which can be true as it applies to our expectations of others. But we can make assumptions about our own lives. Making assumptions means trusting our instincts and acting on faith. We take a leap of faith and move into a situation knowing and believing things will progress for the best.

Rule #5 – Raise the stakes and make unexpected choices. The funnier scenes are those that deal with some kind of conflict or crisis that the players must respond to. "Talking heads" are boring and don't raise the level of excitement. Instead, revealing a secret like, "I'm not your sister, I'm your mother," takes the scene to a different place. Or, if given a suggestion from the audience "bump and grind," instead of going for the obvious strip tease scene, make it about playing pool or being a piece of fruit in a blender, the unexpected choices.

In life, the stakes are often raised without our consent, those unexpected events that can change our life in small or big ways. But how often do you raise the stakes yourself? When was the last time you shook up your life by doing something outrageous or unexpected? We need to do this in order to challenge ourselves and to bring spontaneity and joy to our lives.

Rule #6 – Be consistent and real. Stay in character, establish information and keep mimed objects and locations in play. If a player mimes a chair in the middle of the room, walk around that chair as if it were really there. Also, draw upon your life experiences and knowledge of local and current events to feed the scene. Act as if it were real and it becomes real to the audience.

This final rule is the most important. If we aren't real, consistently and genuinely, we're living lives that are lies. What kind of life is that? You know when you're not aligned with your real self, when you're off purpose.

In the children's book, *The Velveteen Rabbit,* by Margery Williams, there's a conversation between a child's favorite stuffed animal, a velveteen rabbit, and the old horse that's been in the nursery for years. It goes like this…

"What is real?" asked the Rabbit one day when they were lying side by side. "Does it mean having things that buzz inside you and a stick-out handle?"

"Real isn't how you are made," said the Skin Horse. "It's a thing that happens to you. When a child loves you for a long, long time, not just to play with, but REALLY loves you, then you become Real."

"Does it hurt?" asked the Rabbit.

"Sometimes," said the Skin Horse, for he was always truthful. "When you are Real, you don't mind being hurt."

"Does it happen all at once, like being wound up," he asked, "or bit by bit?"

"It doesn't happen all at once," said the Skin Horse. "You become. It takes a long time. That's why it doesn't often happen to people who break easily, or have sharp edges, or who have to be carefully kept. Generally, by the time you are Real, most of your hair has been loved off, and your eyes drop out, and you get loose in the joints and very shabby. But these things don't matter at all, because once you are Real, you can't be ugly, except to people who don't understand."

Our lives are like improvisational comedy…we're constantly making it up as we go. Sometimes it turns out the way we want it to, sometimes it flops. What's important is that we continue on, that we follow the theatrical premise, "The show must go on!"

There was an episode on the "Mary Tyler Moore Show" (*Season 7, Episode 6, Chuckles Bites the Dust*) when one of the television station's characters, Chuckles the Clown, dies tragically by getting crushed by an elephant while dressed as a peanut in a parade. Lou, Murray, Ted, Sue Ann and the other station employees make joke after joke about this, but Mary finds it disrespectful and tries to stop them. Chuckles is eulogized by the minister at the memorial service with these words: *"Chuckles the Clown brought pleasure to millions. The characters he created will be remembered by children and adults alike…Peter Peanut, Mr. Fee Fi Fo, Billy Banana and, my particular favorite, Aunt YooHoo. And not just for the laughter that he provided. There was always some deeper meaning to whatever Chuckles did. And what did Chuckles ask in return? Not much. In his own words—'a little song, a little dance, a little seltzer down your pants.'"* Only then does Mary burst out laughing hysterically, until it turns to sobbing.

Tears of laughter and tears of sorrow come from the same place. We can laugh so hard that we cry or cry so hard that we laugh hysterically. We need to balance these feelings of sorrow and humor. We need to be serious about how we honor our commitments and respect ourselves and others, but not take life so seriously that we forget to let a little joy and humor into it, improvised or otherwise.

The Pleasure of My Company

(2013)

What would bother you more—eating dinner alone at a restaurant on a Saturday night, going to a party by yourself where the only person you know is the host or driving alone on an eight-hour trip without any music or radio playing, in complete silence? I ask these and other questions of my readers in my book, *The Pleasure of My Company: Finding the Motivation and Courage to Spend Time Alone,* published in 2012.

It is my premise that too many people are missing out on Life because they won't do enjoyable things or visit interesting places or try something new simply because they don't have someone to accompany them. There's a fear of being alone in our culture that, I believe, needs to be addressed for several reasons:

- Spending time alone can enhance your relationships
- You can create balance in your life by adding 'alone time' to it
- Solitude enriches you socially, physically and psychologically

One of the most interesting things that draw us to a person is his or her story. Storytelling is timeless--we all do it in one way or another. Stories based upon your personal experiences have the value that can entertain, teach and inspire your listeners.

You need to build up your repertoire of stories. Sitting at home because you don't have someone to go with you to take a class, to work out or to go on vacation—well, those are missed opportunities for creating 'stories' about yourself that you can share with the people in your life. Someone who participates in Life, rather than watches from the sidelines, is someone who develops solid, valued and long-term relationships.

As for balance in your life, Leonardo da Vinci offered us these wise words:

Every now and then go away,
have a little relaxation,
for when you come back to your work
your judgment will be surer;
since to remain constantly at work
will cause you to lose power of judgment.

Go some distance away
because the work appears smaller
and more of it can be taken
in at a glance
and a lack of harmony or proportion
is more readily seen.

When one aspect of your life is monopolizing your time and energy, or if you feel pulled in many directions at once, detachment from your everyday life allows you to take a breather and create the balance referred to by da Vinci. If there are problems you're struggling with, relationships you need to explore or decisions you're putting off, going off alone can help you get the proper perspective on the situation. It helps you clean out the cobwebs so you can return with a clear mind, ready to tackle whatever comes your way.

Finally, for many, the idea of being alone conjures up negative images of loneliness. But there's another, more positive aspect of being alone—solitude—and solitude improves your life socially, physically and psychologically.

According to Ester Schaler Buchholz, author of the book "The Call of Solitude: Alonetime in a World of Attachment:"

"When you're always surrounded by people and living life
in the fast lane and you don't have time to refuel, you're
going to get very irritable and push people away from you.

Researchers say that having time alone can actually improve your social interactions, making you a better spouse, employee and friend."

Psychologist Peter Suedfeld studied the effects of living in extreme solitary situations, restricted from environmental stimulation, such as on a lone voyage or living in a polar station. He claims:

"...the body's physiological response during times of solitude is similar to that of deep relaxation, especially if solitude is combined with reduced levels of sensory stimulation (e.g., the television shut off). This includes lowered heart and respiration rates, lowered blood pressure and muscle tension and reduced production of stress hormones."

Psychologically, solitude provides a special haven, a place where you can "hear" your inner voice and get back in touch with dreams and thoughts that are often drowned out by the outside world. Your self-esteem and self-reliance are strengthened so you can face day-to-day situations with higher resolve and confidence.

Going out to eat alone. Attending a party by yourself. Traveling long distances in silence. These circumstances, and more, await you as adventurous opportunities to enrich your life. My advice? Don't miss out! Enjoy the pleasure of your own company!

Act As If

(2014)

Dear Michael,

I was taking my morning powerwalk yesterday morning when I thought about our dinner at the Outback and how much I enjoyed our time together. I loved the conversation and how you stimulate new thoughts in me and allow me to share my thoughts openly with you without taking them personally or offensively. As I was replaying that conversation in my mind, I realized there was something else I would have shared with you regarding your dissatisfaction with your job. Maybe I would have if we'd stayed for dessert. So pretend we're doing that, lingering over some delicious treat as we continue our conversation.

What I would have shared is a trick I learned years ago and that has become ingrained in me enough that I don't even consciously call upon it anymore—I just do it naturally. I call it the "Act As If" trick. It can be used any number of ways. Let me share an example.

When your dad and I were working at Liberty Industries back in the late 90's, the original owners retired and their son-in-law Ron, his brother and his brother's partner took over. They all lived out of state and their method of operating was questionable and was very much about the bottom line and making money. They operated purely on greed and the office morale slowly went downhill. Your dad finally left in 1998, and I was planning to follow suit. Then, I heard my "inner voice" tell me to *"Sell your house and things, quit your job and go west!"* That's where the "Act As If" trick came into play. I *knew* I was going to leave eventually, even though I hadn't told the bosses that, so I told myself to *Act As If* each day was my last day at the job. Pretend in my mind that I was just finishing one last project before I left. I trusted in my decision to go west and knew that the Universe was getting my 'ducks in a row' so I could finally leave.

Well, as they say, be careful what you wish for because it might come true! I've learned over the years that the Universe has a sense of humor and Its own sense of timing that doesn't always coincide with my plans! In May 1999, all of the owners were in town and one of them called me in his office, I thought to go over some projects. However, as he started talking and saying that Ron was moving back to Youngstown and would be in the office all the time now, I heard that voice in my head say, "He's going to fire you!" Sure enough, he said they were eliminating my office manager position—it was business, not personal. The Universe had done what I couldn't bring myself to do on my own—it got me out of a job that was stressing me and holding me back from properly planning my trip west. By "acting as if" it was my last day, had I actually manifested my last day? My reaction wasn't to get emotional by crying or getting angry, which I think he expected—I just said I understood and proceeded to discuss my projects. I almost thanked him—and I *did* thank the Forces Behind The Scenes that made it all possible.

So, what does this have to do with you? If we were sitting in the Outback right now, I'd be telling you to *Act As If* when you go to work at that dreary carpet cleaning job that you dislike so much. *Act As If* it's your last day. *Act As If* you're just biding your time because something BIG is about to happen in your life. Don't put a time limit on it--just trust that Time will deliver when it's appropriate.

We teased during dinner about you being "Angry Young Man." And, while I get why, I caution you to be careful about the labels you use to describe yourself, even in jest. Words have a lot of power, especially when we internalize them as definitions of who we are. Yes, you may be feeling anger, but you are so much more. You are Talented Young Man, Ingenious Young Man, Caring Young Man, Passionate Young Man and, probably most importantly, Susan's Nephew Young Man, which means you don't limit yourself.

Some labels I *would* use to describe you are Imaginator, Actor, Great Pretender, Illusionist! You see beyond the norm and envision worlds and characters that make people laugh, cry, scream and demand more. So, how about "Acting As If" when you go to work. For kicks, try imagining that you are a superhero who's going to rid the world of carpet crud. You are *CARPET MAN, Defender of Cleanliness and Conqueror of Dirt* in all its nasty forms! You have the power to remove the world's filth from carpets, upholstery and homes so that people can live happily ever after in healthy conditions and beautiful surroundings. Your co-workers are your bumbling sidekicks, who help you in their own inept but supportive way. Wow, aren't you something!?

I know, I know—corny as hell, right? Stupid even! But you're only acting and it's for your own amusement. No one else will know and if you can bring a smile to your face every day as you head off to work so that you feel good for that "last day at work," what's wrong with that? Anyway, you get the idea—although you don't need to take it to the extreme that I did!

It's easy to see what's happening—or not happening—in our lives as being out of our control and start attributing our plight to circumstances and others who are *doing it to us*. And while there definitely are things out of our control, how we choose to react to them and proceed internally is what we *do* have control over. You are responsible for creating a healthier, happier YOU regardless of what job you have, where you live, who you know, what you believe and what others think. Sometimes we have to pretend it's the way we want it to be before it actually becomes what we want it to be— it's a mindset thing. And that's something I have confidence you can do, Michael.

Okay, dessert is over and I'll come down off my soap box. See, even when I'm writing a letter to you, I get passionate and excited. Thanks for bearing with me. I hope you'll glean something of value from this—my intention is *always* to support and assist you in any way I can.

❧ ❧ ❧ ❧ ❧ ❧ ❧

I like to spend alone time with each of my nieces and nephew when I visit them in Ohio, and this is part of a letter I wrote to my 25-year-old nephew Michael after going out to dinner with him during a recent visit. He is dissatisfied with his part-time job and is in a transitional period of his life. Michael is one of those people who "hears a different drummer," and I can relate to him in a so many ways.

The Ant and I

(2014)

Have you ever visited an enchanted forest? I have--the Mianus River Gorge Preserve in Bedford, New York. Of course, it wasn't always an enchanted forest. When I lived in Bedford Hills in the Eighties, it was a place I frequented for long hikes on forest trails, walking alongside or above the Mianus River under a canopy of centuries-old trees. Every now and then, I'd find the remains of a low stone wall that dated back to the 1700s and I'd sit and sketch. There was one place where I'd go off the main path to an outcropping of rocks that looked down on the river about fifty feet below. I'd meditate or read or just listen to the sounds of the forest as I became 'one' with my surroundings.

The forest became enchanted after I'd left the area. The enchantment is the lingering memories of my many visits into its depths. I'll often travel back there in my mind when I close my eyes to meditate. My senses come alive with the sights, sounds and smell that percolate up from the deep recesses of my soul. I see the buds on the trees as they come alive in the spring, the canopy of thick summer branches overhead or the palette of autumn colors as the forest prepares for its winter slumber. I hear the rushing river waters, the rustling branches and the chorus of bird songs. I smell the damp earth, the fragrant foliage and the musky tree stumps. But there's one memory that, to this day, amazes me because of the lessons I learned from one of the forest's smallest creatures—an ant.

It was fall and most of the leaves I'd watched bud and bloom that spring and summer now blanketed the forest floor. I figured this would be my last hike before winter, so I was taking my time and absorbing the experience when something caught my eye on the trail ahead of me. I studied the ground to see what it was, getting down on my haunches, until there, in the middle of the trail, I saw a large carpenter ant. It was dragging a moth that was twice her size over the tops of the dried leaves in a determined march to God knows where.

I was mesmerized as I watched her traverse over leaves and twigs and rocks with her booty in tow. It would be like me climbing K2 with a backpack weighing twice my weight! Did she know I was looking down at her? Did she realize that her eminent demise was but a footstep away? I rooted for her to make it across that path to the safety of her final destination. I saw ahead of her a small twig, about the size of my pinky finger. Hardly noticeable from my perspective but it would be an insurmountable obstacle when she reached it. So, very slowly and carefully, I removed the twig and gave her clear passage. A few minutes later, she disappeared into the forest.

I stood there and thought about what I'd witnessed and I wondered, *Was there a creature looming over me somewhere out there in the vastness of space, watching me trek through the forest? Could this force end my life or change the course I take?* As a 'big picture' thinker, I can't help but be moved by the big picture of that ant's life and how it mirrors the big picture of mine—we're both the center of our own universe while also being mere specs in the vastness of the Universe. It's amazing how I can feel large and small at the same time. Significant and insignificant; valuable and negligible. It's all a matter of perspective, and it reminds me that even though someone else's perspective may be different from mine doesn't make either one's better or worse than the other—simply different.

Lessons come to us from many and varied sources. On that fall day, amidst the acres and acres of trees in that Preserve, my eye was drawn to the forest floor by the subtle movement of a minuscule creature so that the Universe could teach me two lessons. The first was a reminder about my place in the Universe and the importance of perspective. But it was the second one—perseverance—that has stuck with me the most. The ant's doggedness that navigated her across the trail with a moth in tow convinced me that *I* could persevere whenever I faced my own daunting challenges.

That little ant has stayed with me since that autumn day, a constant reminder when I've faced difficult situations, when my patience has run thin, when I've taken on more than I can handle. Unbidden from the depths of my subconscious, I see that ant walking across that path dragging that moth—and I tell myself to persevere, I can do it! Sometimes the answer to the most complex question comes from the simplest source.

Top of the World!

(2014)

It's a beautiful blue-sky day in Sandusky, Ohio, as my 20-year-old niece Rachel and I stand in line. A cool breeze off of Lake Erie tempers the sun's heat that kisses my bare shoulders. We inch forward as the line weaves around the guardrails. We're close enough to hear the operator instruct the next row of passengers on how to get situated in their cars.

The Blue Streak is Cedar Point Amusement Park's oldest wooden roller coaster, circa 1964, and it still attracts long lines of eager riders. It holds its own against all the newer, faster, scarier steel monoliths that have popped up at the park over the past decades. Give me an old-fashioned wooden rollercoaster any day! The clickety-clack of the chains pulling the coaster up that first big hill still sends chills through my veins as we make that jerking, creeping crawl up to the summit before plummeting to earth.

Growing up, rollercoasters were milestone markers of my youth. Every summer, we'd go to Idora Park in Youngstown, Ohio, for the afternoon company outing for my dad's employer, Ohio Edison. He'd go to work in the morning, while my mom would make her infamous fried chicken to add to the picnic basket with her potato salad and other munchies. My sister and I would be so excited we'd almost wet our pants when dad pulled into the driveway to pick us up at noon and take us to the park.

Mom and Dad were rollercoaster enthusiasts and, after dropping off the picnic basket in the pavilion, they headed straight for the two big coasters at Idora—the Jack Rabbit (the smaller of the two) and the Wild Cat. I hated waiting behind with my aunt while I watched their car chugging up that first hill, then whisking down and around the ride in lickety-split time. "One day when you're a little older, Susan, we'll take you on these rides," my mom promised. Then the day came when she kept that promise and I 'graduated' from the kiddie coaster to the Jack Rabbit! I was so excited, sitting beside my Dad, gripping the security bar as his arm came around my shoulders! Wow, what a ride! "Let's do it again! Let's do it again!" I pleaded as Mom and Dad laughed at my enthusiasm. A few years later, I added the Wild Cat to my achievements and have been a wooden rollercoaster nut ever since.

On this summer day in July 2014, I feel that same excitement in the pit of my stomach as Rachel and I step into our car and get locked in. A small voice in my 64-year-old brain is wondering what the heck I'm doing here, defying gravity, putting myself in this precarious position on a mechanical nightmare that could...oh, forget it, Susan! Besides, it's too late now--we're climbing that first hill. Did I mention I have a fear of heights? I don't look around as we crest the summit. But, as we plunge down, picking up speed and whipping around the turns and hills, my hands go up and I'm screaming my head off like that 10-year-old on her first Jack Rabbit ride. Whee! Who said you can't be a kid again? I feel like James Cagney's character, standing at the top of the gas tank at the end of the movie *White Heat* yelling, "Made it, Ma! Top of the world!"

Retirement, Be Damned!

(2015)

A new word crept into my vocabulary a few years ago that's made me feel ambivalent and confused. Just typing it makes me anxious, but here goes … *retirement.* Phew! That was easier than I thought, but the idea of retirement still confuses me. When I entered my sixties (six years ago…you do the math!), people started asking me all these weird questions. *When are you going to retire? Have you signed up for Medicare yet? When are you going on Social Security?* Excuse me…what are you talking about? That's something my grandfather did, not me. After all, I'm only…wait a minute…I *am* my grandfather's age! When did that happen?

If I mention how old I am, the reactions are a little unsettling. "Really? You don't *look* 66!" or "Oh, I wouldn't have guessed you were *that* old." These people have good intentions, but they're starting to irritate me. I've come up with a couple of retorts, like, "Get used to it--this is what 66 looks like now!" or "And I wouldn't have guessed you were *that* clueless!" Okay, I probably don't say that second one out loud, but replying with my own rude, stupid or juvenile retorts like theirs might make me feel better.

I'm sure I speak for other Baby Boomers who are struggling with this concept. What's the saying these days--60 is the new 40? Why can't 60 just be "the *new* 60?" Many of us are healthier and more active physically and mentally than our parents' generation were at this age—we feel like we're still in our forties. And, like me, the thought of *not* working boggles our minds. After having various jobs and volunteer responsibilities for the past forty-eight years, I can't imagine waking up without having some routine or project to fill my days and challenge my mind.

But it's inevitable. So I've been reading books, meeting with life coaches, evaluating my finances and talking to retired friends. One book, "Don't Retire, REWIRE!" by Jeri Sedlar and Rick Miners, offers a concept I find appealing. *Rewire* sounds more positive and fun to me than *retire*, so I've decided I'll rewire my life and create a vision for how I'll live out my third act, the next thirty-some years.

Where does that leave me? So far, I've come up with these ideas:

- Live a year on O'ahu, Hawaii, getting a job as a resort concierge or executive assistant to a resort manager
- Use my book, "The Pleasure of My Company," as the catalyst for workshops to empower women (and men) to be comfortable doing things and being alone.
- Improve my boxing skills. Yes, boxing! I took it up five years ago and love it!
- Travel around the country visiting my many friends
- Continue learning Italian and visit Italy

Shakespeare says, "…and 'tis our fast intent to shake all cares and business from our age, conferring them on younger strengths, while we unburdened crawl towards death." (King Lear, act 1, sc. 1) Yikes! Spare me, please, Will! Oliver Goldsmith makes it a little more appealing with, "Oh, blest retirement! Friend to life's decline! How blest is he who crowns, in shades like these, a youth of labor with an age of ease!" But my favorite quote is from entertainer George Burns, who said, "Age to me means nothing. I can't get old; I'm working. I was old when I was twenty-one and out of work. As long as you're working, you stay young. When I'm in front of an audience, all that love and vitality sweeps over me and I forget my age."

Maybe that's my answer—I'll become a stand-up comedian and let my audience keep me working and young! Or, I'll just be true to myself and trust that, as long as I want to work, work will be there for me in one form or another—*retirement, be damned!*

⁋ ⁋ ⁋ ⁋ ⁋ ⁋ ⁋

I'm writing this commentary on January 22, 2022, while living in the Viewpoint Golf Resort 55-plus community. Yes, I sold my soul to the devil, retired from my job of 18 years at a ski resort in Utah in September 2018 and moved to Mesa, Arizona, on October 1. But I didn't succumb entirely to the retirement lifestyle. I've been working off and on as a temporary administrator for Robert Half Office Team on assignments. I found my own footing in this new lifestyle and even learned to enjoy not working. What I didn't get used to was residing in such a cliquish community of retirees who have a propensity for complaining, judging and frowning. I got my first hint of this when someone said to me after being there two months, "Oh, you're the woman who backs into her driveway!" Seriously?! You're watching me that closely? Get a life! (There were a few exceptions, but not enough to keep me there for long.)

I wanted to be part of the broader Mesa/Phoenix community and interact with people of other ages and cultures. I got involved in outside interests—Unity Church of Mesa; Fresh Start for Women; Mesa Community College Mentor Program; a women's book club and a women's writing group; attending a gym. Yes, there were activities at the resort, but I'm not into golf, water aerobics, pickle ball, dime bingo or weekly Rummikub games.

Anyway, as of three days ago, I sold my house so I can move back to my home state of Ohio to live in the Columbus area near my brother and sister-in-law, their three adult kids and my two grandnephews. During the Covid lockdown, the distance between them and me seemed to increase exponentially; I realized I wanted to be near them at this stage of our lives. I'll continue working for Robert Half there—when I feel so inclined—but the funny thing is, I enjoy those days when I don't have to set the alarm and head to some office. I can admit when I'm mistaken—there may be something to this retirement gig after all!

Love at First Sight

(2016)

Who'd have thought, at the ripe age of 66, I could fall head over heels in love! I met this great guy on social media this past January and it was love at first sight! When I saw his face in that Instagram photo that my brother posted, my heart skipped a beat and I knew a lifelong connection had been made.

His name is James Everett Adams and he was born on January 23, 2016 -- the firstborn child of my niece Christina. I wouldn't meet James until four months later when I visited them in Columbus, Ohio. But I was already madly enamored with this new member of our family!

Time stands still and flies concurrently. We watch the clock's secondhand tick, tick, ticking as we wait anxiously for a long-winded speaker to finish his lecture. We blink--and a child is having children of her own. I met James almost 29 years to the date that I watched his mother being carried off a plane in the Pittsburgh airport. Christina Marie Morrell was born on March 7, 1987, in Wertheim, Germany, where my brother was stationed in the U.S. Army. They returned to Ohio when she was two months old for her christening--I'm also her godmother! --and the immediate, overwhelming love I felt for her I now felt overflowing to her son.

Time also plays tricks on our mind. My grandma Rose was 103 years old when she died, but the last year of her life she was in and out of reality--our reality, that is. Time took her to a transition place where she would talk to loved ones who had died as if they were right there in the room with her. It was hard for my Aunt Toni when her mother didn't even recognize her only living child. She'd desperately correct Grandma when she'd point to my brother and call him Hank, her own brother who had died many years before. "No, Mom, that's Tony, your grandson. Remember?" She didn't remember, not in that moment of Time.

I realized that the "when" that Grandma lived in most of her days was a place I wish I could visit. So I'd play along with the "joke." If she was talking with my mom Gloria, I would talk with her, too. Why not? Who's to say she *wasn't* there, listening in on our conversation? It was much more fun to spend Time with Grandma in this way than to waste Time trying to bring her back to a world she would soon be leaving permanently.

My spiritual viewpoint allows me to believe that little James came to us directly from the loving arms of my mom and dad, my Grandma Rose and Grandpa Todd and all the other relatives who have moved on to Time's other reality. I believe that, until he reaches that inevitable "age of reason" that we teach children to exist in, his little mind will be remembering those loved ones and he, too, may even talk to them as his invisible playmates!

In the blink of an eye, James will be presenting Christina with her first grandchild. In the meantime, I will savor every moment with him and create memories for him to pass on to future generations about his 'silly, sassy Aunt Susie.'

☙ ☙ ☙ ☙ ☙ ☙ ☙

On August 31, 2018, James' brother, Luke Henry Adams, was born. Just when I thought my heart has no more love to divvy up, it proves me wrong. I am in love again with another delightful little boy—or, I should say, little man because that's what their mom calls her sons. She reigns in a household of men and thrives!

Say Nay to Naysayers

(2016)

I've faced my share of naysayers during my lifetime. I didn't realize it early on, but as I started paying attention and looked back in hindsight, I realized just which of my family and friends I could share things with and who to avoid. You know the ones I mean. You have this sudden, bright, exciting notion to go somewhere new or do something creative, and you enthusiastically tell that special person all about it—and then it happens. She looks at you like you've grown a second nose. He shakes his head and starts spouting logical reasons why it won't work. They present a list of "friendly facts" to help you and explain about how you should do this or that instead. Yep, they've burst your joy balloon. You feel deflated and stupid and alone. The Naysayers!

One particular incident in my life really brought this into focus for me. It was a pleasant, late summer day that Friday, the fourth of September in 1998. As the hour approached eight a.m., I was driving along Route 422 in Girard, Ohio, on my way to work, as I'd been doing for the past two years, to my job as the office manager of a pallet broker company. When I turned onto Tibbetts-Wick Road, I had no idea in a matter of minutes—nay, seconds—my whole life would be so drastically changed. As thoughts about my upcoming vacation to Maine intertwined with thoughts about how dissatisfied I'd been with my job and the sense of unfulfillment I'd been experiencing lately, it came to me.

Not as a subtle idea that my mind could play with and coddle. It was not an image that I could hold up and gaze upon from a distance, that I could walk around and see from all sides. It was not a whisper that echoed through my psyche, teasingly, begging to be deciphered and understood. I had no time to decide whether to let it in or to dismiss it, sending it back to the recesses of my mind, never to be dealt with again. No, it came to me like a cannonball. Without warning, it shot through my mind with a loud, thunderous thwack that left me shaken to the depths of my core. It screamed out of me with decisive clarity, leaving no question as to its meaning.

"Sell your house and your things. Quit your job and just go. Go west!"

What? You can imagine my surprise, my utter shock, at "hearing" those words. I actually looked in my rear-view mirror to see if someone else might be in the car yelling at me. Then I heard them again, *"Sell your house and things and go west!"*

I waited for those other voices that would tell me to ignore this incredulous notion. Waited for the self-inquiries asking me, "Are you crazy? You can't possibly be considering this lame-brain idea, can you?" But those voices never came. Instead, I realized the voice I'd heard had come from deep within me—it was my Soul's voice that I'd been listening to and heeding for years, one that I trusted beyond all else. With that realization, overwhelming feelings of freedom and weightlessness and, yes, giddiness washed over me. I heard myself responding, wholeheartedly and with conviction, "Yes! I can do this! My God, I'm actually going to do this!"

By the time I pulled into the parking lot, a mere quarter mile down the road, my life had been transformed. As I walked through the doors of Liberty Industries, unbeknownst to my co-workers, I was already on my way. The journey west had begun. For a number of reasons that I won't go into here, it made perfect sense to me that this was a solution to a number of burning questions I was dealing with at the time about my job, about living in Ohio, about my social life and more. I was excited! Of course, I couldn't burst into my office and make an announcement yet. It was too new an idea and needed to be thought out. Besides, these were just my co-workers; they didn't deserve to hear such astounding news first. My family and friends had first dibs on that.

But I just had to tell someone, and the first person I thought of was my friend Barb—I knew she'd 'get it!' So I called her and do you know what she said to me? "What fun! I can't wait to hear all about your journey!" How's that for a good, supportive friend? No questions asked, she just jumped on the bandwagon with me. The next two people I told were my brother and sister-in-law, Tony and Patty, when they returned from a weekend trip. They, too, understood and acted as if it were the most sensible thing in the world—for me, that is! You see, Barb, Tony and Patty knew me and knew I wasn't looking for answers or approval or resolutions from them—they believed in me and trusted that I'd figure out the *how* eventually. They simply supported the vision!

On the other hand, two weeks later, my childhood friend Kathy visited Ohio with her husband Chan, but I knew I wasn't ready to share this vision with them. As much as they loved me, I *knew* they'd immediately question the logic of it and come up with reasons it would or wouldn't work. Logic? Reason? That's not what is needed to make a vision come to fruition, at least not in its embryotic stage. It needs hope and enthusiasm, magic and faith. So, as much as I loved them, I kept silent about it during their visit. I finally did tell Kathy in a phone conversation five months later, and as expected, Ms. Practical emerged, as did Mr. Logical in an email from Chan the next day. They both talked about how this vision wasn't necessarily a reasonable thing to pursue—maybe a sabbatical from my job would be better. They offered good, reasonable advice for other options instead of quitting, selling and leaving, but as well-intentioned as their advice was (and I *did* appreciate their good intentions and concerns), they kind of missed the point. By then, however, the vision had taken root, and I'd already started planning and solidifying it within my heart, mind and psyche. It was no longer an ethereal idea that could be blown away by reason—I'd laid a foundation for it to happen and it could now withstand the naysayers!

By the way, I wasn't disappointed by their skepticism—because I knew *them*, I had predicted their reactions and I hadn't set my expectations up for disappointment. Besides, they eventually supported me when they realized I was serious, just like I knew they would! Also, they weren't the only ones I didn't tell about my plans—since most people react in the "fix it" mode, I kept my brainstorming and ideas "close to the vest" for quite a while until they started to take form.

One last story about knowing who to trust. A month after my initial "voice" experience, I was in Connecticut on vacation visiting my friend Gail. We went out to dinner with a third friend, Kathy, and I was deciding whether or not to share my idea with them. Finally, I knew it was safe and told them what had happened. And, yet again, I wasn't disappointed—they were excited for me! I mentioned that I'd been brainstorming about what to do on this journey—no plans, just random ideas. One was to volunteer at Robert Redford's Sundance Film Festival in Park City, Utah, in January of whatever year I'd be out there. The next morning at Gail's I found a clipping from the *Parade's* Question & Answer section of the Sunday newspaper under my orange juice glass. The question asked how someone could find out about volunteering at Sundance and the answer was the contact information. Wow! Gail said she'd read this a few weeks before, didn't have an interest herself but felt someone she knew might, and had cut it out and pinned it on her bulletin board. She figured it was meant for me. Talk about synchronicity!

Author Alan Cohen writes in his book, "A Deep Breath of Life," (January 25):

> *In the early stages of a project, it is wise to keep our thoughts and energies contained, not wavering in the air. If we expose our intimate visions to negative influences, we may be knocked down or lose momentum.... No one in the outer world has power over us, but if our vision has not yet gelled, we must nourish it before sending it out into the world. When a farmer plants a tree in a field, he builds a fence to protect it from being trampled by cattle. After the tree has grown strong and firm, the fence is removed, and the cattle can scratch their backs against it and rest in its shade. Honor your tender thoughts and dreams by surrounding them with*

a protective womb. Then when they are born, they will bless everyone.

I'm going to turn the tables now. We can all come up with moments when naysayers have squashed our hopes and dreams. Instead, I want you to ask yourself when *you've* been the naysayer. Because, let's face it, we've done to others what we don't like them doing to us, haven't we? Acknowledging this is important--it's part of human nature to protect ourselves by pulling others down to our level of insecurity, depression and sadness. Having recognized the possibility in ourselves, we can now be aware of when we're about to naysay someone's dream and we can STOP IT! Instead, smile and listen to his or her excitement regardless of what you think about the idea. Be a Yeah-sayer, not a Naysayer!

Listen Between the Lines

(2018)

I'm sure you're familiar with the popular routine, *Who's On First?*, made famous by the comedy team, Abbott and Costello. They're my favorite comedy team. I even have a book of all their routines and the complete set of DVDs of their movies. When I worked for Xerox on the east coast in the Eighties, another trainer and I performed the skit as the opening of some combined training sessions we conducted.

What's funny about this routine, besides the obvious, is that we've all been there, haven't we? We've been in a conversation that seems to be going nowhere and has us ready to pull our hair out or punch the other person! Why is that? My answer to that question is, *We aren't really listening.*

Listening is *not* hearing. *Hearing* is a physical capability using our auditory senses. *Listening* takes hearing to a deeper level. It means turning off the voice in our head that's judging or analyzing what's being said, the voice that has us preparing what we'll say next and how we'll tell *our* story instead of paying attention to the speaker's story.

When I was living in Ohio in the Nineties, I was trained in Compassionate Listening for my Unity church's High Watch Ministry. I learned the importance and value of giving my full, undivided attention to the person coming to me for guidance—the words, the expressions, the tone and body language—so I could fully and effectively respond to what he or she was saying.

Often times, when a spouse or friend comes to us to "talk," he or she is really looking for someone to whom they can vent about a situation or share their fears about something. They aren't necessarily looking for an intellectual, *thinking,* resolution--they are looking for an open heart to acknowledge that what they are *feeling* has merit and should be expressed. Women are commonly much better at this then men. Now, I know I'm generalizing, but let's face it—for the most part, men don't get it…we ladies don't need your *help*, we just need your *attention!*

In 2017, I was trained and became certified as a Life Coach. Like with my Compassionate Listening training at Unity Church, the emphasis for a Life Coach is on *listening*—not advising, not fixing, not healing. We're there to guide clients through a situation so that they can make informed decisions and appropriate changes. When I am truly listening, I take myself out of the equation unless the client asks specifically for advice. Instead, I prompt the speaker to continue talking by asking forwarding-moving questions or making assuring responses that let the speaker know he or she is in a safe environment. Often times, the client draws her own conclusions just by being able to talk out loud to a supportive audience who sends the unspoken message, "I care!"

The art of listening doesn't just use your ears to hear the speaker's words. It also notices the tone of voice and the pacing of the words. The eyes contribute to the conversation as well, as does the speaker's body language—stiff or fluid? Calm or fidgety? A valuable technique when listening during coaching is to repeat back to the speaker what you understood him to say. It gets clarity for you to proceed and it lets the speaker know that you really are listening, not just to the words but to the underlying meaning of those words.

It's important for me to note here that a Life Coach is *not* a therapist or a doctor. Sometimes during a coaching session, it becomes apparent that the client requires the kind of care that only a psychologist or other specialist can offer; so I'll suggest that the client seek that help. The purpose of coaching is to help clients come to their own conclusions regarding whatever situation is being discussed, so they'll usually make the decision on their own to seek that additional help.

But you don't have to be trained or certified to be a good listener. Giving the speaker your undivided, unbiased attention is a gift you are offering to him or her, one that will be appreciated and reciprocated when *you* need an attentive ear.

As for that *Who's On First?* routine, let's listen to the conclusion of Lou and Bud's comedic conversation...

LOU: Let me get this straight. I'm the catcher and the guy at bat bunts the ball. To get him out, I throw the ball to first base. Whoever it is drops the ball, so the runner goes to second. Who picks up the ball and throws it to What. What throws it to I Don't Know. I Don't Know throws it back to Tomorrow---a triple play.

BUD: Yeah. It could be.

LOU: Another guy gets up and it's a long fly ball to Because. Why? I don't know. He's on third, and *I don't care!*

BUD: What was that?

LOU: I said, I DON'T CARE!

BUD: Oh, that's our shortstop

You, of course, *do* care, so you'll remember to listen.

Living on the Plateau

(2018)

There are a lot of metaphors to describe the ups and downs of life, such as, peaks and valleys, a rollercoaster ride and riding the waves. Some people live for the rush of the ups and downs, seeking out those adventures that take them to extremes, and they become bored or frustrated when they find themselves in those quiet times in between. Others prefer to sit on the plateau between the ups and downs for as long as they can, rarely venturing out or trying something out of their comfort zone.

Ups and Downs can happen erratically within a day or stretch out over a short period of time. They can happen within different areas of your life simultaneously and be in opposition to each other. For instance, a personal relationship could be on a high while your career is on a low or your career could be skyrocketing while you're experiencing a health issue.

In the 1970s, the *biorhythm theory* became popular. This pseudoscientific theory was developed by Wilhelm Fliess in the late 19th century and is the idea that our daily lives are significantly affected by rhythmic cycles with periods of typically a 23-day physical cycle, a 28-day emotional cycle and a 33-day intellectual cycle. I'm not going into detail about this theory here, but there's plenty of information on the Internet about it. You'll see how it uses an up/down curved line graph to record these three rhythms for a given day/time, which is why I mention it.

An interesting exercise for you to do is to make a timeline of your life to see when the ups and downs occurred. Check the peaks, valleys and plateaus for patterns that seem to regulate your life. For the intent of this essay, let's focus on the plateaus.

Plateaus in nature are areas of level ground either between two peaks on low ground or two valleys on high ground. For our purposes, a plateau is a state of little or no change following a period of activity or progress. Think about times when we can experience a plateau—when flying, for instance. The take-off and landing are steep up or down stages of the flight that require short bursts of acceleration or deceleration, while the flight itself is the plateau of the journey when we seem to be inactive. Other terms that can be used to describe this are in limbo, in a lull or stagnant.

So, what is the value of a plateau? Do you get impatient when things aren't moving fast enough—when you're not selling your house quickly or you haven't heard about that new job or can't seem to learn that new skill fast enough? Think about learning to ski.

I worked at a ski resort for 18 years and saw the value of plateaus while learning the sport. At first, it was that uphill struggle to get my body and mind in sync to coordinate my movements down the hill. I felt so clumsy and fearful. Eventually, the day came when it all came together and what was once difficult became effortless. It seemed to be sudden, but of course, it wasn't. Once it clicked for me, the challenge now was to not push myself to ski beyond my ability on terrain I wasn't ready for—to do so would put me and other skiers at risk of injury or worse. I couldn't let my ego put me in danger just so I could say I skied that double-blue run. Instead, I had to ski the same runs again and again to create the muscle and brain memory of performing this sport successfully. Eventually, I could challenge myself up to a new level of achievement, which would be followed by another plateau, and on and on.

Another example of allowing the plateau to play itself out is when you plant a garden. It's not always about up and down or speeding things up—it's more about hurry up and wait. You go through all the motions necessary to prep the soil, then you carefully put the seed in its allotted hole in the row of the garden. You cover it with some water and then fill in the hole and pat it down to secure it in place. Now the waiting starts. It seems like nothing is happening and you may be tempted to dig in the soil and see what stage the seed is in. However to do that disturbs the natural process, even if you don't touch the seed. You'll end up stifling it and maybe even killing it. Instead, you wait patiently and rejoice when you see the buds poking out of the soil and slowly growing into the desired vegetable or flowering plant. So worth the wait, right?

One last example—weight management. Usually this means weight loss, but it could also be the need to add weight, both necessary to achieve the healthiest body for *you*, not based on someone else's or society's general definition. For the purposes of this essay, I'll use weight *loss* as the example. If you lose weight at a steady pace, you're excited at your results. So you set your expectations too high, then get frustrated when the results slow down or stop altogether. This is the body's way of adjusting to the new pattern of eating— this is the plateau. However, in your frustration, you may give up, binge and gain back what you lost *and some.* A pattern of yo-yo dieting may follow, creating health risks. Better to congratulate yourself while on that plateau and enjoy the "new" body you currently have instead of worrying about not achieving an even thinner body in the future.

I share these examples of 'living on the plateau' to encourage you to live your life with patience. When you're in a state of limbo and can't get any momentum to move forward, do the following:

- Analyze past decisions and make future plans
- Expand on what you already know, do, think, feel to strengthen your base
- Rest and reap the benefits of the previous high or low that you recently experienced

Plateaus are the bridges connecting the active times of your life— don't bypass them or you may find yourself floundering in the river.

Meet-Cute

(2019)

In the 2006 movie, "The Holiday," actor Eli Wallach's character, Arthur Abbott, explains a meet-cute to Kate Winslet's character, Iris Simpkins.

Arthur: Well, this was some meet-cute!

Iris: Sorry?

Arthur: It's how two characters meet in a movie. Say a man and a woman both need something to sleep in and they both go to the same men's pajama department. And the man says to the salesman, "I just need bottoms.' The woman says, "I just need a top.' They look at each other, and that's a meet-cute.

Well, I had my own 'meet-cute' of sorts in 1983 while traveling in Great Britain for the first time. It was September and I was in Edinburgh, Scotland, on my second day in the country. But before I explain the meet-cute, let me tell you how I ended up in Edinburgh in the first place.

In 1983, I was living in Bedford Hills, New York, and working for Xerox Corporation at their Greenwich, Connecticut, Northeast Region office. In mid-January, the area was bombarded by a major blizzard that kept me homebound for two days. Luckily, the weekend before, I'd done a lot of research at the library for a possible four-week trip to Great Britain in the fall. For those of you "of a certain age" who remember the pre-Internet era, you'll understand what I mean by 'research at the library.' Looking up countless travel destinations, hotels, transportation, etc. via books and little reference index cards in antiquated file cabinets. Talking to Reference Librarians to get their help. Making copies upon copies of pertinent data at ten-cents a copy and checking out travel books. Everything was manual—no online searches or bookings.

Reservations were done by letters, so I had to allow enough time for them to arrive at my destination and get a written response. If places were booked on my selected dates, I'd have to start that process again. Hence, the eight-month lead time I'd given myself.

Anyway, during those two snow days, I plotted my course. I'd start out in Glasgow, Scotland, for one night, then drive on to Edinburgh. Yes, driving on the *left* side of the road! Actually, it wasn't as difficult as I thought it would be—in fact, I had a harder time re-acclimating myself back to driving on the *right* side when I returned home because I wasn't concentrating as hard as I was in Great Britain! But I digress…

I connected the dots of my trip from Glasgow to London, circling the cities on a map that I wanted to stay in or visit on my four-week journey. I then checked out places to stay, which included a castle, manors, inns, hotels and even a haunted estate. Over the next seven months, I got my passport; confirmed all my lodgings; rented my car; bought new clothes and luggage; and got ready for the longest trip by myself and in a foreign country to boot. At least they spoke English, so no language barrier!

On my second night in the country and my first in Edinburgh, I was walking through town along a main thoroughfare, Prince Street, looking for a place to have dinner before heading to a Military Tattoo at Edinburgh Castle, part of the Edinburgh International Arts Festival. At a crosswalk, I looked left down a side street and decided (or was guided?) to go that way. At the next corner, I looked left again and saw the awning of a pub called, "The Blithe Spirit." It called to me! It was a very small pub, with maybe ten small tables and a curved bar that sat six. I went to the end seat of the bar on the far left. I like sitting at the bar when traveling alone so I can chat with the bartender and get suggestions for things to do and see. This bartender was talking to a guy at the other end seat around the curve to the right along the wall. They both watched me take my seat and smiled nicely. So far so good!

After I ordered my beer and baked potato—yes, that's a *huge* potato smothered in cheese! —the bartender commented about my American accent and about my traveling alone. The next thing I knew, the cute guy—did I mention he was a cute blonde with blue eyes and a nice smile? —joined in the conversation, introduced himself as Stuart and asked if he could sit next to me so he wouldn't have to yell across the bar. Dah, of course he could! That was our *first* meet-cute! Of course, I hadn't heard about a meet-cute at the time, but as soon as Eli Wallach described it to Kate Winslet, I thought of how I met Stuart—who ended up moving to New York and becoming my husband fourteen months later and my ex-husband four years after that. But that's a story for another time! Stuart and I walked down Rose Street to another bar for a beer and a nice chat before I said my goodbyes and headed to Edinburgh Castle for the show.

Our second meet-cute didn't actually have the 'meet' element until later, but it sure was 'cute!' The next day, I planned to drive into the highlands to go to the Royal Games at Balmoral. I went into the hotel's restaurant for breakfast first and discovered that guests in the small hotel had a table assigned by their room numbers. I found mine, and I saw a beautiful yellow and pink rose in a juice glass in the center of the table. I looked around, but there weren't any flowers on the other tables. Then I noticed a note under the glass. It was a dart score sheet from the bar and on the back was written a note from Stuart. He'd picked the rose out of a garden, wrote the note for me on the back of the sheet and left it with the bartender the night before to be delivered to my table. It said he enjoyed meeting me, hoped I'd have fun at the Tattoo and that I have a safe trip to Balmoral. Then he left his phone number and address and asked if I'd keep in touch with him on my trip because he was interested in how things went. Okay, cute, right?

So I sent him the occasional postcard from my travels and may have casually mentioned where I'd be staying in the weeks ahead. When I arrived at my hotel in Stratford-on-Avon a week or so later, a letter and a red rose awaited me at the front desk! Ah, another cute moment! He asked if I'd call him when I got to Devon, which I did and where another rose greeted me at the check-in desk. We made plans to meet in London, where I was ending my trip and he 'just happened' to have to go for his business at the same time. And this is where the 'meet' element catches up with those 'cute' ones of the roses! We met in London at the Dr. Watson Lounge in the Sherlock Holmes Hotel *(I couldn't make this up!)* where he presented me with another red rose. Okay, now it's corny—but *he's* cute, so who cares! Long story short—we saw the sites of London together, shared many transatlantic phone calls, he visited me in New York, we fell in love, he proposed, we married, he drank too much, we divorced. The 'meet-cute' of our story doesn't lose any of its charm, however, no matter how the long story ended.

So, a few questions for you, Reader. *One,* have you had a meet-cute and, if so, have you told the story of it to someone? I truly believe it's meant to be shared! *Two,* have you ever traveled to a foreign country by yourself? If so, be sure to share that experience with others, including the little stories that made the trip special. *And three,* were you lucky enough to have a meet-cute while on that trip? Now *that* would really be fun to hear about!

On Turning Seventy Years Old

(2019)

No matter what spin I put on it--*70 is the new 50, Age is a state of mind, You're as young as you feel, Age is only a number* or any of the other adages related to aging—there's no escaping the fact that I've clocked in more years than I have left to live. Seventy years have come and gone since October 28, 1949. I'm currently nine days into my seventy-first year as I write this, and the odds of me living another seventy years to even out the "before and after" years are SO extreme—well, I'm back to my opening—there's no escaping that I have less days *ahead* of me than I have *behind* me.

So, what does all this mean? Why am I writing about this? I'm reading a book with a book club of like-minded women and we're discussing this transition. The book is "The Grace In Aging" by Kathleen Dowling Singh. Talk about depressing! She really lays it out there that we're aging and dying and there's nothing we can do about it so just suck it up and deal with it. Okay, so those weren't her exact words, but the other ladies and I all agree that she's not sugarcoating this stage of our lives.

So, as I'm sitting in my living room re-reading the last chapter we read in our last meeting, entitled "Predictable Sufferings," I found myself thinking—since death is closer than it's ever been to me, why not start planning my death? Well not the *how* of my death or the *when.* What I mean is to create a plan for how I'll live my future years with a full acceptance that death could be around the next corner. Instead of worrying about how I'm aging and bemoaning the changes in my body and mind, I'll honor those changes as just another notch in the "Rest of My Life" belt. Acceptance is key. So are awareness and deliberation.

What it's *not* about is resigning myself to the inevitable and sentencing myself to a bland, boring existence. Nor is it about making a "bucket list" to rush through things I may not even want to do but feel compelled to do to fill the years with significance. No, this plan is about being authentic and honest with myself. In truth, I've pretty much lived my adult life on my terms anyway. My life mantra has been about having no regrets on my death bed and decluttering myself of things and thoughts that no longer hold any meaning to me.

For instance, I used to want to travel to a lot of places, like Australia, Japan and Italy. Now, I'd rather spend my time and money on a return trip to Hawaii, where I'm familiar with the island of O'ahu and feel "at home" there. I don't feel the need to have more countries stamped in my passport. To date, I only have one country stamped in my new passport—Mexico, from my trip to Baja in December 2018 for a workshop at the Modern Elder Academy. I visited Great Britain in 1983 and Germany in 1988, so three countries in total. The idea of a twelve-hour plane ride to a country where I don't speak the language no longer appeals to me. I no longer want to explore places—I'd much rather explore people's minds and hearts.

I feel a subtle shift taking place in my psyche—that is, in my soul, because *Psyche* is the Greek goddess of the soul, not the mind as is often assumed to be the meaning of psyche. Anyway, the shift taking place is about this whole aging process. I can't put my finger on it, but I know myself well enough to recognize that something is churning at the deepest levels of my soul. So, just like I do so often in my life, I'm going to trust the Universe to reveal this shift to me in its own good time. There's an excitement to surrendering—the anticipation, the mystery, the promise—that has always gifted me with incredible life choices, opportunities and experiences. It's about the *quality* of my twilight years, not the *quantity*, right?

❧ ❧ ❧ ❧ ❧ ❧ ❧

As I re-read this for inclusion in my book, I've recently celebrated my 73rd birthday. I'm proud to say that during the past three years I've made some significant changes in my life. Like millions of others, I experienced the isolation and introspection of the Covid 19 lockdown. During those months alone in my home in Arizona, I re-typed a book my mom and aunt wrote in the Seventies but never got published; then, I had copies printed and bound for my family members. That prompted me to gather everything I've written during my lifetime and create the book you are reading.

In October 2021, I started a Weight Watchers program to lose the 40-plus pounds I'd gained during my three years in Arizona and to reduce my blood pressure and cholesterol. I'm again proud to say I successfully reached my goal in April 2022 and have maintained it ever since. As if that wasn't enough, during that same time, I sold my Arizona home and moved back to Ohio in the spring of 2022 to be closer to the family I felt so isolated from during the pandemic. I'm now settled into my darling 71-year-old three-bedroom ranch home in Hilliard. It's survived seven decades with minimal wear and tear, just like her new owner—we're kindred spirits! I've had fun decorating it in my eclectic, artistic style—that means colorful walls, my own paintings (alongside two by Georgia O'Keeffe) and lots of beachy/Hawaiian décor. I've found a boxing gym where I can get back to one of my favorite workouts, I'm working temp jobs in the area and I'm enjoying discovering central Ohio. (I'm from northeast Ohio originally.)

There's lots more I'm planning to do as I'm settling in. What I'm not doing is settling into mediocrity or vacillation. This gal is living what remains of her life the same way she's lived the rest of her life—with vim, vigor and vivaciousness!

Book 'Em!

(2020)

I have a crush on Lt. Commander Steve McGarrett! I admit it—my heart goes pitter-patter just thinking about him. No, no, *NOT* the Jack Lord version from the original television series *Hawaii Five-O* that aired from 1968 to 1980—heavens no! I'm enamored with the McGarrett portrayed by actor Alex O'Loughlin in the rebooted show that ran from 2010 to 2020.

It all began on April 29, 2009. I was watching one of my favorite crime shows, *Criminal Minds.* It was Season 4, Episode 22, called "The Big Wheel." The villain's name was Vincent Rowlings, yet unlike so many of the unsubs on the show, this guy was actually a sympathetic character. *What gives? Who was this actor who was making Vincent so appealing that he had me in almost-tears by the final scene?* Alex O'Loughlin—never heard of him, but I made a mental note of his name and stashed it away for future reference.

Fast forward to the summer of 2010. CBS announces that it's producing a reboot of the popular *Hawaii Five-O* series. *(Quick note here: They changed the capital letter 'O' in the new show to a zero—* Hawaii Five-0—*in order to keep the two shows separate on Internet search engines. I never did understand why the original had the letter, though, and not a number.)* Anyway, the announcement went on to say that the actor taking on the iconic role of Steve McGarrett was Alex O'Loughlin. *Wait a minute—I know that name—think, think—ah-ha—he was Vincent on Criminal Minds last year!* Well, well, they had my full attention now!

The pilot episode aired on Monday, September 20, 2010, and I've been a die-hard fan ever since. O'Loughlin was fantastic as the Navy SEAL who returns to his home state of Hawaii to avenge the murder of his father. The governor asks him to stay and head up a new task force to deal with major crimes, giving him full immunity and means so he could go after his father's murderer as well. At first, McGarrett declines, preferring to go it alone. But after finding some items in his father's garage that seem linked to his murder—and being confronted by Honolulu Police Detective Danny Williams who's in charge of investigating the murder—McGarrett decides he'd take the job. And so began an incredible ten-year run of one of the best shows on television, bar none! (Well, that's one besotted woman's opinion anyway!)

The crush may have begun with McGarrett, but it now extends to the entire show, including what is sometimes referred to as the "other" member of the Five-0 team—the state of Hawaii itself. Seeing the majesty of the islands and the charm of the Hawaiian culture, I knew I had to go there to see this beautiful place up front and personal. I lucked out when I was able to book a week's stay at the Marriott Ko'Olina Beach Club resort using a friend's timeshare.

In October 2011, I arrived on O'ahu, got in my rental car and (thank God for GPS!) hurried to the Halekulani Hotel in Waikiki. *Why,* you may ask, *was I going there and not to the Marriott on the southwest shore of the island?* Well, as more luck would have it, the cast and producers of *H50* (a much easier abbreviation for the show's name that I'll use moving forward) were participating in a two-hour Question & Answer discussion of the show at the Hawaii International Film Festival being held there—and I had booked a ticket! Of course, my luggage was almost the last off the plane and the rental car company got my reservation mixed up, so I missed the first hour of the discussion. Handing off my car key to the valet, I fast-walked to the conference room, slipped quietly into the room and took an aisle seat. Looking up at the stage, I saw him—Steve McGarrett—er, I mean, Alex O'Loughlin. Made it! What was really strange was hearing Alex (we're on a first name basis now—more about that later!) talk—he had an Australian accent because, well, he's from Australia. But he does such a good job of speaking with an American accent on the show that it was a little disconcerting at first. Regardless, he was perfect and my vacation couldn't have begun on a better note!

Oh, but don't think it ended there. Absolutely not! I returned to Hawaii in the fall of 2012 for two weeks, 2014 for four weeks and 2016 for three weeks. But it was my visit in 2014 that earned the title, "My *H50* Vacation Year." Here are the high points:

Saturday, September 13: It had become tradition for CBS to hold a free "Sunset On The Beach" premiere for the fans on Queen's Surf Beach in Waikiki a week or so before the new season began. There was a red-carpet event for fans, photographers and reporters, followed by the season's first episode displayed on a giant screen once the sun had set. I'd watched the televised events the prior years on Hawaii News Live and decided I had to brave the traffic and crowds to experience it myself. I was renting an apartment in Kailua and my landlords, Susan and Claude, said they wanted to go as well. So we parked at their friend's condo away from the busy area and walked to the event. They went off and did "their thing" so I could do mine.

I managed to get a spot on the sand right behind the barrier by the photographer's section of the red carpet. Perfect! Every actor from the show stopped to get their photos taken so I was able to take my own photos—what a collection! Seeing them ten feet away from me was so exciting—I could have reached out and touched them! As it got dark and people were settling in to watch the show, I walked through the adjoining park and saw one of the actors, Dennis Chun, who portrays Sgt. Duke Lukela. *(Another note: His father played Chin Ho Kelly in the original show.)* I asked for a quick photo and he graciously took a selfie with me. I proceeded to find a good spot to stand and watch the premiere episode as the sun set on the Pacific Ocean and the sound of waves created an idyllic backdrop. Sharing this with so many fans who appreciated the show as much as I did—and who would understand my obsession—was so much fun.

Saturday, September 20: This requires a little background information, so bear with me. Early on in the show's first season, I read that one of the extra actors who played a thug in an episode was Egan Inoue and he was Alex's Brazilian Jiu-Jitsu trainer. I researched Egan and discovered he owned a few gyms on the island. When I returned for my second visit in 2012 and was looking for a gym, I remembered Egan's, so I checked into it. I ended up taking his boot camps a couple of days a week, which really put me through the drills! I established a good relationship with Egan and his staff. So when I returned in 2014, I immediately signed up for more boot camps. Not being familiar with Brazilian Jiu-Jitsu, I asked if I could come watch a session. Egan said that the upcoming Saturday, September 20, they were holding tests for all the students to achieve their next-level belts, and I was welcome to come watch.

That Saturday, I pulled into the parking lot and backed into a spot. Since I was a little early, I was checking my phone when a pick-up truck parked to my right. *Wait a minute— couldn't be—was that Alex O'Loughlin?* It took me four double-takes to finally realize, yes, it was Alex! OH. MY. GOD. Trying not to be caught staring, I nonchalantly got out and followed him into the gym. If you're asking why I didn't approach him, well, it's just not my style to infringe on a celebrity's private time. Plus, I don't know if I could have spoken coherently at that point. He immediately went to the men's locker room to change into his gi—the traditional Brazilian Jiu-Jitsu pants and jacket. I stepped up to the front desk to say 'Hi' to Brielle.

"Did you see who came in just now?" she asked excitedly, knowing my fixation with *H50*.

"Yes, and he parked right next to me!" I replied. "Is he testing today?"

"No, he and some of the other adult students are assisting with the tests."

Well, as much as I was interested in observing the belt tests themselves, my attention was equally divided with watching a certain adult student as he assisted Egan with the tests. As the time slipped away, however, and I watched Alex the Man, not Alex the Celebrity, interact with the other wrestlers, I realized that his down-to-earth, approachable and unassuming demeanor had relaxed my nervousness. There's always a risk when you meet someone you've admired from afar—will they live up to your imagined persona or be complete jerks? Well, Mr. O'Loughlin did not disappoint from what I observed.

A few hours later, as the students and families dispersed, I lingered with the hopes I'd somehow meet Alex. Egan saw me then and came up to ask what I thought of the sport and did I think I'd want to try it. Before I could answer, he turned to his right and called out, "Alex, come here...there's someone I want you to meet."

Even as I type this, I'm feeling the goosebumps that traveled down my whole body when I realized that Alex O'Loughlin was walking toward me with a cute smile on his face and his hand extended as Egan introduced us. To this day, I don't know exactly what I said, but I hope it wasn't the "blah-blah-blah" I heard in my head. Egan got called away, and Alex was asking me why I was there, did I know someone taking the test. I told him I was just observing to see if I would want to try it out and that I was taking Egan's boot camps. He laughed and said that anyone who could survive those could do Jiu Jitsu. I told him I boxed and his face lit up. "Really? That's cool!"

Egan walked up then and asked if I wanted a photo with Alex. Dah! So he handed my camera to Brielle and the three of us took this great photo, which allowed me to put my arm around Alex's waist as he draped his arm over my shoulder and leaned in for a smile. Be still my beating heart! We said our goodbyes and I walked—no, floated! —to my car. I was too excited to drive right away and kept looking at the photo of the three of us.

As I sat there letting the parking lot clear out, Alex appeared to my right and got into his truck. He didn't notice me and I didn't honk my horn or wave my arms to get his attention. He was just a regular guy who was participating in his gym's belt testing event, not the star of a popular television show— and I liked him like that! What I realized later was that I never mentioned *H50* or having seen the Sunset On The Beach premiere. It was just about Alex and me and how friendly he was to a perfect stranger who was also a friend of Egan. *(Final note: I printed an 8 x 10 of the photo we took and sent it to the film company's office in Honolulu with a letter to Alex. I asked him to sign it and I shared what I never got a chance to say that day we met. Going snail mail, and knowing how busy he and the show's staff were, I was very pleasantly surprised when I received it back about six months later, signed and with an accompanying short note from him thanking me for my support of the show and wishing me luck with my boxing—he remembered!)*

Wednesday, September 24: I had booked a reservation to take a walking tour of Honolulu's 1940s brothel district in Chinatown. We were meeting the tour guide in front of the Hawaii Theater on Bethel Street at 9 a.m., but I decided to arrive early to make sure I found a parking lot and could walk around on my own for a while. So at 7:30, having parked nearby, I found the theater and got my bearings. Then I noticed a police car pull up and put a barrier on a nearby side street, where I also noticed a blue Chevrolet Silverado parked. I asked the police officer what was going on and he explained that there was an H50 location site on Fort Street Mall.

What?! Could I be so lucky?! I immediately headed to Fort Street Mall and, sure enough, there were people all over with loads of filming equipment—cameras of all shapes and sizes, and booms and cranes and microphones and other stuff I didn't know the names for. There was a fake farmers market set up along the block and a long line of vendor trucks from supposed food supply companies making deliveries. At the back of the last truck, a series of crates and ramps was set up as well. Across the street were a lot of extra actors gathered and being directed by people with headsets to go here or there. Then to my delight, they began filming a scene. Someone who looked suspiciously like McGarrett appeared from the side street, ran onto Fort Street Mall, jumped on the lowest crate and climbed up the ramp, where he proceeded to run across the tops of the vendor trucks to the end of the line. Holy moly! It was Alex's stunt double, Justin Sundquist! Which begged the question—*was Alex nearby ready to do the closeups?* I struck up a conversation with one of the crew on the sidelines, Sean, who explained that the stars wouldn't be there until later in the afternoon when all the main stunts were done, if today at all. He said I'd have plenty of time to go on my walking tour.

I watched some more of the location activity, which included a guy on a motor scooter racing past the line of trucks through the food market, knocking down food carts, near-missing customers as McGarrett chased him from the tops of the trucks. I guessed the takedown would happen at the other end of the street later in the day when the actors arrived. Location activity also involved a lot of waiting around for next shots to be set up. I eventually headed for the Hawaii Theater and met up with my tour group. The two-hour tour was fun, but my mind kept wondering if I was missing anything back on Fort Street Mall. I ended up spending the rest of the afternoon meandering along the street behind the barriers, watching take after take. I found a restroom at a nearby Walmart and some lunch at a Subway, but for the most part, I just walked and observed. These behind-the-scenes people and extra actors really have tough, boring, active, tedious, dangerous, interesting jobs. When the whole crew took a lunch break, I noticed one guy standing on the street next to a big pile of carrots. I asked why he wasn't going to lunch and he said he was guarding the carrots—so that they were all in the exact same place when they started filming. Talk about taking things seriously! But that exemplifies the professionalism of the film crew for this show.

Finally, around 3:30 p.m. as I stood at the far end of Fort Street Mall where the final showdown would take place, Sean signaled to me and told me that the stars were scheduled to arrive in about 15 minutes. *Thanks, Sean!* Sure enough, as I stood in the front of a group of observers looking at the front of the truck line, I saw my hero, Steve McGarrett, walk to the front of the line, dressed in his black jeans, navy blue T-shirt and Kevlar vest, strapped with his weapons. There goes my beating heart again! *Hey,* I thought, *I know that guy! I've talked to that guy! I shook hands with that guy and wrapped my arm around his waist! I even have a photo to prove it, so there!* They began filming the takedown, where Alex's stunt double jumps down off the truck as a black SUV pulls up to cut off the motor scooter. Out jump Lou Grover and Danny Williams (actors Chi McBride and Scott Caan). Cut! Then Alex steps in to replace the stunt double and the three proceed to arrest the bad guy! They did a few more takes before the director said it was a wrap and the actors walked back down Fort Street Mall. (Season 5, Episode 8)

Well, that was a day well spent! How often do I happen upon the filming of an action scene for a television show? I loved it! I walked back in the same direction as the actors, noticing Alex and his bodyguard walking in the street. Should I work my way over and say Hi? Would he even remember me? No, I couldn't—he was working and I respected that. I wasn't going to push my luck and ruin what had been an enjoyable experience by being hauled off by security guards. But it wasn't over yet!

At the end of the block where the side street turned off to the left, Alex stood next to the blue Silverado. He was getting ready to make a run for it as if just jumping out of the vehicle to chase the guy on the motor scooter—this was the beginning of that scene—and Alex ran to the stacked crates and stopped—this was where Justin took over—cool! They had actually filmed segments of the scene in reverse order. I watched that a few more times, then Alex walked toward a parked van with the *H50* logo on the side. He took off the navy T-shirt—one more time for the beating heart! —put on his plaid shirt and entered the van, where Chi and Scott awaited him so they could head back to the studio for some indoor filming.

I slowly headed down the side street toward the parking garage where I'd arrived over nine hours earlier, only to come upon yet *more* filming. This time I was stopped at an intersection where they were filming the motorscooter guy racing down one street, turning left toward Fort Street Mall and the Silverado in close pursuit. Does it never end? Yes, for me that was the end of an exciting, unplanned *H50* adventure.

So, that's the story of my 2014 *Hawaii Five-0* vacation. The television show was beginning its fifth season that fall and went on for five seasons more. I own the DVD for every season and have watched them many times. What I loved about the series, besides the lead actor, supporting cast and good storylines, was that the producers paid tribute to the original series in subtle and obvious ways. For instance, they reshot an episode called "Hookman" (Season 1, Episode 15), filming in some of the exact locations and from the same angles as the original episode in 1973. They even used the same colors and fonts for the title and credits, and the original episode is included in the DVD for Season 1 as an extra feature. Since the first show had the killer trying to kill Steve's father, John, when he was a police officer, they had to change it a little for the reboot so that the killer was now after the cops who put him in prison years before for bank robbery, as well as deceased John's son, Steve. Another nod to the times was the killer's forearms that were blown off during the botched bank robbery. He wore primitive prosthetic arms with hooks in the original show compared to the advanced mechanical prosthetic hands in the reboot.

Another "call back" to the original series was actor Ed Asner. He portrayed a rising world-class smuggler named August March who was captured and imprisoned in the 1975 episode. He returns for Season 2, Episode 19, of the reboot as the now-reformed March who was recently released after spending thirty years behind bars. They tied the two together by having Steve McGarrett approach March for help on a current jewelry smuggling case. March hears his name and asks if he's related to John McGarrett—then explains that a cop named John McGarrett took him to prison and wouldn't accept a bribe to let him go. They even inserted clips from the original episode as flashbacks for the March character.

I could go on and on with more interesting trivia about the show, but I think I've made my point—I'm an avid fan! I'm also a sad fan because, after ten entertaining years, the last episode of *H50* aired on Friday, April 3, 2020. I'm writing this on September 20 because it's the tenth anniversary of the show's first episode. Since there's no Season 11 starting this month—although it probably would have been delayed like so many other shows due to the Covid lockdown—I'm going to start binge-watching my 10 DVDs today.

Spoiler Alert: *I'm about to write some revealing comments about how the show wrapped up, so if you don't want to know, skip down to the last paragraph and commentary.*

The truth is the show ended on a high note, the reason being that Alex was ready to call it quits after years of physical hits doing some of his own stunts. He also wanted to spend time with his family-- he'd married a local woman in 2014 and they had three sons, one each from previous relationships and a son together. During the final season, it was still ranking high in the ratings and gaining new popularity in syndication on TNT, then ION. The storyline woven through the final season's episodes were well-written, bringing Steve McGarrett full circle from the death of his father in the pilot. Over the years, he has suffered the loss of his parents (John and Doris), his mentor (Joe White), his Aunt Deb and other close associates; he's experienced innumerable physical trauma, including a liver transplant and radiation poisoning; and his paramour, Catherine, has been absent from his life more than present as she followed her Soldier mentality that "God and country" come first, regardless of how much she loved Steve. He decides it's time to get away from the islands for a stretch, to find some long-elusive peace. It was obvious during the goodbye scene with his team in the final episode that the farewells were not just between characters but between the actors as well. The final scene was the best: Steve's sitting on the airplane when a voice in the aisle says, "Is this seat taken?" I squealed with joy—Catherine was joining him! "Catherine," says Steve, to which she replies with her favorite greeting for him, "Hey, Sailor." His smile in profile as he takes her hand and the scene fades out is precious and speaks volumes to how much he loves her and is ready to move on with his life.

So that concludes my long-winded tribute to my favorite show. I hadn't meant to go on like I did—and there's so much more I could share! Instead, I'll close now. I hope whoever reads this enjoyed my exploits and insights.

❧ ❧ ❧ ❧ ❧ ❧ ❧

As I'm re-reading this on December 30, 2021, to include in my book, I'm wondering—do you, Readers, have stories like this that need to be written down and shared? Television often gets a bad rep as a non-sophisticated media that doesn't contribute to viewers' overall wellbeing. While I agree that there are shows that would leave me brain dead if I watched them, I mostly watch television because it offers me some good escape time and entertainment, along with some unexpected tutelage. For instance, I've learned so much about the Hawaiian islands by watching H50; about the Hawaiian culture of aloha *and* ohana; *and about some specific historic incidents, such as the Japanese internment camps on the islands during World War II, the leprosy isolation colony on Molokai, and the native Hawaiians' movement for sovereignty. My visits to the islands, especially my favorite O'ahu, have given me memories from which I'm still reaping the benefits. Writing about the ending of the show was both emotional and enjoyable for me back in 2020. Perhaps you have some favorite TV shows that have had inspiring or motivating effects on you in unexpected ways.*

Getting to Know Dad Again for the First Time

(2020)

Tuesday, April 21, 2020, 8:55 a.m. I started crying this morning for no apparent reason. Well, that's not entirely true—I was thinking about my Dad.

I was sitting at work at a temporary assignment, performing the repetitive, mundane task of entering data, while Tchaikovsky was playing in the background on my computer via a YouTube collection of his greatest hits. When I was little, I used to roller skate around our basement to classical music and Tchaikovsky was one of my favorites. The music was provided by my Dad—he bought classical albums from our local grocery store. A new composer would come out every week or so, and the album case included pages on the biography of the artist.

As I'm typing away, my body is responding at a visceral level. Deep within my muscles and mind and memories, I can feel my body wanting to float around the room like I did while skating, responding to the crescendos and decrescendos. My favorite piece—Edvard Grieg's *In the Hall of the Mountain King* from the Peer Gynt Suite No.1, Op. 46—had a slowly-building tempo ending with climatic crashing cymbals.

Then my mind goes to those albums and asks, *Why did my Dad buy those?* And, as the mind tends to do, it rambled on and on about Dad. He was an electrician by trade, yet he was so much more. He loved playing baseball as a catcher. He gave blood regularly. He was a popular bartender at the Slovak Club and Knights of Columbus hall. He spent hours in our garage making wooden weaving frames with nails, so we could create yarned placemats and such. He carved out Yahoo board games for family members. He dressed as Batman for a Halloween party, wearing his electrician belt and dyed long underwear. He cried on my shoulder after his grandmother's wake because he loved her so much. And he bought classical music albums at the grocery store.

And then I started crying, yet not for *no* apparent reason. The reason is I love and miss my Dad who has been dead for almost 41 years, and I want so much to talk to him about his loves and interests and hobbies. I was 29 when he died. What twenty-something child thinks about having a discussion with her Dad about weaving frames and classical music? My self-absorption in *my* life ignored the details of his life, the details that made him the man I never got to know as an adult as well I could have, should have. He caught for Satchel Paige! I didn't find out about that until he'd been dead a few years. Why didn't he ever tell me? Or did he and I just never realized the importance of that and how much it meant to him?

So I'm writing this to capture this enriching moment in my life when I got to know my Dad again *and* for the first time. Too bad it took forty-one years.

A Quick Glimpse

(2021)

It's Saturday morning and I'm sitting in the recliner in my office slash meditation room, coming out of a peaceful meditation. I glance up at the wall over my desk where I have framed photo collages of old family photos from my childhood and earlier. I look at a photo from my first communion day taken sixty-four years ago—a simple black and white, 4 x 6 image of my parents standing behind eight-year-old me and my five-year-old sister—and in the blink of an eye, my heart skips a beat, my breath goes ragged and my eyes tear up. In the blink of an eye, I am overwhelmed by unbidden feelings and memories.

How can a quick glimpse of an old photo of my mom and dad create these escalating feelings so suddenly? How does what the eye is *physically* seeing trigger these *emotional* responses? What part of the corporeal brain houses the thinking mind and the emotive heart, and allows them to conjunctively react in the blink of an eye to a quick glimpse? Why am I feeling this concoction of love and sadness and wonder simultaneously? Have I crossed over some ethereal boundary where I'm sensing my parents' spiritual entities?

This is how my mind works. It starts with a simple thought or idea, then dissects it layer by layer in search of its deeper meaning or the intricate mechanics behind it. As a 'big picture' thinker, I like stepping back from the scene I can see through a lens to take in the surrounding countryside. When I navigate, I look behind me to see where I've been, whether looking in the rear-view mirror while driving or physically turning around while walking through a woods or a mall. I "see" in 360-degree perspective. I don't know why. Maybe reading all those Nancy Drew mystery books as a child got me questioning the *who, what, where, when, why* and *how* of things. Maybe my left brain is analyzing and nitpicking the fine points while my right brain keeps everything in balance by creating a broader point of view.

Anyway, my mind went on an inquisitive journey due to that quick glimpse this morning, wondering about the correlations between my *physical* brain, my *intellectual* mind and my *emotional* heart and how those connections operate so efficiently and autonomically. Then I added to the Body/Mind/Heart triad the role of Spirit or, if you prefer, the Soul. I wondered how I could feel such a wrenching at my emotional heart as I thought of my mom and dad that I could physically react with tears when it's been thirty years since my mom died and forty-two since my dad passed away. The feelings, the reactions, were immediate and Now, as if I had just lost them again. Intellectually, I knew this wasn't the case, but that's not how I was responding—that quick glimpse transcended the Time/Space continuum so that I yearned to hear them speak to me, to hold me, to be with me again. *That's* the power of the Soul—that fourth element that also transcends Time and Space.

So what does all this mean? What have I learned from this contemplative exercise today? I think for me, it's not so much that I've learned something new, but I've learned to view what I know and believe from another perspective. I've peeled away another layer and affirmed my comprehension of just how valuable the 'big picture' way of thinking and processing is to me. As for how I felt when I took that quick glimpse of my parents from sixty-four years ago—well, they're still my Mommy and Daddy regardless of the years that have gone by or the physical state of our beings. The skipping heart, ragged breath and tearful eyes were just ways of us saying to each other, *I love you.*

A Soulful Conversation

(2021)

For weeks, I'd been questioning the limbo I felt my life was in and trying to figure out what I was supposed to do next. I was reading Julia Cameron's book, "The Listening Path," and free-flow writing my daily Morning Pages when this "conversation," in answer to my inner turmoil, flowed freely onto the paper with no forethought or conscious thinking. This message from the depths of my Soul helped me to get past my concerns and to trust in the overall plan that's in motion for me. It's worked for me before and I know it's working again!

Okay, it's my turn to write now. Your Soul Mind has control of the pen and paper now, Conscious Mind, and here's what I want to share with you. You *aren't* wasting your life now. Just because you're not working or volunteering or working on some big project doesn't mean you're wasting your life. You call this a plateau, remember? You're on a plateau now. You've done so much already. — *Have I really? Like what?* — Don't interrupt me. You already know what you've accomplished, so don't get me to write about everything now just to feed your ego. Now is the time for you to think—no, to experience—the quiet "not doing" of your life. It doesn't mean it will be like this until you die, which is a long way off, by the way— No, I can hear your questions now and I can't tell you when or how and where that will occur. Just know that you're not done yet. Sometimes things have to simmer before they come to a boil. You've been used to time moving faster between "projects" or life changes. This pandemic that had to happen for a global experience has put you in an unusual holding pattern. But can you imagine what it would have been like to be going through it somewhere or sometime else? You've had temp work and you live alone and you could take the time to sort through things. Yes, there were times of distress and anxiety—that comes with being human—and you came through them just fine. You had the foresight to relax, breathe, meditate, walk and talk to your doctor.

So, that's what happens when a global crisis gets handled by an individual. She calls upon—*you* called upon—your life's lessons and teachings to practice what you've been preaching. You coached yourself through this. You also reached out to friends you haven't reached out to before and made conscious efforts to fill your days and your heart and mind with those connections, both for yourself and for them. You don't realize the impact you have on people, Susan, but you have to trust and believe that it's all good. You may not see the results, but think of it like a stone thrown into a pond— the ripples go out there even if the stone can't see them. You are a stone, Susan—you are a rock. And that's one of the reasons you're here in this persona now—to live by example and trust that those who need to hear and see the messages you are conveying are getting them. The controller in you wants to control the details and be prepared for any contingencies. But trust Me that just *being* and *doing* are sufficient for the purpose you are here. I can hear you— *what are you to learn this time around?* You are an older, wiser soul, Susan. That's why you aren't attached physically to a husband or children—to a conventional family or lifestyle—you are meant to reach out beyond those confines and spread your wings to fly higher and see farther. You ARE that falcon from your story. Yes, it seems like you've come to a stop because of where you now live and how your days are playing out. You feel lazy and useless—but you're not! We're giving you the gift of your own company, just like you wrote about in your book—the pleasure of being with yourself. Let go of your worries and concerns about whether you're wasting your life—you're NOT! Trust me when I say, there's more joy and happiness ahead. Let me set the groundwork in motion with the other Souls and when the time is right, I'll call on you to take action, just like I have in the past. I love you, Susan.

❧ ❧ ❧ ❧ ❧ ❧ ❧

I wrote this on May 19…today is January 22, 2022. Three days ago, I sold my house on the same day that it was listed, a cash offer for my asking price, which was twice what I'd paid for the house almost four years ago. And the buyers agreed to my closing date of April 15. Once again, my trust in Universe and the concept of "let go and let God" has proven to be well placed.

I'd decided last summer to move back to Ohio to be near my family. I set the move in motion when I met with a realtor in Columbus in October just to let her know my long-term plans, which were to sell the house in the winter or early spring and move to Ohio in the spring or summer. I wanted to spend one last winter in Arizona and I didn't want to be traveling back to Ohio and looking for a house there during wintry weather. When I got the text the afternoon of January 19 that the house had sold with the first showing to a couple anxious to live in the retirement community where I was located, I couldn't believe it happened SO fast—but I really could believe it happened because that's how I've lived my life for decades. Thanks to all the Powers That Be for your continued support and guidance. I'm off that plateau!

Crazy Ivan

(2021)

I love hindsight! According to Internet dictionaries, the definition of hindsight is, *"considering or analyzing the past with the knowledge that one has now; the ability to understand, after something has happened, what should/could have been done or what caused an event."* I've found myself using this word so many times over the years as I've explained my behaviors or decisions "based on hindsight."

I also love introspection! I like to delve into my psyche and learn more about how I process life. Introspection gives me the information I need to understand so many of the *whys* behind what I've said and done over the years. It's helped me recognize patterns in my behavior so that I can make changes or enhancements to that behavior in the present moment.

Another word for hindsight is *retrospection.* Retrospection and introspection are two sides of the same coin—hindsight is the best place to visit to learn about myself so I can then introspectively see the 'big picture' of my life and adjust or plan accordingly. You may know this as soul-searching or contemplation or self-analysis. Regardless of what name you give this, using that "-spection coin"—retro and intro—is a valuable way to improve one's life, alleviate concerns and create balance.

I believe that people tend to repeat behaviors just because "it's the way I've always done it" or it was the way they first learned it. Often, it was how it was modeled to them by their parents, teachers and others. It's like getting your car tire stuck in a rut that you can't get out of because you just keep putting pressure on the gas pedal instead of getting out of the car to find a different way to solve your problem. How do you 'spin your wheels' in your life, repeating behaviors in rote fashion and getting the same unsatisfactory results? What worked in the past may not be what will work now.

Albert Einstein said, "Insanity is repeating the same behavior and expecting different results."

This not only applies to how you behave or do things, but to how you relate to others. Your reason for believing or not believing in someone in the past may actually change based on new information. Unfortunately, many people won't think of changing their minds about someone because of how it might look—what it might say about their original opinion. Being able to admit that your initial impression of someone was wrong or no longer applies is a step toward becoming a more compassionate, understanding individual.

There was a segment on the August 1 episode of *CBS Sunday Morning* about how we navigate today versus in days past, referring to the use of GPS and other technology and no longer using compasses or paper maps. A park ranger was taking the commentator on a hike through the forest and showing him how to use a compass, when he stopped and told the commentator to turn around. He said it's important when hiking to turn around and see where you've been so you can create points of reference for your return trip. *Hindsight!* I was so excited when I heard that because I've been doing that for years. I have very good navigational skills and love reading maps to see not only where I'm going but where I've been. When I'm driving in a new area, I'll look in the rearview mirror to see what I just passed so I'll have landmarks when I go back. It's part of my 'big picture, 360° mentality.' Anyway, it's just another way that hindsight plays an important part in our lives.

In the movie, "The Hunt for Red October," there's a scene where a U.S. Seaman tells his Captain that a Russian submarine they're chasing has just done a 'crazy Ivan.' He explained that it's a sharp turn made by a Russian submarine to look behind it with sonar.

Do you make 'crazy Ivans' in your life? Do you take the time to scrutinize your past, to look behind you in order to make smart choices ahead of you? Do you allow yourself to be retrospective and introspective so you can learn more about yourself and your life's paradigms? The Covid-19 pandemic of 2020 has certainly given us all a lot of time to be contemplative. Perhaps as we come out of this unprecedented period of our lives, we can act on some of what we've learned about ourselves and create exciting new adventures.

Inked

(2021)

As the title suggests, I'm about to tell you about getting my tattoos. Yes, I said, *tattoos*—three in all—and I got them all after I turned fifty-nine!

It all started when I was visiting my family in northeast Ohio. My older niece Christina was there for the weekend from Columbus, where she was a student at Ohio State University. I excitedly pointed out a small tattoo on her ankle of a Celtic cross. She indicated that her parents weren't happy about it, but I liked the fact that she was expressing herself and her independence, something I fully supported. I'd never given tattoos a second thought other than associating them with convicts and bikers. However, they were becoming fashionable, especially for women, so I was intrigued and the seed of an idea took root in my brain—I want one, too!

So when I next went home a few months later (and a few weeks after my 60th birthday), I flew into Columbus first to pick up Christina so we could drive up to Warren for the Thanksgiving weekend *and* so that she could take me to her tattoo artist to get *my* tattoo. I got a triquetra, about an inch and a half wide, on my upper right hip, just below my waistline. *Why there?* you ask since no one would see it. And why a triquetra? Well, I was working at a ski resort in Park City, Utah, which didn't allow their employees to have visible tattoos, so I 'hid' it just below my waistband so I could reveal it discreetly when I wanted to show it off. It was my little secret knowing it was there! However, I proclaimed that as soon as I retired from the resort, I was going to get a visible tattoo on my ankle.

As for the triquetra, the 'power of three' was something that I'd embraced for a long time because of its spiritual symbolism for me of Body, Mind and Spirit. The popular TV show *Charmed* used the triquetra as its symbol for the three sister witches who, as the Charmed Ones, shared the collective power of three, said to be the strongest kind of magic. But TV fantasy aside, an online search will result in many other *three* collectives. I could probably compose an essay on the *Power of Three* alone because the list goes on!

- Past, Present, Future
- Power, Intellect, Love
- Father, Son, Holy Spirit
- Thought, Word, Action
- Faith, Hope, Love
- Legislative, Judicial, Executive
- Life, Liberty, Pursuit of Happiness
- Blood, Sweat, Tears

But back to tattoos. I lived with that lone tattoo for over twelve years. When I finally did retire in the fall of 2018 and moved to Mesa, Arizona, one of the first things I did was explore the town itself. As I was strolling along Main Street, a sign hanging over the sidewalk in front of a small establishment caught my eye— *Naysayer Tattoo!* If you haven't already read it, there's an essay in the book about saying 'nay' to naysayers, so the word holds special meaning to me. Was the sign a *sign* for me? I walked in and a young man approached to welcome me to the shop. Whatever I was expecting, this greeter looked more like Prodigy/Special Agent Dr. Spencer Reid of the TV show *Criminal Minds* than a tattoo artist, so I wondered if I was in the right place! Then my mind was put at ease when I saw the two tattooed tattoo artists working on clients. They graciously answered my questions about time, cost, appointments, pain level, etc. and one of the artists told me, "Feel free to come in any time and we'll take good care of you." He said his name was Neil and I told him he'd hear from me for sure.

Well, as things happen (work and a health issue), I didn't make my appointment with Neil until February 2020 for Saturday, March 21. Then something even bigger happened—Covid 19 and lockdown! So my tattoo got put on hold for another year. Finally, on April 17, 2021, Neil gave me my second tattoo—a nautilus shell—on my outside left calf just above my ankle. It's about two inches long and

1.5 inches wide, a simple black graphic and I love it! On May 29, my third tattoo joined the other two—the power of three again? — and I had the words *Be still* tattooed on my right arm just above my wrist. I wanted some kind words or quote that epitomized who I was and, if you read some of my other essays, you'll know the importance of meditation, silence and solitude in my life. I designed the tattoo so that the phrase repeated itself—one faced me so I could look down and read it and the other faces the other way so I wouldn't have to be a contortionist twisting my arm for someone else to read it. Clever, right?

Are you curious as to why I wanted to get a tattoo, let alone three of them? I'll admit, I've asked the same question of myself. I know that part of it is my rebelliousness, the "quite contrary" woman who seeks out ways to do something unexpected or out of the box. However, I think it's mostly about expressing myself on the *outside* through symbols of my *inner* persona. I've already explained the triquetra and the words, so here's why the nautilus shell. I've always been drawn to the shape of a spiral, like those simple swirl designs found in a lot of artwork, logos, sculpting and more. The book I published in 2012 has a nautilus shell on the cover and, as a collector of seashells, my favorite is the nautilus shell with its spiral effect both inside and out.

Another reason is that I look at the Life/Time continuum as a spiral, circular pathway instead of a linear timeline. I imagine that there are periods in a lifetime that repeat their experiences or opportunities in order for me to grow—it's as if I'm on a spiral staircase moving upward. There are times when I'll be living on a stair that looks down on another stair several levels below that is in perfect alignment but that took place years or decades earlier in my life. For instance, the Terrible Twos are aligned with the Turbulent Teens, which are aligned to Mid-life Crisis—not *my* terms for these periods, by the way; I find them too negative! All three are about rebelling and stretching and testing boundaries. As a retired woman, I find myself on a fourth level aligned to these three because Retirement has also felt like a time to rebel internally—against the assumptions of what a "person of this certain age" should be doing with her life while simultaneously shedding the habit and rigidity of a working life in order to create a new, more enriching lifestyle. Hence, getting tattoos at this stage of my life makes perfect sense, right?

So, that's the story of my three tattoos. I think it's important to note that I got the second two when I was seventy-one years of age. So, if you're feeling the urge to be rebellious or to stretch your nonconformist muscles, I say go for it! Oh, if you're wondering how painful it was, it wasn't at all...really. The needles are *so* tiny that the little pricks were barely noticeable, and each tattoo took about thirty minutes or less to complete. Of course, I had simple, black outlined artwork—I imagine that the more elaborate, colored or filled-in designs would sting a little more!

Lessons of A Lifetime

(2021)

I've been doing a lot of introspective pondering lately. I've always been one for analyzing the 'big picture' and finding the 'why' behind something in order to better understand that big picture. I like to step back and look at things in hindsight to identify what I've learned, what I've contributed and what I've still got to work on. Since I moved to Arizona in October 2018 upon my retirement from an eighteen-year job at a ski resort in Utah, I've had time to be introspective and retrospective about my life, both to date and for what's happening next. Of course, during the Covid 19 pandemic, I've had plenty of *(too much?)* alone time to "contemplate my navel" and get philosophical about my existence. Whoa, just typing that sentence shows how far I've gone with this, but it is what it is!

Let me share three experiences I'm currently involved in that will shed some light on these self-examinations. First, on May 11, I started an eight-week webinar with author Alan Cohen based on his book, "Soul and Destiny." The subtitle of this book is, "Why You Are Here and What You Came to Do." I mean, who hasn't asked that big question, *Why am I here? What purpose does my life serve?* What's been most satisfying from the five weeks we've met on Zoom so far is that a lot of my beliefs and choices have been affirmed and strengthened because I'm able to share my experiences with like-minded people. I think I'm at the point in my life where nothing is really *new* to me, just presented from a different perspective. That's not to say I don't learn something from these encounters—there's *always* something to be learned, whether it's new information to add to my cache, a new point of view to consider or a new awareness from an 'ah-ha' moment. Being able to share my stories and having the participants comment how my sharing has helped them have a moment of clarity is what I'm most excited about.

During the webinar, I shared the following comment with a participant who was struggling with whether she was a victim or a martyr: "Victim and Martyr are two sides of the same coin. The first blames others for his problems and the second blames herself for them." The key word here is *blame*. As noted in Lesson 9 below, we should take ownership for our lives and not focus on placing the blame outside of ourselves. We shouldn't use circumstances to get the attention of others, to pass the buck or to try to make others feel guilty.

Simultaneously, I discovered a new book by Julia Cameron called, "The Listening Path: The Creative Art of Attention," around the same time that I started Alan's webinar. Julia wrote a book years ago entitled, "The Artist's Way," that introduced me to Morning Pages, and she uses them again in the new book. In Julia's own words,

> *"Morning Pages are a daily practice of three pages [of] stream of consciousness, [hand]written first thing upon awakening.... The pages are about anything and everything. There is no wrong way to do them. They range from the petty to the profound.... are like a little whisk broom that you poke into all the corners of your consciousness."*

In her latest book, she focuses on the importance and value of *listening.* That's what appealed to me when I saw her book on the Barnes and Noble bookshelf. As a forty-six-year veteran of meditation practice, as well as being trained in Compassionate Listening at Unity Church and as a certified Life Coach, I've come to appreciate and understand the significance of listening in our lives. She has a quote by Alfred Brendel at the beginning of the Week 6 chapter on Listening to Silence: *The word "listen" contains the same letters as the word "silent."* I almost had that tattooed on my right arm recently, but decided to condense it to my favorite phrase, "Be still," which is also the name of a CD of guided meditations that I co-produced with the musical director of Unity Chapel in Park City, Utah. Anyway, the Morning Pages have unearthed some interesting thought processes for me that synchronize (not *coincide* because there are no coincidences spiritually!) with my webinar studies as well as with another book I'm reading.

The third parallel experience of this period of introspection is the book, "Journey of Souls," by Michael Newton. My cousin Tina and I were discussing her mom's recent death in April and how we both believe her soul will somehow reunite with all her relatives—her parents, husband, sister (my mom) and brother-in-law (my dad), all of whom had preceded her in death. She recommended the book as one she'd read years ago (first edition, 1994) and had suggested to her sister as a way to deal with their mom's death. So, because I was signed up for Alan's webinar on the soul anyway, I bought the book.

While I don't believe verbatim anyone's writings about what happens when we die because no one can know for sure, I do believe in a Force beyond our human existence and a connection within me to that Force—my soul—that returns to the source of life. Notice how generic I'm being with my words—it's impossible to talk about this subject with our limited supply of words because anyone who reads or hears them has their own definition or interpretation of a given word. For instance, I grew up Catholic and the word "God" had a certain meaning to it. But as I've evolved spiritually (not religiously, mind you), I may still refer to the Universal Force as "God" just because it's a short, easy word that I'm used to but to which I now connote a different meaning altogether. So I hesitate to use "God" when speaking to others because they will put their spin on what God means to them and assume that's my meaning as well. But enough about this--I could go on and on about the semantics of this topic but won't. Suffice to say, the book is adding complementary data to my webinar workshop and to my wellspring of knowledge.

So, these three synchronicities being explained, I want to share something that I've compiled as a result. I'll just call them "Lessons I've Learned During This Lifetime," or what I've come to believe spiritually and humanly. They are not listed in any particular order of importance, but as I randomly wrote them in my notes. Here goes!

1. *Less is more.* Clutter blocks movement in all aspects of life—physical, mental and emotional.
2. *No regrets.* Either do it or let go of it and move on—don't dwell on it.
3. *No guilt or embarrassment.* I won't let others decide how I should react to my thoughts or actions—what others think won't deter me from my authenticity.
4. *I'm not a victim.* No one has power over me. I make my own choices and only *I* have power over my life.
5. *Time and Money have no meaning.* The Universe doesn't keep Time linearly nor does it count Abundance monetarily. A minute, a year and a century are the same. A penny, a one-thousand-dollar bill and a billion dollars worth of diamonds are the same.
6. *Gratitude is a forward action.* I say 'Thank you' to the Universe before receiving anything and trust I'll receive what I ask for or need—or better.
7. *Listen to my Inner Voice.* Pay attention, let go of doubts and trust my Soul's voice.
8. *Acknowledge differences.* There's not always a 'right' or 'wrong' way to do things or to be—just a different option, a different perspective.
9. *Diffuse the situation.* Take ownership—apologize—forgive—move on.

I could go deeply into each one of these Lessons, but for now I'll just let the readers come up with their own interpretations and decide for themselves what works and what doesn't for them. These are *my* lessons—what are yours?

The Beast Within - The Story Behind the Poem
(2021)

While compiling material for this book, I found a poem I'd written in 1974 called The Beast Within, which can be found in the Poems section. I wrote this poem a few months after Tom McGuire—the love of my life…the one who got away—ended our relationship. I know it sounds like a cliché, yet I was truly devastated because I was so much in love with him, and he with me. I can hear you thinking—if he loved you so much, why did he break up with you? Why did he hurt you? The thing is, I understood the why from his perspective—he was an honorable man, a good Catholic man, who valued the state of matrimony. Let me explain…

Tom and I met in July of '73 at Gulliver's, a nightclub that straddled the border of Port Chester, New York, and Greenwich, Connecticut. This cute guy with a smile that sparkled in his blue, blue eyes asked me to dance, we hit it off right away and started dating the following weekend. We were inseparable, often double-dating with my best friend, Kathy, and her fiancé, Chan. The four of us especially enjoyed playing cards together, always ending the evenings laughing and planning our next date. By the time our birthdays rolled around in October—his on the 16th and mine on the 28th-- we'd declared our love for each other. We were happy.

In January, that happiness was shattered. Tom came to my apartment after work one evening late in the month. I'd been home sick with the flu for a few days, so was surprised by his visit, but glad to see him. He wasn't his usual smiling, witty self, but I wasn't prepared for the reason why—he told me that his ex-wife of two years, who had cheated on him with his best friend, wanted to get back together with him. She was sorry. She wanted another chance.

The thing is, I'd sensed this might be coming about a month earlier when Tom told me he'd received a Christmas card from her out of the blue with a note asking for his forgiveness. My female "spidey senses" went up, and I'd asked him then if he was breaking up with me. He said 'no,' but he wanted to be upfront about what was happening. He admitted that he wanted to at least meet with her to see what was going on and determine if there was still something between them. Like I said, he valued the marriage vows he'd taken and felt he owed it to himself to find out. And he didn't want to do it behind my back, which is why he was telling me about it.

I know, I know—it's easy to judge him and tell me I should have dumped him right then and there. But I was living in that moment and believed he was torn between her and me. I wanted to be the mature woman who listens to her man when he's struggling with a life dilemma. I wanted to give him a chance to choose, not be the one to tell him he had to choose between us immediately—not make it just about me. I wanted—I hoped—that his curiosity would reveal there was no longer any love between them and that he wanted to stay with me. He was honest with me from the start and I couldn't fault him for that, nor did I have the courage to end it with him. I wanted to play it out. Unfortunately, my gamble didn't pay off.

We just sat on the couch in each other's arms, both sad and crying and realizing what a mistake this could be. Trust me when I say, because I'm the one who knew him, he was truly upset and he wasn't being duplicitous. I didn't blame him—but I did blame her. Once he finally left, I cried for hours and blamed her incessantly. She'd had her time with him. She'd broken his heart. She shouldn't get another chance—it was my turn—it wasn't fair!

In April, I had a gloomy day and the poem flowed out of my lethargy. During Kathy and Chan's wedding reception in May, I kept hiding out in the bathroom to cry and reapply my mascara, seeing Tom everywhere and nowhere. But the months went by and the pain did eventually subside as I recovered from my devastation and moved on. Then, on the evening of July 1, I was surprised to get a call from Tom. He started out with, "Oh, thank God, you're alright!" Then he asked me, "Did you hear about the fire at Gulliver's?" Yes, I'd heard about it at Sunday mass the day before. It had happened in the early hours of Saturday morning—twenty-four patrons were killed and dozens injured. Tom had called because we'd met there, and he knew I still went there with friends. He was worried that I'd been there, and worse. I could hear the concern and the relief in his voice and wanted so much for him to reach through the phone lines and comfort me as we shared our grief. Hearing his voice again had churned up some of the embers still burning in my heart. It was the last time I ever talked to him.

So, was Tom McGuire really the "love of my life?" In truth and in hindsight, yes, he really was! Oh, I've had relationships since, I've been in love—I was even married for almost four years in the Eighties. Here's the thing—a lasting relationship for me needs more than love. *Falling* in love, that's the easy part. *Staying* in love requires two other components—*like* and *trust*. I may love a guy, but I may no longer like him because differences that revealed themselves threw the relationship off balance. I may love him, but if I can't trust him--well, that's a deal-breaker for me. Tom was someone I loved, liked and trusted completely.

For Tom to be the *love of my life* doesn't mean we have to be together for that love to continue. I've come to know that Love—with a capital 'L'—is fluid and exists regardless of how it's being experienced by us. It simply *is*. We can make it difficult or hurtful by the expectations and demands that we place on it and on our relationships. It's said that we have to 'work at' love, but what we really have to work at is creating a space where we can be aware of Love without the expectations or limitations we place on it. Therefore, when I say that he's the *love of my life*, I mean that the love we shared was so potent it has influenced and inspired how I've lived and loved all of my life—it's still a part of me at the deepest level. I wasn't *discouraged* about love because of us breaking up—I was *eager* to love again and experience the joy that Tom's love taught me was possible. When I've thought of him over the years, it's brought a smile to my face. Images of him float across my mind on October 16th if I remember it's his birthday. If I hear of a ravaging fire in a building like the one at Gulliver's, I remember meeting him there and his phone call to see if I was safe. He and I would continue with our lives separately, but the love we shared was already embedded within us forever.

In the bigger scheme of the Universe, our time together was simply a blip on the radar. But that blip was passionate, loving and memorable, and I was blessed to have experienced it. Yes, I may still be carrying a torch for Tom and I'm okay with that. I hold no grudge nor have any regrets. The thing is, I know with all certainty, if Tom were to show up at my front door—almost 50 years older, with white hair and liver spots and a little paunch—if his smile still sparkled in his blue, blue eyes, I'd let him in.

To Quote Meghan O'Rourke...

(2021)

My mother, Gloria, died on December 9, 1991, at the too-young age of sixty-three years. She found out in June of that year that she had liver cancer that had metastasized from cancer of the colon and not been found soon enough to treat. We had six and a half more months with her—not nearly enough time.

Over the years, I've written about her, about our relationship, about how much she influenced my life. The summer after she died, I awoke crying from a dream about her, then grabbed a tablet and pen and wrote a short folk story about our relationship. It's called *The Woman and the Falcon,* and it describes the metaphor I'd created a few months before her diagnosis about our relationship—how she's the falconer to my peregrine falcon because she was always there for me to 'come home' to for love and support.

In 2012, I read a book by Meghan O'Rourke called *The Long Goodbye: A Memoir*, which is about the death of her mother and her period of grief the year following it. I found this book to be poignant and aligned with my own experience of my mom's death, so I highlighted passages that held special meaning for me. Since Meghan did such a wonderful job putting my same thoughts into her words, I'm going to let them speak to you, too. (Riverhead Books; Reprint edition [April 3, 2012]; Page numbers in parentheses.)

- ...the Person Who Loved Me Most in the World was about to be dead (69)
- What had actually happened still seemed implausible: A person was present your entire life, and then one day she disappeared and never came back. It resisted belief. (139)
- It was what *wasn't* there that made it different. An absence that becomes a presence, like the shadow cast by an oil lamp

on a stormy night...I had memories of her, but I no longer had her secret sense of the world... (172)

- And even if death doesn't lead to extinction, it still means that, in the best of circumstances, one will never see one's loved one again in this form--never be able to share jokes, hug, have a glass of wine. I don't just miss my mother's soul, after all. I miss her laugh, her sarcasm, and the sound of her voice saying my name. I miss her hands, which I shall never see again...That loss is not recuperable, regardless of what one believes about the afterlife. (187-188)

- Yet the reality of her *being dead* was so different from her death. (199)

- You remember her in flashes. The flashes hurt. They light up your stomach. Then you breathe, look out again...And I thought: I am becoming someone whose mother is dead. Then a cool sadness flooded me. It was true. I was getting used to her being dead. My mother was gone. And I: letting her go. (202-203)

- I had tried to find a metaphor for my loss in the weeks after my mother's death. (217)

- I reached for the phone. And realized--I couldn't. From now on, I would have to answer questions myself, through trial and error. (236)

- The moment when I flash upon my mother's smile and face and realize she is dead, I experience the same lurch, the same confusion, the same sense of impossibility. A year ago collapses into yesterday in these moments. Periodically for the rest of my life, my mother's death will seem like it took place yesterday. (266)

- Perhaps it is fitting, too, that while my grief has lessened, my sense of being motherless has intensified...as each new day arrives, I find myself, though suffering less acutely, feeling *more* unmothered. (294)

- ...said that at moments I had reminded them of my mother. *If only*, I thought. Then I thought, *If so, it's not my doing, it's hers*...I think about my mother every day, but not as concertedly as I used to. She crosses my mind like a spring cardinal that flies past the edge of your eye: startling, luminous, lovely, gone. (295)

- The bond between a mother and child is so unlike any other that it is categorically irreplaceable. *Unmothered* is not a word in my dictionary, but I often find myself thinking it should be. The "real" word most like it is *unmoored.* The irreplaceability is what becomes stronger--and stranger--as the months pass: Am I really she who has woken up again without a mother? Yes, I am... Who else do I share this history with? No one. Because she is not there, I must mother myself. (295-296)

- ...and then she breathed once more, the last breath, and we were there and she was not, and even now I think, Come on, Mom, stay another night, stay the night---Stay the night. (297)

As I write this, it is thirty years since my mother's diagnosis and death. She's missed so much—her granddaughter Christina and grandson Michael growing into incredible adults; the birth of their sister Rachel two years after she died; the birth of Christina's two sons, James (5) and Luke (2); the deaths of her mother 11 years ago, her daughter Sandy last year and her sister Toni earlier this year. I've missed so much, too, especially seeing her with her grandchildren and great-grandchildren and being able to talk to her about publishing a book, romantic relationships, menopause, aging and retirement and all that Life has dished out to me over the years. Because, even at the wise age of seventy-two years, there are still days when I want my Mommy.

Years ago when I asked her if she minded that, as the oldest child, I wasn't married while my sister had just tied the knot and my cousin already had two children, her response was, "No! I'm living vicariously through you, so don't ever feel you have to get married or have kids for my sake. When you're ready, I'll be there and enjoy it, but do it for yourself, not for me." I've come to realize just how exceptional my mom was because she didn't force me to conform to some societal norms like a lot of her friends did with their children. I've come to realize what a 'functional' family I grew up in. Oh, we weren't perfect, by any means! But I was never made to feel inadequate, unattractive, insufficient, unloved or stupid. I was never made to feel that I had to live my life in such a way as to make my parents look good—their love and support of me always told me that they were proud of me.

So, I'm wondering as I type this—what else would she want me to do with my life as she lived vicariously through me? What can I do now, Mom, that I haven't done yet, something you would have liked to experience through me? I've already published a book, a project you and Aunt Toni tried to accomplish but didn't. I've performed improvisational comedy on stages, following in your thespian footsteps. I've moved around the country, living in new cities and making an incredible cache of friends, which you seemed able to do so easily. In fact, I've been telling people lately that I've *become you* because I talk to strangers everywhere like you used to do. Remember when we kids would wait for you in a store because you were talking to someone and how, when we asked, "Who was that" you'd drive us crazy when you replied, "I don't know—we were just talking?"

Anyway, Mom, I'm sending that question out into the Universe— *What can I do now on your behalf?* --and expecting it to reach your spirit. I know you'll send me a sign somehow because you never let me down!

∾ ∾ ∾ ∾ ∾ ∾ ∾

As I prepare this for the book's publication in November 2022, I'm happy to report that since I wrote this essay my Mom has lived vicariously through these accomplishments in my life:

- *I edited and retyped a novel she and her sister wrote over forty years ago but never got published; then I had it printed and bound into copies for my family members—she was looking over my shoulder the entire time!*

- *I lost over 40 pounds so I could be healthier in my later years, something she would have wanted for me.*
- *I moved from Arizona back to Ohio to be near my remaining family, a move I know she would have been excited about.*
- *I'm publishing my second book—and she's thrilled being a published author again through me!*

Vulnerability Part 1 – Of Body

(2021)

I debated about whether or not I should include an essay about this experience in the book. Most of my material is light-hearted or lovingly emotional. This story, however, is neither of those things. Yet I feel I need to share it because, first of all, it is a significant part of my story; and second, I've kept it to myself for too many years and others need to be aware of how situations like this affect a person for the long term. What I'm talking about is date rape.

Did you cringe when reading those last two words? Before you decide to skip this essay, I ask you to pause and ask "why" then move beyond that and read on anyway. I won't be explicit about the details, but I will be explicit about the effect it's had on my life.

When this happened to me in the fall of 1970, the term "date rape" hadn't even been created yet. Its prevalence slowly grew in studies, books and magazines in the Eighties, but first attracted media attention in 1991 when two women came forth publicly with their experiences. One was an unnamed 29-year-old woman who accused William Kennedy Smith of raping her on a beach after meeting in a Florida bar. The other victim was Katie Koestner, who started speaking out in 1991 about being raped by her date the year before on the William and Mary campus. In 1970, in northeast Ohio, the notion that a guy having unwanted sexual relations with his date was considered rape was unheard of. But allow me to tell my story.

I worked in the computer department at a bank in my hometown in 1970. One of my co-workers was having a Halloween party and I decided to ask the new guy in the Loan Department to go with me. That act alone—a woman asking a guy out—was a new concept prompted by the women's movement in the Sixties and Seventies. Anyway, Ron agreed to go with me. We had a fun time, but as someone new to drinking alcohol—I'd turned twenty-one three days earlier—the Harvey Wallbangers I consumed amidst the games and dancing and conversing took their toll on me. The mix of Vodka, Galiano liqueur and orange juice goes down sweetly while knocking you for a loop as they ferment inside you. By the time Ron and I left, my head was spinning and I felt nauseous on the drive home.

Only we didn't go right to my home. This is where the details get really fuzzy. In trying to recreate what happened that night, images and sounds came intermittently over the next few weeks and over the years. A string of motel rooms near a highway. The weight of a body on top of mine. Grunting sounds as I tried to push the weight off of me. The realization that I was naked when I got up to vomit in the bathroom. Pain where there shouldn't be pain. And blood. The quiet of a VW bug as I huddle against the passenger door. Hugging the toilet in my house as my mom taps on the bathroom door to ask if I'm alright. But I was still reeling from my over-consumption of drinks that I didn't even think consciously and went straight to bed.

That was Saturday night. Sunday, as the alcohol wore off, the flashes of what happened started slipping into my thoughts, but I never—to this very day—remembered exactly what happened from the time we left the party to the morning when I woke up. Only flashes and the pain of having been physically assaulted had me asking, "Did we have sex?"—and knowing *he* did.

I told no one. What was I supposed to say? I was his date. I'd asked him out. I flirted with him at the party. Going into the bank that next Monday was excruciating for me because I didn't know what to expect from Ron or how I was supposed to act. As happens in these kind of circumstances, I thought I was somewhat responsible because of initiating the date and then overdrinking. And, since I couldn't really remember the details, it would have been a "he said/she said" situation. So I acted nonchalant and never once confronted Ron about that night for the next two years that we both worked at the bank before I moved to New York. Part of me thought I was being so modern and mature by ignoring my suspicions and moving on. What I know *DIDN'T* happen was *I NEVER SAID YES!* I was a virgin who was naïve enough about sex to have misjudged his intentions. However, I never had a say in where we went after the party or what we did in that sleazy motel room. But it wasn't until 1990, as Katie Koestner was publicly talking about her date rape experience on the campus of the College of William & Mary in Williamsburg, Virginia, that it all came rushing back to me—that happened to me! Ron had *raped* me that fall night in 1970!

I cried and cried for days whenever it crossed my mind. But I still didn't talk to anyone about it. What purpose would it serve? I couldn't go back to Ohio and file charges about a twenty-year old assault. Besides, Ron had left the bank, bought a bar and was killed one night while closing up by a thief who shot him in the face. Karma? Part of me hoped so. It wasn't until I attended an eight-week personal development workshop in Utah in 2015 that I shared the experience with a young man with whom I was paired. We were instructed to share with our partners something we hadn't shared with anyone before. He told me about being attacked and raped by a few men in an alley a few years earlier—and, because of his frankness, I found myself opening up to this stranger about my own experience. *And it felt so good to finally release it and not be judged or reprimanded or counseled about it!* Those of us who were able to open up to our partners were encouraged to call someone else during our lunch break to share the story again. I called a friend who also didn't judge me, but offered a loving ear and a supporting voice.

Since then, I've shared my story with a select number of women in my family and my life when it was appropriate to do so. What I learned was how many others have had similar circumstances happen to them. They weren't all full-out rapes, but any type of physical, emotional or psychological abuse falls into the same category—*unwanted assault on our bodies, minds and souls!* We are left feeling vulnerable, a vulnerability that can work its way into other aspects of our life and stifle our creativity, relationships and power.

Just how *did* this affect the broader scope of my life? I have no doubt that the brutal experience is why I shied away from some intimate relationships in the years following the date rape, stopping a guy before "going all the way" or ending a too clingy relationship. I needed to say 'NO!' *before* it went too far and I needed to be heard—because I hadn't been heard in 1970. Then there was a period when I needed to be the assertive partner, the initiator, for a sexual relationship, taking the lead, having the control—because I hadn't been in control in 1970. At times, I'll admit, I could be a sexual tease, sending signals of compliancy then enjoying it when I'd say, "NO!" to stop him in his tracks—because I couldn't stop him in 1970. I didn't realize all of this at the time and I'm not proud of the times when I was purposely mean and hurtful--they weren't conscious decisions on my part. I reflected back on those past relationships, however, about how they ended or never got started. Fortunately, I eventually recognized how destructive my blemished behavior was to me and to the men, so I adjusted it accordingly and finally shared some passionate liaisons with some really nice guys.

So, that's my story and I'm glad I've included it here. I hope I didn't shock, embarrass or enrage you—that wasn't my intent. I *did* want to elicit a thought-provoking moment for you through my honesty and authenticity. Is there a secret you are keeping that needs to be released to the Universe so that you can be your authentic self? Do you feel vulnerable and don't know how to empower yourself? I strongly urge you to seek guidance and support that will allow you to release your secret and move on with your life, whether it's a professional therapist or a trusting friend, a spiritual advisor or in the privacy of your own space.

Vulnerability Part 2 – Of Identity

(2021)

On Saturday, August 28, I placed an order on the Victoria's Secret online store for a new sports bra, and I received the usual order confirmation that all was well and I'd receive my order on September 5th. Then, on Sunday, August 29, all hell broke loose. I received an email from Victoria's Secret saying my order was cancelled—only the order they were referencing wasn't mine but it had been placed on my account! I tried to access my Victoria's Secret Credit Card account online but couldn't get into it. I immediately called their Customer Service department who said there were over $500 in charges on my account to ship to a Florida address—were these mine? "No!" I exclaimed and was transferred to their Fraud Department at Comenity Bank, who handles the VS credit card accounts, and my eleven-day nightmare began!

I've heard about or read the stories about identity theft and how people have had their accounts cleaned out or had charges racked up in their name on store or credit cards. I know there are people out there who have the technical savvy to hack into accounts and do this. I'm also savvy enough not to click on links in emails or texts that I don't recognize or to answer phone numbers that aren't in my Contacts list. Yet somehow, someone had wormed their way into my account and it only got worse as the days progressed.

The biggest scare, and the one that had me taking Lorazepam to calm the anxiety that I'd wake up with, was when my retirement IRA at my investment company (name withheld for obvious reasons!) was compromised! This person or persons had submitted a withdrawal from the account for $9,000 in the form of a check—but it was to be mailed to me! Also, they opened a second IRA in my portfolio and tried to transfer funds *into* that account from two different banks. I was alerted to these transactions by Experian credit bureau, as well as by my investment company itself, as suspicious activity. My conversations with the Fraud Departments at both institutions helped to alleviate my concerns because they immediately began investigations and prevented any losses and negative credit reporting on my files.

The other big account that was affected was my Amazon account. I didn't have Amazon Prime or an Amazon credit card, but I had saved my two commercial credit cards on my account to use when I made purchases. Only the last four digits of the card appear, so no one could actually get access to the credit card, but they managed to place several small orders. Also, Experian received credit inquiries from two banks for a new Amazon Prime Store Card and an Amazon Visa Signature Card, both to be mailed to a post office box in Florida. Again, the Fraud Department stopped the orders and began an investigation. They also closed my account and told me to open a new one a few days later. Needless to say, I did *not* add my credit cards to the account file, and I went into other vendors, like airlines, rental cars, stores, etc., and removed the card information from there as well.

The Fraud Departments at these places were all so professional, friendly, patient and efficient in getting everything cleaned up for me. I couldn't have survived the stress of this ordeal without them. I learned so much—much more than I'd ever thought I'd need to know—about how these things happen and what I should do to prevent them in the future. I was instructed by all of them to have my laptop computer cleaned of any viruses, etc.—thanks to Geek Squad at Best Buy for doing that—and to have my cell phone checked as well, which Verizon Tech Support did for me.

The one thing that I immediately started doing that first Sunday when this all began was to change the passwords on my accounts, starting with the financial institutes. I called my niece, Christina, because of her computer savvy and she gave me some great ideas for how to form strong passwords, so over the next eleven days I ended up going into all my accounts to upgrade my security even more, adding two-step verification where I could.

On Wednesday, September 8, I had my last conversation with Amazon and Victoria's Secret, and no new emails or alerts have come my way—my accounts are safe! I still wake up anxiously thinking, *What new alert will I get today?,* but I know that won't last for long. Now that it's over, I can't help but wonder the *why* behind this happening to me. I don't mean specifically about the hacking, but about the spiritual lesson behind all of this. As a 'big picture' thinker, I'll always question this and what lessons I learned from the experience.

One thing I'm proud to admit is that my organizational skills had a lot to do with why I didn't lose a dime. I *know* all of my accounts and wasn't afraid to call them when I realized they'd been compromised or could be threatened in the future. Also, I'm not a confrontational customer because I've been on the other end of those phone calls and can empathize with those representatives. The old adage about honey versus vinegar works wonders, too, and creates a positive interaction. A few of the Fraud reps told me that my immediate call in to them had a lot to do with how quickly they could get the situation remedied—I'd done 'good'!

So, why am I writing all of this in this essay for my book? Well, I think part of it is my way, as a writer, to purge myself of any residual negative fears or feelings about what I went through by putting the words to print and leaving them there. Also, I want my readers to take warning that this can happen to *anyone* so take the steps to safeguard your accounts.

Finally, I needed to face the vulnerability I experienced. I was scared and anxious, I admit it. So typing the events in this analytical way helped to detach the emotions from them. Feeling vulnerable is *not* pleasant, especially when, as a single, retired woman, my finances are in jeopardy of disappearing. More than anything, I know that I'm grateful to all of the people I spoke with who resolved this issue and to the Universe for keeping my abundance intact.

A Constant in My Life

(2022)

As I've been compiling this anthology of my written works, I've been reminded fondly of the many people in my life who have celebrated the high points with me and have consoled me during the low points. They've helped me navigate those highs and lows, and one person in particular stands out as a constant in my life—my "forever friend," Kathy Hoynos Reuschenberg.

Kathy and I first started hanging out together in the seventh grade, while trying out for the cheerleading squad for St. Mary's Middle School basketball team. We realized we lived three streets from each other, so we either walked home together after practice or had our parents take the other one home. We once figured out that we actually met for the first time in the third or fourth grade at Jackie Drennen's birthday party. I knew Jackie from the public school we both attended and Kathy lived across the street from her. I remember going to a party there and Kathy said she did, too. So it stands to reason we met. But just prior to me starting fifth grade, my family moved and I changed to St. Mary's School—that's when we became classmates. It took two years for Fate to bring us together as friends.

There are so many stories popping into my head right now that I could share, but to keep this book down to one volume, I'm going to restrain myself and only disclose a couple that demonstrate how we've kept the fire of friendship burning brightly all these years. For instance, who else would drive miles off our course with me to attend a rock music festival in Canada?

I got a job at a bank in our hometown of Warren, Ohio, after high school graduation and Kathy went to Bowling Green University in Findlay, Ohio, following in the footsteps of her sister and some cousins. We always planned a vacation during her summer breaks. It was August 1970 and we were driving up to Montreal, Canada, for a week in my baby blue Volkswagen bug. We arrived at the

Niagara Falls border between New York and Canada around nine o'clock at night and noticed an influx in vans and cars with other young adults. We also noticed that a number of cars were randomly being pulled over by the border guards so they could be searched. Did I say randomly? There were suspiciously more vehicles with groups of young adults inside being detained than families or older couples. Sure enough, when I pulled to the front of the line, the guard waved me over and told me to park by the building and get out of the car.

Kathy and I couldn't believe it—we were being searched for drugs! We were innocent Catholic girls from Nowheresville, Ohio—the last thing we would have stashed in our packed bras or sneakers were drugs! As we stood there and chatted with some of the other "alleged smugglers," we learned that most of them were going to the Strawberry Fields Festival, a rock music concert, being held at Mosport Park Raceway in Bowmanville, Ontario, about sixty miles east of Toronto. We watched the border guard in astonishment as he shook our bottles of vitamin pills and manhandled our clothes. Then we looked at each other, grinned and nodded—not a word spoken but we knew—we've been searched so we're going to that festival!

A few hours later, we pulled off the highway to Montreal and followed a stream of vehicles heading to the Raceway. The parking lot was filling up fast and I squeezed my bug between a couple of vans. Long story short, the gates were closed for the night, we didn't want to hang around until the gates opened again in the morning because we still had a long drive to our final destination. So, we visited with some of the die-hard concert-goers for about an hour, then drove past the continuous incoming line of traffic to get back on the highway. Now I ask you, is that not the kind of friend you want to travel with and get busted with for smuggling drugs? (Just kidding about that last part!)

Of course, being best friends didn't keep Kathy from almost shooting me!

In 1979, I was living in Suffern, New York, a small town in Rockland County. About five miles away lived Kathy and her husband Chan. Their house was buried in the woods off of Route 202, a big, secluded old farmhouse. Kathy was expecting their first child and was about eight months pregnant that fateful night. Chan was in Wisconsin where he'd started a new job and was setting up a house for Kathy and their baby to move into once she delivered.

Around eight o'clock, Chan called me and asked if I'd heard from Kathy—he'd been trying to call her but wasn't getting an answer. Remember, it's 1979 and all we had then were landlines, which could easily go down in storms or rural areas. He asked me to drive to the house and check on her, which, of course, I agreed to do. I drove through the dark woods, over the little bridge above the little stream and parked by their back door. The downstairs of the house was dark, but there were lights on in the upstairs bedroom and I saw shadows moving around—a good sign. I knocked while I unlocked the door with my key and called out to Kathy as I walked through the kitchen to the living room and the staircase going upstairs. She never answered, but I kept saying calmly so as not to frighten her, "Hello—Kathy. It's me, Susan. Just checking on you."

As I reached the bottom of the staircase and looked up, the hall light went on and I froze—then screamed as I back-pedaled away from the steps. At the top of the landing, dressed in a long nightgown, her damp hair askew, her glasses half on and half off, stood Kathy— holding a double-barreled shotgun resting on her pregnant belly and pointed directly at me! I yelled. She yelled. I called out, "Kathy, it's Susan! Don't shoot me!" She called out, "What are you doing here? You scared the hell out of me!" As we calmed down—and she put the gun down, thank God! —I walked up the stairs and helped her onto her bed so we could both catch our breath. When I told her Chan asked me to check up on her because he couldn't reach her on the phone, she said she was taking a long shower and never heard the phone. Once we'd calmed down and hugged and were able to joke about her almost shooting me, I told her to please call Chan immediately. I said my goodbyes, drove back to my apartment and poured myself a cold beer as I thanked my lucky stars the baby hadn't kicked her trigger finger.

Kathy and Chan are still happily married, have two grown daughters and four darling grandchildren. They live in Katonah, New York, now and are both retired. I haven't seen them since 2010 when I visited a bunch of friends in New York, Connecticut and New Jersey—I can't believe it's been twelve years! A week ago, Kathy and I had a two-and-a-half-hour phone conversation, catching up on our families and our health. Sharing books we've read and shows we're watching. Bragging about her grandchildren and my grandnephews. Reminiscing about the crazy situations we got into when we were single and traveling around. Long conversations like that are not uncommon for us, whether on the phone or in person. Chan will just walk into a room where we've been sitting for hours gabbing, shake his head and walk back out. He can't understand what we could have to say for all that time! Actually, we've been carrying on the *same conversation* for over sixty years because no matter how much time passes between those calls or visits, we simply pick up where we left off the last time. That's just how it is between me and my BFF—a true constant in my life.

Love you, Kath!

❧ ❧ ❧ ❧ ❧ ❧ ❧

I finally saw Kathy again this year when I convinced her to come to Ohio for a visit so we could go to our 55th John F. Kennedy High School reunion! What a great time we had! She flew to Columbus to see my new home in Hilliard, then we drove up to Warren for a two-night stay at the local Holiday Inn. On the way, we stopped at Kent State University to visit the May 4th (1970) museum and see the memorials for the four fallen students from the shootings that year. I'd been there before but she hadn't—it was somber yet satisfying to see how the university commemorates that tragic event.

The reunion had a casual icebreaker event on Friday night and a slightly more formal buffet dinner on Saturday night. I'd been attending and even coordinating reunions in the past, but she hadn't seen most of these people since the 25th reunion that she attended. Friday night, she admitted to being a little nervous about recognizing and remembering people, but I had no doubt she'd be fine—and before long she was mingling and chatting up a storm! By Saturday's dinner, we were laughing and having a blast with our long-time friends.

Saturday afternoon, we met a fellow classmate and friend, Barb Murray Heiss, for lunch at Charley's Restaurant & Pub. (Barb graduated with us but never attends the reunions—to each her own, but I think she's missing out on a good time.) Anyway, we had a great time at lunch, listening to Barb share stories about the antics of her family.

Home Run!

(2022)

LOU: I'm really looking forward to seeing the Yankees play today, Bud.

BUD: Well, it's a perfect day for baseball, Lou!

LOU: Before we go in, I'd like to learn the players' names on the Yankees' team.

BUD: Sure, I can tell you. Who's on first, What's on second, I Don't Know is on third.

LOU: You know the players' names?

BUD: Yes.

LOU: Well, then, who's playin' first?

BUD: Yes.

LOU: I mean the guy's name on first base.

BUD: Who.

LOU: The player on first base.

BUD: Who is on first.

LOU: Well, what are you askin' *me* for?

BUD: I'm not asking you---I'm telling you: Who is on first.

LOU: I'm asking *you*---who's on first?

BUD: That's the man's name!

LOU: That's who's name?

BUD: Yes.

LOU: All I'm trying to find out is what's the guy's name on first base.

BUD: Oh, no, no, What is on second base.

LOU: I'm not asking you who's on second.

BUD: Who's on first.

LOU: That's what I'm trying to find out!

BUD: Now, take it easy.
LOU: What's the guy's name on first base?
BUD: What's the guy's name on second base.
LOU: I'm not askin' ya who's on second.
BUD: Who's on first.
LOU: I don't know.
BUD: He's on third. We're not talking about him.
LOU: How did I get on third base?
BUD: You mentioned his name.
Etcetera…

I'm sure you're familiar with this popular pun-driven sketch performed so successfully by the comedy team, Abbott and Costello. They're my favorite comedy team. I even have a book of all their routines and the complete set of DVDs of their movies. But there was another comedy team who performed this sketch quite successfully, too. Have you ever heard of Morrell and Wallace? No? Hmmm, maybe we weren't as good as we thought. That's right, I'm Morrell and my friend Gail is Wallace. Here's the scoop.

In the early Eighties, I was an administrative trainer at Xerox Corporation's Northeast Region office in Greenwich, Connecticut. There were three trainers in the department and we taught employees in the sixteen branch offices in the northeast. Gail Wallace taught the employees who processed sales orders and scheduled deliveries of copier and duplicator sales; I taught the employees who handled the billing and related questions or adjustments of the monthly invoices; and Bob Berger taught the ones who handled accounts receivable for those invoices. It was important that our trainings supported each other because each facet of the three administrative processes in a branch needed to understand and back up the other two—orders needed to flow from sales to installment to billing to payments as flawlessly as possible.

One year, Gail and I were going to be doing a joint training in all of the branches to teach them about a new program being directed by the headquarters office in Rochester, New York. A key element for the success of this new program was exceptional communication between the two departments, Equipment and Billing. At the time, Gail was the newest member of the training team, and she and I only knew each other from work functions. So it was important that *we* had exceptional communication to pull off these trainings at each of the sixteen branches. How were we going to make the mundane data being mandated by headquarters interesting and memorable? Then I had an idea—what if we performed Abbott and Costello's "Who's On First?" routine as an icebreaker? Talk about an example of how *not* to communicate exceptionally! When I suggested it to Gail, she immediately said, "Yes!" And that's when the seeds of our forty-years-and-counting friendship took root!

Gail and I have shared some funny and fun moments, whether we're hanging out at her place in Greenwich, taking vacations together or traveling for business as trainers. A good example of how well we fit together was during a three-day training trip to Boston. During the day, we spent time with our separate departments in the branch, but we got together for dinner. The first night, we ended up near Faneuil Hall at a Mexican restaurant called GuadalaHarry's. Scrumptious nachos, delicious frozen margaritas and Ms. Pac Man game tables—who could ask for anything more? Gail was a fanatically fantastic Ms. Pac Man player, so she had a roll of quarters in her purse already to go. We spent a few hours chowing and imbibing and chasing those little dots around the board.

The next night, we asked for some suggestions about where else to go for dinner, then looked at each other and said, "GuadalaHarry's!" So we repeated the previous night's menu selections and even got the same game table. Finally, our last night in town and we wanted to do it up big—so of course we went back to GuadalaHarry's! By then the bartender and waitress knew us by name and by order. Only good friends could be as in sync like we were on that trip. We still talk about it.

While I was living in Park City, Utah, I had the good fortune to have two friends, Mary and Edo Bernasconi, who owned a membership in a timeshare program, which they generously offered to me since they hadn't used it in the few years they'd first invested in it. So I graciously accepted—and shared it with my traveling buddy, Gail. We spent a week in southern California, right across Highway 1 from the beach. I took my first trip to Hawaii in 2011 using the timeshare. Then, when I decided to return to Hawaii in 2012 for *two* weeks, I ended up renting an ohana cottage through VRBO in Waimanalo on O'ahu and invited Gail to join me for one week since I knew she'd never been to Hawaii. Now this is how solid our friendship is—when I invited her, I told her we could share the cottage for one week, but I wanted the second week to myself. She understood completely and we had fun exploring the island that week.

What I learned on that Hawaii trip is that Gail likes to visit museums in every new city to which she travels—me, not so much. But friendship is about compromise, so one day we visited the Honolulu Museum of Art. We split up, and it didn't take me long to bypass most of the artwork to check out two exhibits I'd seen advertised at their ticket office. One was a series of photographs taken by a female soldier whose subjects were locals and comrades she'd encountered during her tours of duty in the Middle East. The other was the history of Hawaiian tattooing. Tattooing is a custom that has been practiced within the Hawaiian culture for thousands of years. It uses the images of myths created from a combination of geometric shapes and swirls resembling the land and waves. Up until that time, I had no experience with tattoos, but the intricacy and stories behind their designs were so beautiful that I think that's when the idea of getting my own tattoo took up residence in my mind.

Gail has become a great traveling companion, but there's so much more to our friendship. One of the most valuable contributions she has made to my life is our shared firm belief in an omniscient Spirit and the synchronicity of the Universe. Whenever I tell her about something synchronous that happened to me, I don't have to explain synchronicity first to her—she already gets it! —so she's one of a few people I know who I can share these experiences with indisputably. For instance, two weeks ago I was going to a thrift store to drop off some bags of clothes I was donating. As I drove along Main Street, I thought to myself, "Look for that Chinese restaurant you got takeout from last year that you can't remember the name of and you haven't been able to find again since." So I checked out every strip mall and shopping area that I passed with no luck—it must be on a different street.

I found the thrift store, dropped off the bags in the back and was weaving my way through the maze of stores in the plaza, trying to get to a certain cross street for my next destination. As I approached the driveway leading onto that street and glanced to my left at the last business in the strip mall—you guessed it—it was the Chinese restaurant! Oh, my God—and thank you, God! I quickly pulled over and just sat there laughing out loud. I took a picture of the place so I'd remember the name this time. I immediately called Gail to share with her what happened and she so got it—just like I knew she would! I know my friends well enough to know that, while the others might laugh and be happy for me, only Gail got the more significant meaning of how the Universe had guided me out of that maze in that direction for a reason. These were not simply coincidences. Trust me, the silly, smaller synchronous happenings in your life are just as significant as the life-changing moments—the Universe doesn't measure or count what it provides, it just produces results and gifts us with surprise blessings. We have to be open to recognizing and receiving even the smallest gesture in order to appreciate the larger ones.

Well, I got off track there a little—sorry. Getting back to the Abbott and Costello routine that Gail and I performed, we recorded our own parts for the other person, allowing blank air so she could interject her own dialogue when she practiced alone. Then we rehearsed together in front of our friend and Xerox manager, Chuck Alfini, who loved it. Soon, we were at the first meeting. I opened up the meeting, greeting everyone until Gail walked in and interrupted me, saying she needed to know the names of the players on the Xerox softball team. I apologized to the audience, then proceeded to tell her, "Who's on first, What's on second, I Don't Know is on third…"

It was a home run! And even though we didn't have the same fame and fortune of Bud and Lou, we've sure had the same great friendship!

Synchronicity

(2022)

syn·chro·nic·i·ty | \ ˌsiŋ-krə-ˈni-sə-tē , ˌsin- \
plural synchronicities

Definition of *synchronicity*

1: the quality or fact of being synchronous

2: the coincidental occurrence of events…that seem related but are not explained by conventional mechanisms of causality

> --Merriam/Webster online dictionary

My life has been filled with synchronicities—from the phone calls from a friend I was *just* thinking of calling to having actor Alex O'Loughlin park right next to me at a gym where we were both going! Sure, it's easy to shake your head and say, "Oh, it's just a coincidence!" Many times those everyday occurrences can be just that. The definition above even used the word *coincidental* in its description. However, I've chronicled my life's experiences enough and in such detail that I've noticed patterns of "coincidental occurrences" that go beyond everyday occurrences to life-altering incidences. These patterns are driven by something other than happenstance. They go beyond the every day to the grander design of Time and Space. No, I'm not talking about Fate, which implies a plan that I don't have a part in creating.

Imagine the Universe as a hugely complex, four-dimensional game board. Multiple games are taking place simultaneously, but all the moves being made impact the entire game. The players can't see or determine the effect they are having on the grander design, but they often know at some level that what they do is important in the bigger scheme of things. One life—my life, for example—is merely a speck amidst the gazillion of specks playing this game. A grain of sand amidst all the grains of sand on all the beaches around the world. A flicker of light indistinguishable in the vast array of a fireworks display. Now, imagine what has to happen in this titanic 'game' in order for a series of related events to occur simultaneously in one person's life. Mind-boggling, right? These related events are synchronicities, and Whatever or Whoever the Master Gamester is, these synchronicities are put in your life for a reason. What you choose to do with them is entirely up to you.

I choose to pay attention. I've learned not to be surprised but to take notice and move on accordingly. That doesn't mean I sit back and wait for the Universe to do it all for me. This is a partnership. There's an old joke about a guy who prays to God every night that he would win the lottery, but he never did. Finally, when he meets God in Heaven he asks, "I prayed and prayed to you to let me win the lottery. Why wouldn't you answer my prayer?" And God's reply is, "Why didn't you buy a lottery ticket?"

We all have our part to play. It's a fine balance between participation, control and releasing control. We need to know when to be active and when to let go and be passive. Those periods of waiting can be difficult, but they're often the most important. I'm sure you've heard the old saying, "a watched pot never boils." If you have a hard time waiting, think of it as a recess or a time off from the 'work' of your project or situation.

Synchronicities are simply little signs of the bigger picture of your situation playing out. They're not forced on you nor do they require any response on your part—they just *are*. What you choose to do with them determines at what level you'll play the game and what you'll get out of it. There's not always a right and wrong way, just different options. The Universe is always offering assistance, lessons and support—you decide if and when you want to be a team player or play solitaire.

This morning as I sat to begin my daily meditation ritual, I experienced a perfect example of what *I* mean by synchronicity because it holds a deeper meaning for me than a couple of simultaneous happenings. It has inspired this essay for the book because it exemplifies my spiritual philosophy.

I start each day sitting in the recliner in my office where I read from two books before doing my meditation. For years, I've been purchasing a "book of the year" that has daily inspirational messages. Some of my favorites have been Alan Cohen's *A Deep Breath of Life* (Hay House, Inc. © 1996) and *A Daily Dose of Sanity* (Hay House, Inc. © 2010), Marianne Williamson's *A Year of Miracles* (HarperCollins Publishers © 2013) and Derek Lin's *The Tao of Joy Every Day* (Penguin Groups Ltd © 2011). The book I chose for 2022 is called *Until Today!* by Iyanla Vanzant (Inner Visions Worldwide Network, Inc. © 2000). I also subscribe to Unity's *Daily Word* magazine (Unity Publications), a little booklet that helped me through a troubled marriage and divorce and led me to Unity Church.

Rather than tell you about today's synchronous occurrence, I'm going to type out today's entries from both books and see if you can discover it for yourself.

<u>Until Today!</u>

January 2, 2022

Life will work for me when *I realize…*

I must make myself available to life.

The highest form of service you can offer to yourself and God is to spend time each day in silence. This is time to spend with your true Self. It is time spent being available to the Source of your life and the Force behind your life. Time spent in silence is time spent in contemplation of your purpose in life. It is time spent to gain clarity and build confidence. It is time spent strengthening your mind, clearing your heart and fortifying your spirit. Time spent in silence each day serves the greater You and is, therefore, time well spent.

The highest form of love you can offer to yourself, to God and to those you love is to spend time each day calling on the presence of God, the name of God and the light of God. Time spent calling on God's presence strengthens you. It is time spent in recognition of your dependence on the Creator and giver of life. Time spent calling on God's name opens your soul to be filled with the essence, the energy of God. Time spent calling on the light of God cleanses you. It gives you access to the sweetness of life without the struggle and drama we humans are accustomed to experiencing.

The highest form of praise you can offer to yourself, to God and to the world is to spend time each day expressing gratitude. It says to God that you are aware and appreciative of grace. It says to life that you are acknowledging its awesome presence in you. It says to yourself that you are worth the time it takes to be healed. Time spent in silence, contemplation and gratitude is time spent in devotion to a higher calling and a more loving state of being.

Until today, you may have been trying to squeeze God into the rest of your daily activities. Just for today, give God a full ten minutes of your time when you silently call upon God's love, God's name, God's light and God's presence in your life.

Today I am devoted to spending quality time with God.

Daily Word

Sunday, January 2, 2022

--- Clarity---

Time spent communing with God gives me clarity.

When I gaze toward the heavens on a moonlit night, I expect to see twinkling stars and constellations. But if I use a telescope, I can see details with much greater clarity.

This example could describe my spiritual life as well. I may go about my day mindful of my blissful feelings and kinship with all the people. These things and more are the fruits of my faith.

But I find clarity during times of intentional contemplation, when I meditate upon the truth I feel the presence of God fill my consciousness and touch my heart. This clarity informs my thoughts, words, and actions, bringing my faith to vivid life.

For now we see in a mirror, dimly, but then we will see face to face. Now I know only in part; then I will know fully, even as I have been fully known.

-1 Corinthians 13:12

Do you see it? Do you see how the topic of both pieces is sending me the very same message? Even the choice of words is the same— *time spent*. That caught my eye, and tugged at my soul, the minute I read the opening line of the Daily Word's message because I'd just read those same words in Ms. Vansant's passage. *Time spent calling on God's presence...Time spent calling on God's name...Time spent calling on the light of God...Time spent in silence, contemplation and gratitude* and *Time spent communing with God...* How could I *not* feel the significance of the words when they were coming from two completely different sources?

I'm sure there are those of you who are still arguing on the side of coincidence—and that's your prerogative. I, on the other hand, have lived a life believing in a Higher Power that flows through me and the Universe. This Power is organizing, harmonizing, aligning, arranging, coordinating, authenticating—dare I say it! —

synchronizing the information, circumstances and encounters of my life so that I can make wise choices, appreciate my blessings and live my life to its fullest! Who wouldn't want that kind of camaraderie as we navigate our lives?! I'll take synchronicity over coincidence any and every day!

In case you're asking yourself, "Okay, so I get the synchronicity of the two passages, but what did they actually mean to her? Why was this such a significant moment?" To understand that you'd have to know a lot more about me than I'm able to reveal in this essay, not that I wouldn't want to share but who has the time to write it or read it all! You'll get insight into me as you read through the rest of this book. Know this—I'm planning on moving from Arizona to Ohio this year and will begin the process of selling my house here, moving across the country and purchasing a house there. A lot to think about and plan and organize—and the timing of everything is significant. You can be sure I'll be spending time listening to both corporeal and spiritual messages in order to create a smooth transition.

As for today's immediate significance, the moment affirmed my strong belief in the way synchronicity keeps me attuned to the spirituality of the Universe. Today's readings simply reminded me to keep placing my trust in the Universe; to be grateful *now* for what's to come; to recognize what I'm supposed to do to create change in my life; and to accept the contributions of others when offered. If all of this has you scratching your head and thinking I've lost it, again, that's your prerogative. I'm waging, though, there are a lot of you who 'get it'!

∾ ∾ ∾ ∾ ∾ ∾ ∾

So, how did synchronicity play out with my move to Ohio? Allow me to explain:

1. *Fall/Winter of 2021/2022 in Mesa, Arizona: I'd been debating when to contact the realtor about putting my home in the retirement community on the market so I could stay for the winter and be back in Ohio in late spring/early*

summer. When I woke on Tuesday, January 18, I was compelled to call her, so I did and we met to get things rolling. She called me the next day to ask if she could come over with her partner to take photos of my house and to ask if they could show it that afternoon. I arranged to be out of the house at 1 p.m. I was just about to place my lunch order with a waitress when I got a text from her saying the house had sold! The buyers accepted my price (twice what I'd paid for it three years earlier), were paying the full amount in cash and agreed to my closing date in April! Now that's what I call synchronicity!

2. *Fast forward to early May in Ohio. I've been living with my brother and sister-in-law since April 21 as I looked for my new house. It's been several weeks with disappointing results as bid after bid is rejected as 'too low'—due to the competitive market, buyers were bidding way over the asking price and I couldn't keep up. On a rainy Friday, May 6, my realtor and I looked at five properties that were five 'no-gos.' I went home disappointed. I sat down, meditated and put out to the Universe, "Thanks for showing me all those homes today because now, even though I didn't like any of them or get any of the others, I'm that much closer to the house that will be my home." An hour later I found a new home on the listings that was going on the market the next morning. I immediately contacted my realtor and scheduled to see it at 9 o'clock the next morning. By 6 o'clock that evening, my bid was accepted and I was on the way to getting the perfect house for me! I closed on May 27 and have been living in it and loving it for over five months now. No one can convince me that the Universal power of synchronicity doesn't exist!*

Tin Soldiers

(2022)

Tin soldiers and Nixon coming.
We're finally on our own.
This summer I hear the drumming.
Four dead in Ohio.

Gotta get down to it,
Soldiers are cutting us down.
Should have been done long ago.
What if you knew her
And found her dead on the ground?
How can you run when you know?

These are lyrics to the Crosby, Stills, Nash & Young song, *Ohio,* which has been called one of the greatest protest songs of the Vietnam War era. Neil Young's haunting words evoked the mood of outrage that had befallen the nation after the shooting of four students at Kent State University on Monday, May 4, 1970. It's one of those moments in history that people ask, "Do you remember where you were when you heard about the Kent State shootings?"

Well, I absolutely remember where I was because I watched the National Guard deploy from their armory in downtown Warren in convoy fashion to drive the thirty miles to Kent State University that morning. I was twenty years old, the same age as many of the students enrolled at Kent—I had friends who attended the university. So you can imagine my shock at seeing these military vehicles converging on that campus. What the hell was going on?

You have to remember, it was 1970. No Internet. No cell phone videos. No social media. No instant news, real or fake. I was working in the Loan Department on the third floor of Second National Bank across from Courthouse Square in downtown Warren, Ohio. When I'd come in that morning, I went to the cafeteria on the lower floor first to get a cup of coffee and was surprised to see two loan officers there dressed in full National Guard garb. Their macho egos where on full display as they boasted about being "called up."

"Where are you going?" someone asked them.

"To Kent...to the university. Some protesters are causing trouble," they replied, swaggering back and forth.

"The university? Are you kidding?" a few of us responded, as the two buffoons sashayed to the elevator. Why did they even bother to stop at the bank if they didn't have to work? The answer to that was simple—to show off!

When I got to the loan department, a number of transistor radios had been turned on and we spent the morning trying to pick up stations that might be reporting on what was happening at Kent. Evidently, a peace rally had been officially scheduled for noon to protest the expansion of the Cambodian Campaign by President Nixon on April 30. No details as to what prompted sending in the National Guard— it would take months of investigation and years of analysis to answer that question. In the moment, however, the state and the nation were getting fragments of information that only increased our anxiety.

We were speechless as we stood by the windows and watched that convoy leave Warren to advance on the unsuspecting little town of Kent. Unbeknownst to us, other battalions of the National Guard were also being deployed there from the Cleveland area and other bases in Ohio. Around 1 p.m., we started hearing stories on the radios of shooting on campus. Still no details until later that afternoon when sporadic reports of some student deaths were reported. Was there truth to these reports or were they just rumors and exaggerations? Could this really be happening in Ohio, at Kent, just forty-five minutes away? It wouldn't be until the evening news that the full stories and verifications confirmed the worst-case scenario—four students had been shot down at various locations on the campus, some not even participating in the rally, and an undetermined number had been injured.

What you have to realize is that Kent State University was basically a commuter school in 1970--most of the students lived nearby, commuted to and from their homes during the week and had been away for the weekend. Those returning to campus on Monday morning were unaware of incidents of unrest that weekend in the town itself. They didn't know the peace rally that had been scheduled the previous Friday for noon that day had been cancelled that morning. Some weren't even aware a rally was to take place— they were simply back for the grind of classes. They may have bypassed the knoll where students were still gathering, or they may have stopped out of curiosity. They didn't know a "perfect storm" was looming.

The rest, as they say, is history and I don't need to relate it word for word, incident for incident, here. Just like with any situation of this magnitude, experiencing it from your little corner of the big picture makes it impossible to know the whole story until you step back from it. What is it they say, "You can't see the forest from the trees," right? I lived through that day and its aftermath from a close-up perspective. It wasn't until twenty-three years later that I was able to step back from the trees and see the whole forest.

It was 1993 and I was enrolled at Youngstown State University where I was finally going to get a college degree in my early forties. I was in a mandatory American History class and, let me tell you, I really felt the age difference between me and the other college students—we were studying periods in our American history that I had lived through myself! I had more in common with the professor than those students! Anyway, we were given an assignment to pick one of a dozen contemporary events that the professor had selected and write an in-depth analysis. The paper was to discuss both sides of the issue and give a personal evaluation and opinion. I chose the Kent State shootings.

I'm not going to go into detail here about my findings—I wish I still had my composition to share because I got an 'A' on it. Suffice it to say that a lot had happened on many different levels, from many different viewpoints, for many different reasons—all of which escalated to the powder keg that exploded on that campus that afternoon. I will say that my personal opinion was that Governor Rhodes should *not* have ordered the National Guard to go to Kent State University. Many of the troops sent—most of whom were the same age as the students and were students themselves—had spent that weekend and the weeks prior controlling a wildcat teamsters' strike near Cleveland. They were tired, stressed and overburdened— not a good combination when facing a group of riled college students on their home field. It was an accident waiting to happen.

Why did I feel compelled to write this essay just for this book? A month ago, my friend Kathy and I stopped at Kent State University on our way to our 55th high school reunion. I'd been to the memorial on campus a couple of times, but she'd never seen it. Walking the grounds, seeing the monuments where the four students had fallen, touring the visitor center and watching the 30-minute film summarizing the events—everything brought back the emotions associated with the shootings. So, if I'm sharing events in my life that affected who I am as a person, this would be one of them. Living through it stamped the anger, sadness and fears indelibly on my heart and soul. The realization that, *That could have been me—that could have been one of my friends,* lingered for months. I shouldn't have been thinking about my mortality at the too-young age of twenty, but I was. So, yes, I had to write this essay, if for no other reason than to purge any residual emotions from my psyche.

What about you? What major event that you've lived through and been affected by needs to be purged from *your* psyche? Why not grab a pad and pen, then write about it—you'll feel better for it, I promise.

Whodunit?

(2022)

Our bed-and-breakfast hotel sat in the middle of a neighborhood of quintessential Victorian structures in Cape May, New Jersey, the only city in the United States wholly designated as a National Historic Landmark due to the predominance of said Victorian architecture. But my friend, Diane, and I weren't there to tour the city's historical sites—we were there to solve a murder.

It was the summer of 1980-something and we had arrived at our hotel late on Friday afternoon. The exterior of the hotel showcased the typical gingerbread scrollwork and ornate decoration prevalent in its style, and that extravagance carried into the interior. Wallpaper with profuse patterns of flowers and birds assaulted our eyes while large pieces of carved oak, mahogany and rosewood furniture created a claustrophobic feel to the place. Our room felt like a briar patch with its enveloping displays of roses on the walls, floor and bedding. It's no wonder I prefer minimalistic contemporary home décor after spending two nights in that oppressive environment.

After we settled in, we followed the instructions to meet our fellow "detectives" at one of the larger homes for a briefing on the weekend's events. An air of anticipation permeated the large dining room as strangers became acquaintances. Whispered conversations increased in volume when the unfamiliarity waned, creating a more relaxed informality in the congregation. As dessert was being served, our host stood to address us.

"Welcome to our Cape May 'Murder to Go' weekend adventure!" he exclaimed, which got an immediate round of applause from the enthusiastic audience. Yes, Diane and I were attending this latest creation of playwright and screenwriter, David Landau—interactive mystery plays. And what a weekend it was!

I'm going to spare the play-by-play details of that weekend because I could never capture in enough words what all transpired nor can I recall those details after almost forty years. However, I recently found buried in a file the four-page, full-color article from *Life Magazine* that covered the event—and it triggered memories that I haven't thought about in years. Those memories weren't just of the event itself but of the bond that Diane Bowden and I shared and how easily we'd gone from co-workers to friends.

We met in 1978 when I moved back to the New York area and got a job as traffic coordinator at Falcon Steel Industries in Montvale, New Jersey. Diane was the nineteen-year-old receptionist, nine years my junior. It was a small office with four other employees, named Milt, Jim, Austin and Jerry (owner, traffic manager and two salesmen). Despite the difference in our ages, Diane and I clicked and complemented each other. Over the years we've travelled together, hosted "Game Night" parties, played *lots* of cards (to her mother's chagrin!) and even roomed together for a few months until I found my own place when I followed her to the Chicago area. It's been forty-four years since we met in that office in Montvale, and during all those years she's been there for me. Whether I've needed a gal-pal to pat my back as I cried on her shoulder or a partner-in-crime to laugh with—and we've done a lot of laughing!—Diane has never left me hanging.

As I study the photos in that magazine article, I can see our faces in the crowds that surrounded the murder scenes and during the "whodunit" reveal. Were we really that young? Oh, well! Regardless, whenever we get together, we revert back to those laughing young women as we shuffle the cards for yet another game of Spite and Malice. (Sorry, Mrs. Bowden!)

Writing Prompts

(2022)

As a writer, I find that being given an assignment of *what* to write about, like homework, helps take the onus off me to find that interesting topic—I simply do what I'm told and the words seem to flow. Recently, while cleaning out my books in anticipation of my upcoming move from Arizona to Ohio, I came upon a book of writing prompts called "642 Things To Write About." Now, that's a lot of prompting!

Skimming through the book, I discovered that I hadn't been as motivated to write as I thought I would be when I bought the book— I only did thirty-six of them! Some of my responses were quick phrases or lists. The prompts requiring a fictional response were my most challenging because that's not my genre of choice, but there were those that I found insightful or creative. I thought I'd write this essay to share them with my readers just to let you peak into the mind of a writer trying to exercise her writing muscles. Also, why don't you "play along" and try writing *your* responses to the prompts?

You are an astronaut. Describe your perfect day.

I've seen the universe in ways most humans could never imagine. I've felt as small as a grain of sand and as large as the world. So my perfect day involves being in a movie theater alone or with some good friends. We're going to watch the entire Bourne series of movies first. Then after a leg-stretching bathroom break, we watch all of the Abbott and Costello movies. We end the day watching "The Champ" with Jon Voight. There's laughter and tears. But mostly there's closeness and a sense of being near things.

I spend enough time in my job feeling the expansiveness and infinity of the world. My perfect day is about putting up the walls and boundaries. I don't want to see forever. I want to see the walls and edges and feel like I'm inside instead of outside.

What could have happened to you in high school that would have altered the course of your life?

The nuns were insistent that I take the math courses that would get me admitted to college. I was insistent that I wasn't going to college. I was going to join the Women Marine Corps. It wasn't that I'd always dreamed of being in the military—I just saw it as a way to get a college education without costing my parents anything. I even went to the Marine recruiting office to learn about their college program and how much time I'd have to commit to serve.

Then, my Aunt Emma called from California and asked if I'd want to live with them while attending Pasadena City College. Seventeen-year-old high school senior, southern California, two-year college—that was an easy decision!

But, what if she hadn't called me…

You bring someone back from the dead. Who is it?

Dad, so I can have the kind of conversations with him that I had with Mom. He died when I was twenty-nine, before I had evolved from my twenty-something selfishness to my adult introspectiveness. I want to know what his dreams were as a young man. Did he want to play baseball professionally? What was it like to catch for Satchell Paige during that public relations promotion for the Negro League? Who were his heroes? What did he think when he first met Mom?

You get to be any singer you choose and sing one song in a live concert.

I'm Bette Midler and I'm singing, "The Wind Beneath My Wings," because it's the song I associate with my mom and the metaphor I created for us—I'm the falcon and she's the falconer. She's the wind beneath *my* wings. As I sing it, Mom's spirit fills the concert hall and then manifests into corporeal form. She smiles at me and we cry with love and joy.

You track down an old boyfriend/girlfriend.

It's been forty-five years since I last saw Thomas McGuire. Finding him on Facebook was a surprise—that I'd actually recognized his photo was incredible. And he's widowed. It took me a few days of thinking and many "almost" posts of the IM before I finally sent the message asking how he was. Even more of a surprise was his immediate reply— "I'm doing okay. How are you?"

Back in my court. What do I say now? This is hardly the forum for summing up forty-five years of my life! And where exactly do I expect this to lead us? "I'm okay, too," I finally reply. Then I'm honest and add, "This is so awkward and unexpected, so I'll make it even more so—here's my phone number—call me—I'd love to talk."

You are a serial killer. What TV shows are on your DVR list? Why?

First and foremost, *Criminal Minds,* so I can keep on top of the FBI's methods and maybe even get some ideas from the "unsubs."

Second would be *Supernatural* because those two guys are after villains that make me look like Pollyanna!

Finally, reruns of "The Mary Tyler Moore Show" to remind me why I prefer killing to the mundaneness of a steady job.

A present from your mother.

My mother gave me Nancy Drew. When I was ten years old she gave me two of her books from her childhood, then bought me more books that totaled fifty-four by the time I'd outgrown them. But Nancy was *literally* my 'best friend' during those years and shaped me into the independent, self-reliant woman that I am today. So thanks, Mom, for the best present—Me!

Re-create your earliest childhood memory.

The aroma of fresh-baked bread and pastries floats through the air from Warren Bakery into the windows of the house next door where I live with my mom, dad and younger sister. I am four-years old. My mom gives me some change, and I walk to the bakery.

There in the glass-enclosed case is the brown square I have my mind set on—a delicious chocolate brownie! I point to the brownie—although I think she knew what I wanted from previous visits—and reach up to hand her the money. She picks up a brownie with a crinkly slip of paper, puts it in a little white paper bag and hands it over the top of the counter to my outstretched hands.

Walking home with that brownie in the little white paper bag is incredibly joyful!

Write a story in which each sentence will begin with a different letter of the alphabet, beginning with the letter A and moving sequentially, i.e., B, C, D, and so forth to Z.

Alex looks at her with surprise and a devilish grin.

Being new to Hawaii, she asks, "Is this Egan's gym?"

"Coming to test for your jiu-jitsu belt?" he teases.

Dare she flirt with him?

Eager to keep his attention, she replies, "Only if you're my tester!"

Feigning alarm, Alex then laughs and leads her to the gym.

"God," she thinks, "am I really walking beside Hawaii Five-0's Alex O'Loughlin?

How will I be able to keep my cool during the testing?"

Inside the gym, kids and adults are warming up for the tests.

Jiu-jitsu is a sport she isn't familiar with.

Keeping to the side of the room, she can feel Alex next to her.

"Looks like we have a full session today," he says.

"Maybe you could join me for coffee afterwards?" he asks.

Not wanting to appear too excited, she nods.

"Oh, yes, that would be nice," she replies and smiles coyly.

Placing a hand on her arm, Alex looks her in the eyes and says, "Good!"

Quickly, he goes to the locker room to change into his Gi.

Racing heart and quick breaths kept her standing quietly by the wall.

Soon the belt testing begins as Egan calls out moves and checks students' forms.

Too often, she finds herself watching just Alex as he helps the students.

Under two hours later, the testing and the belt awards ceremony end.

"Victory!" Alex yells with the rest of the group as he walks over to her.

"Wait right here while I change, okay."

"X-ray eyes would be nice now," she thinks unabashedly as he heads for the locker room.

"You ready—oh, by the way, what's your name?" Alex asks when he rejoins her.

"Zelda."

Poems

Poems are written with a special cadence, whether rhyming or free form, therefore I suggest that you read them aloud to better appreciate them. There's a certain liberty taken with grammar and punctuation—poetic license!—in order to create that cadence. I've always thought that less is more, and this holds true for how poems can tell a story so succinctly.

The End of a Beginning: In Memory of Robert F. Kennedy

(1968)

I search feverishly for a light to lead me.
I am lost in a world of gloom, sorrow and desperation.
My heart cries out for a hand to guide me.
I know there is something better,
but I'm blinded by the darkness that surrounds me.

And then I see him.

He walks tall and speaks proudly of justice, truth and love.
I follow him eagerly, listening to his every word.
I no longer fear the turmoil in which I live.
He's given me a feeling of security and hope.
His eyes are my guiding light.
His hand reaches for mine with compassion and understanding.
His nearness makes me feel fresh and clean and new!

A burst of fire!

And his eyes no longer shine,
his hands are closed forever.
And I tumble back into the darkness,
and I weep.

‽ ‽ ‽ ‽ ‽ ‽ ‽

I was eighteen years old when Robert F. Kennedy was assassinated. While I wasn't old enough to vote in that year's presidential election, Kennedy was my candidate of choice, the first person I supported politically as an adult, just as my parents had supported his brother John.

I went to bed the evening of June 5th knowing he had won the state of California in the presidential race. My mother woke me up for work the morning of June 6th and told me he'd been shot. I was devastated! I stopped by St. Mary's church on the way to work to pray. The next morning when my mom woke me up again, she told me he'd died. Another stop at the church, only this time I wasn't only sad, I was mad. I asked God, "Why?" I think—no, I know—this was the impetus for my period of religious questioning and the onset of my spiritual awakening.

Divine Interrogation

(1968)

What is God?
God is the wind that caresses the trees,
        the sea that washes to shore,
        the mountains that touch the sky.
He is the bitterness of winter,
        the freshness of spring,
        the warmth of summer,
        and the crispness of autumn.
God is Life.

Where is God?
God is in the wheat fields of the Midwest,
        the rice paddies of China,
        the jungles of Brazil
        and the deserts of Africa.
She is in the cathedrals, the temples,
        the chapels and the mosques.
God dwells in us.

When is God?
God is yesterday, today
        and tomorrow.
He is every minute in the hour,
        every hour of the day,
        every day of the year.
He is the seasons,
        the centuries, the ages.
God is Time.

Who is God?
God is the Creator,

the Protector, the Comforter.
She is the barber, the teacher,
    the executive, the vagrant.
She is man, woman, and child.
God is Everyone.

Why is God?
God is for strength when our hearts grow weary,
    warmth when our hearts grow cold
    and understanding when our hearts have doubt.
He is so the birds can sing,
    the rivers can flow
    and the stars can shine.
She is because we need all the love we can stand,
    with just enough sorrow to know the difference.
God is Love.

How is God?
There is no answer in the minds of Humankind
    as to how there is God.
It is only for God to know
    and us to believe.

⥽ ⥽ ⥽ ⥽ ⥽ ⥽ ⥽

I wrote this in the fall of 1968. Earlier that year, Robert F. Kennedy had been assassinated, and I began questioning my religious beliefs because I couldn't understand how the Catholic God I'd grown up with could let something like this happen. I was an 18-year-old woman who was beginning to form her own adult opinions when he was killed. I changed from idealistic to cynical in the flash of a gun—and I wanted answers. Upon reflection, my disillusioned soul was gifted with these answers, which have held fast for me ever since.

The Beast Within

(1974)

It comes without warning from somewhere deep in my soul,
from some dark, lonely place that harbors unrelenting sorrow.

It surges through me, uninvited, unrestrained,
like a beast running rampant through an unsuspecting village.

Its long, bony fingers clutch at my heart,
strangling it in its cold, unmerciful grasp.

Every fiber of my body recoils in its presence.
The pain. The excruciating pain.

My breaths become gasps. My skin becomes ice.
My nerves are charged to the point of exploding.

Then, from the same dark depths that gave birth to this torment,
comes a scream. An agonizing, wrenching shrill.

It echoes off my bones and surges through my veins,
racing for my vocal chords to be heard beyond the confines of my
body.

Some instinct still untouched by this cruel invader
stifles the sound, forcing it back to the source of its insurrection.

Then, as quickly as it came, the beast is gone.
In its wake are tears and sobs and shards of broken flesh that once
was my heart.

Will the pain of losing him never subside?

Intuition

(1989)

In the time it takes to count to "one,"
I see our lifetime come undone—
Sitting alone, I cry and wait
  through endless years
    of endless nights.
Feeling my love turn into hate.
  His drinking. My anger.
   Our fights.

From deep within I hear a voice
that tells me I must make a choice.
Listen to my mind's direction
  and stop the wedding
    right away?
Listen to my heart's emotion
  and take my chances,
    come what may.

In the time it takes to count to "two,"
I choose my heart and say, "I do."
For three plus years, love is blind,
  but there's just so much
    I can stand.
I finally listen to my mind
  and give him back
    the wedding band.

❧ ❧ ❧ ❧ ❧ ❧ ❧

In September 1988, my husband Stuart and I got a divorce, just two months shy of our fourth wedding anniversary. I wrote this poem on November 24, 1989, which would have been our fifth anniversary.

It tells of the message my intuitive Inner Voice sent me while driving from New York to Ohio for our wedding, with Stuart sleeping off a drunken stupor in the passenger seat. "This is what it will be like if you marry him," It told me. In a matter of seconds, I deliberated, I vacillated, I rationalized. Then I responded with, "But I love him," and I drove on. The poem sums up those four years in twenty-four lines of rhyme. I pay better attention to my intuitive Inner Voice now.

Chicago

(1992)

Chicago. Pulsating. Vibrating. Scintillating.
Captivating. **Chicago.** Rush Street. Magnificent Mile.
Oak Street. You *Make Me Smile.* **Chicago.**
Sears Tower. Water Tower. Money, politics, and power.
Chicago. Ness. Capone. Prohibition.
O'Leary's cow. The conflagration. **Chicago.**
You're the Inspiration. Elation. Sensation.
Jubilation. **Chicago.** The Cubs. The Bears.
The Bulls. The cheers. **Chicago**.
Rushing people in a group.
Rush-hour traffic. Loop the Loop.
Chicago. *Saturday in the Park.* Grant Park.
Lincoln Park. Comiskey Park. **Chicago.**
Museums. Restaurants. Theater.
Art. Music. Architecture. **Chicago.**
Old Town. Chinatown. Greek Town.
Toddlin' town. **Chicago.** *Colour My World.*
Blues bars. Gold Coast.
Green Door Tavern. White Sox.
Chicago. Meigs Field. Soldier Field.
Wrigley Field. Marshall Field. **Chicago.**
Only the Beginning. U. of I. U. of C.
Northwestern University. **Chicago.**
Energetic. Dynamic. Fantastic. Romantic.
Chicago. C.T.A. What a beat!
Rockin'. Singin'. Dancin' feet.
Chicago. *Twenty-five or Six to Four.*
Windy City, je t'adore. **Chicago.**
Oprah. Opera.
Frank Sinatra's "My Kind of Town Chicago is"…
et*Cetera*, etc., etc.

≈ ≈ ≈ ≈ ≈ ≈ ≈

I wrote this poem to celebrate the rock band Chicago's 25th anniversary and my favorite metropolitan city where I lived from 1989 to 1991. In October 1992, I sent the poem, an anniversary card for the band and a birthday card for my favorite musician, Robert Lamm, in a package to the Front Row Theater in a suburb of Cleveland, Ohio, and asked them to present it to the band when they arrived for a concert that month. I attended the concert as a birthday present with my brother and sister-in-law. After the show, we waited outside to get autographs and see the band board their touring bus. I stretched my arm through the crowd and handed my copy of the poem to Robert Lamm who signed it quickly and sent it back through the fans. Then my brother and I stood behind a barrier and I called a roadie over to us.

"Can you do me a favor?" I asked.

"I'm sorry, but you can't talk to the band members," he immediately replied.

"No, I don't want to talk to them. I sent them a small gift by way of the front desk. Can you please ask them if they received it?"

"Sure...hang on," and he walked to the bus and boarded it.

As I was gawking around, my brother elbowed me and pointed. Robert Lamm had gotten off the bus and walked halfway to where we were standing.

"Yes, we got the poem and the cards. Thanks a lot!" He smiled and waved, and I said something like "Blah-blah-blah-blah," although my brother assured me I responded with a friendly "You're welcome...and great show tonight." Even a 43-year-old woman can be a groupie!

Moments

(1992)

Working diligently one afternoon,
I rearrange the living room and call her to see it—
      but in a second,
I remember she is gone, that I can't share it with her.

Sitting at Grandma's kitchen table,
I turn to where she always sits as a thought crosses my mind—
      but in the blink of an eye,
I remember she is gone, that I can't share it with her.

I forget the name of a character on *Guiding Light*,
and I think to myself, "Mom will know it"—
      but in an instant,
I remember she is gone, that I can't share it with her.

I run into relatives we've not seen in years,
and say to myself, "Wait until Mom hears about this!"—
      but in that same breath,
I remember she is gone, that I can't share it with her.

So many trivial, inconsequential moments.
But moments are like threads that weave together,
      creating the tapestry of our lives.
And moments take on special meaning when shared with someone
you love.

Yet, the spark, the enjoyment,
the spontaneity of these moments
      are lost to me forever
when I remember she is gone, that I can't share them with her.

It is at these moments that I miss her the most.

❦ ❦ ❦ ❦ ❦ ❦ ❦

I wrote this on June 14, 1992—188 days after the death of my mother—after a particularly sad moment of missing her.

Oreo Cookies

(1996)

I eat Oreo cookies whole and complete.
I don't twist them apart.
I don't lick the cream filling
then eat the chocolate wafers.
I eat Oreo cookies whole and complete.

I don't drink milk.
It can flavor my coffee,
soften my cereal,
and fluff my mashed potatoes,
but I don't drink milk.

I do dunk my Oreos in milk.
I plunge the cookie in the glass,
my thumb and forefinger skimming the surface,
as tiny brown flecks speckle
the opaque white liquid.

Dunking an Oreo is an art.
Retrieve too soon, and it's too hard.
Submerge too long, and—plop!
I test it with a pinch: gooey on the outside,
yet firm in the center.

Placing the morsel upon my tongue
like a communion wafer, I close my mouth.
No chewing. No biting.
I just savor the feel of it
between my tongue and palate.

Cocoa and lactose scents caress my nostrils.

Mushy pulp oozes around my teeth.
My mouth salivates,
my jaw gyrates,
and my tongue licks my lips.

The Oreo cookie,
still whole but transformed,
dissolves
and fills me with delight.

If you want to love me,
love me like an Oreo cookie—
whole and complete.
Don't twist me apart.
Don't dissect me, keeping what you like
and trying to change the rest.

Love all of me.
Love the hard and soft of me.
Love the in and out of me.
Taste me. Savor me.
Delight in me.

Then,
if you want to love me,
if you want to be
the milk that melts my heart,
I'll submerse myself in you—
wholly and completely—
like an Oreo cookie.

This poem received an honorable mention award in the Poetry category at the Midwest Writer's Conference in Canton, Ohio, in 1998. I dictated it into my tape recorder on the way home from a poetry class one day when the words just came to me unbidden.

Sleep's Back Door

(1996)

His body slouches in the threadbare recliner,
resisting the sweet temptations of Sleep.
His eyes struggle to stay open, barely able
to focus on the eleven o'clock news.
His body, mind and emotions feel numb
from hours spent at his ex-wife's bedside.
He lingers on the fringe of consciousness, thanking
God for sparing her life and relieving her pain.
If only he'd not caused her heart so much pain!
If only he could rewrite their lives so he could
earn her trust and deserve her love once more!
He falls at last under Sleep's hypnotic powers.

Sometime during the still June night—
as his father and mother lie sleeping down the hall;
as his beloved recovers in her hospital room;
as his children dream of pleasurable pastimes—
the fragile nerves in his heart go haywire.
Blood pulsating through his veins stops pulsing.
Oxygen coursing through his brain stops flowing.
Life surging through his body stops—
Death takes him out through Sleep's back door.
His mother discovers him early that morning,
his blue eyes closed and forever unfocused,
his body slouched in the threadbare recliner.

∾ ∾ ∾ ∾ ∾ ∾ ∾

*This poem was written for a poetry class at Youngstown State
University and is in memory of my father, Frank Anthony Nyitrai,
who died of a heart attack in his sleep on June 16, 1979. He had*

fallen asleep in a recliner at his parents' apartment, after visiting my Mom in the hospital. She'd been in since Monday when she had a tumor removed from her right lung. They were separated at the time, but amicable, so he held vigil over her hospital bed all week. We got the "all clear" from the doctor for Mom that Friday and Dad passed away in the wee hours of Saturday morning.

The Blister

(1996)

The glass slipper magnified the palm of her hand.
She held it gently, careful not to drop it
on the wooden floor where it would shatter
into thousands of shimmering slivers.

She gazed into the slipper
as if it were a crystal ball,
seeing images of the evening past
flicker in its iridescence…

Her stepsisters,
flitting to and fro,
their gaudy gowns crinkling
like crumpled paper when they walked.

Her stepmother,
trying one last time to convince her to join them
while herding her daughters to the carriage
like a mother goose with her goslings.

Her godmother,
arriving uninvited,
satin gown and glass slippers in hand,
insisting she attend as well.

So much for a quiet night at home alone!
So much for sitting by the fire
with a glass of Chablis
and a good book!

She donned the gown,

and stepped into the slippers,
feeling a pinch
in her left heel.

The royal ball.
Music flowed, candlelight glowed,
and guests showed off their finery,
wondering which eager maiden would win the prince's fancy.

The prince.
A handsome man, for sure.
Tall and lean and muscular.
His hair, the color of raven's feathers.
His eyes, the sheen of his Toledo sword.
His smile, the luster of flawless pearls,
beguiling, transforming even matrons into giddy girls.

His personality—
alas, dull.
Shallow and vainglorious.
Boring and boisterous,
at least, in her opinion.

She endured dancing with him until,
at the stroke of midnight,
she could endure no more.
"A headache. So sorry!" she declared,
fleeing from the ballroom,
running down the palace steps,
losing her left slipper in her haste…

The clop of hooves on cobblestones,
the squeak of carriage hinges,
the rap of a brass knocker—
brought her out of her reflective state.

The prince had arrived,
searching for a bride to fit the lost shoe.
She need only present its mate
and the prince and his kingdom would be hers!

She gazed again into the glass slipper,
looking for a sign.
As she paced the bedroom floor,
the blister on her left heel throbbed.

"They don't fit me anyway,"
she thought, as she loosened her hold.
The slipper shattered on the wooden floor
into thousands of shimmering slivers.

⇝ ⇝ ⇝ ⇝ ⇝ ⇝ ⇝

I wrote this poem just for fun—no class assignment. It's my fractured take on a popular fairy tale.

Who Will Stop the Rain?

(1996)

Rain hits the roof
like BB pellets spilling on a linoleum floor.
It's the kind of rain that makes my toenails grow.
Standing on the porch, I inhale the smell of steamy pavement.
Cool water penetrates the skin of my outstretched hand
and tastes like acid when I lick my fingers.
I hear seedlings struggling to break the soil's surface
in the water-soaked geranium pots.
Credence Clearwater Revival's *Who Will Stop the Rain?*
echoes in the back alleys of my mind,
and I remember London in the spring.
I've never been to London in the spring.
I wish I could someday.
I wish I could play Mozart on piano
or prestidigitate like Copperfield.

If the rain continues on forever, I'll sprout fins.
I'll swim to Australia and waltz with Matilda.
Doing somersaults across the rooftops,
I'll travel through town and through time.
One day, I'll meet Keanu Reeves
and cartwheel to the moon and back.
Thunderous clouds of judgment pass sentence
on the populace, electrifying the air with silence.
Oh, satanic rain, you wash away the sins of the world!
Mea culpa, mea culpa, mea culpa.
Rain keeps tumbling down,
daring me to step into his embrace.
So, I skip barefoot through his puddles
and feel my toenails grow.

℣ ℣ ℣ ℣ ℣ ℣ ℣

I wrote this poem for a Poetry class. We were instructed to follow the template below, using as many prompts as possible in the same order. Skipping one or two is allowed though—I skipped 13-15 and combined 16 and 17.

Jim Simmerman's Template for Poem Construction

- Begin the poem with a metaphor.
- Say something specific but utterly preposterous.
- Use at least one image for each of the five senses.
- Use one example of synesthesia (mixing the senses).
- Use the proper name of a person and a place.
- Contradict something you said earlier in the poem.
- Change direction or digress from the last thing you wrote.
- Use a word (slang?) you've never seen in a poem.
- Use an example of false cause-effect logic.
- Use a piece of "talk" you've actually heard (preferably in dialect and/or a word that you don't understand).
- Create a metaphor using the following construction: "The (adjective)(concrete noun) of (abstract noun).
- Use an image to reverse its usual associative qualities.
- Make the persona or character in the poem do something he/she could not do in "real   life."
- Refer to yourself by nickname and in the third person.
- Write in the future tense so seems to be a prediction.
- Modify a noun with an unlikely adjective.
- Make a declarative assertion that sounds convincing but that finally makes no sense.
- Use a phrase from a language other than English.
- Make a non-human object say or do something human. (personification)
- Close the poem with a vivid image that makes no statement, but that "echoes" an image from earlier in the poem.

Counterpoint to Szymborska's Four in the Morning

(1997)

The hour from night to day.
The hour from innocence to wisdom.
The hour for those who contemplate.

The hour swept clean to the crowing of cocks.
The hour when the universe absorbs us.
The hour when wind blows from invisible stars.
The hour of and-what-if-everything-begins-with-us.

The wondering hour.
Still, fertile.
The pivot point of all future hours.

One can feel good at four in the morning.
If some don't feel good at four in the morning
--feel pity for them. Five o'clock comes soon enough,
and we go back to living.

Four in the Morning

by Wiskawa Szymborska

The hour from night to day.
The hour from side to side.
The hour for those past thirty.

The hour swept clean to the crowing of cocks.
The hour when earth betrays us.
The hour when wind blows from extinguished stars.
The hour of and-what-if-nothing-remains-after-us.

The hollow hour.
Blank, empty.
The very pit of all other hours.

No one feels good at four in the morning.
If ants feel good at four in the morning
–three cheers for the ants. And let five o'clock come
if we're to go on living.

*We read this poem in a Poetry class at Youngstown State
University, along with many others. That night, we were instructed
to write a poem that shared some of the elements of one of the
poems we'd read. My counterpoint poem precedes this one.*

Finest Glory

(1997)

Learning to swim at twenty-five;
    then, fencing at thirty-one.
        Donating blood so someone survives.
          Touring Great Britain alone.

Asking a guy to a wine-tasting bash—
    a true "new woman" trait.
        But, better yet, not being abashed
          when he comes with his very own date!

Changing careers at forty-two
    to attend university.
        Loving the academic milieu—
          an English major I'll be.

Discarding the "old," and discovering the "new."
    Meditating and doing Tai Chi.
        Enriching my life by expanding my views.
        Recognizing the God-life in me.

These moments, and more, I'm proud of, you see.
    These moments *are* me somehow.
        So, in choosing my moment of finest glory,
          I submit that that moment is now!

ℒ ℒ ℒ ℒ ℒ ℒ ℒ

Instructed to write a poem for a Poetry class about an incident that exemplified one of our finest moments, I wrote this one because I couldn't choose one moment when I've been blessed to have so many!

If Children Ruled the Earth

(1997)

Imagine that, for a time or so, children ruled the Earth,
    and their one decree was, *"All must act as we.*
The world will be one playground, a place of joy and mirth,
    and everyone upon it will be free."

At first, we would be hesitant to venture from our nooks,
    huddled safe in our familiarity.
But soon some would step forward, bearing cautious looks,
    drawn out by their intense curiosity.

Before too long we'd find ourselves playing, side by side,
    with those that share our special interests.
Diversities in language, culture, politics—and pride—
    no longer act as barriers to our quests.

The adversities of Yesterday—well, they would be no longer,
    and Tomorrow would be miles and miles away.
The attraction of the Present would prove to be much stronger
    when we learn to live our lives day by day.

Earth would resound to the heavens in a cacophony of voices
    as our laughter and our singing fill the air.
We'd acknowledge both our differences and affinity of choices,
    recognizing in ourselves the bond we share.

This bond is known by many names—God, Allah, Christ or Tao—
    but a rose by any name is still a rose.
This unifying spirit, which children sense somehow,
    is the magic that creates friends from our foes.

The world would be a peaceful home if nations forget to fight,

involved, instead, in creating a place of worth.
We'd learn to forgive, exist for Now and live in constant delight
if, as children, we could learn to rule the Earth.

❧ ❧ ❧ ❧ ❧ ❧ ❧

I wrote this after my nieces and nephew spent a weekend at my house. They keep me grounded and help me remember to live in the present moment and find joy in everything and anything. Their simplistic way of being teaches me such complex lessons of Life, Love and God. They are my angels, my spirit guides, my gurus.

Ten

(1997)

I'm ten! I'm ten! I'm ten! I'm ten!
I'll never be one digit again!
It's not that that's so very bad.
My life so far has made me glad.

Aunt Susie came to join the fun
in Germany when I turned one.
And number two was quite a drama
as I discovered Alabama.

By the time that I was three,
my brother, Michael, had joined me.
My fourth was in a brand-new town.
Grandma Glo and Sandy lived two doors down.

When I was five, I started school.
The teachers learned I was no fool.
And in the year that I was six,
my sister, Rachel, joined the mix.

In the years of seven and eight,
I mastered baseball, cycling and skates.
I'd have to say that being nine
has suited me so very fine.

But now that I am turning ten,
I'm crossing a bridge I won't cross again.
It goes from the Land of Number Midgets
to the wonderful Land of Double Digits!

In Double Digit Land, you see,

there are many more numbers I will be!
In three short years, I'll be a teen.
Mom and Dad groan—what does *that* mean?

Twenties and Thirties and Forties and more!
By then, I won't even want to keep score.
So from now until I'm ninety-nine,
I'll live a good life and have a good time.

Then, in two thousand eighty-seven,
before I take that trip to heaven,
with snow-white hair and wrinkled hands,
I'll visit Triple Digit Land!

∾ ∾ ∾ ∾ ∾ ∾ ∾

I wrote this poem for my niece Christina's tenth birthday. When I was 12, my Aunt Toni wrote this similar poem for me:

Dear Susan,

Today you are twelve—how time does fly!
It seems by a day since we heard your first cry.
You came into our lives on a bright autumn day.
Yes, into our lives and our hearts, too, to stay.
To see you today, so grown up and tall,
It just doesn't seem that you ever were small!
But deep in my heart there's a picture I hide.
You're running to greet me with arms stretched out wide.
So if there are times that I taunt you and tease
It's 'cause years do not matter—you're my little niece!

Aunt Toni

Ever Watching

(1998)

High above and all around us,
Never, never far away,
They are watching, ever watching,
Ever with us still today.

In the wind that brushes by us.
In the sunshine on our hair.
In our hearts, we feel them beating.
In our minds, we know they're there.

How we long to hear their laughter!
How we wish to see each face!
Oh, so close, yet, oh, so distant!
How we yearn for their embrace!

Sensing how we miss their presence.
Seeing how our lives transpire.
These two friends high up in heaven
Get together and conspire.

"Let us bring our girls together,
And some good times they will spend.
Let them feel our love abounding
Through a friendship without end."

So it happens on that morning,
In a classroom, chair by chair,
Barb and Susan, reacquainted
After some odd twenty years.

First some small talk, then some girl talk,

Then some talking from the soul.
Each fulfilled within the other
Something that would make her whole.

A nine-hour lunch. A birthday party.
A week in Jersey and one in Maine.
Countless hours of loving moments.
Never would we be the same.

There's a bond that lasts forever
Known as mother and daughter.
Through our friendship, they join with us
In our tears and our laughter.

High above and all around us,
Never, never far away,
Pat and Gloria, ever watching,
Ever with us still today.

∾ ∾ ∾ ∾ ∾ ∾ ∾

I wrote this poem for Barb Murray Heiss for her 50th birthday. Our mothers were close friends and both had died. Barb and I hadn't seen each other in over twenty years, having gone our separate ways, living different lifestyles. We met again in a Sociology class in January 1994 at Youngstown State University—and fast became close friends like our moms had been. We truly believe that our moms, Pat and Gloria, pulled some strings from on high to bring us together again.

Night of the Round Table

(1998)

One by one, or in pairs, they come,
      driving their forged steel carriages.
The lady of the manor greets them at the door,
      takes their coats, directs them down
Into the basement. Divorcees, widows and some
      still united by the bonds of marriage,
they gather at the round oak table. Their banter
      is eager and friendly, witty and loud.

With piles of quarters laying before them,
      each hopes the cards will give *her* the advantage.
The dealer shuffles like a veteran gambler,
      calls for antes and deals the cards all around.
For hours they play, body parts going numb.
      Gossip flowing in a steady barrage.
Quarters change hands—some have more,
      some none—but regardless, good spirits abound.

Halfway through the evening, hunger overcomes
      them. The hostess serves open-faced sandwiches,
coffee and soft drinks and dessert du jour—
      pineapple cake baked upside-down.
The game soon continues. The room
      becomes smoky from Benson & Hedges.
Though weariness sets in, the ladies play on for
      several hours, until the final showdown

At midnight when they each get one
      last deal. No one gets rich,
but it seems not to matter.
      Friendship's the prize without a doubt.

After goodbyes, seven of them head home.
    In a week, though, the refreshed assemblage
will meet at another's house, for nothing deters
    these Ladies of the Table Round.

▬ ▬ ▬ ▬ ▬ ▬ ▬

A poem about my Mom's poker club meeting at her house--eight ladies rotated hosting duties of their weekly game. The most they could lose was a ten-dollar roll of quarters—if they ran out, they played "on poverty" until they were able to win a pot and recoup their losses. They had fun!

Orchids

(1998)

Gnarled and misshapen
     like the roots of an old-world tree,
     Grandma's hands
betray her ninety odd years.

Moving in slow, rhythmic motions,
     they squeeze a purple rubber ball,
     easing her arthritic pain,
pumping blood through purple veins.

Translucent skin,
     stretched across protruding bones,
     resembles the delicate petals of orchids
growing on the hills of Maui.

Massaging a hand in mine,
     fondling loose flesh with my fingers,
     I wonder, so I ask,
"Does the purple ball help at all, Grandma?"

Her blue eyes meet my blue gaze,
     though I'm not sure they see only me
     as she replies,
"Only when I dance the hula."

℞ ℞ ℞ ℞ ℞ ℞ ℞

I wrote this after spending the morning visiting my 92-year-old Grandma Rose and massaging her soft, smooth, arthritic hands.

Pirouettes in Cowboy Boots

(1998)

Deep within my mind,
like old photographs in a shoe box,
dwell the memories,
those fragments of time that
fuse to create our friendship.

IBM and Nynex.
Savin and Xerox.
Falcon Steel.
Pirouettes in cowboy boots.

Casino night. Spite and Malice.
Grandma's finger.
Playing Hearts.
Broken hearts and loving hearts.

A Caribbean cruise. Miami Beach.
Dave and Ken.
West Side Story, Improvisation
and Dutch-treat dinners.

New Jersey, Ohio
and New York.
Connecticut, Atlanta,
and Chicago.

A surprise 30th birthday party.
A Christmas party in July.
Cold beers. Warm welcomes.
A hot fire.

Carrying home a Christmas tree
in Oak Park.
Solving a murder mystery
in Cape May.

Singles Gourmet, personal ads
and blind dates.
Ray and Chuck and Jim and Stuart.
A bartender named Pete.

After-dinner walks
and midnight talks.
Laughing so hard
we'd end up in tears.

Eighteen years of sharing and caring,
laughing and crying, loving and giving.
Eighteen years as work mates,
playmates, roommates and soul mates.

The Scorpion and the Libran.
Where I am aloof, you are convivial.
When I take risks, you take heed.
I acquiesce and you compete
I am abstract to your concrete.

To Fate, I sing my gratitude
for acquainting us,
for recognizing in you the traits
that complement mine.

My light would not shine
so bright today,
my friend, Diane,
had you been absent from my life.

ക ക ക ക ക ക ക

I wrote this poem for my friend Diane Bowden Pricola's fortieth birthday, twenty years after we met at Falcon Steel, a stainless steel brokerage firm in Montvale, New Jersey, where I got a job when I moved back to the tri-state area in 1978. I was the traffic coordinator and she was the receptionist. I was 29 and she was 20, but despite the age difference, we clicked and formed a lasting friendship.

Simply a Playwright

(1998)

Shirt the color of evergreens,
       sleeves rolled haphazardly to the elbows,
              buttoned-down collar opened at the neck.
Slacks the color of desert earth after a misty rain,
       held aloft by a brown leather belt,
              their loose fit giving evidence to their name.
The hair, combed but not impeccably coifed,
       kisses the buttoned-down collar
            and hugs the spectacles as they wrap
               around the curve of the ears.
Silver-haired and
       silver-tongued and
           quicksilver wit.
A statement of non-fashion
       imparting an aura of informality.

Leaning on the podium, never quite still,
       the lightweight form shifts
           from one leg
     to the other
         and back again.
Arms cross and rest on the lectern,
       then separate.
           Then cross,
       then separate.
Fingers fidget and toy with—something—
       an obscure object that demands his attention
           on some subliminal level.
One perceives an aloofness,
       perhaps even a sadness,
           despite attempts at familiarity.

There—that smile.
Enigmatic.
Fleeting.
With cheeks drawn back in deep creases
        and the tips of a shaggy moustache curled upward,
                the face is transformed into a puckish expression
                        that illuminates the stage—
                then evaporates with the flicker of an eye.

The voice,
        hinting of its northeastern roots,
                projects effortlessly to the depths of the theater.
A resonant, throaty, masterful voice,
        with an ever-so-slight nasal quality,
                reminiscent of Victorian tutors and
        William F. Buckley.
Pleasant and smooth,
        it captures the attention of all within its realm.

And emanating from that voice are words,
        wafting through the air,
                creating a verbal vapor that pervades the room.
        Drifting,
                drifting…
The words invade the body,
        penetrate the senses,
                enshroud the mind and soul with images
        so vivid,
                so alive,
they are almost tangible.

Emotions,
        aroused to climactic proportions
                cry out!
Deliciously.

Deliriously.
Leaving one both satisfied, yet unfulfilled,
      all-consumed, yet lusting for more,
           so much more.

I am a playwright,
      nothing more,
           simply a playwright.

Oh, the effrontery!
      The understatement!
Does the sorcerer dare to call himself apprentice?
No, it is a master magician that stands before us,
      conjuring up literary treasures,
           regaling us with histrionic tales,
      our beings overflowing with inspiration and delight.

He casts his spell with hypnotic eloquence,
      and we sit transfixed in its embrace.
Bewitched.
Enraptured.
So much so that at his parting,
      we experience a wrenching at our hearts
           and a rending of our spirits,
giving testament to the genius of this man,
      this playwright,
           this personage known as
Edward Albee.

∾ ∾ ∾ ∾ ∾ ∾ ∾

I wrote this after hearing playwright Edward Albee address the attendees of the Midwest Writer's Conference in Canton, Ohio, in 1998. He absolutely held that audience captive and mesmerized us with stories about his life and his works.

Rachel's Laugh

(1999)

Floating in the sound of Rachel's laugh.
Dancing across the room in Rachel's steps.
Echoing in the song that Rachel sings.
Twinkling in the sparkle of Rachel's eyes.
Mom—is that you?

Imparting a wisdom beyond her six years.
Exuding enthusiasm that infects us all.
Comforting our hearts with one brief smile.
Dealing poker like a riverboat gambler.
Mom—is that you?

But, she is not you, this child so fair!
Unique is she, and all her own.
Yet, glimpses of you, in expressions we see;
In her hugs, her smile, her tenacity.

Dare I give credence to this thought?
The soul, the spirit—so sublime.
Have you, in some wondrous way divine
Returned in part, if not in whole?

I probe my mind for what to know.
I search my heart for what to feel.
And from the depths of my own soul,
You speak the answer that is real.

Yes, Rachel's laugh echoes my own.
Yes, Rachel shares my soul with hers.
As God is part of everyone,
I'm here, in her, and everywhere.

I cannot help but wonder now,
with this new truth revealed to me,
when Michael does his silly jig—
Dad—is that you?

≈ ≈ ≈ ≈ ≈ ≈ ≈

My younger niece Rachel was born in October of 1993, twenty-two months after my mom died. Her Dad and I have noticed uncanny resemblances to our Mom in Rachel's young demeanor and interests—and toyed with the notion that maybe Mom had returned to us as Rachel! I don't really think so, but I have no doubt that their two souls collaborated before Rachel was born and Mom gave her some pointers on how to drive us crazy! Her brother, Michael, who's four years older than her, has hints of my Dad in his physical mannerisms, hence the last verse.

Boxes

(2000)

Boxes.
Everywhere, boxes.
Big boxes and little boxes.
Brown boxes and white boxes.
Boxes with lids and boxes with flaps.
Boxes.

Everywhere.
In my living room,
there's a wall of boxes.
In my basement,
there's a fortress of boxes.
Everywhere, boxes.

The bookcases are empty.
The dresser drawers are empty.
Tabletops and closet shelves.
Desks and cupboards.
All empty.
All in boxes.

A box that once held eggs
now contains my video tapes.
Boxes from the liquor store
now are filled with many books.
Pots and pans and platters
in boxes that held motor oil.

These boxes hold my life.
My life is many boxes.
My life's boxes bear many labels.

Daughter box and sister box.
Student box and worker box.
Friend box and lover box.

I've learned to live outside the "box."
I've learned to value originality.
I live beyond the boundaries
and seek the unknown elements.
I draw from all my boxes
to create the box that's me.

Many boxes and many moves
and many changes in my life.
A life that's filled with many things
in many different boxes.
Everywhere.
Boxes.

ↄ ↄ ↄ ↄ ↄ ↄ ↄ

This is my reaction to packing up my house in Warren, Ohio, the summer of 2000, as I prepared for my trip west. What didn't get sold (most of it) or donated got packed and put in a storage unit, where it sat for four years until I'd settled in a new apartment in Park City, Utah.

The Sweater Red

(2001)

The night I went to bed with Ed
I wore a sweater of bright red.
The sweater red lay on the floor
with bra and pants and shoes and more
between the front and bedroom doors.

"To bed with Ed?
That's what you said?
Or is this a lie that we are fed?"
"To bed with Ed," was my reply.
"To bed with Ed, I'll not deny."

"But tell us how this came to be.
Tell us now, for you can see
to us it's quite a mystery."
"A mystery to me as well,
but listen to the tale I'll tell."

The party at the lodge was fine.
The music. The food. The beer. The wine.
But then it ended, right at nine!
Ended right at nine, you see.
Right at nine—too soon for me!

Where can we go to have some fun?
Where is some fun
'cause I'm not done?
Not done enjoying the night, not me.
Where can we go? was my query.

"To Mulligans," said Ed, I believe.

"To Mulligans," repeated Steve.
To Mulligans we'll take our leave!
At Mulligan's we'll have some fun
Because this evening is not done!

At Mulligans I entered in.
I entered in to quite a din!
The din, it went from door to door
as patrons packed each inch of floor.
I wondered if it could fit more!

I looked around and I could see
amongst the crowded revelry
folks from Deer Valley just like me.
And as I looked from head to head
I saw the head I knew as Ed.

He beckoned me to join him there.
To join him at the bar for beer.
And so we stood and had a brew.
And then we had a brew times two.
A brew times two plus one more, too.

We talked with Blair and Noel and Pat.
We talked with Matt, who drives a CAT.
We talked of this, we talked of that.
And by the time the clock struck one,
we realized we'd had some fun!

"You can't drive home," was what Ed said.
"You can't or you could end up dead.
Come sleep on my recliner instead."
And so we ventured out the door
to walk up Main Street a block or more.

"I'm parked down here," I heard me say.

"You do not want to go that way.
Come with me, with me you'll stay."
Then without warnings or alarms
he held me close within his arms.

And as his lips touched on mine,
I felt a shiver down my spine.
The shiver down my spine was fine.
He kissed me, oh, so passionately,
that in his bed I wanted to be.

Not another word from me,
the rest's our private history.
For tell you more I will not say.
Suffice to say when all is said,
I liked it there in bed with Ed.

ലി ലി ലി ലി ലി ലി ലി

The Story Behind This Poem

(2022)

Ah, yes, my first one-night stand. It was my first winter working at Deer Valley Resort in Park City, Utah. The annual employee mid-season party was held on a Sunday night in mid-January after the busy holiday season had ended. Monday was my day off, so I didn't have to rush home to get a good night's sleep—I wanted to party with my new friends. When the moment came to decide "go home or go with Ed," in that split second I thought, "Go for it, Susan! You're an unattached woman who deserves to enjoy herself!" So I went and I did!

No strings. No relationship. No embarrassment. Just mutual, adult consent to enjoy ourselves—as they say today, we 'hooked up'—in fact we hooked up a couple more times that year before going our separate ways. The next morning, after Ed and I—well, you know! —we walked to a coffee shop down the street from his place, then he walked me to my car in the parking garage.

This poem came to me when I got back to my apartment, while taking a shower. As I was standing under the hot water, I started giggling remembering the party and being with Ed. Had I really done that? Had I actually allowed myself the pleasure of a night of unbridled sex with a guy seventeen years my junior? Oh, yeah—I did that! I laughed out loud. Then the first verse of this poem just came out of my giggling mouth, then the second verse, and after I'd dried off and gotten dressed, I sat down to complete the poem.

Braille

(2008)

Her body is a book in Braille,
and his fingertips read every word,
moving slowly,
       effortlessly,
             thoroughly over it,
                  inch by inch.
Never has she felt so charged!
Never has she experienced
such a sweet pain of desire!

Just when she thinks
she can take no more,
he finds another unread passage,
his touch sending chills and fire
through her body simultaneously.

God, I can endure it no longer!
Yet, even as her thoughts cry out,
her body writhes and arches,
letting him know
she wants him to read on.

And he does.
His lips follow where his fingers tread.
His breath is warm.
His tongue is moist
as it licks a path
       from the base of her neck,
           down her spine,
              to the small of her back.

His hands reach beneath her,
playing with her taut nipples
while his teeth nibble
the soft curves of her buttocks.
She arches her head back,
and a moan escapes her lips.
Now! her mind screams.
   Please, now!

He rolls her onto her back
as if slowly turning a page,
and she pulls him to her,
wanting desperately to satisfy
the primal need deep inside her.

But he continues in his deliberate fashion.
Licking.
  Kissing.
    Touching.
      Fondling.
Electrifying her senses.

His mouth begins to drink
of her sweet, buried nectar,
and she opens herself to his thirst.
Her hunger intensifies.
Her body, mind, and soul fuse and soar,
exploding again,
  and again,
    and again
      until…
   gradually,
  slowly,
she floats back to earth.
Back to the bed, to his arms that hold her
pressed against his long, lean body.

Smiling,
she snuggles her face into his sinewy chest.
Sighing,
she succumbs to the strength of his embrace.
Sleeping.
she knows a serenity that transcends all else.

Until the next time he takes her off of her shelf
        and reads again her sensual saga.

Erotica inspired by "302 Advanced Techniques for Driving a Man Wild in Bed" by Olivia St. Claire (Harmony, 2002)

And the Aspens Weep

(2012)

High above the soil,
Reaching up and spreading out,
The branches of the aspens
      separate into many trees
         of beauty and joy.

Deep beneath the soil,
Reaching down and spreading out,
The roots of the aspens
      entwine as one entity
         of life and love.

A heart that is soiled,
Cutting down and cutting out
Twenty aspen saplings,
      ripped from the sacred soil,
         torn from the embracing roots.

A mind that is soiled,
Slashing down and slashing out
Six mature aspen trees,
      hacked in their prime,
         torn from the embracing roots.

Cries of horror from the soil,
Penetrating down and penetrating up,
Every aspen in the pando
      feels the fatal cuts
         of death and desecration.

And the Aspens weep as one.

& & & & & & &

In memory of the Sandy Hook Elementary School massacre victims—twenty children and six adults. Newton, Connecticut - December 14, 2012

Freedom to Be Me

(2019)

Don't think.
Don't plan.
Don't organize.
Let it flow.

Be impulsive.
Be spontaneous.
Be quick.
Let it flow.

Water flows.
Air flows.
Words flow.
Thoughts flow.

I am impulsive.
I am quick.
I won't plan.
I won't think.

I soar.
I fly.
I float.
I drift.

I let it flow.

I attended weekly sessions of a women's writing group at Unity Church of Mesa the summer of 2019. The facilitator of the group selected poems to read for the evening and we'd discuss them. Then we'd have fifteen to twenty minutes to write something, anything, that the poem inspired from us. Nothing was coming to me and I told myself to just let it flow…and this is what came out of me!

From the Chairs' Perspective

(2019)

Forlorn? Oh, how wrong is he!
We look forward to these hours alone
Without a body weighing us down,
Without the heels of their leather shoes
Leaving scuff marks on our legs.

Usually, the man plops down
And sighs after mowing the lawn,
Placing a sweating glass of iced tea
On the table between us,
His sweaty arms sliding onto our arms.

Soon, the woman joins him,
And sighs after doing the laundry,
Straightening up the bug repellant candle
And matches on the table
Before she sits down and closes her eyes.

Neither one speaks.
She pulls on our arms and lifts up
To align her chair with his, just so.
She's very tidy and very exact.
He's very satisfied with things as they are.

But it's so nice to be empty once again.
The late fall wind blows leaves
That gather in our spines or around our feet.
The last birds of summer fly south
To where the man and woman spend their winters.

We are at peace as we await

The evening's peaceful sunset,
As we look forward to the snow
That will soon settle on our laps.
Vacant? Yes, and loving it!
Forlorn? Oh, no, not us!

The Chairs That No One Sits In

by Billy Collins

You see them on porches and on lawns
down by the lakeside,
usually arranged in pairs implying a couple

who might sit there and look out
at the water or the big shade trees.
The trouble is you never see anyone

sitting in these forlorn chairs
though at one time it must have seemed
a good place to stop and do nothing for a while.

Sometimes there is a little table
between the chairs where no one
is resting a glass or placing a book facedown.

It might be none of my business,
but it might be a good idea one day
for everyone who placed those vacant chairs

on a veranda or a dock to sit down in them
for the sake of remembering
whatever it was they thought deserved

to be viewed from two chairs
side by side with a table in between.
The clouds are high and massive that day.

The woman looks up from her book.
The man takes sip of his drink.
Then there is nothing but the sound of their looking,

the lapping of lake water, and a call of one bird
then another, cries of joy or warning—
it passes the time to wonder which.

❧ ❧ ❧ ❧ ❧ ❧ ❧

We read this poem at a Women's Writing class at Unity Church of Mesa, and it is preceded by my counterpoint poem from the chairs' perspective.

Life Through the Hourglass

(2019)

I'm at a loss
For what to say,
For what to do,
For whom to be.

I'm poised at the neck of my hourglass
With grains of sand
From days gone by
Piling up on the floor below.

With grains of sand
For days to come
Pushing me from up above,
But I'm blocking their flow.

I pause to think of
What to say and
What to do and
Who to be.

I'm at a pivotal point in my life
And Time has stopped
Her grains of sand
And given me a chance

To pause,
To think
Before I choose exactly

What I want to say and

What I want to do and
Who I want to be.

I think it's time
To turn the hourglass over
And shake things up a bit!

❧ ❧ ❧ ❧ ❧ ❧ ❧

I attended weekly sessions of a women's writing group at Unity Church of Mesa the summer of 2019. I wrote this poem during one of the fifteen minute writing periods—it speaks to the adjustment of retiring, moving to Arizona and wondering what this new phase of my life would look like.

Unc

(2019)

Remi Romelo is his name.
Silver haired and
Silver tongued and
Quick-silver wit.

Enjoying life is his game.
Player of trumpet,
Driver of semi rigs,
Canner of hot peppers.

Special uncle is his role.
Thumb-sucking niece
Recalls thumbless hands
Playing silly games.

Exuding fun from his soul.
Devilish laugh and
Zany smile and
Playful ways.

Where have you gone, Uncle Remi?
Do you hear me calling your name?
Do you know how dear to me you are?
Does my love penetrate your coma's veil?

Screaming out to me in desperation,
he's a prisoner held captive within
the confines of his shrinking form
and diminishing mind.

I long for the laughing, loving man

who made this little girl giggle,
who loves life so unconditionally.

Remi Romelo is his name,
But he'll always be Unc to me.

❧ ❧ ❧ ❧ ❧ ❧ ❧

My favorite uncle, Remi Romelo Rechedy, died on April 3, 2003. He was my mom's brother-in-law. He was born without thumbs, yet he played the trumpet in a jazz club and drove an 18-wheeler cross country. I was a thumb sucker as a child, and my Mom and aunt would try to get me to stop by telling me, "Look what happened to Uncle Remi!" He'd wink at me behind their backs and shake his head 'no'—and I kept right on sucking that thumb! After my Grandpa Todd died in 1973 and my Dad in 1979, Uncle Remi became the patriarch of our little family, a role he was born to play!

Goodbye, Sister

(2020)

I'm waiting for my sister to die.
I cry.
I sigh.
I say goodbye
as I wait for my sister to die.

Does she know?
Does she realize death is near?
I spoke to her three days ago
and she didn't say,
"I'm dying."
She didn't say much—
I did the talking.
When I said goodbye, did she know
it was for the last time?

I knew.
I felt it.
I heard it in the few words she did speak.
I sensed it, yet I pretended all was well.
But I told her I loved her
and I missed her
and I got choked up.
So, did she sense on some level why?

The sadness surprises me in waves.
Knowing she's been sick
and knowing she wouldn't get better
is not the same as
knowing she's going *now*.
Knowing she's unconscious

and ventilated
and basically gone.

Yet I'm waiting for her to die.
To breathe her last breath.
Will she have a moment of clarity,
of knowing what's about to happen?
Will she say my name? Or Tony's?
Or will she simply breathe out
one last time?

She's all alone in that hospital bed
in Youngstown.
I'm here in Arizona.
Tony's in Columbus.
There's no one there to hold her hand—
and that makes me sad
and I'm crying again
because *I* don't want to die alone!
God, this sucks so much!

But it sucks more for her
even if she doesn't know it.
Be at peace, Sandy.
Say 'hi' to Mom and Dad for me.
Say 'hi' to all the others who are waiting
for you wherever.

Goodbye, sister.
Goodbye, Tahney.
I love you.

ও ও ও ও ও ও ও

My sister, Sandra Rose Morrell Parry, went into the hospital in early February in 2020. We presumed it was just another round of treatment for various ailments she'd been experiencing since moving into an assisted living facility. I was living in Arizona, so I called her when I heard. She sounded sedated, so we didn't talk for long. I wrote this poem a few days later.

Over the next six weeks, her condition fluctuated from bad to good to in between, until mid-March when her body suddenly shut down completely. Our brother Tony and his wife Patty arrived from Columbus the night of March 13 and were with her throughout that next day. She died a few hours after they left the hospital on the evening of March 14, 2020. I'd like to think she knew they were there and knew it was okay to finally let go and join our parents and grandparents.

Love in Raindrops

(2021)

I sent my love in raindrops.

Raindrops flowing down my street,
    vaporized by the Arizona heat,
        evaporating into the troposphere,
            transforming into eastward-floating clouds.

Clouds eventually drifting over central Ohio,
    bloated with renewed precipitation,
        gushing forth upon the town
            in a pitter-patter of raindrops.

Raindrops mesmerizing two little men
    watching from their living room window,
        being held prisoners indoors
            as clouds release their cargo.

Cargo gently flowing downward,
    splish-splashing into the hearts
        of two mesmerized little men,
            showering them softly with

The love I sent in raindrops.

It was pouring rain one morning here in Arizona, and it made me think of a photograph of my grandnephews, James and Luke, taken from behind as they stood by their picture window watching it rain outside their Columbus home. I imagine my rain ending up as their rain and sent love to them through the raindrops.

Queries

These shorter essays were written for a blog that never materialized, and they're meant to goad you into thinking about the subject matter. The trainer/life coach in me likes to stimulate my readers to think for themselves about certain topics. I think everyone should spend time contemplating their lives in depth, to get to "know thyself" as some guy named Socrates liked to say.

Salieri's Torment

(1982)

SALIERI: *It started simply enough: just a pulse in the lowest registers—bassoons and basset horns—like a rusty squeezebox. It would have been comic except for the slowness, which gave it instead a sort of serenity. And then suddenly, high above it, sounded a single note on the oboe.*

It hung there unwavering, piercing through, till breath could hold it no longer and a clarinet withdrew it out of me and sweetened it into a phrase of such delight it had me trembling. The light flickered in the room. My eyes clouded! The squeezebox groaned louder and over it the higher instruments wailed and warbled, throwing lines of sound around me—long lines of pain around and through me. Ah, the pain! Pain as I had never known it. I called up to my sharp old God, "What is this?...What?!" *But the squeezebox went on and on, and the pain cut deeper into my shaking head, until suddenly I was running—*

dashing through the side door, stumbling downstairs into the street, into the cold night, gasping for life. "What?! What is this? Tell me, Signore! *What is this* pain? *What is this* need *in the sound? Forever unfulfillable, yet fulfilling him who hears it, utterly. Is it* Your *need? Can it be Yours?...*"

Dimly the music sounded from the salon above. Dimly the stars shone on the empty street. I was suddenly frightened. It seemed to me that I had heard a voice of God—and that it issued from a creature whose own voice I had also heard—and it was the voice of an obscene child!

This soliloquy is from Scene 5, Act One, of Peter Shaffer's play, *Amadeus*. I saw it at the Broadhurst Theater in New York City on

May 8th, and this passage so moved me that I bought a copy of the book so I could read and re-read it. I also researched Salieri at the library to find out how much of the story was based on fact.

Antonio Salieri was a modestly successful Italian composer in Emperor Joseph II's court in Austria in the late 18th century. Enter upstart child composer, Wolfgang Amadeus Mozart, whose talent feels like a slap in the face from God to Salieri. The soliloquy is the moment he hears Mozart's music for the first time and can't believe God has given this extraordinary talent to an "obscene child."

I walked away from that play wondering if there's a talent God has bestowed on me that I have yet to discover in myself. At thirty-two years of age, I'm hardly done learning. A lot of artists and famous people didn't achieve fame or recognition until their later years. If I had a choice, what talent would I like to cultivate? A language? Definitely Italian. An instrument? The saxophone, perhaps. I'll have to give this some serious thought.

What new talents would you like to pursue? Have you recently developed a new skill? If so, why do you think you were drawn to this (or any particular) talent? How have you put it to its best use?

Miracles

(2001)

I'm struggling with writing about *miracles*, prompted by a query in my daily meditation booklet, and I'm tempted to abandon the project altogether. Yet perhaps my struggle is a sign that I should continue contemplating this subject. Maybe there's something I need to define or understand that will come out of this exercise, so I will just sit here and type away as my thoughts come to mind.

My first struggle comes from asking whether or not I *believe in* miracles. My immediate response is, 'Yes, how could you not believe in them?' After all, they are around us every day. We read or hear about extraordinary events taking place in medicine, science, rescue efforts, births, near deaths and more. Events that cannot be explained by anything 'natural,' so we attribute them to some supernatural agent.

Growing up a Catholic, miracles were the exclusive domain of God or God's elite emissaries in the form of Jesus Christ, his disciples and saints. The common man or woman would not presume to think they could perform such remarkable works. Does that theory still hold true for me today? I think not.

I think we all have it in us to perform miracles. We just don't have the belief in *ourselves* to do so, at least not the kind we attribute to those early Christians who raised the dead, healed the sick and turned water into wine. So how *do* I perform miracles? On an unconscious level, my body's daily functions are miracles-- breathing, thinking, turning food into energy, moving me from place to place, allowing me to sense the world around me. I am fascinated by my body's ability to heal itself. Have you ever watched a cut heal? Isn't it amazing how the body reconnects the skin layers and seals the wound until you can't even tell where the cut was?

But what miracles have I performed consciously, if any? This one stymies me. I don't know if the things I create and do--writings, crafts, ideas, sports--could be considered miracles. That I could survive a marriage gone wrong. That I could endure the loss of both parents. That I could make the choices I've made and see them through. Are these miracles? For those who can't do them, maybe they are, yet I'm hard pressed to consider them any more than my life experiences.

What of the things that happen in my life that come unannounced and unbidden, but provide me with just what I need at that particular moment? Synchronicities. Some would call them coincidences, but I don't believe that things happen accidentally. The Universe seems to know what I need and when I'm ready to accept help and when I'm not. Rather than say that I believe in miracles, I can honestly say that I believe in synchronicities. If I didn't, I wouldn't have lived so much of my life "letting go and letting God." I've come to trust in the Spirit that guides me. When I truly let go of the need to control and the fears associated with a current situation, I am blessed by those people, events and things that appear "miraculously" in my life to assist or reward me. Ah, yes, those are *my* miracles.

Maybe we need a new word to define the extraordinary things we humans do to separate them from the extraordinary things that occur in nature and in our lives without any human interaction. Mother Nature's creations--sunrises and sunsets, changing tides, blooming flowers and trees, thunderstorms, snowflakes--are miracles in that we can't reproduce them. Yet they are simply natural occurrences of the universe. It's all a matter of perspective.

So, where has this exercise gotten me? I guess I'd have to say that, to paraphrase a familiar saying, "miracles are in the eye, and heart and soul, of the beholder." One person's indifference is another person's awe. We must each determine for ourselves what and when a miracle occurs. But I have no doubt that for all of us, miracles do happen.

How about you—what's your take on miracles? Can you point to incidents in your life that happened miraculously? Would the words *wonders, phenomena* or *marvels* work better for you than the religiously-implied word, *miracles*?

Quote...Unquote

(2005)

Last week, my manager and good friend, Mary Bernasconi, gave me a refrigerator magnet that reads, "WE PLAN...GOD LAUGHS!" This quote isn't new to me, but it is absolutely in sync with my philosophy on life, something that Mary has been learning about me in the past four years since we met. She knows I believe in a "let go and let God" way of planning and operating. Planning for me first involves releasing control of a situation to the Universe, then asking for guidance as to when and what I'm supposed to do to support the Universe's plan, not the other way around. I looked up the origin of this quote today and learned it is from an old Jewish proverb, "Man plans and God laughs." You can find other variations in an Internet search, and others who claim to have come up with it first. Regardless of where it began, I'm sure it will be around for a long time to come.

This quote has been an inspiration for me for decades, as has another quote since 1979. That year, I was hired back to Xerox Corporation's Northeast Region office in Greenwich, Connecticut, by Don Holborn. Don and I started at Xerox together in 1972 in White Plains, New York. I'd eventually transferred with the company to Phoenix in 1975, left the company in the spring of 1976 to spend the summer in Las Vegas and moved back to my home state of Ohio in the fall. When I moved back to New York and Don hired me at Xerox in 1979, I wasn't surprised to learn he'd worked his way up the corporate ladder.

I tell you this because I want you to understand my history with Don and with Xerox. In June of 1979, just a few months after I'd started back there, my father died in his sleep and I had to go home for the funeral and to help my mother because she was in the hospital at the time recovering from major surgery on her lung. Even though I didn't have vacation time built up, Don worked it out for me to spend a couple weeks in Ohio to help my mom.

Then, in September, my aunt called me on a Sunday to tell me that my sister, Sandy, had tried to commit suicide by shooting herself in the head. I immediately called Don to tell him I wouldn't be at work the next day because I had to go to Ohio again. I was in shock, he heard it in my voice and he took over. After asking what airports it would be best for me to fly out of and into in Ohio, he booked my flights, drove from Stamford, Connecticut, to Suffern, New York, with his girlfriend and took me to Newark Airport. Again, he said to take as much time as I needed—we'd work out the time off later. When I got back to my desk two weeks later, there was a 2" x 4" marble paperweight from Don on my desk with the words, "When life gives you lemons, make lemonade." My hero!

These two simple quotes have gotten me through some tough times. They're perfect reminders of how important it is to make the best of bad situations and why we need to laugh, too, when it feels like all hell has broken loose.

Do you have favorite quotes that keep you grounded, that remind you how simple life can be if you let go of the need to control it and trust that everything will work out?

What Frightens You?

(2008)

I think I must have been buried alive in a past life. I think this because I find it difficult to catch my breath when I lay flat on my back. Also, when I'm in a confined space, like the window seat of an airplane, I feel trapped. Sometimes, just being in the dark suffocates me because I can't see out far enough to know that I'm safe—I feel restrained by the blackness. Being in crowds where I can't move my arms or move away from the people—phew! I'm getting hyper just typing about it!

I am of two minds in those moments. One mind panics and makes me try too hard to gasp a breath or get free, which only worsens the situation. *"What if I never get another breath?"* my mind screams. The other mind is trying to create calmness out of the chaos. It's telling me, *"Relax. Slow down your breathing. Inhale...exhale."*

There are words to describe these feelings--*Claustrophobia* is the fear of confined spaces and *Cleithrophobia* is the fear of being trapped. With claustrophobia, the fear is related to actually being in an enclosed space, while cleithrophobia is less about the size of the space and more related to being unable to leave or move. For example, imagine someone being inside of a closet. If this individual had claustrophobia, sitting in the closet would be distressing. In contrast, if the individual had cleithrophobia, he would only experience panic if the closet door was locked. If he could open the closet door, he would likely not experience anxiety.

Another fear I have is heights, also known as *acrophobia.* That's a tricky one for me because it depends on the type of height that affects me, not just the measurement of the height. I'm not afraid of flying, but looking out the window of the airplane and seeing that there's nothing below me—yikes! I'm an "aisle only" person. At an amusement park, I love riding wooden rollercoasters but don't even try to get me on a Ferris wheel. I think it's the difference in the speed of those two rides. I can stand on a mountain and look *out* at a beautiful vista, but I won't get near the edge of that mountain—I have no interest in seeing the Grand Canyon in person, thank you! I can ride an elevator, as long as it's not glass, but if it opens on a high floor near windows, I'm pushing that *Down* button immediately.

I remember watching the movie *The Towering Inferno* (1974) and learning that the highest a firetruck's ladder could reach is around the seventh or eighth floor. I've made sure to only book lower floors in hotels ever since. What's hard to believe, however, is that I've been to the tippy-top of the Empire State Building and the crown of the Statue of Liberty! I think this fear has intensified as I've aged— maybe because I'm wiser and know how crazy it is to be that high, duh! One friend pointed out to me years ago that I could be afraid of heights because subconsciously I want to fly and I'm afraid I'll act on that desire. Heaven help me if that's true! And I'm aware of the dichotomy between fear of heights and identifying myself with the peregrine falcon. Okay, this is getting too confusing—and I'm making myself dizzy!

One of my favorite television shows was *Monk,* who was a former police detective with obsessive issues and phobias exacerbated by the tragic murder of his wife a few years prior to the pilot episode. He claims to have 312 fears and will somberly run through a list of his top ten phobias, from germs to crowds, sometimes changing their order and sometimes overcoming them (heights) to save his assistant's life. While Monk is a fictional character, there are people who unfortunately experience serious phobias, so my intention is not to make light of them.

When I'm experiencing one of the fears I've referenced above, the quieting mind eventually prevails and I return to normal. But what can I learn from these moments? Don't lay flat on my back? Avoid tight places or always carry a flashlight? Stay on the ground? Perhaps. But I think fixing the external factors doesn't really resolve what may be going on at a deeper level. What exactly am I afraid of? The one common element seems to be that I'm not in control or

I'm at the mercy of someone or something else. Now THAT scares me—and irritates me! Maybe it's a mortality thing as I mature—that fear of dying. Or maybe I *was* buried alive or thrown off a bridge in a past life!

How about you? Are there fears in your life that repeat themselves and make you wonder if they are remnants from a former lifetime? Have you examined the meaning at a deeper level? And just what do we do with this insight once we discover it?

On Purpose

(2011)

Did you always know what you wanted to be when you grew up? Have you achieved that dream or are you a 'work in progress?' Me? I used to worry because I never aspired to *be* anything or *do* anything in particular. Oh, as a pre-teen, I wanted to be an amateur detective like my literary friend Nancy Drew. And there was a brief moment my senior year in high school when I wanted to join the Marines and actually talked to the recruiting officer at the local post office. (In hindsight, that may have been me rebelling against the nuns at my school who insisted I had to go to college 'with grades like yours!')

But, in truth, I was never drawn to any one career enough that I wanted to go through the schooling and devote the time to developing in that one area. As I got older and our culture was espousing such concepts as 'finding our life's purpose' and 'following our passion,' I tried to zone in on *my* passion and life's purpose. But they were illusive and hard to define, kind of like reaching for smoke and having it dissipate and shift when trying to grasp it. Instead of taking on a specific role--like teacher or doctor, mother or actor—I ended up following my heart to *places* where I wanted to live and near people who mattered to me at the time. I managed to find jobs that matched my skills and I enhanced those skills over the years so that I could better define the kind of job I wanted to find, but I never *became* something particular. I also enrolled in varied and sundry non-credit classes—fencing; American sign language; painting; boxing; tarot card reading; ballet dancing; acting; improvisational comedy and more--to become a "Jane of all trades, Master of some."

What I did discover is that I have a talent for conducting workshops or classes, and one of my favorite jobs was as an administrative trainer at Xerox Corporation. I realized that I'm not afraid of public speaking; and I liked stimulating people's minds, getting them to have those "light bulb" moments when they learn something new. Consequently, I've conducted a variety of workshops over the years, usually based on books, which have included *The Artist's Way* by Julia Cameron; *Pleasurable Weight Loss* by Jena La Flamme; and, *Younger Next Year for Women* by Chris Crowley & Henry S. Lodge, M.D. My style is not to lecture but to create a participatory ambiance so the students can share their stories related to that week's lesson—adults teaching each other and me!

At one point in my life I identified my soul's journey as being a teacher, then later I expanded that to teacher *and* student. I've come to the realization that my life's purpose isn't about one career or one singular accomplishment. In hindsight—and, now, in foresight—my *life focus* is discovering what my soul wants to learn in this lifetime and my *life plan* is actually learning it.

What about you—did you identify your life's purpose early on and achieve your goal? Have you changed your roles over your lifetime? What do you still want to do or who do you still want to be?

Grandma's Birds

(2013)

Isn't it amazing how the aroma of a particular food can pull a memory out of the attic of your mind? The memory's been tucked away there in some box or pushed into a dark corner under the eaves. Maybe spiders have crocheted cobweb doilies around it.

Today, the waft of a co-worker's fried egg sandwich tickled my nostrils and – poof! The memory escaped, and I returned to my Grandma Rose's kitchen on a Saturday morning where eggs and sausage are sizzling on the stove top. I'm sitting in my chair by the wall, talking to Gino the Parakeet, who's walking around the kitchen table and nibbling on the butter set aside on a little plate just for him. Grandpa Todd is seated at his usual place, putting milk on his corn flakes and checking the baseball scores in the newspaper to see the stats of last night's game when his beloved Cleveland Indians got trounced. And Grandma? She's standing at the kitchen sink, looking out the window at the birds in her backyard.

Grandma's birds were infamous. The word had spread throughout the avian community over the years that the scraps at 1736 Bonnie Brae were to die for. When Grandma threw out morsels of pancakes, sausage, French toast, doughnuts, Easter bread, pasta, birthday cake or other delights, her backyard looked like a scene from Hitchcock's film, "The Birds." Blue Jays. Robins. Blackbirds. Cardinals. And a plethora of brown wrens. Some days, they'd line up on her clothesline or on the garage roof or in the apple tree, waiting to see what scraps were going to be served to them. It was an ongoing joke that eventually those birds wouldn't be able to fly away because they were too chubby.

But, while the backyard was a gourmet restaurant for birds, anyone who was unfortunate enough to be at the receiving end of Grandma Rose's wrath might be threatened with being thrown "out to the birds!" for his or her indiscretion. Grandma may have been a diminutive five foot zero inches in height, but that little Bohemian woman could put the fear of God in people—even Grandpa Todd! One minute, she was all sugar and spice and everything that's nice about a grandmother. But when something "pissed her off" (her words, not mine!), she could rattle off a list of expletives that would make a sailor blush!

Grandma Rose lived to be 103-1/2 years old, dying of old age in 2010. Unfortunately, about five years before she died, my aunt had to move her to an assisted living facility. I wonder how long the birds kept coming back to her backyard after she left, looking for their daily treats. Did they pass on stories to their descendants about the "woman on Bonnie Brae" who served them mouthwatering delicacies?

I have a lot of loving, funny, poignant memories of Grandma Rose in the attic of my mind. And I don't need the smell of a coworker's egg and cheese sandwich to conjure them up. But it's always a delight when one comes bursting out of storage unexpectedly and leaves me feeling nostalgic for those childhood times.

What smells conjure memories for you? I hope they're as savory as mine!

Step Outside Your Box

(2013)

What is it about boxing that appeals to me? I've asked myself that question a number of times since putting on the gloves a few years ago. I was never an aficionado of the sport, except to watch some great movies with boxing as the theme—*Million Dollar Baby, Raging Bull, Girl Fight, The Champ, The Fighter*. But I was looking for some way to 'shake up' my exercise routine, to improve my overall strength and balance while doing some good cardio work. And, being the 'think outside the box' woman that I am, I asked my trainer, Aaron, if he could teach me to box. He told me to buy a pair of gloves with gel-padded knuckles and he'd put me through the drills.

I soon learned that boxing is more than a good left hook or right uppercut. It's leg exercises and jumping rope and core work and machine-gun punching drills. Aaron taught me the correct stances and punches, as I took aim at the big blue mitts he wore to catch my hits. Well, I got what I wanted—I shook up my routine and have been punching away ever since! After a while, he said my punches were strong enough that I should get myself some regular boxing gloves.

About the same time, I discovered a gym in a nearby town where a female professional boxer had set up business and offered classes. So I switched to her gym and bought the girly pink hand wraps and gloves—I was making a statement after all! I spent that summer working out weekly in her classes, sometimes in a real ring. She was one tough cookie! But as winter approached, I didn't want to make the drive to her gym.

Coincidentally, a new trainer at my regular gym was starting a cardio boxing class, so I jumped in. But I didn't particularly enjoy that class. We'd move from one workout station to another in two-minute drills—pushups, punching bag, tire balancing, medicine ball, etc.—and take turns doing sparring drills with the trainer, Shane. That was my favorite part, so I asked if he did private lessons, which he did, and the rest, as they say, is history. I've been working out almost weekly with Shane ever since.

I never had any aspirations to compete. I just wanted to get the full-body workout that boxing provides me. But I told Shane recently that I'm ready to move to sparring with someone else at my level if he knew of anyone. In the meantime, I've been watching those boxing movies with a keener eye, really dissecting the fight scenes and actually understanding the lingo now.

I shared this with you because it's a perfect example of taking yourself out of a comfort zone and challenging yourself to something new. In my case, it was boxing as a form of exercise. What's important is that you listen to your body, mind and/or spirit when it whispers ideas about doing something new. What would it be for you? Are you ready to step outside *your* box? Have you ever tried something for the sheer thrill of it? What was the result?

What If Someone Gave You a Pen?

(2015)

Let's play a little game…*suppose someone gave you a pen*. A sealed, solid-colored pen. You can't see how much ink is in it. It might run dry after the first few tentative words or last just long enough to create a masterpiece that would last forever and make a difference in the scheme of things. You don't know before you begin to write. Under the rules of the game you really never know. You have to take a chance.

Actually, no rule of the game states that you must do anything. Instead of picking up and using the pen, you can leave it on a shelf or in a drawer or in your purse where it will dry up, unused. But if you decide to use it, what would you do with it? How would you play the game?

Would you plan and plan before you ever wrote a word? Would your plans be so extensive that you never even get around to the writing?

Or would you take the pen in hand, plunge right in and just do it, struggling to keep up with the twists and turns of the torrents of words that take you where they take you? Would you write cautiously and carefully, as if the pen might run dry the next moment? Or would you pretend or believe (or pretend to believe) that the pen will write forever and proceed accordingly?

And what would you write about: Love? Hate? Fun? Life? Death? Family? Work? Nothing? Everything? Would you write to please yourself or to please others, or to please yourself by writing for others?

Would you even write? Once you have the pen, no rule says you have to write. Would you sketch, scribble, doodle or draw? Would you stay in or on the lines or see no lines at all, even if they are there?

There's a lot to think about here, isn't there?

Okay, now suppose someone gave you a *life*.

છ છ છ છ છ છ છ

This is paraphrased from Jack Canfield and Mark Victor Hansen's book Chicken Soup for the Soul (1993).

Are You a Risk-taker?

(2016)

One of the reasons I wrote the book *The Pleasure of My Company* was to dispel the fear I sensed in people who responded to my life's experiences by saying they could never be so brave to take such risks.

Risks? Yes, I'll admit that some of my major life changes involved taking risks. What change doesn't? But did I consider myself a risk-taker at the time? Does 'controlled chaos' count as being a risk-taker?

I like jumping off the deep end of a pool as long as I can see the edge close by…no swimming in an ocean or a lake for me. I enjoy flying in an airplane, suspended above a bank of fluffy clouds in the pure azure sky…but you won't catch me standing on solid ground on the edge of a mountain cliff or tall building looking down. I like spiders…but keep those 'tobacco-splitting' grasshoppers away from me.

I've lived a life that many people have called adventurous and risk-taking and, often times, I do these things in my own company. That's what prompted me to write my own book, subtitled *Finding the Motivation and Courage to Spend Time Alone*. In the spring of 2012, I took a risk and set myself a goal to finally get my book published by December or take it off my "list of things to do before I die." Having tried the traditional publisher route over the ten years since I'd written the book, I decided to independently publish it and, on December 3, I held the first copy of the book in my hands! Now what? Self-publishing involves self-marketing and self-promoting. But instead of allowing Control to have his way by creating stress and impatience with getting the book sold, I'm letting Chaos have her day with it in her own good time—whatever happens, happens. I'll do my part, but mostly I'm just hitching a ride on her coattails. Would that be risk-taking? Maybe. For me, it's kind of like getting in the last seat of an old wooden roller coaster—hands up and ready for one helluva ride!

Are you a risk-taker? Do you take risks or watch from the sidelines? Have you shied away from some really good experiences by letting Fear keep you from taking that leap of faith? Perhaps you don't even think of yourself as one but someone else might. What do you do that's outside 'the box' and has people commenting, "I couldn't do *that!*" Maybe you *are* a risk-taker after all!

Hurry Up and Wait

(2016)

Have you ever had a "hurry up and wait" moment? You rush through the steps of a project only to come to a screeching halt just before completion because of some technicality that has to happen first that's outside your realm of control. You speed down a highway that's clear of traffic with the knowledge that you'll arrive at your destination with time to spare, only to come upon a traffic jam that sets you back hours.

On page 101 of my book, *The Pleasure of My Company,* is the following subtitle:

> *The journey is not the adventure…*
>
> *The destination is not the adventure…*
>
> *Life is the adventure!*

I believe Life presents us with "hurry up and wait" moments so we'll remember to appreciate *all* aspects of our journeys and to take in the 'big picture' of what we're experiencing. I've always been a 'big picture' person, so maybe this is why this appeals to me. But it doesn't mean I don't have my frustrating, impatient moments as well. When I heard 'the Voice' inside me say, "Sell your house and things, quit your job and go west!" on that fateful morning of September 4, 1998, after the initial 'Who said that?' reaction, I knew enough to trust it and said, 'Okay!' I was ready to go then and there! I wanted to take that giant leap!

But the Universe held that carrot out in front of me for two years before I could leave Ohio on my westward journey. I had 'little steps' to take first--sell my house, sell my things, save money, bond further with my nieces and nephew, get a new vehicle, leave a job at a firm whose owners had become unethical in their practices, map out where to go and what to do. It's kind of like Monopoly. You're on GO and roll a '2' to Community Chest and get the "ADVANCE TO GO (Collect $200)" card. Not bad except you've missed out on buying properties, drawing cards and landing on other player's properties…all part of the fun of the game.

In her book, "Journey to the Heart," Melody Beattie says, *"Stay present for each step of your journey. Trust each stage. Many things are possible for you if you accept that the fastest way is one step at a time."* (Beattie 135-136) Do you stay present or are you a leaper? What experiences in your life would you like to live over so you could take the time to experience the 'little steps' along the way?

Cruise Control

(2017)

I never used the cruise control on cars when I'd rent them. For years the vehicles that I owned didn't even have this feature. I didn't like the idea of relinquishing control of a two-ton piece of machinery.

In 2011, I purchased my Subaru Legacy, which had cruise control. Soon, I found myself trying it out when there was very little traffic on the highway. It felt good to relieve my right foot of the pressure to maintain a certain speed. Eventually, I was using this feature in local traffic as a way to keep at the lower speed limit to avoid getting a ticket. Now, cruise control is my trusted traveling companion—it saves on gas as well. I've come to trust it and myself when using it.

Of course, the symbolism of cruise control isn't lost on my introspective, spiritual self. I've actually been operating with cruise control most of my adult life. I learned long ago the importance of surrendering to a Higher Power and trusting that things will go as they should in my life. Whenever I've worked too hard at controlling the events of my life, or when I've created anxiety about how events *should* be happening, I've learned to stop and let go in order to allow things to transpire as they are meant to do. I've put my life in cruise control, releasing my foot from the gas pedal and going along for the ride as the Universe guides me on my journeys.

Just like in a car, I don't let go of the steering wheel when I'm in cruise control. I'm still guiding myself in the general direction that I want to go. I'm taking responsibility for the part I have to play in maneuvering the vehicle of my life. My free will is a navigator on my journeys. But I'm no longer putting pressure on myself to maintain a certain speed. I'm trusting that things will settle to a right result and get me to my desired destination safely and smoothly. And, when it's the right time, I'll release the cruise control button and be in control again.

Do you use the cruise control feature in your car? How about in your life? Where do you feel you have the most control and where do you feel out of control? Do you trust in an omnipresent life force that works in partnership with you as you drive through Life's obstacle courses?

Imagine That!

(2018)

Did you have an imaginary friend when you were a child? My imaginary friend was a pair of twins, both named Kathy--one who always annoyed and contradicted me and the other who always sided with me. As luck would have it, when I was 12 years old I met a classmate who would become my best friend for life and her name—you guessed it—was Kathy! We've been friends for over 50 years now, yet I think our friendship is just a continuation of our souls' journeys.

I have a theory that imaginary friends aren't made up at all. I think maybe they are connected spirits from the "other side" where our souls exist and that we communicate with while we are still young and innocent. Before the 'age of reason' tells us no such things exist. Before we're told to grow up and be serious. It's only now, as I review my life and remember my "friends" Kathy and Kathy that I realize being serious isn't necessarily the natural way of things. The innocence of childhood—the imaginary friends, the wonder at the simplest things, the joy of playing—was a time when the soul that took on this persona was living closer to the surface, so to speak, and not muffled by grown-up thinking. Then logic and practicality replaced imagination and spontaneity.

Did you have an imaginary friend? Do you still allow yourself the luxury of playing? How do you treat the child deep inside of you—with respect or with skepticism? Remember what we were told as children—be nice—so be nice to your child-ish self!

Daddy's Tears

(2019)

On a chilly February evening, at the age of nineteen, I felt my father's tears in the deepest recesses of my heart. He bent slightly and rested his head on my shoulder as his arms wrapped around me and held on so desperately. "I'm going to miss her so much, Susan," he sobbed into my ear.

I'd seen my father cry before, mostly those "happy tears" that adults let flow when they're pleased or, well, happy. When he was proud of me for getting into National Honor Society or when his son was born. The men in my family—especially on my mother's side—were big softies behind their macho statures. Grandpa Todd would cry at the Macy's Thanksgiving Day parade when the marching bands performed with precision and when Santa Claus appeared at the end of the procession. Dad cried with Mom when John F. Kennedy was assassinated.

Tonight, we'd just returned to our house from Grandma Lena Galambos's funeral and wake. It was just after sunset and the streetlights had come on. He and I had come home together while Mom was following with my sister Sandy and brother Tony in her car. Dad and I got out of the car and approached the back stoop when he stopped, turned to me, took me into his arms and began crying.

He was especially close to his Grandma Galambos growing up. She called him her "Feddy Fe-om"—I have no idea how to spell her nickname for him in Hungarian, but this is what it sounded like phonetically—or her little Frankie in her strong Hungarian accent. This six-foot-tall electrician and baseball player would do anything for his grandma. Now she was gone, and he cried unabashedly on my shoulder.

In that moment of his sorrow, I felt such joy that I could offer comfort to him and share in his vulnerable sorrow.

Are you willing to share your vulnerability? Or do you keep your sorrows and uncertainties to yourself so you don't appear to be weak? My father's willingness to expose his sorrow to me was not a sign of weakness—it was a sign of inner strength and love. How can you better nurture your inner strength?

What Would I Change?

(2019)

At a session of a women's writing group that I recently participated in, we were presented with a writing prompt that asked, *If you had your life to live over, what would you change in your life if you could?* We had twenty minutes to respond and, after struggling to pinpoint one thing I might change, my reply was:

If I had my life to live over, how do I decide what I would change? Would I stay in California in 1967 and finish my associate degree at Pasadena City College instead of moving home to Ohio after two months? Then I wouldn't have learned computer programming. And I wouldn't have been in town to see the National Guard convoy taking soldiers to Kent State University one fateful day in May 1970, where friends went to classes, unsuspecting the tragedy to come.

Should I have stayed in New York instead of moving to Phoenix in 1975, sight unseen? But then I wouldn't have gotten over my fear of water and learned how to swim or learned Transcendental Meditation, which I'm still doing over forty years later. I wouldn't have dated a nice guy named Bruce, who was six years my junior. I wouldn't have experienced my own phoenix rebirth and metamorphosis at the age of 25.

Would I have walked straight along Prince Street in Edinburgh in 1983 instead of going left, then left again, to end up at the Blithe Spirit Bar where I met a Scotsman named Stuart who I'd marry and later divorce? Yes, I could have avoided the pain of his drinking, but I'd have missed the love of his touches.

Maybe I would change my mind about staying in Park City, Utah, to work a second winter at Deer Valley Resort instead of driving to my original destination of Arizona that spring of 2001. But then I'd have missed the eighteen years I lived there and all that I experienced during that time, like performing improvisational comedy, producing a meditation CD, publishing my book and meeting my soul sisters, Mary and Geri, and other great friends.

If I change just one little thing, what domino effect would I create? Where would I be? And who would I be? I like ME as I am because of what my life has been. So, no changes for me, thank you, except I might be aware sooner of those precious moments that come and go so fleetingly so that I could live in their bliss a little longer. I might smile more at strangers at a younger age and see myself in them like I do now. I might appreciate sooner the spectrum of Life and how there really is no right or wrong, just different perspectives.

Our lives are enriched by every moment that we live, even if those moments are tragic or sad or unfulfilling because it's how we *respond* to everything that happens to us that creates the learning and teaching experiences.

So, I turn the question to you, Reader—what would *you* change about your life if you could live it over? Or would you?

I Get it, Grandpa Todd!

(2020)

"I get it, Grandpa Todd!" I found myself saying this out loud to my deceased grandfather as I wiped away tears after watching a segment on *CBS Sunday Morning*—I get why he cried at commercials!

Let me back up here. My Grandpa Todd, my mom's dad, was one of the nicest men I ever knew. Growing up, I was very close to him and Grandma Rose. I'd spend Monday and Saturday nights at their house, which was next door to ours. I had my own drawers in the dresser in their one spare bedroom and kept a spare "blankie" there to sleep with on those nights. I'd play Scrabble with Grandma Rose, sipping a taste of her Sauterne wine. On Saturday nights, Grandpa and I were treated to a meatball on a slice of Italian bread from Grandma's batch of fresh spaghetti sauce that was simmering on the stove for Sunday's family dinner—her tasters, she called us!

In the summer, I'd go on road trip vacations with them to destinations that included Calumet horse farm in Lexington, Kentucky; Gettysburg battlefield in Pennsylvania; Lookout Mountain in Chattanooga, Tennessee; the Rockettes at Radio City Music Hall in New York City; and various cities for Grandpa's bowling tournaments. Grandpa would sometimes pretend to be surprised to find me hiding in his coat closet when he came home from work or exacerbated because I was going with them yet again on vacation. But I knew it was all in fun because I felt the love that he and Grandma had for me and never doubted it. From the time I was brought home from the hospital to *their* house, I was attached to them. Often in Italian families, a child will live with her parents when she first marries until children start showing up. That's what happened with us—Mom, Dad and I were there until I was about two-years-old and my mom was pregnant with my sister. Hence, my close attachment to these grandparents. But I digress...

Grandpa Todd was a "man's man." He was a life insurance salesman who visited his clients by going door to door as it was done in the Fifties and Sixties. He was an avid bowler and one of the first bowlers inducted posthumously into the Ohio Bowlers' Hall of Fame. He was a member of the BPOE—Benevolent and Protective Order of Elks--or as it was affectionately nicknamed, Best People On Earth or simply the Elks Club. He loved the Cleveland Indians and Lawrence Welk.

His gruff manly demeanor housed a gentle, loving heart and soul, which brings me back to my opening statement. As he got older, it wasn't unusual to find him hiding tears—while opening his Christmas presents, hugging his beloved wife, watching a marching band or watching a Kodak commercial on TV. Yes, even touching TV commercials would find him scratching his semi-bald scalp and sniffling as the tears welled up in his eyes. He was a big softy!

So today, I was watching a story on *CBS Sunday Morning* about a two-year-old girl who was being treated for leukemia and was highly susceptible to disease and infections. On Halloween night, her parents put a sign in their front yard for Trick-or-Treaters that read, "No candy this year—child with cancer inside. See you next year!" What happened that night was remarkable: children started leaving their candy on the lawn by the sign! No adult told them to do this—they did it just because they wanted to share! I was brought to tears and realized I'd become my Grandpa Todd. And I'm just fine with that!

Do you find yourself mimicking mannerisms of a family member? Are you surprised when you hear yourself telling your kids how to behave *exactly* the way your Mom told you? Do you walk with the same lumbering stride as a dearly-departed uncle? Now think about how *your* own words and behaviors may be repeated by your children someday—makes you think more about what you say and do, doesn't it?

In Other Words

(2021)

I love words.

I love how some words roll off my tongue, like *salubrious* or *precocious.*

I love the sound of some words, like *conundrum, aloof* or *oboe.*

I love the look of some words, like *scintillating, Hawaii* or *mesmerize.*

Think about it. The English language has twenty-six characters—52 if you consider the lower and upper case versions—that we call 'letters.' These random characters are jumbled together and combined to form 'words.' And words combine into phrases and sentences that join together into paragraphs, then into complete articles, essays, poem, books, etc.

Words convey messages, relate information, record history, tell stories, lyricize tunes, educate students, impart feelings…the list goes on and on. But what I love most about words is the myriad—another word that I like to say—of meanings that one word can convey. In other words, I love semantics.

Complexly put, *semantics* is the branch of linguistics concerned with meaning, including *formal* semantics (logical aspects), *lexical* semantics (word relations) and *conceptual* semantics (cognitive structure of meaning.) Simply put, *semantics* is the study of *meaning.* And meaning is all in the eye of the beholder and the ear of the listener.

In my roles as writer, trainer, speaker and life coach, I've learned the power that words have in communication. Their meanings create perceptions that form our belief systems, propel our behavior and, eventually, construct our world. How we respond emotionally to words that we read, hear or say determines the power ascribed to them. I've become very aware of others' reactions to certain words, and I'm adept at choosing my own words carefully when trying to get a point across.

There are two words that have special meaning to me because they are words used to describe me by two completely different men under two completely different circumstances. The first is *aloof.* I grew up believing I was shy. When I was young, I didn't particularly know what the word meant, but I'd hear my Mom tell a teacher, "Susan's a little shy," or my Dad explain why I buried my face in his leg when approached by one of his friends, "Oh, she's just shy!" So, as words tend to do, the word *shy* took root in my subconscious. As I came to understand what it meant, I lived up to its meaning. I *shied* away from large groups of kids or adults. I *shyly* walked around a party until I found a person I knew and could latch onto for the evening. I denied myself opportunities to shine because I just knew I was too *shy* to be successful at them.

In 1972, I moved to White Plains, New York, to work at Xerox Corporation's northeast region office. About a dozen of us twenty-somethings were hired by a new manager who was creating a department to administratively support the sixteen regional branches. The office was a wide open space where our desks were lined up like a spreadsheet in rows and columns, but without the confining cubicles so we could interact easily. Every day around 10 a.m. and 3 p.m., a coffee vendor would roll his wagon off the elevator and provide refreshments and a break for all the employees on that floor. It's not that we couldn't take breaks any time, but this service made it easier for us. One afternoon about two months into my employment, as my department paraded down the hall for a quick respite, I stayed at my desk. A few minutes later, Chuck Alfini was tapping on the front of my desk. (By the way, Chuck became a really close friend whom I've kept in touch with for fifty years. We spent hours in phone conversations during the 2020 Covid pandemic discussing our favorite authors and more.)

"You know you're allowed to take a break, too, Susan?" he teased.

"Yeah, but I'm fine…need to get this done," I said, tapping away on my calculator.

"Oh, come on," he persisted. "Stretch your legs and join us."

"I'm not that into coffee klatches. I'm shy that way," I insisted.

"You're not shy," he immediately retorted.

"Yes, I am!" I *unshyly* and adamantly replied.

"No, you're not," Chuck persisted. "You're aloof!"

"I'm n---*what?*" I said, giving him a puzzled look.

"You're aloof. Shy means you're afraid, but I don't get that about you. You're reserved—friendly, but detached. You choose when and if you'll join in on your own terms, not ours. Aloof!"

"Aloof," I said softly to myself, as he walked away smiling and I let what he said sink in. At that moment, my whole internal definition of myself shifted. I felt myself sitting taller, getting stronger, being confident. *I'm aloof!* The fact that I'm writing about that incident today is proof of its impact on me and how I think of myself.

The second word is *stoic.* I heard it in a hospital room at Mt. Kisco Hospital in Mt. Kisco, New York, in April 1986. The morning before, I'd had excruciating pains in my lower abdomen and my then-husband Stuart took me to the emergency room. I spent the day lying on a gurney while nurses, doctor's assistants, doctors and lastly the surgeon prodded my abdomen asking, "Does this hurt?" *Yes, you freakin' idiots, it hurts like hell!* (I may have actually yelled that once in my fevered frenzy.) Finally, they wheeled me into the operating room to remove my appendix before it burst, which I'm sure it would have done eventually from all that poking. The next morning, the surgeon came into my room to check on me. When I said I felt a lot better, he commented, "You're one stoic patient.

Most people would have been screaming in pain from all that prodding. Your appendix was highly inflamed."

Stoic, I thought as he left the room. I think I know what that means but I'm going to have to look it up to make sure it was a compliment, not a jibe. When I confirmed that I'd been complimented, I decided that I liked being stoic. It kind of went along with my aloofness and said that I was a strong, independent woman. Not a bad thing at all!

I shared these two incidents because I wanted to stress the importance of the power words have to change your whole life. We carry around recordings in our brain of everything that was said *to* us and *about* us during our lifetime, from childhood on. Some of those recordings were implanted by often well-intentioned outside sources—parents, teachers, bosses, friends, strangers—and some were programmed by our own minds. We replay them over and over to the point of believing they are *truths*, when in fact they are just words we've clung to for whatever reason. We make decisions and take actions based upon these recordings, but recordings can be taped over or erased. You can change them internally simply by deciding not to give them the power over you any longer. When I'd tell myself I couldn't approach a guy at a singles bar because *"I can't do this because I'm shy,"* I'd immediately stop myself and say, *"No, I'm aloof...I* can *do this!"* When I faced the end of my marriage and wondered how I'd regain my identity, I told myself, *"You're stoic...you'll endure this and move on."* It may take some time to reprogram your way of thinking, but it is *so* worth it.

Have you ever been in a conversation with someone who just wasn't getting it? You keep explaining your point of view, they retort with something completely contrary to what you were talking about and an argument ensues. A trainer in a workshop I attended told a story about a disagreement he and his wife had about *dogfish.* He said it went on for almost an hour until they realized they were talking about two different things, and he refers to that kind of communication now as a "dogfish conversation." Imagine two people passing each other in the same room, completely oblivious of each other, he told us—that's what happens when we talk without listening or don't pay attention to the words being said to us. It created a visual for me whenever I find myself in such a discussion. If he and his wife had been more explicit early in the discussion, they could have avoided the argument.

Clarification is key to ensuring that your words aren't misinterpreted. This can happen between two individuals or while addressing an auditorium full of people. There will be a disconnect between the speaker and the audience if what is *understood* by the listener is different from what was *intended* by the speaker. What I do when presenting something that is open for interpretation is to ask my audience, "What do you think I mean when I say [blank]?" Or, if I hear something that sparks a certain meaning to me, I may ask the speaker, "When I hear you say [blank], that means [blank] to me. Is that what you meant?"

One of the most controversial, misinterpreted words for me is *God.* Every person has his or her own meaning attached to those three letters. Wars have been started based on the meaning assigned to the word or any of its variations. I don't intend to get into a whole theological discussion here—I'd risk misrepresenting a religion or culture because of my ignorance and I don't want to insult or incite my readers. What I offer is simply *my* experience with this little word, G-o-d. You'll notice throughout the book that I use interchangeable words when I'm talking about God—Spirit, Force, Powers That Be and, my favorite, The Universe. My Catholic upbringing has evolved to a more broad-minded spiritual philosophy, and the vocabulary I use to express my spiritual beliefs has expanded. It's important that I don't convey the wrong impression of fitting into a boxed definition of my beliefs, from extreme fundamentalism to non-believing atheism. If I say, *"I trust God to set things in motion for me,"* one person may presume I prayed to an omniscient being separate from me while another may decide I've gone off the deep end to think an outside entity controls my destiny. Neither are true. I *don't* believe in the separation of God and me and I *don't* believe in Fate where I have no control. So I choose my words delicately and wisely based upon my audience.

That leads to my love of semantics—it opens the door for profound, in-depth conversations where those involved in the exchanges share their thoughts, reasons, ideas and beliefs. Oftentimes, it also creates an opportunity for the individuals to learn about themselves as they dig deeper into their psyches to understand the *why* behind their viewpoints. As with the two words that I reprogrammed into my internal recordings—*aloof* and *stoic*—we can change our minds about beliefs and reprogram our thinking, changes that usually happen over time and with the wisdom of age. Also, we can become more accepting and no longer judge others based upon *our* definitions of the words they use or don't use. We can create better relationships and, dare we think it, a better world!

So my query to you, Reader, is three-fold. First, what are your favorite words to say, hear and see? Second, what words are you using internally to define yourself and which of those words need to be reprogrammed because they are outdated or never really fit? Finally, how do you plan on becoming a better communicator now that you understand the power of those twenty-six little characters when concocted into words?

Role Models Part 1 – Nancy Drew

(2021)

When I was about twelve years old, if asked what I wanted to be when I grew up, my response was a detective like Nancy Drew. I read Nancy's books avariciously, often sequestered in my closet for the utmost seclusion, a flashlight hanging from the clothes rod, a pillow under my butt and a glass of water outside the sliding door. Nancy's adventures intrigued me and opened up worlds of possibilities for a young girl's imagination. While I never did become a detective, Nancy was one of my first role models, and I attribute my independent spirit, self-confidence and determination for solving problems to her.

Role models are funny creatures. We don't go out seeking them and we often don't recognize them in the moment. It's usually in retrospect that we realize how much a certain person has influenced our thinking and our lives. Sometimes, the role model is someone we know personally, like a teacher who inspires us to pursue a particular field of study or a family member who supports us in following our dreams. Oftentimes, the role model is someone famous, either a contemporary from our lifetime or a historical figure whose accomplishments resonated with us. Regardless, these role models hold an esteemed place in our hearts and minds when we're thinking about what makes us tick.

I won't go into my list of role models and why they are so for me, except to honor the women in my family, all of whom demonstrate strength, love, individuality and humor. Reigning over all of them is my mother, Gloria Marie Christina Lucille Morrell Nyitrai. She was the falconer to my falcon, the proverbial 'wind beneath my wings,' and I lost her too soon at the age of sixty-three to liver cancer. It was with her in mind that I've wondered about what kind of a role model *I* am. While I don't have children of my own, my brother's children—Christina, Michael and Rachel—are 'my kids' and provide me with my best job ever, that of Aunt Susie. I've consciously thought about how I'm living my life so that I'm the best example for them. What's the most important message I want them to get from my life? Be authentic and honor yourself above anyone else because if you don't treat yourself with love and respect, you won't be able to offer authentic love and respect to others nor should you expect others to be loving and respectful towards you.

Why is this so important? I have always been an introspective woman, questioning my intentions, analyzing my motives, looking at the clues of my life to understand my beliefs, decisions and thoughts. My Nancy Drew detective skills serve a purpose when I scrutinize my life in order to create the 'next best thing' for myself and my loved ones. Knowing which people have played a role in forming my moral basis helps tremendously in this introspection.

Okay, enough about me. I turn the question now to you. Who are your role models and why? What have these individuals offered you in the way of inspiration and support? I'm sure you've given some thought to this over the years. This time, really dig deep into the *why* these people are so important to you—then let them know!

Role Models Part 2 – Auntie Mame

(2021)

In my query, *Role Models Part I*, I wrote about Nancy Drew being a role model for me in my childhood. I also honored the women in my family, especially my mother, and I mentioned how being Aunt Susie to my two nieces and a nephew has kept me consciously aware of being a role model for them. I'm also consciously aware that I had an amazing role model for being the best aunt that I can be— Auntie Mame!

Auntie Mame is a fictional character created in 1955 by author Edward Everett Tanner III, under the pseudonym Patrick Dennis. The book was adapted into a Broadway play from 1956 to 1958 starring Rosalind Russell as Mame Dennis; and in 1958, Warner Brothers produced the first film adaptation, with Russell reprising the starring role. I don't remember when I first saw it, but it would have been as a teenager and it would have been on television, not in the movie theater. What I do know is I immediately fell in love with the flamboyant, exuberant woman who lives life on her terms and whose favorite quote is, *"Life is a banquet, and most poor suckers are starving to death!"* She has a huge, loving heart and triumphs over her vulnerabilities as a consummate survivor. *I want to be her!* I remember thinking.

I matured from teenager to young adult, from living under my parents' wings to spreading my own independent wings. I explored the life of a single working woman in the suburbs of New York City, then in Phoenix, Arizona. During these years, I often asked myself, *What would Mame do?* In 1975, I transferred with Xerox Corporation to Phoenix, Arizona, without ever having been there just because I'd visited Tucson for a week in February and fell in love with the desert. A few years later a friend in New York told me that, when she was facing a major change in her life, she remembered how brave I was to make that move. *Brave?* I didn't feel brave making that decision—I just did it. Then I realized that maybe I *had* been brave and maybe some of Mame's gumption had sneaked its way into my subconscious thinking. I'll be darn!

Then, in 1987, I learned that the banquet of Life has a funny way of fulfilling your dreams, even those that you'd simply put out into the Universe as an impressionable teenager. *So, you want to be Auntie Mame, do you? Well, how does Aunt Susie sound?* On March 7, 1987, my niece Christina Lynn Morrell was born in Wertheim, Germany. My brother was stationed there in the Army and the family had to wait two long months to see her when they flew to Ohio for her christening. They asked me to be her godmother! (My husband/now ex-husband Stuart is her godfather.) Godmother *and* Aunt—two roles I take very seriously.

In 1990, I presented Christina and her parents with a book I'd written for her called, *Dear Christina.* It was a letter to my three-year-old niece and goddaughter that told her about our visits together over her first three years and imparted things I wanted to share and lessons I wanted to teach her just in case I never got the chance. I included some of my favorite photos of her that so captured her spirited personality. There's a passage that describes a spiritual moment I experienced with her on the first night of their two-week stay in Ohio. That moment made me realize how close infants are to God as newborn souls and how I wished she could answer my questions about what it was like "over there." I realized that toddlers and young children have that pure innocence of believing in imaginary friends and angels and Santa Claus because they probably *are* still seeing or sensing spiritual entities. It's as they get older and the adults in their life teach them to be logical and realistic that those imaginary entities fade away. Oh, to be that innocent again!

I've digressed a little from the topic of *role models* and Auntie Mame. The point is, I *did* become Auntie Mame for Christina, her brother Michael (1989) and her sister Rachel (1993). Every decision I've made since they've become part of my life has been with them in mind—I want to be an example for how to live their lives to the fullest and how to be true to oneself. I tease my brother and sister-in-law that I'm grateful for them having *my* kids for me—being an aunt gives me the fun and joy without the expense and responsibility! I just hope that the three of them are having as much fun and getting as much out of our relationship as I am. As Auntie Mame would say, *"You've got to live, Live, LIVE!"*

So I'll turn this back to you. To whom have you been a role model? Do you consciously make decisions about your life that you know may influence these loved ones? What would you do differently now that you realize how impactful your choices may be on someone else? It's a lot to think about and a lot of responsibility—and a lot of fun!

What is God Dreaming for You?

(2021)

This morning I was reading Oprah Winfrey's latest book, *The Path Made Clear,* and this passage in a piece from Wintley Phipps's conversation with Oprah affected me emotionally, brought me to tears and had me contemplating my life—something that happens a lot when I read these types of books:

> "When you watch the things you dreamed of as a kid come to reality, those are moments of destiny. But I've realized that moments of destiny are *moments* for which you were created, but they're not the *reasons* you were created. The reason for which we were created is to grow every day to more resemble, reflect and reveal the character of the one who created us. Let me tell you, God is the ultimate dreamer, and when He dreams, He also dreams about us. He dreams about you. He dreams about me. And the most amazing thing that can happened in the life of a human being is to catch a glimpse of what God's been dreaming of for you." (Page 40)

"...to catch a glimpse of what God's been dreaming of for you" Wow! What a thought! What *has* God been dreaming for me? Am I honoring that dream? Have I understood what God has been hoping happens to me and for me?

I pride myself on having created an incredible relationship with the Universal Force that guides me and supports me as a spiritual being. I talk to this Force all the time. I ask for clarity, voice my confusion, complain about apparent non-responsiveness, acknowledge being hasty in my judgements, laugh about silly ideas that crop up and, mostly, express my gratitude. But I'd never given thought to what God's been dreaming for me.

Therefore, this morning I decided to open up to my god and let Her know that I'm prepared to receive whatever I need to receive in order to fulfill this dream. I accepted that what *I've* decided is the best timing, best direction, best person, best choice may be prohibiting what I truly need to have appear in my life. I've surrendered my life in the past and seen extraordinary opportunities and agents for change emerge. I just needed to be reminded that I should do that again during this new phase of my life, perhaps more frequently due to the irregularity of my days now as a retired woman.

So, in answer to the title of this query, what is God dreaming for *you,* what comes to mind? We all have our own ways of conversing with God, regardless of what name or spiritual ideology you prefer. Ask yourself the same questions I asked myself above and be ready to listen. Then, be ready to take ownership of that dream as your own—because it is!

<u>EPILOGUE</u>

Why?

I must have been one of those kids who drove her parents crazy asking *why* all the time. *Why? You ask. (Pun intended!)* Because reviewing all the material for this book made me realize just how often I've been doing that my entire life!

No matter what I called it—introspection, retrospection, hindsight, contemplation, navel-gazing—it's all been about searching for the *why* behind my behaviors and thoughts, behind what's happened to me or what's not happened. I became Nancy Drew after all as I looked for clues beneath the surface of my life. That Wizard in Oz wouldn't have stayed hidden for long if I'd been there because I'd have pulled aside that curtain to see what was behind it. I enjoy watching television shows that explain how and why things work, whether it's an assembly line making and packaging Hershey's Kisses or an intricate operation of a human body.

I realize as I'm writing this that my role as a Life Coach is a perfect match for my *why* fixation. As a Life Coach, I don't fix things or offer resolutions—I listen to my subjects and ask probing questions that allow them to take that deep dive for the answers. I'm encouraging them to ask "Why?" or some variation so that they can arrive at the conclusion or solution themselves—and own it! It resonates as a deep-seated, personal choice rather than hearing it as *my* choice, which can be accepted or rejected.

So has all this *why* business paid off for me? Do I have all the answers I've sought over the years? Well, my life has been enriched by everything I've learned from those deep dives. Of course, there's still a lot that stymies me—like exactly how *does* Santa Claus visit every child's house around the world in one night? Or why does the pain of losing a loved one feel like a fresh wound to the heart even decades later? I guess some things are just meant to be part of the Great Unknown—and I can live with that. After all, I do love a good mystery story!

I hope you've enjoyed this Falcon's peregrination through her life's significant and trivial moments as she rediscovered herself. More importantly, I hope you've taken your own journey, discovered some of the *whys* of your life and been enriched by them.

Be well, Readers, and remember, Who's on first, What's on second, I Don't Know…

<u>ACKNOWLEDGEMENTS</u>

There have been many influencers in my life for whom I am grateful. They run the gamut from classmate to ex-spouse, in-person relationships to celebrities I've admired from afar and even some fictional characters. We may have shared a day or decades. While there's no way I can list all their names here, I am going to give kudos to a "few" who have played a significant role in my life. (To those whose names are not listed here, please know that it's no reflection on our association but merely the need to conserve time and space. You know who you are, and I hold you in my heart in fondest memory.)

Family: Frank and Gloria (Morrell) Nyitrai, parents; Sandra Parry, sister; Anthony and Patty Morrell, brother and sister-in-law; Rose and Todd Morrell, maternal grandparents; Emma and Menyhart Nyitrai, paternal grandparents; Lena Galambos, paternal great-grandmother; Toni and Remi Rechedy, maternal aunt/godmother and uncle; Emma Clark, paternal aunt; Christina, Michael and Rachel Morrell, fraternal nieces and nephew; Shaun, James and Luke Adams, Christina's husband and sons; Lorraine "Chickie" Grabosky and Lynette "Tina" Dudek, maternal cousins; and the rest of my extended clans.

Friends, Schoolmates and Co-workers: *Childhood:* Barb Heiss, since we were infants and our parents were good friends; Kathy Reuschenberg, my BFF since seventh grade cheerleader tryouts. *Most Significant Relationships:* Thomas McGuire, first love; Stuart Pawluk, ex-husband. *Along the Way:* Allen Gentry; Allison Sandler;

Anne Tompkins; Bob May; Bruce Cohen; Chan Reuschenberg; Chuck Alfini; David and Gail Teasley; Dee Macaluso and my *Off the Top* improvisational comedy troupe; Diane Pricola; Don Holborn; Dorothy Leone; Ed Patterson; Gail Wallace; Geri Nielsen; Isidra Mencos; Jean Miles; JFK Class of '67; Joanne and Dave Breier; Johnny Cocca; Kathleen Whelen; Kathy Stanger; Marie Creaturo; Mary and Edo Bernasconi; Mary Holt; Mary Lou Davies; Marylou Mylet; Oscar Crawford; Pete Wills; Rev. Guy Lynch; Rev. Paddy Wood; Rick Warmbold; Sam Bixler; Sam Fossaceca; Shane Heaps; Sue Razzetti; Virginia McDonald.

Renowned: Alex O'Loughlin; Barbara Walters; Bud Abbott and Lou Costello; Danny Kaye; Egan Inoue; Georgia O'Keeffe; Glenn Frey (Eagles); Jesus of Nazareth; Katherine Hepburn; Maharishi Mahesh Yogi; Moody Blues; Oprah Winfrey; Paul O'Neill; Peter Noone (Herman's Hermits); President George W. Bush; President Jimmy Carter; Robert Downey, Jr.; Robert F. Kennedy; Robert Lamm (Chicago); Rosalind Russell; Val Kilmer; Vincent Van Gogh.

Authors/Poets: Alan Cohen; Anne Morrow Lindbergh; Carolyn Keene; Catherine Gaskin; Chip Conley; Dale Mayer; David Baldacci; Harlan Coben; Jena la Flamme; Julia Cameron; Kate Aster; Neale Donald Walsch; Nelson DeMille; Peter Shaffer; Richard Bach; Rod McKuen; Sara Davidson; Scott Sanders; Sofia Segovia; Toby Neal; Victor Frankl; Vince Flynn (Kyle Mills); Dr. Wayne Dyer.

Fictional: Bruce Wayne, Batman; Doreen Montgomery, amateur sleuth; Elizabeth Bennet, protofeminist; Jo March, writer; John Corey, NYPD detective; John Puller, CID investigator; Lei Texeira, Hawaiian police detective; Mame Dennis, Auntie Mame; Mitch Rapp, CIA operative; Myron Bolitar, sports agent/P.I.; Nancy Drew, girl sleuth; Scott Drayco, crime consultant; Sophie Ang, tech security specialist; Steve McGarrett, Hawaii Five-0 commander *(the reboot)*; Tony Stark, Iron Man; Will Robie, CIA operative.

Thanks to each and every one of you for the contribution you've made to my life—real or imagined, past or present tense, short-lived or long-term—because *every* interaction matters. I hope I've been a good influence in your lives as well. (Although, I doubt that Tony Stark has me on his list!)

Postscript

I'd like to explain the change in surnames for me and my immediate family from *Nyitrai* to *Morrell*, in case you're wondering. My siblings and I were born with our father's surname, Nyitrai, and carried it proudly for decades, as did my mother. Our father died at the young age of fifty-one in 1979, when my brother, Tony, was sixteen years old. Before his senior year in high school, Tony approached my mother about changing his last name to her maiden name of Morrell.

His reasoning was three-fold: one, there were Nyitrai males to carry on the name but no males to do the same for the Morrells; two, he was closer to his maternal relatives than to the paternal ones, especially after our father died; and three, he intended to change it when he turned eighteen years old, but thought it would be easier to do so sooner so it would be on his high school transcripts for college and the Army. My mother was willing to do this, but she wanted to discuss it with her mother-in-law first so she wouldn't be blind-sided. Grandma Nyitrai was a little disappointed, but she understood and gave her blessing.

Hearing of this while living in New York, I decided that I would also change my name; and then my sister followed suit. Not only would it be easier for us all to have the same surname, but *Morrell* was a much easier name to pronounce and spell. We haven't regretted our decision, although I sometimes miss the uniqueness of *Nyitrai.* BTW, it's pronounced *Nee'-try-ee.*

<u>LIGHT BULB MOMENTS</u>

These are *your* pages, Reader. Record your thoughts or feelings here as you read, then turn your "light bulb moments" into shining stars in whatever manner you feel inspired!

<u>LIGHT BULB MOMENTS</u>

<u>LIGHT BULB MOMENTS</u>